that I use
lo...

"I think you'll admit that my dreams were rather detailed . . . and just a little risqué," Lettie whispered, glancing up at him. When her lips tilted in a mischievous smile, he seemed to forget the fact that he'd been trying to button his shirt.

Savoring each second as if it were delicate wine, she unfastened the last button, looked up to gauge Ethan's expression, then laid her hands flat against the flesh of his chest.

Ethan took a shuddering breath. "Dammit, Lettie, this isn't a good—"

"This is a fine idea, a wonderful idea," she interrupted smoothly, her thumbs extending to rub against the soft brown patches of his nipples. His skin was warm and firm beneath her palms.

Their lips met in hungry anticipation, made all the more sweet by the fact that it had seemed so long— too long since they had held each other this way and touched, embraced. Lettie held him tightly against her, until the combined heat of their flesh seemed to meld together in a tantalizing manner.

"Damn you, Lettie, why can't you leave well enough alone," he whispered more to himself than to her, his voice thick with his own desire.

"Because I can't bear to see you aching . . ."

SILKEN DREAMS

LISA BINGHAM

POCKET BOOKS

New York   London   Toronto   Sydney   Tokyo   Singapore

This book is a work of fiction. Names, characters, places and incidents are either the product of the author's imagination or are used fictitiously. Any resemblance to actual events or locales or persons, living or dead is entirely coincidental.

An *Original* Publication of POCKET BOOKS

POCKET BOOKS, a division of Simon & Schuster
1230 Avenue of the Americas, New York, NY 10020

ISBN: 0-671-72806-7

First Pocket Books printing February 1991

10 9 8 7 6 5 4 3 2 1

POCKET and colophon are registered trademarks of
Simon & Schuster.

Printed in the U.S.A.

Dedicated to Joyce and ElMont.

Thank you for teaching me that dreams can come true,
love truly exists,
and nothing is impossible.

Prologue

*O*verhead, the crash of thunder built to a shuddering climax, then subsided in a relentless, jagged echo. As if the sky wept in silent commiseration with my torment, I ran down the path just as the rain began to fall—huge, iron-gray drops that pelted into the dust with relentless force.

But I didn't care.

Without thought for the moisture that seeped into the silk of my gown, I ran toward the abandoned stables, knowing he would be there—he had to be there.

Already the path was beginning to grow slick from the rain that pounded to the earth in a solid sheet of moisture. Long before I'd reached the halfway mark to the distant paddocks, the careful sweep of curls over my ear became sodden, the hem of my ivory gown grew black with mud. Pausing for a moment, trying to catch my breath, I scooped my skirts up above my knees and raced toward the side door of the stables. The weathered portal was slightly ajar. As if he'd left it that way for me.

With a final burst of energy, I dodged inside, slamming the door closed. Vainly, I sought the shadows for his familiar form—though my eyes had not yet grown accustomed to the darkness. But long before I could see for myself, the emptiness that flooded my heart warned me that he wasn't there.

A quick sob tore at my throat. I knew I mustn't surrender to the fear that began to twine within me. Despite my inner protestations, a chill began to seep into my bones. Long before, I had accepted the fact that I'd fallen in love with the Highwayman, but I'd never been able to accept the fact that he could be caught.

Even as the thought of his possible capture raced through my mind, the cold fear began to take hold. Something had happened. Something must have happened to him or he would have met me. He'd always been here before, always when I needed him most.

Fighting to breathe against the tight lacing of my gown, I stepped into the musty warmth of the stables, absorbing its shelter, its security . . . its hollowness. Walking down the earth-packed center aisle between the stalls, I slipped the fichu from the neckline of my gown and used it to blot the moisture from my face. But with each brush of the cloth, I found myself remembering the strong breadth of his chest, the narrow span of his hips. And his lovemaking . . .

His lovemaking.

Suddenly, the door behind me slammed open. A gust of cold rain blew into the stable, and without turning, I knew it was he. My breathing quickened in relief. The hand that held the fichu grew lax and the silk scarf dropped to the ground, leaving the firm swells of my breasts all but exposed above the low square of my gown.

"Letitia," he breathed, his voice low, intense. The mere sound of my name on his lips caused my breasts to ache.

I sighed, and though I fought to contain them, the words "Kiss me" tumbled from my lips.

From behind, I heard his firm bootstrides against the earth and straw. Sweet anticipation swelled within my loins and my pulse began to pound. I knew what would happen next, and my fingers lifted to begin plucking the *fastenings of my bodice free. After his journey he would be tired, hungry . . . and lusty. Impatient and aroused, he would jerk me into his arms. His hands would slip around my waist and pull me tightly against him. So tightly the studs of his shirt would dig into my flesh, the hilt of his saber would press against my stomach, and his hips . . . he would lift me until his hips ground against my own, while his hands impatiently tugged at the skirts that would bunch between us.*

Already burning with need and eager anticipation, I closed my eyes. Without turning, I could feel him stop behind me, feel his hand reach out . . .

1

Letitia Grey screamed when a very real, very warm, very wet masculine hand closed upon her shoulder. Her nut-brown eyes flew open, and the elegant paddocks of her fantasy scattered as the dingy reality of the barn plunged into view.

The fingers on her shoulder tightened and she nearly strangled upon the gasp that lodged in her throat. Moving nothing but her eyes, she darted one quick look at the hand that held her. A firm hand, covered with a light dusting of dark hair.

Her breath escaped in a high squeak of fear and she whirled away, rushing toward the opposite side of the barn, where a pitchfork leaned against one of the weathered stalls. "Get back," she said, spinning in the straw and holding the pitchfork in front of her, its tines lifted toward the intruder.

The man who'd touched her regarded her in surprise, his hands lifted, palms out, as if to show he was unarmed, despite the gun belt strapped low to his hips. "Whoa, I just—"

"Quiet!" Lettie snapped, wondering how long the dark-haired man had been there, how much of her daydreaming he'd seen. A hot flush rose to her cheeks

4

when she realized she'd been so deep in her fantasies that she'd actually unfastened a good number of buttons on her bodice—enough so that the smooth flesh of her bosom could be seen through the delicate tatting of her camisole.

Lettie nearly moaned aloud in embarrassment, then became still, her eyes growing wide and startled as they focused on the stranger who stood in the dim light. By all that was holy, it seemed as if her Highwayman had somehow materialized in front of her. In the flesh.

The man's gaze deepened slightly, dipping to study the unbuttoned portion of her bodice. "I wondered if you could help me."

"Ah-ah!" Lettie warned when he took a step forward.

The man stopped, but his study grew even more intent.

The pitchfork wavered in Lettie's grip ever so slightly. Her eyes grew wider, darker; her breathing became shallow and quick. He wasn't a terribly big man—just under six feet, she'd wager—but there was something about him that exuded a sense of latent power. Water dripped from the dark hair plastered against his head. His eyes were intense, their color all but indistinguishable in the near darkness.

Lettie shivered slightly, though not entirely from the cool, rain-kissed air. In all her imaginings, the Highwayman had looked the same as the man before her. *The same!* Dark-haired, lean . . .

Sensual.

Her fingers tightened around the rough wood in her hands. Despite the overwhelming similarities with this man, there was something different separating him from the Highwayman of her fantasies. Something *real*.

The stranger took another step and his hands began to drift down to his sides.

"Don't come any closer!" she warned, jabbing into the air in front of her with the pitchfork.

Once again he stopped. Then his eyes narrowed and his jaw hardened. "Letitia Grey," he murmured, his voice low and deep, like velvet thunder. "As I live and breathe, you're Jacob Grey's little sister, aren't you?"

"Yes."

He knew her? But how? If he were truly a figment of her imagination, she could believe his familiarity with her. After all, her Highwayman had been a constant imaginary companion for years. But this man was no illusion. He was flesh and blood.

Wasn't he?

Although she knew she was behaving recklessly, foolishly—even wantonly—Lettie took a cautious step forward, then another. And another. The man stiffened, evidently distrustful of her actions after she'd threatened to skewer him with the pitchfork. But Lettie needed to get closer. Just a little bit. Just enough to assure herself that he was no dream.

"Who are you?" she demanded softly.

The man didn't answer; his jaw remained tight. His glance flicked toward the approaching tines of the pitchfork before he took a step back.

Lettie's gaze dropped. His wet boots gleamed in the near darkness. The muscles of his thighs were firm, strong, the denim of his pants wet. And his hips . . .

Laws! The man had the hips of the Highwayman. Narrow, masculine. Firm.

Realizing she was staring at the all-too-masculine bulge in the front of his pants, Lettie forced herself to look up. But that action was worse. So much worse. The pelting rain had saturated the thin blue cotton of his shirt so that each line, each indentation had been lovingly molded to his skin. The front lay open nearly to his waist, exposing a healthy expanse of firm, muscular flesh spattered ever so lightly with dark hair.

"Who *are* you?" she demanded again, her tone a little more forceful. He was so close now, she could see the moisture beaded in the dark strands of his hair and on the harsh, square planes of his face. Yet the pitchfork could have been a matchstick between them for all the power it had in convincing him to speak.

Since he refused to answer, she decided to try another tack: "How do you know who I am?"

When he still didn't speak, she jabbed the pitchfork toward him.

The man lifted his hands in a defensive gesture and muttered cryptically, "Your brother and I were ... passing acquaintances a few years back." For a moment his eyes glittered in the dim light. "I made it my business to learn everything about him." After a slight pause he added, "And those he cares about."

Her eyes narrowed. "Have you come to see Jacob?"

He hesitated before responding. "No. I stopped for directions."

"For what?"

"The road to Eastbrook."

"Why?"

Once again, he refused to talk.

Lettie stepped forward, effectively trapping the man against one of the stalls. For the first time in the murky light of the barn, she could see that his eyes were blue. A clear, azure blue. Yet they were eyes that saw the world from an emotional distance—missing nothing, seeing everything, while remaining detached. Wary.

When he still refused to answer her, Lettie pressed the pointed tips of the pitchfork against his chest in a none-too-subtle attempt at persuasion.

He didn't try to step away. Instead, one of the sharp points dug into the flesh of his left breast and a bead of crimson welled from the spot.

A soft gasp spilled from Lettie's lips only moments before the man swore. Obviously impatient with her actions, he grasped the pitchfork, tossing it into the stall beside her.

Lettie made the mistake of twisting to watch it plunge to the hilt in a mound of soft hay. When she turned back, the stranger had moved away.

"Don't!" she called out when he stepped toward the side door.

The man turned to face her again, and Lettie found herself moving toward him on limbs that were slightly shaky—but not from fear. Try as she might, she couldn't help thinking this man was only a continuation of her

7

fantasies about the Highwayman, the man she had fabricated in her head years before when reality had become just a little too monotonous. She couldn't let him go. Not yet.

Not without touching him. Just once.

The man hesitated, and Lettie closed the distance between them with a wariness she might show to a less-than-housebroken tomcat. When only a few scant feet separated them, she nervously licked her lips, speaking quickly in an effort to prevent the man from leaving before she knew something more about him. "Eastbrook is south of here. If you take the main road through the center of town, then turn left at the bank, you'll see the . . ."

Her words trailed away and she fought to breathe, her hand lifting toward the stranger ever so slightly. *She was so close now!* So close. Every pore of her body seemed to absorb the warmth of his body. She had only to reach out and touch him.

The man's eyes flicked from a lock of honey-brown hair that clung moistly to her cheek, to her eyes, to her slightly parted lips. Lettie could tell that he thought her daft for acting so strangely. But how could you tell a man he was a dream come to life?

She took another step forward. Two. Her skirts brushed against the toes of his boots, then pressed against his thighs. The air she drew into her lungs smelled of male musk and rain, reminding her all too eloquently of just how near she'd managed to stand to this stranger.

Her Highwayman.

Slowly, cautiously, she reached out to touch the placket of his shirt with her finger. The blue chambray was wet. Soft.

Her gaze lifted.

Brown eyes locked with blue.

Lettie was torn between fear and some strange emotion she wasn't sure she could name. Her skin seemed to grow hot, then cold, and her stomach tightened.

"No one's ever going to believe me this time. They'll say I conjured you from the air and you never really

8

existed," she whispered to herself, but the man evidently heard her, because his dark brows creased into a scowl.

Still marveling at the fact that this man had to be real—flesh and blood—Lettie used the same finger to push aside his shirt and touch the small puncture high on his chest.

The man's fingers snapped around her wrist, jerking her hand away, his grip bold, firm, and faintly calloused. The dim light winked against the ruby signet ring he wore on his right hand, the flash of crimson echoing the bead of blood that clung to the tip of her finger.

"Wha—" She couldn't finish what she'd been about to say, couldn't *remember* what she'd been about to say. The stranger had moved forward, his expression growing fierce.

"Don't play games with me, Letitia Grey."

"Get away from her," a low voice rasped. The snap of a revolver being cocked split the near quiet of the barn.

The man stiffened. His eyes became guarded, his muscles tense. Though his features remained inscrutable, Lettie sensed a brittle caution settling into his frame.

Slowly, he released her wrist. Air swirled between them, cold and thick with the scent of rain.

"Back away from her, nice and easy," the voice ordered again, and Lettie cringed, knowing for a fact who had interrupted them. Twisting her head to peer over her shoulder, Lettie wasn't sure if she should growl in frustration or wither in embarrassment when she found her brother, Jacob, sighting down the barrel of a Colt revolver.

Jacob lifted the weapon ever so slightly, as if correcting some slight error in his aim. His dark eyes gleamed in the blue-gray light of the barn and his expression unnerved Lettie. Although she was Jacob's junior by nearly six years, she'd learned to avoid that look.

"Lettie, get into the house," he barked.

"But—"

"Do as I say!"

"Jacob, you don't understand!"

Without warning, the stranger's arm snapped around Lettie's neck and the cool tip of a revolver dug into her temple.

"Put the revolver down, Grey," the man behind her snarled. His grasp became tighter. The harsh grate of the hammer being cocked seemed to ricochet in the heavy air.

Lettie saw her brother tense, and a dangerous light entered his eyes. "Damn you," he whispered.

"Put it down!"

Slowly moving his arms out to his sides, Jacob released the hammer of his revolver, then bent and carefully set it in the straw.

"Now back away." When Jacob hesitated, the stranger ground the end of his revolver more tightly into Lettie's flesh. "Back away!"

Jacob's eyes narrowed. "You've never shot anyone before."

"I'm willing to start now. Back away!"

Jacob's boots rasped through the straw as he moved into the shadows.

Still holding Lettie tightly, the man moved toward Jacob's revolver, dragging her behind him. His grip loosened only for a moment as he scooped the weapon from the dust and shoved it into the back of his waistband.

"You're coming with me," he muttered softly, pulling her toward the side door.

"Dammit! If you take my sister, I'll kill you."

"Shut up, Grey. As long as your men don't follow me, she won't be hurt."

The man dragged her through the side door and toward a bay gelding that waited patiently beneath the eaves. Barely giving her time to think, the stranger grasped her waist, lifted her onto the saddle, then swung up behind her.

"Hold on," he growled into her ear, and dug his heels into the animal's sides.

Lettie clung to the mane of the animal as they bolted into the rain. The stranger led his mount in a tangled

10

course through the back streets of town, then out past the creek, and into the scrub.

But Lettie paid little attention to where they were going. Instead, she tried to absorb the fact that she had just been abducted. By a man who looked very much like her Highwayman. With the warmth of his body against her back and the strength of his arm around her waist, Lettie was oblivious to the rain that pounded around them.

Without warning, the stranger pulled on the reins and brought his mount to a stop. Finally lifting her head to gaze around her, Lettie realized that they were at the crossroads three miles out of town.

The man behind her shifted. "I'm sorry, Letitia, but you'll have to walk back."

She glanced over her shoulder, then grew still and tense. Although she had been entertaining fanciful imaginings about the man behind her, it was obvious that he was bent upon much more practical matters.

The hand around her waist tightened, and he lifted her from the saddle. She stiffened, her fingers curling more tightly around the horse's mane. Then she realized that this was not her Highwayman but a stranger. A cold, hardened man who had threatened to kill her.

A chill wracked down her spine and she pushed away from the horse's neck and slid to the ground. The moment her feet hit the earth, she began to run. But after only a few yards, she stopped and turned toward him. "Lettie. They call me Lettie."

His dark hair lay plastered against his skull. His azure eyes regarded her from a face that was all planes and angles. And Lettie knew she would never forget the expression that crossed his blunt-hewn features. There was no doubt that this man was hard and unyielding. But for a moment—one fleeting moment—she thought she saw a glimmer of something softer within his expression. Something that looked very much like regret.

Gathering the reins, he turned his mount, then hesitated and glanced over his shoulder. "Don't stay out here too long then, Lettie Grey. Go back to the house and get out of the rain. Promise?"

"Promise," she whispered, surprised and a little confused by his concern.

His hand lifted, his fingers touching his forehead in a gentlemanly salute. Then his lips twitched in what she thought was a smile, and he rode away.

Lettie wrapped her arms about her and blinked against the rain as the man who'd looked so much like her Highwayman disappeared into the trees. Finally, when she couldn't distinguish his shape anymore, she turned and began to walk back into town.

Halfway there, she was met by Jacob and six other men.

When Jacob saw her, he galloped toward her, slid from his horse, and grasped her arms. "Are you all right?"

"I'm fine."

His eyes narrowed. "You're sure he didn't hurt you?"

"Yes. I'm fine."

Jacob wrapped his arms around her and held her tightly to his chest as if to assure himself of her well-being, then he drew back. "When he left you, where was he headed?"

Lettie hesitated only a moment before saying "Bluffdale."

It was the first time she could ever remember lying to her brother, and a twinge of guilt curled within her when Jacob apparently took her words at face value.

"Rusty, take her home. We'll meet you on the road to Bluffdale."

After gently squeezing her arms once again, Jacob helped her onto the horse behind his deputy, then mounted and signaled to his men. The posse thundered away.

In the wrong direction.

As Rusty turned his horse toward town, Lettie thought she saw a shadow moving in the trees beside the creek. The shadow of a man on horseback.

Though she couldn't explain her actions or her reasons, Lettie suddenly knew she'd done the right thing.

* * *

Within an hour, Jacob Grey and his posse returned, having been unable to find any leads to the stranger's whereabouts. After leaving his men at the jailhouse, Jacob mounted his horse and rode five miles out of town to the abandoned Johnston farm. Reining his mount to a halt beside a huge, lightning-blasted oak tree, he hesitated only a moment before withdrawing a metal canister and inserting a single piece of paper into the damp chamber. Then he replaced the canister and rode back in the direction he had come. Within two hours, he knew his message would be relayed to the other members of the vigilante group known as the Star Council of Justice:

Proof positive that Ethan McGuire has entered the state of Illinois. Begin necessary procedures to notify the Star Council. Must know if evidence of guilt has been obtained. If so: apprehend through legal channels? Or deliver to the Star?

2

Lettie never discovered what Jacob knew about the Highwayman—as she'd begun to call the stranger she'd encountered in the barn—but after that day, she didn't see the man again. He disappeared from Madison as if he'd never come, and no one could tell her exactly who he was.

But she wondered.

And secretly, she wished he would return.

Much to Lettie's relief, Jacob never told her mother what had happened, although she'd had to suffer through one of his Lettie-you're-too-trusting-and-too-much-of-a-dreamer lectures. In time, he seemed to forget the event himself and stopped staring at Lettie as if she'd be safer locked up in one of his cells.

But Lettie didn't forget. Each shimmering moment she'd spent with the stranger lay etched in her memory like a patch of ink that waited only for a drop of water before it emerged again, fresh and shiny. Tiny things triggered her thoughts: the smell of rain, the musty warmth of the barn, the texture of splintered wood against her palms.

Without at first being conscious of the action, Lettie began to catalogue each day according to the memory.

14

When she awakened in the morning she would think to herself: *It's been three whole days now. Two weeks. A month.* Each night before she went to bed, she curled into the window case of her garret bedroom, intending to write her poems. Yet, time and time again, instead of writing, she'd find herself staring out at the barn, remembering the scent of his skin, the warmth of his grip.

Always blessed with an abundant imagination, Lettie found her fantasies of the Highwayman becoming more lifelike than ever before. The locations of their meetings became more exotic, the anticipation more enticing.

Each time she thought of him, her imaginings would end with a hint of a smile. That brief, gentle smile. Then the daydream would vanish, the image of the man would dissipate into the air like smoke in the breeze, and she would turn, expecting the stranger to appear behind her as he had once before.

But he never did.

Instead, she would awaken to her surroundings feeling . . . strange. Restless. Where once her dreaming had proven to be an escape, now her fantasies became an obsession until soon, without her being aware of the change, spring melted into summer and something blossomed within Lettie. Something . . . hungry.

Hungry.

Setting a basket of sodden laundry on the top step behind the boardinghouse, Lettie paused to swipe back a lock of honey-brown hair from her damp forehead and squinted up at the sun that drooped wearily on the edge of the horizon. As if a tangible echo to her thoughts, her stomach rumbled noisily, reminding her that she hadn't eaten since sunrise, and now the day was nearly over.

Shrugging away the impulse to grab a piece of bread to tide her over until she could fix something a little more hearty, Lettie grasped the basket and determinedly marched down the back steps. Though it was getting late, she'd finally finished the last batch of laundry. All that remained of the task was clearing the clothesline of the items that had dried in the hot summer air and exchanging them for those in her basket. And by darned, she wasn't going to take a moment longer than necessary! She wanted the task done as soon as possible. Then Lettie could find herself something to eat and slip upstairs to finish her latest poem, "Ode to a Highwayman," while the sheets and pillowslips dried on the line before dark.

A hot gust of air tugged at her skirt and the tail of her braid, seeming to tempt her into returning to the house, but Lettie would have nothing of it. Somewhere along the chain of years she'd spent washing linens in boiling baths of lye, Lettie had come to the conclusion that dirty clothes were a bit like rabbits: If left untended long enough, they multiplied to three times their original number.

Dropping the basket onto the grass beside the clothesline, Lettie swatted her thick plait over her shoulder and began unpinning the garments that had been drying since late afternoon. On the outer lines were the men's slacks and workshirts. Moving inward were the table linens and dishcloths. Then, discreetly separated by a line of bath sheets, were items of feminine clothing, the more delicate unmentionables properly shielded from view by the long, voluminous petticoats of Miss Alma Beasley, one of the maiden ladies who'd lived at the boardinghouse for years.

Despite her efforts to hurry, Lettie huffed in irritation when the wind seemed to mock her, whipping at the clean laundry and trying to snatch it from her fingers before she could fold things and put them in one corner of the basket, exchanging the dry for the damp.

She'd finished little more than a third of the clothesline when, peeking over the top of the wires, Lettie noted Mr. Randolph Goldsmith lumbering through the grass toward her like a white-suited tug boat in full steam, his hairpiece slightly askew on top of his head and his forehead bathed in perspiration. Behind him, like a tall, slender shadow, trailed Ned Abernathy, his assistant, carrying their sample cases of buttons and lace. They'd evidently left their buggy in the barn after a full day of drumming in some of the neighboring towns.

"Trouble with the wind, Letitia?" Mr. Goldsmith intoned when he caught sight of her behind the flapping garments.

Lettie fought back a smile and reached for another clothespin. "No, I can manage. Thank you."

Mr. Goldsmith nodded, then grabbed for his hairpiece when it slid dangerously forward on his head. Flushing a brilliant shade of crimson, he pushed his hair back into place and wheezed to a stop. "Even so, you'd best hurry if you're to make the poetry reading at the social hall." Still gasping from the exertion of walking up the hill, he reached into his pocket for a huge handkerchief, then used it to blot some of the moisture from his brow.

Lettie reached for another clothespin, more slowly this time. The mere mention of the poetry reading still managed to jab her with a sharp pang of disappointment and frustration. "I won't be going." Despite her effort to sound unaffected, her words emerged clipped and filled with the dregs of her private anger.

"What? Not going?"

"No." She jerked a pair of socks from the line and savagely rolled the tops so that the mates would stay together. "Someone has to stay at the boardinghouse," she answered curtly, too embarrassed to admit that she'd been forbidden to attend by her mother, due to the "suggestive elements of the poet being presented." But she couldn't admit that fact to these men, so she waved her hand in a sweeping gesture. "Besides, there's all this yet to do and . . . you know how busy things can get sometimes."

"Oh. I always thought . . . what with all that poetry you write . . ." Goldsmith gazed at her first in confusion, then in dismay. After a moment, he glanced at his assistant, who towered above him by a good six inches. "Ohhh," he breathed, as if just now realizing her confinement in the house was by force, not by choice. Then he turned to regard her again with blatant pity. "Oh, we're sorry. So sorry. Aren't we sorry, my boy?"

Lettie glanced again at Mr. Goldsmith's assistant. Although Ned offered her a brief, sympathetic nod, she couldn't read much in it. For as long as she'd known him, Ned Abernathy had existed with a quiet, sober expression that seemed to have been carved from a gaunt tree branch, making him seem much older than his twenty-three years.

Mr. Goldsmith slipped his watch from his pocket, then wheezed. "My, we'll be late if we don't hurry." He threw Lettie a guilty glance, then cleared his throat. "Come along, Ned. Evening, Letitia."

Goldsmith lumbered toward the back stoop and Lettie moved back to her laundry, but after a moment, she became aware that Ned hadn't moved. Turning, she found him watching her with his almost colorless gray eyes. Lettie waited, expecting him to speak, but when the air around them lay unbroken but for the snap of the laundry and the low moan of the wind, she finally prompted, "Ned?"

Finally, his eyes flicked to the setting sun, then back. "There'll be a storm," he murmured, his voice low and slightly husky, as if he weren't accustomed to speaking aloud much.

Lettie smiled, glanced at the clear, cloudless sky, then shook her head. "Oh, I don't think so. There's a bit of wind, but the sky is clear."

"You be careful tonight," he murmured as if she hadn't spoken. Then, after throwing her a quick half-smile, he turned, climbed the steps, and disappeared into the house.

Lettie watched him, her fingers curling into the trousers she held until they wrinkled. A sharp gust of wind tugged at her skirts and caused the laundry to snap like a bullwhip, forcing her to return to her task. Although she tried to banish Ned's warning, she couldn't help noting the twisting contortions being made by the grass at her feet and the heavy weight of the sun in the sky.

The screech of Madison's incoming passenger train reverberated against the stone stationhouse and weathered walkways with a strength to wake the dead. Then the thick evening air stifled the noise, leaving only the breathless pant of the engine and the whine of brakes as the six o'clock express ground to a weary halt.

18

Almost immediately, travelers began to disembark, greeting family and friends before moving toward the baggage-collection area. Those passengers who were not stopping in Madison emerged as well, taking advantage of the fifteen-minute waterstop to stretch their legs or grab something from the cafe to eat.

From within the last passenger car, Ethan McGuire waited until most of the travelers had disappeared toward home or the scant comfort of the stationhouse. He watched them scurry away from the train like soot-stained ants intent upon the anthill, until all that remained were a few harried porters and those too tired to step from the cars.

With a loose-limbed grace that belied his dusty clothes and disreputable beard-darkened jaw, Ethan pushed himself to his feet. His eyes swept the railroad car, with its leather-tufted seats and faded chintz blinds, but those passengers who remained on board paid him no mind.

Denying the weariness that cloaked him as surely as the tenacious layer of soot on his jacket, Ethan bent to scoop his hat from the seat, settled it over the dark, ash-brown waves of his hair, then reached for the saddlebags he'd brought with him for his trip. Slinging another small valise over his shoulder, Ethan moved down the length of the railroad car onto the rear platform.

For a moment he paused to study his first glimpse of Madison in nearly a month. He breathed deeply of the heavy air, thick with its scents of dust and heat.

Since he'd met up with Jacob Grey on his last pass through Madison, Ethan had sworn to himself that he wouldn't come within twenty miles of the sleepy town until he had a pardon from the governor safely tucked into his pocket, a pardon for Ethan's more youthful peccadilloes—mainly his overt skill at opening safes and removing their contents.

Nearly ten years before, Ethan had developed that skill into an art form, making a certain trademark for himself and his work. A trademark more distinctive, and damning, than a personal signature could ever be. His daring midnight robberies had caught the attention of lawmen and journalists, preachers and sinners alike. Even the newspapers had given outlandish accounts of his exploits and coined Ethan with the title of the "Gentleman Bandit."

But now someone else was using that self-same trademark to trap Ethan like a rat in a hole. And after nearly three months of trying to find the person responsible, Ethan kept butting head-on with the fact that all of the thefts had occurred within a twenty-mile radius of Madison—while Madison itself had remained untouched. And damned if Ethan didn't have a horrible idea of just who might be responsible.

The fact that his stepbrother had been rooming at the Greys' boardinghouse for nearly a year now had not escaped Ethan's attention. And ten years before, Ned had known every detail of Ethan's methods.

Ethan had tried to see Ned on his first trip through Madison, but Jacob Grey had prevented the meeting before it could ever happen. Since he'd been unable to talk to his stepbrother, Ethan had tried to dismiss the robberies as a fluke coincidence, reassuring himself that the thief would be captured in a matter of days.

But three robberies had occurred in the past two weeks alone, all using the methods of the Gentleman Bandit. Each heist had proven to be more damaging to Ethan's "retirement" and the well-being of his pardon. And it was only a matter of time before some of the more experienced lawmen began remembering that their most likely suspect for the Gentleman years before had been Ethan McGuire.

Ethan's eyes narrowed and his gaze swerved in the direction of Madison's city jail. Marshal Jacob Grey would be one of those lawmen. Five years before, as a part-time deputy in Chicago, Jacob Grey had been the first man to come within spitting distance of catching the Gentleman Bandit in the midst of a midnight robbery. Yet because of a careless act on the deputy's part, Ethan had escaped unscathed, and the only thing Jacob had been able to salvage from the evening was his suspicions.

But Ethan had lived too long on the edge of the law to discredit the other man as harmless—even though Jacob Grey had never come forward during the years to apprehend him. Regardless of the passage of time, Ethan couldn't help wondering when Jacob would realize his theories had indeed been fact. But most of all, Ethan couldn't help wondering if Jacob could also uncover the means of proving his guilt.

No matter how he looked at it, the time had come for Ethan to make a decision. Soon enough, he would have to weather the storm of suspicion and fight for his pardon, or cut his losses and leave the country.

Ethan had just about decided to cut his losses.

But he had to talk to his stepbrother first.

Ethan's eyes lifted and scanned the station yard with a restlessness he'd developed at an early age. Although he saw nothing untoward in the area, a tension formed deep in his gut. He couldn't place his finger on it, but there was something unsettling about this small, sleepy town. Something more than a town marshal who stood only a breath away from sending Ethan to prison, or a stepbrother Ethan hadn't seen in years, or a bewitching woman-child who had threatened him with a pitchfork.

But Ethan had returned. Regardless of the risk.

His jaw tightened, and he stepped from the platform onto the rough boardwalk. The swirling pant of steam from the train twined about his feet like a cat, seemingly bidding him to stay away from Madison and all it entailed—an omen, his mother would have said. But Ethan had never been a man who paid heed to omens. He was a man who believed in the importance of survival and the necessity of wits. He'd learned the harsh realities of that lesson too early on to forget it now.

No, he'd never liked the feeling of being hemmed in, and he knew he'd like prison even less. So if someone were truly intent upon trapping him and seeing him arrested for crimes that weren't his own . . .

Ethan wasn't about to sit back and wait for it to happen.

Hiking his saddlebags more securely onto his shoulder, Ethan strode toward the rear cars to retrieve his mount, his mind already bent on the job that awaited him. Since Ned probably wouldn't be home until after dark, Ethan intended to ride out to the creek where he could hide for an hour or two and perhaps even snatch a little sleep. Then, once darkness had fallen, he would try to survey several of the banks in town. Though he had no proof, Ethan felt the Gentleman was about to strike again. It had been days since his last heist, and one of the nearby banks would be his most logical target.

Ethan could only hope his luck was beginning to turn and that he'd find the man responsible. Soon.

Ned Abernathy's prediction proved true. Within an hour, the wind had begun to whine and moan like a banshee, bringing a load of dust on its back that caused the air to become gritty and thick. Not until Lettie stood tight-jawed, watching the departure of those destined for the poetry reading, did she remember her laundry on the back line. Cursing under her breath, she ran through the house and emerged with her basket, only to find her clean linens coated with a layer of grime.

Since it would serve no purpose to fold things—they would have to be rewashed anyway—Lettie unpinned the linens and wadded them into the basket, fighting the wind that seemed determined to rip the precious items from her hands.

Finally, with her eyes stinging from the grit and her mouth filled with dust, she heaved the basket against her chest and hurried into the house. Gasping air into her lungs, she stood in indecision for a moment, listening to the moan of the wind through the eaves and the distant slam of a loose shutter against the side of the house.

All at once, she grew still. The house seemed so quiet. Hollow. With seven permanent boarders—and often times double that amount, due to people who stayed only a night or two—the boardinghouse was rarely silent. Tonight, since all of the boarders had gone to a reading of Poe hosted by a well-known circuit actor, the house was completely empty.

Except for Lettie, who hadn't been allowed to attend.

After setting the basket of clothing on the floor of the pantry, Lettie marched through the kitchen to the front parlor. Lifting the delicate lace curtain, she glared through the window, which had already been coated with a slight layer of dust. By squinting her eyes, she could just see the shimmering gaslights at the end of Main Street where the assembly hall was located.

When she thought of all the townspeople gathering in the auditorium for the performance, a bitter frustration flooded her, then a fiery anger. This had been her first chance to attend a professional poetry reading. And since Lettie had aspirations of publishing her own work, she'd been so excited. Imagine such a golden opportunity coming here. To Madison!

But from the very start, her mother had put her foot down, claiming Poe wasn't a good influence on a young woman. *"Poe is much too sensational for a girl your age, Lettie,"* she'd said. *"He's entirely too moody. Too frank."*

Lettie's mouth tightened in frustration. Sensational or not, Celeste Grey had gone to the reading.

With a huff of irritation, Lettie glared at her own reflection in the glass. What her mother didn't seem to realize was that Lettie wasn't a child anymore. *No one* seemed to realize it. She'd just turned nineteen, the same age Mama had been when Jacob was born.

So why couldn't Jacob and her mother see she wasn't in need of their coddling and fussing? Landsakes! Many of the girls in town her age had been married and had a baby or two by now! She was more than capable of making her own decision as to what was right or wrong, proper or improper. And if she made mistakes—fine. At least they would be *her* mistakes.

Making a face at her reflection, Lettie turned away from the mocking gleam of lights in Madison proper, absorbing the creak and shudder of the house and the low moan of the wind as it banged against the house and threatened to rip it from its very foundations Once again, her hands tightened into balls of frustration. The evening's atmosphere was perfect for Poe: gloomy and grim. Lettie could almost imagine the spectators huddling in their seats as the actor recited "The Tell-Tale Heart" or "The Raven."

Whirling in a flash of petticoats and black cotton stockings, Lettie lifted her calico skirts and crept dramatically through the parlor toward the lamp she'd left on the side table. Lowering her voice to an eerie murmur, she slowly repeated, "Once upon a midnight dreary, while I pondered, weak and weary/Over many a quaint and curious volume of forgotten lore . . ."

Although her mother had sought to protect her from the effects of Poe, Celeste Grey had never realized that Lettie had not only read his "sensational" literature, she'd memorized most of it as well. Her voracious appetite for poetry and literature caused her to borrow whatever books might find their way into the boardinghouse, and whenever possible, she tried to commit the shorter poems to memory or at least copy them down.

Lettie reached out to grasp the lamp and hold it aloft like a heroine in a lurid dime novel, then continued her macabre recitation, carrying the lamp back into the kitchen.

"While I nodded, nearly napping, suddenly there came a tapping,/As of some one gently rapping, rapping at my chamber door."

As if on cue, the wind banged against the loose shutter at one of the upstairs bedroom windows. Lettie nodded in satisfaction, then snorted when a fine sifting of straw and grit drifted down from her hair. Realizing the wind had coated more than the laundry, she placed the lamp on the table and crossed to retrieve the kettle of warm water that was always left on the stove for the boarders.

Still quoting from "The Raven," she splashed a bit of water into a china basin and carried it to the vanity by the back door. Outside, the wind howled. The loose shutter banged like a madman trying to break free. Lettie shivered in delight.

"Deep into that darkness peering, long I stood there

wondering, fearing,/Doubting, dreaming dreams no mortal ever dared to dream before;/But the silence was unbroken, and the stillness gave no token,/And the only word there spoken was the whispered word, 'Lenore!' ''

That was Lettie's favorite part, and she made a low, evil laugh deep in her throat to add to the dramatic tone of her recitation. Quickly unbuttoning her bodice and folding it neatly over the back of a chair, Lettie took a cloth from the rack beneath the mirror and splashed water on her face, scrubbing her skin of the faint layer of grit left by her dash outside. Then, with her torso clad only in her corset and camisole, she sponged the rest of her limbs clean.

The hot water dripped through her fingers and down the fullness of her chest, easing tense muscles and stilling the nervous fluttering in her stomach. Sighing, Lettie dropped the cloth into the basin, closed her eyes, and reached for the thick honey-brown braid that hung down her back. Inch by inch, she began to free her hair from the intricate plait, her movements slow, poetic. If only the Highwayman could see her now.

The back door slammed open and Lettie screamed, clutching the bath sheet to her chest and whirling to face her assailant. A gust of wind extinguished the lamp, plunging the kitchen into darkness.

With her heart pounding in her throat, Lettie crept through the dark kitchen, keeping her eyes carefully trained on the black shape of the doorway. No one was there, she repeated to herself over and over again. The door was known for its faulty latch, and she'd merely scared herself with all her "Raven" nonsense.

No one was there. No one was there.

But she couldn't be sure. Inching sideways toward the extinguished lamp, Lettie held a hand to her eyes, squinting against the force of the wind that came from the open door. Outside it was so dark. So black. The wind had blown a scudding layer of clouds across the sky, obscuring the faint sliver of moon so that only a single finger of light stretched from beneath the swinging door that led into the hall, but the rest of the room lay huddled in blackness.

Easing toward the table, Lettie was finally able to find the lamp and the matchbox in the center. With hands that trembled, she managed to light one matchstick, carefully shielding it with her fingers and lifting it high so that its feeble light stretched toward the door.

No one was there.

Hesitantly moving forward, Lettie reached out to close the door. Long before her hands could touch the rough wood, the matchstick flickered and died. Moving more quickly, she lunged the last few feet and slammed the door shut, then turned and leaned heavily against it, eyes closed, gasping for breath.

It had just been the wind.

Her eyes opened and she screamed. The door to the hallway had been propped open. Silhouetted in the faint light was the clear shape of a man.

3

"Damn, you're not—"

The man stepped forward, and the light from the hall spilled around his features, highlighting the dark hair, firm chin, slim nose.

Lettie's scream died beneath a gasp of disbelief. *He'd come back!*

Almost before the thought had formed in her head, Lettie became aware of the way the man cradled one hand awkwardly against his stomach. Even as she took a step forward, she saw something drip from his hand and splash on the floor.

Blood.

"What happened?"

"Shh!" The man's forehead creased in impatience and he lifted his hand, revealing the revolver he'd held hidden behind the line of his thigh. Cocking his head, he seemed to listen intently for a moment, his entire body focused on the activity. The dim light gleamed on the dark, ash-brown waves of his hair.

Then Lettie heard it, too: the muffled thunder of hooves.

The man's gaze darted back, pinning Lettie to the

door. She sensed a dangerous purpose in his azure eyes and a fierce will to survive.

How many times had Lettie lived through just such a predicament in her fantasies? How many times had she imagined herself confronting the Highwayman only moments before his capture?

As if her imaginings had been as real as the man who faced her now, Lettie found herself reacting instinctively to the situation.

Shoving the table aside, she whipped the braided rug away from the floor to reveal the trapdoor that led into the cellar. Yanking on the rope handle, she gestured to a set of rickety stairs.

"You've got to hide."

She glanced up to find the man regarding her with narrowed blue eyes. Obviously wary of her actions and her immediate solution to the problem, he seemed to battle with himself, wondering if he should trust her. Her idea of a hiding place would also serve as the perfect trap.

The sound of approaching horses grew nearer. Reaching out, she took the man's arm and yanked him toward the cellar. Handing him the bath sheet she'd clutched in front of her for protection, Lettie instructed, "Wrap this around your hand to stop the bleeding." The stranger disappeared into the blackness of the cellar, and she hurriedly added, "And whatever you do, don't make any noise!"

Dropping the trapdoor, Lettie dragged the rug back into place, tugged on the table, then quickly lit the lamp and settled the chimney into place.

The back door slammed open and Lettie gasped, whirling to press her back against the table. This time when she glanced up, the doorway wasn't empty.

A shape stepped forward, and a betraying squeak tore from Lettie's throat before the man had moved into the dim light and Lettie recognized her brother.

"Jacob! You nearly scared the life out of me!"

Her brother didn't speak. He stepped into the room,

his revolver raised, his eyes carefully scanning the shadows before returning to glance at Lettie.

"Are you all right?"

"Of course I'm all right!"

"Where is everyone?"

When three other men moved to enter behind him, Jacob swore and barked an order for them to wait on the porch, motioning for Lettie to retrieve her bodice.

"They've gone to the poetry reading in town." Lettie avoided her brother's gaze, looking down to pay strict attention to the task of buttoning her bodice.

"Have you seen anyone tonight?"

Lettie's fingers fumbled. "Anyone?" she repeated vaguely. She glanced up to find Jacob staring at her curiously, then returned her attention to her buttons. "Do you mean boarders?"

"Strangers. Have you seen any strangers?"

The bodice completely fastened, Lettie shook her head. "No. I haven't seen any strangers." She felt a small twinge of guilt at the lie: the Highwayman wasn't *really* a stranger.

Jacob motioned for his men to move into the house. One crept toward the parlor, while the other two took the back stairs, heading toward the bedrooms. Her brother waited until they had disappeared from sight before turning, finally looking her straight in the eye. "You're sure?"

"I'm sure." Quickly crossing to the other side of the room, Lettie hurriedly added, "Would you and your men like some coffee? Maybe a piece of pie?"

Without waiting for her brother to answer her, she reached for the gooseberry pie in the pie safe and placed it on the counter, grasping the butcher knife kept on the counter of the dry sink.

"There's plenty. I made it just yesterday." When her brother didn't answer her, Lettie turned. She quickly bit her lip to keep from making a betraying sound when she found her brother squatting on the floor, his finger reaching out toward the splash of blood on the polished floorboards.

Lettie's eyes widened in fear. Upon closer examination, she could see the way the drops of blood led to the edge of the rug. If Jacob were to suspect the man of coming here, it would only take a moment for him to realize where he was hiding.

Whirling away from her brother, Lettie took the knife and, closing her eyes, drew the edge over the pad of her finger. Clenching her teeth, she held her hand out so that a few drops of blood splashed onto the floor at her feet and dripped onto the counter. Then, taking a dishcloth, she pressed it tightly against her finger to stop the flow of blood.

"Jacob?" she asked again as casually as she could. Turning, she smiled. "Do you want some pie or not?"

Her brother glanced up, his eyes probing her expression in the dim light of the kitchen. He rose slowly to his feet and stepped toward her. "Are you sure you're all right? Has anyone bothered you?" he asked softly. So softly, no one could have heard him more than a few inches away. His gaze moved to peer into the dark corners as if some sense warned him of the Highwayman's presence.

Lettie smiled brightly, cocking her head in mock confusion. "All right? Of course I'm all right." She tried to laugh and held up her hand. "Unless you count cutting myself with the knife earlier this evening. I was peeling a potato and the blade slipped and—Jacob?"

Her brother glanced from her hand, with its evident wound, to the floor, to the edge of the rug, to the streaks of blood on the counter. Lettie held her breath, trying to smile, though her jaw ached with the effort of attempting to appear natural.

"Jacob, what's wrong?"

He took a deep breath and stepped toward the door, staring thoughtfully into the darkness. "Another robbery."

Lettie turned back to her pie. "Oh?" When her brother didn't elaborate, she was forced to turn back. "What happened?" she prompted, trying to keep her voice as normal as possible.

Jacob turned to look at her over his shoulder. "The

thief escaped with five thousand dollars in gold." He paused, as if reluctant to continue.

"And?" she asked casually—too casually.

A trace of huskiness entered Jacob's voice. "And then he exploded the safe. A deputy was injured in the fire."

Lettie sucked in her breath in horror. "Where?"

"Carlton."

Only eight miles away.

"After receiving their telegram, we joined the posse from Carlton. About two miles back, we found a horseman hiding in the trees by the creek. When he saw us, he lit out and we followed him here, then lost him in the darkness." Jacob's eyes became piercing.

"How horrible," Lettie murmured.

Jacob moved toward her, his features creased with worry. "You're positive you haven't seen anyone tonight? Anyone at all?"

Lettie hesitated. The stranger's skin had been dirty, his jacket dusted with soot.

For a moment she stared at her brother, her lips parted as if to speak. Jacob was always telling her she was too impetuous, that she burst into action before her mind had time to catch up. Perhaps he was right. Perhaps she did rely too much on intuition and not enough on logic.

Lettie's heart pounded and her hands curled into tight fists before, without conscious thought, she found herself saying "No. No one."

"Jacob!" His men came clattering down the back stairs. "There's no one upstairs, no sign of anyone trying to slip in one of the windows. I checked the locks to make sure."

At the noise, the third man stepped in from the hall. "No one on this floor or any suspicious tracks around the perimeter of the house."

Jacob nodded, still regarding Lettie with eyes that were dark and concerned. "Let's go then. He has to be out there somewhere."

His men filed outside, but Jacob lingered in the kitchen.

Finally, he sheathed his revolver and stood with his hands on his hips, studying her intently.

"See to it that all the doors and windows are barred. Once Mama and the boarders return, let them in. Then don't answer the door for anyone else until morning. Understand?"

"Yes, Jacob."

"And Lettie?"

"Yes, Jacob?"

Silence shuddered between them, broken only by the whine of the wind and the distant pounding of the loose shutter.

"Be careful, little sister."

She flashed him a grin, but it felt stiff on her own lips. "I'm always careful."

Rather than being teased from his somber mood, Jacob stepped toward her, his expression grim. "No. You're not. Sometimes you don't think before you act."

"Jacob—"

"Listen to me, Lettie. The world isn't as pretty as you see it. You imagine everything to be simple and sweet." His tone grew gentler. "Just like you're simple and sweet."

"Jacob—"

"Don't let anyone into the house, Lettie. Please." Jamming his hat onto his head, Jacob turned on his heel, slamming the door behind him so that it rattled, then grew still.

Long moments later, Lettie heard the men disappear in the darkness, yet she still waited several agonizing minutes until she was sure they were gone. Then she moved to check each window, shielding the glass with her hands and peering into the night. Though she couldn't see much, she was almost certain that her brother had truly gone. Still, she had the feeling that someone was out there. Watching.

Dousing all the lamps in the house but one, and checking the locks just as her brother had asked, Lettie adjusted the wick on the remaining light so that it burned dimly, casting the kitchen into shadow. Then she pushed the table aside and rolled back the rug. Hesitantly reaching toward the rope handle to the trap, she lifted it away and held the lamp over the opening until its light fell on the dark-haired man who peered up at her from the cellar.

Although he must have heard Jacob leave, he still held his revolver in his good hand, aiming at Lettie with deadly intent. His features were cast in shadow and light. Smooth planes, rough hollows.

Lettie gazed down at him for long moments, amazed at how much he resembled the man she'd fabricated so long before. Yet in so many ways he was different. Disturbing.

She knew nothing at all about this man, she realized. Not even his name. She had no guarantee that he hadn't set fire to the bank in Carlton. Or that he hadn't tried to murder the deputy.

Or that he wouldn't try to murder her.

"Who are you?" she finally demanded, her voice little more than a whisper.

The man in the cellar studied her intently, rising from the sack of potatoes he'd been using as a seat. Still holding the revolver at the ready, he eased up the steps, his gaze furtively searching out the corners of the room before he brushed past her to peer around the edge of the kitchen door into the hall.

"They're gone," Lettie reassured him. "Though I wouldn't be surprised if Jacob has a man waiting a few yards away from the house. My brother tends to be a bit of a mother hen." Her words trailed away as she realized that, in this instance, Jacob had a right to worry about her safety.

The stranger finally sheathed his revolver and turned to regard her, his expression guarded, his gaze carefully masked. Although Lettie knew she should probably fear this man, in the dim lamplight he made a beguiling picture. His eyes gleamed a hot azure blue. His hair lay dark and damp against his sweat-beaded skin.

Lettie glanced at the man's hand, taking in the crease that cut across his wrist. Though he must have felt her

33

gaze, the man offered no explanations, no excuses. Instead, he waited in the shadows of the room, no doubt expecting a flood of accusations. But Lettie had seen enough bullet wounds in her day to recognize the graze on the man's hand. And she knew better than to ask how the wound had occurred when he'd evidently been eluding Jacob's posse for the better part of an hour.

"We've got to take care of that injury," she stated instead, brushing past him.

His fingers snapped around her wrist.

Lettie bit back a gasp. There was a leashed violence to his touch and, conversely, a buried sense of control.

He gazed at her long and hard, taking in the braid-crimped length of her honey-brown hair, the smooth slope of her brow, the warmth of her nut-brown eyes.

Then, without speaking, he released her.

Lettie crossed toward the stove, taking a cloth from the rack and dampening it with some of the warm water left from her washing. When she turned, the stranger stood with his head slightly cocked, listening to the darkness.

"Where are the boarders?"

Lettie didn't comment on the fact that he seemed to know more about her than she about him; she merely supplied, cryptically, "Poe."

His brow creased, and without speaking, he somehow forced an explanation.

"There's a reading of Poe at the town hall. Everyone in Madison has gone." Lettie gestured for the stranger to sit on one of the trestle benches beside the table. "Please. Sit down and I'll take care of your hand."

The man's eyes grew cautious, and his head shifted so that the lean planes of his face seemed obscured in shadow. Lettie's heart began to quicken slightly when the silence shivered in the room. The distant banging of the loose shutter only seemed to make her more aware of the empty house.

"Why are you doing this for me?" he asked, his voice filled with suspicion.

"I need to wash and bandage your hand or it will become infected."

She took a step forward and reached for his injured hand, but he pulled it away.

"No, why are you—"

"Protecting you from my brother?" she interrupted softly.

"Yes." His eyes narrowed as if he wished he could peer into her mind. Eyes so clear and blue Lettie wondered why they gave the impression of allowing a person to see through to his very soul, while in reality they hid any hint of emotion or vulnerability.

"I don't know," she answered, her voice echoing with sincerity. She gestured to the hand cradled against his lean stomach. "But it appears you need some protecting."

The curve of his lips twitched in an unwilling smile.

"Sit," she whispered again.

With obvious reluctance, the stranger sat, but not before setting his revolver on the table beside him.

Lettie's eyes bounced from the revolver to the man's face. Once again, he regarded her with inscrutable eyes.

Hunted eyes.

Drawing away, Lettie gathered her mother's basket of ointments and bandages from the kitchen hutch, placing them on the table beside him before retrieving a basin and filling it with warm water from the stove.

She reached for his hand, surprised by the sudden burst of need she felt to touch him. *Just to see if he's real.*

Her glance darted up to see his reaction to her touch and became entangled in his own gaze. Her fingers trembled slightly. She looked away.

Though it should only have taken a moment to wash the wound, apply an herbal ointment, and bind the cut, Lettie found herself lingering over the task. Never had she realized that a man's hand could be so fascinating. So absorbing. His fingers were strong, blunt-tipped. His hands broad, his wrists supple.

Soon, however, her task was completed, the wound covered. And Lettie had no excuse to touch him.

"You have a gentle touch."

At the unexpected sound of his voice, she glanced at him, then quickly looked away and busied herself with tidying the basket and putting it back on the hutch. When she turned, it was to find that the stranger was making preparations to leave.

"Thanks for the kindness."

"No!" When he stepped past her, Lettie reached out to grab his arm. She couldn't let him go. Not yet. "You've got to stay."

The man's eyes narrowed. Despite the shadow of beard beginning to darken his skin, the square stubborn shape of his jaw was clearly evident. "Why?"

Why? She couldn't tell him how she'd begun to embroider her abduction into elaborate proportions. She couldn't tell him how she'd hungered for his return to break the endless pattern of her days, how she'd dreamed of kissing him, just to see if the tingling sensations she'd imagined with the Highwayman could also become reality.

She hurriedly scrambled for a logical excuse. "I—I told you: My brother worries about me like an old maiden aunt. He probably has someone watching me from just beyond the house. The minute you step out that door, you'll have a posse breathing down your neck."

"I can't stay in the cellar."

Lettie frowned, realizing that was true.

From out on the road, she heard the distant scrabble of hooves on the gravel and the muffled chatter of people beginning to drift home from the poetry reading.

"Come on!" she whispered fiercely, dragging him out of the way, slamming the trap closed, and moving the rug and table back into place.

"Where?"

"My room."

"Lettie? Where are you, child?"

Lettie just managed to shove the Highwayman into her bedroom, slam the door, and race down the back

36

staircase before the front door creaked open and her mother began to search for her.

Moving as quickly and quietly as she could, Lettie darted through the kitchen, then slowed to a more respectable pace as she moved through the hall to the vestibule. "Here I am, Mother."

"But I just—" Celeste Grey regarded her daughter in confusion, her lips tightening in disapproval. "Were you in the pantry? I went—" She waved her hand in a dismissing gesture. "No matter. I met your brother on the road; evidently there's been more trouble." Shaking her head at the audacity of the world outside the boardinghouse, Celeste drew her cape from her shoulders. "I don't want you out alone until this is settled. Day or night. Understood?"

"Yes, Mama."

The door burst open and the Beasley sisters spilled inside, their faces flushed and their eyes bright with excitement. Both Alma and Amelia Beasley had lived at the boardinghouse for years, and Lettie couldn't remember a time when she hadn't seen their sweet, apple-withered faces wreathed in smiles and breathless excitement. With hair the texture of spun sugar and a suspicious shade of pale blue, no one could guess the age of the two sisters—though Lettie had an idea that they were much closer to seventy than either would admit.

"Oh, my! Lettie, you should have been there tonight. It was so . . . *magnificent*," Alma, the elder of the two, breathed, regarding Lettie from her unusual height.

Amelia, who served as her sister's endless echo, smiled and nodded, her petite frame fairly quivering with remembered enjoyment. "Magnificent!"

"I simply adore Poe."

"Adore him!"

"I shan't sleep a wink tonight. I just know I shan't."

"Nor I!"

Lettie merely smiled. The Beasleys were always losing sleep over something, whether it was a serial story in the *Atlantic Monthly* or a new hat they'd seen at the milliner's.

"I'll bring you some hot milk," Celeste offered, moving to hang her cape on the coat closet under the stairwell. The stiff fabric of her gown rustled as she walked, and the scent of lemon verbena sifted into the air behind her.

"Oh!" Amelia gasped in delight. "Hot milk! I'd just love a cup of hot milk."

Alma pinched her smaller sister for her lack of manners in accepting so quickly, shooting Amelia a warning glance. "Celeste, we couldn't let you do that," Alma demurred politely, though the sparkle of her eyes clearly revealed the fact that a hot cup of milk before bed was a special treat at the boardinghouse and not something to be denied.

Celeste's lips twitched, but she managed to control her smile. "I insist. It will only take me a moment."

"No!" Lettie burst out. Then she smiled, adding graciously, "Let me." She had to keep her mother out of the kitchen until she could mop up the droplets of blood and hide the stained towels. Moving to wrap a concerned arm around her mother's shoulder, Lettie turned her away from the kitchen and led her toward the staircase. "You've had a late night, Mama. You should go to bed."

"Well, if you're sure you don't mind."

"I'm sure."

"Thank you, dear." Her mother smiled. "I am a bit tired. And with all the baking tomorrow . . ."

"You sleep. The Misses Beasley don't mind if I heat their milk, do you?" Though the boarders were rarely given kitchen privileges, the Beasleys had been staying in the house so long that they were regarded more as family than paying guests, and her mother occasionally stretched the rules on their behalf.

"Oh, no." Alma made a fluttering gesture with a slightly withered hand. "You go to bed, Celeste."

"Please," Amelia chimed.

"Very well." Celeste leaned close to plant a kiss on Lettie's cheek. When she drew back, her eyes narrowed ever so slightly and a suspicious light gleamed in her hazel eyes. "Just don't take too long going to bed yourself, Letitia. None of your daydreaming, and none of your poetry. Not tonight."

"Yes, Mama," Lettie answered meekly, hoping her mother wouldn't take it upon herself to check on her. Since the man upstairs was probably hungry, Lettie intended to see to it that he got a slice of her famous gooseberry pie once she'd cleaned up the kitchen. Then she'd go about finding him some extra linens and blankets.

"Lettie?"

"Mmm?"

"Mr. Goldsmith and Mr. Abernathy are bringing Mrs. Rupert and the Grubers. Once they're inside, I want you to bolt the door, then go straight to bed."

"Yes, ma'am."

Celeste stepped onto the first tread, turned, and offered a slight smile. "Good night, then." And she climbed the rest of the stairs, the train of her dress rustling behind her.

"You should have been there, Lettie," Alma whispered when Lettie's mother was out of earshot. "Jonathan Brooks gave an inspiring performance."

"Inspiring!"

The two sisters removed their cloaks and handed them to Lettie, then climbed the stairs at a snail's pace, talking to Lettie over the edge of the railing.

"For his rendition of 'The Mask of the Red Death,' he came onstage wearing nothing but a pair of tight, *tight,* leggings—I swear they looked like a pair of long johns—and a flowing shirt slit clear down to his—" Her hand waved in the general direction of her stomach, and she giggled.

"It's true!" Amelia gasped in delight. "I've never seen such legs on a man before, all tight and muscled. And his—"

"Amelia, you go too far!"

"But Alma, you yourself said on the way home that the man had a—"

"Amelia! Letitia is a little young to be hearing such talk from you."

Amelia blushed and then giggled. "Pardon me. I forgot myself. You shouldn't participate in the talk of such things until after you're married."

Lettie chuckled and turned toward the kitchen, intent upon hanging up the Beasleys' wraps, then heating their milk. "How can that be, ladies?" she teased. "You two aren't married, but you seem to talk about such things all the time."

Dissolving into girlish giggles, the Beasleys disappeared up the stairs toward their rooms, still whispering to each other. Letitia had just hung up their capes beside her mother's when the door opened again and Mr. Goldsmith gallantly stepped aside to usher Dorothy Rupert into the house.

"There you are, madam. Safe and sound, just as I promised."

"Thank you, Mr. Goldsmith. Good evening, Lettie."

Lettie smiled and moved forward to take the older woman's wrap. Dorothy Rupert was a fairly new member to the boardinghouse, having lived there for only a few months. Tall and graceful, a sadness lingered in her pale blue eyes, and the somber colors of mourning she wore denoted some tragedy that she'd never confided in any of the residents.

"Did you enjoy yourself, ma'am?"

Dorothy offered her a small smile. "As a matter of fact, yes. I've always adored Poe's poetry. Of course, his stories are a little gloomy."

"But since I spent the evening at your side, what could a woman such as yourself fear?"

Dorothy's eyes gleamed briefly with secret amusement. "Yes, of course, Mr. Goldsmith. You were very gallant. But now I must see about preparing for bed." She nodded to them both and climbed the stairs, her black dress melting into the darkness at the top of the stairs.

Randolph Goldsmith waited until the lap of her skirts had disappeared down the hall before leaning close to Lettie and whispering in her ear, "I think she likes me. Don't you think so?"

Lettie bit back a smile as he hurried up the staircase, one hand clamped over his hairpiece to keep it from slipping off the back of his head.

The door swung open again. "But dear, I wish you had abandoned your duties to attend. Then even *you* could have seen the inherent symbolism of the piece." Natalie Gruber smiled regally at Lettie, turning her back to her stocky husband.

Silas Gruber reached out to clasp her wrist, his thumb brushing back and forth beneath the edge of her sleeve. His voice dropped to a murmur: "Perhaps you and I could discuss it more tonight. In my room."

Natalie threw her husband a look of barely concealed impatience. "I think not. I'm very tired tonight, Silas. *Very* tired."

Silas's lips tightened in evident irritation, but he did not speak.

Natalie twisted free from her husband's grip and swept her cape from her shoulders in a single elegant movement. She draped the garment over her arm in such a way that Lettie could not help noticing it was new, as was Mrs. Gruber's gown, her shoes, and her hat. "Good night." Lifting her skirt ever so slightly, Natalie climbed the steps. "Oh, Lettie?"

"Yes, Mrs. Gruber?"

"Could I entreat you to bring me a cup of tea?"

Lettie opened her mouth to refuse; her mother would not have granted the request of a special pot of tea being made at this hour of the night. But since Natalie would no doubt see the hot milk she brought to the Beasleys, there was no way to refuse without appearing churlish. "Of course. Just this once, Mrs. Gruber."

Natalie regarded her in evident surprise when her request was accepted. "Well! I'll be waiting for you, then."

"Yes, Mrs. Gruber," Lettie mumbled under her breath, then she pulled a face and turned toward the coat closet as Mr. Gruber followed his wife toward their rooms. Separate rooms.

Since Ned Abernathy would probably be coming in

through the kitchen after putting Mr. Goldsmith's horse and buggy in the barn, Lettie hung up the wraps, bolted the front door, and then rushed into the kitchen. Using some of the hot water on the back of the stove, she mopped up the blood from the floor, muttering to herself when she discovered the stains had soaked into the wooden panels. But soon she had washed them enough so that the darker spots blended into the wood and were hardly noticeable. She was just about to hide the dish-cloths with the other dirty linens when the door creaked open behind her.

Lettie whirled, hiding the cloths behind her back as Ned stepped into the room. He regarded her with silver-gray eyes, closing the door behind him and twisting the latch. The click seemed loud in the deserted kitchen, reverberating like the snap of a trigger.

"G-good evening, Ned."

He merely nodded, his eyes quiet and warm.

"Mr. Goldsmith told me you enjoyed the poetry reading." Brushing past him, Lettie shoved the towels into one of the drawers in the hutch and turned with a smile. "I was just about to make some tea for Mrs. Gruber and heat some milk for the Misses Beasley. Would you care for anything?"

Ned shook his head. "No. Thank you." He hesitated for a moment, his fingers curled tightly around the brim of his hat. Finally he stepped toward her, lifting a hand toward a strand of hair that had fallen across her cheek. Long before he actually touched her, his hand dropped and he turned away, moving toward the hall door.

"Miss Lettie?"

She whirled to face him. "Yes?"

"You'll be careful, won't you?"

Lettie felt a chill spread through her. How did he know? How had he guessed about the Highwayman?

"With all the trouble, you shouldn't wander off alone."

Lettie managed a shaky smile when she realized Ned had been referring to the trouble in town and not the man in her bedroom. Since she'd once confided in Ned about her writing and her habit of dreaming down by the creek, she was touched that he was concerned about her welfare.

"I'll be careful."

Ned regarded her a moment longer, his eyes deep pools of gray beneath his brows.

"Good. I wouldn't want anything to happen to you." Offering her a slight smile, he backed from the room. "Good night, Miss Lettie."

"Yes. Good night."

Ned turned and moved into the hall, intent upon his own room. The moment his footsteps disappeared up the staircase, Lettie sagged in relief. *Laws!* She had to stop sneaking around like this. Her nerves just weren't what they used to be.

4

It took Lettie a few moments to heat the milk for the Beasleys and the tea for Natalie Gruber, but finally she arranged the respective cups on a tray. Taking a lamp from the kitchen, she hurried up the back staircase.

Moving down the hall, she reached Amelia's room first. After tapping on the door, she placed her lamp on the floor and entered, only to find Miss Amelia sleeping amid a mound of frothy pillows, her glasses perched on the end of her nose and a playbill from the evening's performance lying laxly between her fingers.

Smiling to herself, Lettie placed the tray on the bedside table, then leaned over to lift Amelia's glasses from her nose, stowing them within arm's reach. Then she slid the playbill free, pulled the covers up to Miss Amelia's chin, and blew out the lamp, leaving the playbill beside her glasses.

Tiptoeing from the room, Lettie repeated the same procedure when she found Miss Alma dozing in bed with a tattered copy of Poe's poems resting against her chest.

Finally, she moved to Natalie's room. She had already knocked on the door before she realized that Silas Gruber was in his wife's room, and the two were arguing.

44

". . . Is he, Natalie?"

"Go to bed, Silas. *Your* bed."

The voices stopped and there was a long silence before the door opened. Though his cheeks flooded with a ruddy glow, Silas Gruber nodded politely at Lettie, then brushed past her, intent upon his own room down the hall.

Lettie stood for a moment in awkward silence before stepping into the doorway. "I'm sorry, I didn't know . . ."

Natalie merely waved her apology aside as if the interruption had been of no importance. "If you'd be so kind as to place my tea on the bureau there," she instructed from where she sat at her dressing table. One by one, she removed the elaborate switches from her coiffure and lay the swathes of hair in front of her so that they resembled a bizarre collection of horsetails. "I hope I didn't cause you too much trouble."

Lettie didn't answer. She merely hoped her mother wouldn't find out about this and scold her for waiting on the boarders. *"You're not a servant, Letitia Mae. You provide the boarders with a room, hot meals, and clean laundry. The rest is their own responsibility."*

Lettie set the pot of tea on the bureau beside a crisp linen napkin and delicate cup that Natalie herself had provided. Her lips tilted in wry amusement. Natalie Gruber always drank her tea from a "dressy" cup, always sat in a "delicate" chair, always walked on the "feminine" side of the boardwalk, far from the mud and manure. And that was why Lettie often found herself envying the other woman with an intensity that bordered on dislike. Natalie was always so . . . perfect. She ate right, she dressed right, she talked right. She even *looked* right, for heaven's sake, with dark eyes and black hair that curled into natural ringlets.

Frankly, Lettie had never developed a taste for tea, she sat in whatever chair was available, and usually found herself charging down any old side of the boardwalk she pleased in a most unladylike gait. And her hair and eyes were brown. Just brown—not chestnut, not walnut, not mahogany. They were just plain brown.

"You should have come tonight, Lettie."

"Yes, ma'am."

"It was wonderful. Very stimulating."

"I'm sure it was."

"I never tire of hearing a reading of poetry, do you?"

Once again, Lettie felt a stab of frustration and anger. *She'd* never been to a poetry reading. But since she couldn't tell Natalie that fact, she merely smiled in a vague way.

"It's too bad about the trouble in Carlton."

"Yes, ma'am."

"I don't suppose the thief would ever come here, to Madison."

Lettie's gaze locked briefly with Natalie's in the mirror, then bounced away again. "I would hope not," she answered carefully, fighting the urge to peer up at the ceiling. Since Lettie's room was in the garret, her bed would be situated just about . . .

Right over Natalie's head.

"So would I."

"Mmm?" Lettie jerked her attention back with some difficulty.

"I said, I would hope that a thief like that wouldn't come to Madison," Natalie repeated. She stood up, and the delicate lawn and lace wrapper she wore swirled about tiny feet encased in down-edged slippers. "With my husband serving as director of the new bank here in Madison and all, I would hope the thief would never come to rob him."

Lettie gazed at Natalie with wide eyes, suddenly feeling cold all over. She wasn't sure if Natalie was warning her, or simply talking off the top of her head.

"Good night, Lettie. And thank you for the tea."

Once again, Lettie jerked her attention back to the older woman—though Natalie could not have been more than five or six years her elder. She offered her a quick smile that felt shaky on her own lips, then hurried toward the door. "You're welcome, Mrs. Gruber. Sleep well."

She was nearly out the door when Natalie called to her again. "Oh, Lettie?"

Lettie hesitated, then slowly turned to face the other woman. "Yes?"

Natalie turned back to her dresser, retrieved a small book, then moved toward her, the fabric of her wrapper rustling against the floor. "I believe you once expressed an interest in borrowing this."

Lettie glanced down at the book of poetry in Natalie's hands. Natalie's long, slender, perfect hands. Lettie's hands were small, and calloused from the work at the boardinghouse.

"Well, yes."

"Go ahead. Take it. Keep it as long as you'd like."

Lettie looked at Natalie in surprise. "Thank you. I'll take good care of it."

"I know you will." Natalie flashed her a quick smile. "You take care of everything so well. It amazes me how you cook and clean here at the boardinghouse and take care of the boarders as if they were your family instead of . . . strangers." Lettie felt herself straighten a little at the compliment, until Natalie continued: "You're just like a . . . a mother possum."

Lettie felt her face grow stiff. "Thank you for the poetry book," she muttered, then slipped out the door, closing it tightly behind her.

"A mother possum!" she whispered fiercely to herself, stomping down the back stairs. Then, after glancing over her shoulder to make sure no one could hear, she muttered an unkind word that would have made her proper mother faint.

Lettie's irritation toward Natalie was soon forgotten. Within moments, she had raided the kitchen and gathered a piece of pie, a few slices of cold meat, and a portion of homemade bread, wincing when the actions caused the cut on her finger to throb. She was about to hurry up the back stairs when she came to an abrupt halt.

What if he'd gone?

Her heart began to pound thickly within her chest at the mere thought of such a possibility. It would have been easy for him to slip from the house while she'd been attending to the other boarders. But even if the stranger hadn't gone, there was nothing to prevent him from disappearing again the moment the house was quiet and she was asleep. And then it would only be a matter of moments before one of Jacob's men saw him and apprehended him.

Lettie felt a shiver of foreboding at the mere thought of his capture. No. She couldn't let that happen.

Looking about her for some solution, Lettie's gaze fell upon the pantry door, and she quickly set the tray on the table and rushed toward the small storage room. Pulling a low stool toward the far side of the pantry, she climbed on top and reached for one of the quart-sized crocks of milk covered in a wet dishcloth. Taking it out into the kitchen, she hesitated only a moment before grasping a vial of her mother's sleeping powder from the kitchen hutch.

After opening the milk, Lettie hesitated, biting her lip. She had no guarantee that the Highwayman was still in her room. And even if he were, she wasn't sure that she should keep him there by force.

Shrugging away her own misgivings, Lettie uncapped the vial of sleeping powder and sprinkled a healthy measure of the substance into the milk. Her mother took about a teaspoon in her tea when she had one of her migraines.

But the Highwayman was larger than her mother— Lettie eyed the crock in her hands—and there was a lot of milk.

Taking a deep breath, she dumped half the vial into the milk. Better to be safe than sorry.

After grating nutmeg on top to disguise the taste, she placed it on the tray with the rest of the food and the untouched cups of warm milk left from the Beasleys. Then she covered the tray with a napkin and raced up to the rear wing, which housed the men. At the top of the stairs, she took a sharp turn to the right, where another door opened up to a narrow staircase that climbed to the garret.

Originally, the room had been Jacob's, but when he'd begun sleeping in the small house behind the jail, which was provided for the town marshal, Lettie had been given the garret as her own. Although the area was large and spacious, its sloping ceilings and seasonal temperatures made it too uncomfortable to use for boarders. But Lettie found herself grateful for the room, since it provided her a sense of privacy she'd never had before.

Slipping through the door, Lettie closed it behind her and hesitated, quickly running a hand over her hair and smoothing the wrinkles from her clothing. Her heart fairly pounded from her chest in excitement. *He had to be here!*

Assuming her best imitation of Natalie Gruber's lady-of-the-manor smile, she straightened her spine, pushed her bosom out to its best advantage, and glided up the stairs as elegantly as she could. "I'm sorry it took me so long."

The room lay silent and dark.

Her bosom fell and her breath left in a *whoosh*. He'd gone. Somehow, despite the boarders' presence, he'd managed to slip out of the house.

An arm whipped around her neck, and the cool snout of a revolver pressed against her temple.

Lettie opened her mouth to scream, but the hand that held her quickly covered her mouth.

"Where is he?"

She sagged in relief when she recognized the smooth tones of the Highwayman's voice, but he continued to hold her tightly against him, digging the revolver into her skin.

"Where is he?" he asked more fiercely.

Lettie tried to struggle against him, but since her grasp of the tray made the fight nearly impossible, she finally lifted her foot and brought her heel crashing down over the stranger's instep.

The man swore and released her, hobbling a few feet away and muttering under his breath.

"Be quiet, man!" she whispered as he groaned. "Do you want to bring the whole house in here to see what's causing all the commotion?"

The man was immediately silent, but when he glanced up, his eyes fairly seethed with anger and suspicion. As if to underscore his emotions, the man lifted a finger to jab the air in front of her. "You little brat! You set a trap."

"I did no such thing!"

"Then why did you bring your brother?"

"I did not bring my brother."

"I heard male voices."

She huffed in impatience. "This is a *boardinghouse*."

The stranger opened his mouth, hesitated, then closed it again. "Where is he?"

"Who?"

"Your brother."

She sighed in irritation, placing the tray on the bedside table. "I *told* you. He isn't here."

The man grasped her elbow and whirled her around to face him. His eyes were stormy and dark. "You wouldn't defy your brother by hiding me like this."

"I'm not defying my brother. I'm simply . . . avoiding any unpleasantness."

The man clearly didn't believe her explanation.

"Look," she inserted, when he seemed about to argue with her again, "would I be feeding you if my brother were about to come and drag you into jail?" She pulled the napkin aside to reveal the laden tray.

The man continued to eye her in blatant suspicion, but the soft growl of his stomach betrayed him.

"Just as I thought," Lettie murmured, surprised by the wave of protectiveness that rushed through her. "You probably haven't had anything to eat all day."

"I'm not hungry." The man turned away, and the set of his shoulders became stiff and proud.

"You *are* hungry, and we both know it. You need to eat something. I'm not about to poison you, you know." Lettie clasped her hands behind her back, surreptitiously crossing her fingers and silently assuring herself that she wasn't really lying. She was only going to *drug* him, not poison him. There was a difference.

"This is some kind of a trap, isn't it?"

Lettie froze, wondering how he'd been able to tell she'd been stretching the truth, but before she could speak, the man continued.

"You'll wait until I've got my mouth full of food, then your brother will come charging through the door."

"That won't happen."

"You told him about me, didn't you? You and he hatched some kind of trap."

"I did no such thing!"

The air shivered between them. The stranger watched her closely, evidently still hesitant about trusting her.

"Why not?"

Lettie opened her mouth to issue some pat answer, then paused before saying truthfully, "Because I don't want to see you hurt."

"Why?"

"I don't know!" she snapped, but then she quickly lowered her voice. "If you don't want anything to eat, fine! Just sashay on out of here with an empty stomach and forget I ever tried to help you."

A heavy silence fell between them until, finally, the man lowered his revolver. His gaze darted toward the tray of food.

"Eat," she urged again.

Turning, she grasped a slice of bread slathered with sweet butter, then shoved it into his hand. The man stared at it a moment as if it were some foreign object, before he hesitantly lifted it to his mouth and took a bite. Within moments, he was hungrily finishing the last mouthful and reaching for the other items on the tray.

Lettie backed away, watching the stranger with tingling satisfaction as he sank onto the edge of her bed and ate with one hand, his revolver lying laxly in the other. He was a handsome man, she thought, though not for the first time. The lean strength of his features and the crisp waves of his hair were compelling. Alluring. With only a tiny bit of effort, Lettie could imagine this

51

stranger dressed like her Highwayman, in a flowing silk shirt, tight breeches, shining Hessian boots. . . .

My Highwayman came to me for protection. I found him in the garden, bleeding and in need of sustenance. Without a word, I drew him through the French windows and bade him lay upon my bed. Slowly, piece by piece, I removed his shirt, his boots, his breeches. I bathed him, dressed his wounds, and fed him. Yet, when he still gazed at me with a deep, insatiable hunger, I knew it wasn't the food he needed most. But me.

Me.

"What are you staring at?"

Lettie jerked back from her fantasies to the hot, ordinary confines of her bedroom. The wispy foundations of her dreams slipped into the darkness.

Silence shuddered between them, heavy with words and sensations best left unexplored.

"Nothing."

The stranger glanced down at his chest as if searching for flaws. "You keep watching me like I'm a bug on a pin," the man muttered. His glance flicked in the direction of the door to her bedroom.

"I've got to go, you know," he murmured, his voice low and silky smooth, but a thread of steel lay buried in his tone nonetheless. He chewed and swallowed, then reached for the crock of milk. "I can't stay here tonight."

Lettie watched wide-eyed as he lifted the crock to his lips and quaffed a third of the contents. She nearly warned him of the sleeping powder, but something within her forced her to remain silent.

When the stranger looked at her, she offered him a halfhearted smile. "Good?" she asked weakly.

He glanced at the crock in his hand. "It's been a long time since I've had fresh milk with nutmeg," he murmured, an almost regretful tone tinging his words.

He drank again, and Lettie watched with wide eyes. When she'd laced the milk with so much of the sleeping powder, she thought he'd only drink a sip or two.

Not half a quart.

The stranger set the crock on the tray and reached for

a slice of roast beef. For several long moments, neither of them spoke, but as Lettie watched the stranger eat, she saw the drug beginning to take hold. It evidently worked much more quickly when there was such a large quantity.

"How old are you, Lettie?" the man asked, breaking her free from her study.

"Nineteen."

"Nineteen," the man echoed. He blinked, shook his head, then murmured, "I remember nineteen." After a moment, he added, "Vaguely."

The quiet of the night enveloped them in a hot cocoon of tension. Bit by bit, Lettie watched as the stranger's eyes began to lose their intensity, their guardedness. She was surprised by the haunting loneliness she saw hidden in their summer-blue depths.

"What's your name?" Lettie finally whispered.

The man's posture began to weave a little, and he leaned back, resting on his elbows.

Lettie moved toward him, inexplicably drawn by the weary set of his shoulders and the pallor of his skin. She was only a few inches away when he suddenly looked up.

"Nineteen," he whispered, so softly that she propped her knee on the mattress and bent down to hear him.

One of his hands lifted. A finger brushed against the back of her wrist, then skimmed up her arm. When he reached for her shoulder, he tugged on the fabric of her dress, forcing her to sit on the bed beside him.

Lettie nervously licked her lips.

"What's your name?" she whispered, when his gaze became a little too piercing.

He frowned as if finding it hard to grasp her words. Then he suddenly offered her a devilish grin and reached out to stroke her hair. "Yes," he murmured. "Nineteen is a very good year."

The way he said the words, like a verbal caress, caused gooseflesh to rise on Lettie's skin.

His opposite hand lifted as well, and both palms reached to frame her face, pulling her inexorably closer.

Lettie's breath snagged in her throat. Her gaze flicked from his lips to the azure power of his eyes. He was watching her the way a man watched a woman. Just before he kissed her.

The stranger's grip remained firm, but gentle, and he lay back upon the ticking, pulling her with him.

For a moment, she faltered, losing her balance, but he pulled her even closer. Her hands flew out to brace themselves on his chest. She had barely a fleeting expression of firm masculine flesh, then he drew her head toward him. Only a hairbreadth separated them now.

"Your name," she breathed.

He merely smiled, drawing her the last remaining distance.

Lettie knew he was going to kiss her. And she knew she shouldn't let him. But her heart was hammering, her breath came in shallow gasps, and a tiny voice whispered *just this once,* so she closed her eyes.

His hands slid down her arms to clutch her elbows. His breath brushed against her lips. And then . . .

Nothing.

Her Highwayman was fast asleep.

Lettie pushed away from him in frustration and stood beside the bed. "Oh, blast and bother!" she muttered to herself, staring down at him with hands on hips.

Lettie looked at the man in her bed, absorbing the masculine wave of his dark hair, the clean-hewn features. He lay in such a position that one hand had been flung above his head, while the other—despite his drugged state—still firmly clasped his revolver.

"Damn, damn, damn," Lettie muttered. Although she'd meant to ensure the Highwayman stayed the night, she hadn't wanted to send him into oblivion. At least not without learning his name first.

Her gaze slipped to absorb the breadth of his chest, the flat plane of his stomach, his hips. As she had before, Lettie felt something warm and tingly settle within her.

She took a quilt from the railing that surrounded the

staircase and gently laid it over her guest, drawing it up to his chin. He didn't even stir.

Lettie tried to remove the revolver from his hand, but when he shifted, moaning deep in his throat, she reached toward the bedside table, retrieved the napkin, and lay it over the weapon. If she couldn't set the blasted gun on the floor, the least she could do was cover it up so she didn't have to look at it.

After only a moment's hesitation, she lifted the quilt aside and tugged off his boots. The man was so drugged by now that he didn't stir, though she'd had to yank and grunt in order to get them off. He didn't even fuss when she reached out a finger to touch one bare toe, which poked endearingly from a hole in his sock.

Her stomach fluttered a little when she realized that there was nothing more intimate than caring for a man's wounds or undressing him for bed. And there was certainly nothing more intimate than knowing the condition of a man's socks. It was something only a woman with a special relationship would know. A wife.

That thought caused Lettie to shiver in delight. Such an intimate awareness was something to be savored and locked deep in her memory until—

Savored. Another word for her list.

Backing away from the bed, she crossed to the wardrobe and slid open one of the bottom drawers. The wood squeaked and she glanced over her shoulder, but the Highwayman continued to sleep.

Reaching deep into the drawer, tunneling beneath her underdrawers and petticoats, Lettie withdrew a dog-eared book and carried it to the rocker in the corner. A secret anticipation began to flood her limbs as she briefly caressed the marbleized paper on the cover, then opened the pages and removed the stubby pencil inserted into a paper pocket she'd pasted to the flyleaf. Hurriedly skipping past the scribbled snatches of her poems, journal entries, and the accounts of her better fantasies, she finally reached her list of "vocabulary."

On the last two pages, painstakingly written in her most elaborate script, lay column after column of words

Lettie didn't want to forget. Some day, after she had suffered sufficiently, Lettie intended to become a poet. One of the world's greatest poets. To do so would involve a new set of words. Words like *conjugal* and *insatiate*.

So far, Lettie didn't know what all of the words meant exactly; she only knew that the Beasley sisters whispered some of them behind their fans and blushed. One day, Lettie had tried to look up a few of the more challenging words in her mother's dictionary, but when Celeste had caught her looking at the definition of *consummation*, she'd hidden the book.

A heavy sigh of disappointment escaped from Lettie's lips at the memory, but she pushed the emotion away. Some day, she and her mother would travel to Chicago, just as Celeste had promised, and then Lettie would take her list of words to the lending library and spend the whole day looking them up.

After carefully printing *savor* in the list of words she already knew, Lettie glanced up at the stranger, then smiled when her heart began to pound and a brilliant idea flashed through her head. Judging from his speech, the man had a decent education. No doubt he could tell her the meanings of the words she didn't know; that way her literary career wouldn't be stunted in its very beginnings.

A slow smile spread across her features. *Yes,* she thought in delight, *I'll ask him.* After all, a man as worldly and handsome as he could surely tell her the meaning of words like . . . Her eyes skipped to the page. Words like *nebbish.* And *slaked.*

Perhaps even . . . *consummation.*

After closing her notebook and replacing it in the drawer, Lettie gazed again at the stranger. A tingling began to radiate through her body.

Her Highwayman was here. Really here. In her bed.

Easing onto the edge of the rocker, Lettie reached down to untie the laces of her shoes and pull the high tops from her feet, all the while watching the sleeping stranger. Then, even though she knew the man wouldn't wake for hours and hours, she tiptoed around the edge of the bed and gingerly sat on the opposite side.

The man didn't stir.

Feeling a dangerous thrill of the forbidden, Lettie eased her legs beneath the quilt and propped her back against the footboard.

The man didn't awaken.

Very slowly, she reached to touch his shoulder. The muscles beneath her fingers were firm and resilient. She smiled, then ran the palm down his arm to his elbow. *Laws!* She'd never known such a thundering burst of anticipation could shoot through a person's body at the simple exploration of a man's arm.

The man muttered something and she snatched her hand away, as if fearing a sudden bolt of lightning would fry her on the spot.

But nothing happened.

Smiling to herself in delight—but deciding not to tempt heaven any further than she already had—Lettie settled back against the headboard and drew the quilt over her chest. Then, reaching for a cup of milk from the tray beside her, she held it aloft in a silent toast.

"To mother possums everywhere."

5

Even from the depths of my slumber, I could hear the distant grumbling of thunder and the patter of rain against the windows of my bedroom, and I frowned. Dread settled within me like a leaden weight, pulling me from my sleep. It had been months since I'd seen him. Long, long months. Yet the sound of rain and the scent of fresh-washed earth never failed to bring back the memories. And the pain.

I'd known for some time that he was in danger, but lately, I'd heard rumors of his capture. And his hanging.

A hot knife seemed to sear through my stomach, and I groaned, wrapping my arms around my waist and turning to bury my face in the downy pillows beneath my head, my hair spilling about my shoulders like a silken curtain. How would I bear life if the news were true? How would I find the strength to live out each day, knowing that I would never see his face, his smile?

Deep sobs wracked my chest, dry heart-wrenching sounds made all the more painful by the lack of soothing tears.

"Shh."

The sound came to me like the whisper of a summer breeze. Whirling against the pillows, I opened my eyes to find him silhouetted against the weak light that seeped through the French windows. Around him, the delicate lace curtains danced in the rain-kissed breeze as if jubilant at his return.

My Highwayman!

Slowly, I pushed myself upright, staring at him, hoping that this was not some specter of the night that would vanish if I were to reach out and touch him.

My heart began to pound, my breathing came in jagged sobs. "Are you real?" I managed to whisper, my voice choked with desperation and need. "Or are you merely a ghost come to torment me?"

A smile creased his features. A smile laced with humor and a tinge of inner pain. "Nay. No ghost, madam. But a man. A man who has longed for your smile, your joy, your sweet healing caress."

As if to underscore his reality, he slowly unbuckled his saber from about his hips. Narrow, masculine hips that I longed to have crushed against my own.

He set the saber on a nearby chair, then whipped the cape from his shoulders, dropping it in a black puddle beside his sword. He took a step toward me. Two. The weak light of dawn played against his back, emphasizing the dark hair clinging wetly against his head and drawn back in a queue against his nape. Water dripped onto his shoulders. His shirt, which usually flowed about the muscled contours of his torso, lay plastered against his chest. The lacings had evidently worked free during his ride, because the fabric gaped open nearly to his navel, revealing the dark hair that delineated the firm shape of his chest, then stretched down, down, down, like an ever-narrowing ribbon toward his waist.

Real or not, I found myself responding to his nearness, growing hungry for his touch. My fingers lifted to tug at the delicate satin tie of my nightcap, and I slid the cap from my hair, dropping it onto the floor.

His eyes blazed with pleasure. Eyes the color of a hot summer day, yet twice as warm, needy.

"If you be some ghost or demon from hell come to taunt me with my pain, tell me not of my lover's death,"

I whispered through a throat grown tight with unshed tears.

"If this be death, then may I never live."

I gasped at his words, my fingers reaching to pluck free the ribbons of my nightshift, moving from my throat, to my chest, to my underbust. His eyes followed every motion with the intensity of an actual caress, and despite the delicate silk fabric of my gown, I ached at his whispering glance as it passed across the fullness of my breasts. I longed for the moment when he would push the nightshift aside. And touch me.

The bed sank beneath his weight. The scent of rain and wind and his own masculine fragrance filled my lungs. Holding my breath, I reached out a tentative finger. I had to touch him, to see if he was real, or merely the product of my anguished soul.

"Touch me, love," he whispered. "Touch me!"

With a choked sob, I closed the distance between us and lay my finger against his cheek. I encountered warm, masculine flesh, slightly stubbled, but real nonetheless.

His arms whipped around my back and he bent toward me, holding me so that I was pressed against him, breast to breast, hip to hip. . . .

Lettie jerked awake, her lashes flying open when she felt a crushing weight pressing against her chest. Briefly, she became aware of being pinned beneath a man's torso, his head resting on her shoulder, his thigh flung over her hips.

His hand covering her breast.

Instinctively, she reared back and shoved him away. The man's weight left her suddenly as he woke with a start, floundered, then dropped to the floor with a loud thump.

"Dammit all to hell!"

Lettie peeked over the edge of the bed to see him staring blearily at the ceiling, holding his head as if it might explode.

"Lettie?" The voice of Lettie's mother floated up from the floor below.

Glancing at the window, Lettie realized it was dawn and another day had begun at the boardinghouse.

"Lettie? Are you all right?"

Laws! Her mother!

Scrambling from beneath the covers, Lettie raced around the bed and grasped the stranger's hand, yanking him upright and pushing him toward the wardrobe, which stood awkwardly against one sloping wall of the garret bedroom.

"My hell, woman, what are you doing?"

"You've got to hide!" she hissed, whipping open the door to the wardrobe. "Get inside."

"But—"

"Get inside!" Reaching out a hand, she pushed a swathe of garments aside, then gestured for him to climb in. When he hesitated, she grasped a handful of his shirt and yanked him toward the open door. "That's my *mother!*" she whispered fiercely. "If she finds you here, you'll be lucky if they only hang you for the robbery."

The rattle of the doorknob at the bottom of the stairway seemed to convince him, and he wriggled inside. Lettie quickly dumped an armful of dresses over his head, then slammed the door closed. Glancing down, she groaned silently to herself when she realized she was still dressed in yesterday's clothes, and once again she'd managed to unbutton half of her bodice while dreaming of the Highwayman.

Quickly ripping the rest of the offending buttons free, she tore the garment from her shoulders, opened the wardrobe, threw it inside, then reached for another bodice. She had only one glimpse of the Highwayman's startled features before she heard her mother's footsteps on the stairs and slammed the door closed again.

"Lettie?"

"Ye—" She cleared her throat when her voice emerged too high. "Yes, Mother?"

"What on earth is going on up there? It sounds like a herd of buffalo has been stamping around." Her mother stopped on the last tread, peering over the edge of the railing that surrounded the stairwell. Her lips pressed together in displeasure. One cardinal rule of the boardinghouse had always been, Never waken the boarders until absolutely necessary.

"Well?"

"I—I fell."

"You fell?"

"Well, actually, I stubbed my toe first, then while I was hopping around the room . . . I fell." The words sounded weak in Lettie's own ears, and she hoped her mother wouldn't catch her in the act of lying. She'd never been a good liar, but with her mother, she was notoriously bad. And if caught, her mother would gaze at her with a look of such supreme disappointment that something within Lettie always shriveled up in shame.

This time, however, her mother seemed to take her words at face value. "Are you all right?"

"Oh, yes. Fine."

Her mother regarded her again with narrowed eyes. "Be careful, will you? I don't want you hurting yourself."

"Yes, Mama."

Her mother's eyes fell to Lettie's rumpled skirt and the bodice she clutched in her hands, then her eyes skipped to the bed. Lettie cringed, wondering if there was some way a mother could tell if a man and woman had slept in the same bed together simply by the way the sheets lay in careless disorder. But her mother merely turned to regard her again in confusion.

"Did you sleep in those?" she asked quietly, gesturing to Lettie's skirt and camisole. Her lips once again pressed into a disapproving line. The second cardinal rule of the boardinghouse: Always appear neat and well-groomed.

"I was just getting dressed."

Her mother opened her mouth as if to remonstrate her, then closed it again. "Perhaps you'd better choose another skirt. That one is a trifle . . . gritty."

"Yes, Mama."

Her mother looked at her again, her dark eyes probing in the weak morning light. "A proper young woman is always careful of her mode of dress, Letitia. She should wear things that are neat, freshly ironed, and clean. Otherwise, one tends to make the wrong impression and attract the attention of the wrong sort of people.''

"Yes, Mama.''

Evidently finished with her remarks, Celeste turned and moved toward the steps. "We've got baking to do today, and after all the noise this morning, the boarders will probably be coming down early. Don't take too long."

"No, Mama.''

"Your brother came by this morning. He wanted to speak to you, but one of his men called him away. He told me to tell you that he'd be by later.''

"Yes, Mama.''

Celeste reached out a hand to grasp the banister, then paused when her eyes fell on the tray that still lay on the bedside table. The bits of leftover food and drink could be clearly seen, as could the two cups.

Lettie opened her mouth to explain, but her mother merely glanced at her and shook her head in bewilderment. "Lettie, one of these days you're going to have to stop your foolish daydreaming" was all she said before she lifted her skirts and retreated back down the stairs.

Lettie waited until long after she'd heard the squeak of the door and the click of the latch before sagging against the wardrobe in relief. It was some moments later before she heard a low rap from inside the armoire.

Spinning around, Lettie yanked open the door, confronting the sight of her Highwayman sitting in the bottom, with half a dozen garments tangled over his head.

"May I get out now?" he muttered tightly.

"Yes, of course.''

She helped him pull the clothing out of the way, then stepped aside to let him pass. Very carefully, he swung his legs to the floor and pushed himself free. Then he turned on her, his eyes blazing with a blue fire.

"Just what kind of a game are you playing?" he demanded.

"What?''

"I knew your brother was desperate, but I didn't

think he'd stoop so low as to offer me his sister for the night, just to ensure my whereabouts."

Lettie gasped and her hand whipped out, slapping him across the cheek. "Of all the ungrateful things to say!"

She moved to stalk past him, but he grasped her arm, yanking her hard against him. Hard enough that she could sense the careful control of his breathing, feel the leashed power of his anger. The red imprint of her hand seemed to glare at her from the firm contours of his cheek.

"Damn you! What's your brother trying to prove?"

"Nothing! If you'll remember, I hid you from him last night."

"You also drugged me, didn't you? *Didn't you?*" He clasped her elbows and shook her.

"I—"

"Don't lie to me!"

"All right! I drugged you."

"Why?"

She clamped her jaw together in obstinate silence.

"Lettie"—he shook her in warning—*"why?"*

"I knew you'd try to leave. The house was being watched. I couldn't let you try to escape."

"I don't believe you."

"It's the truth."

The room shuddered in silence as the man who held her seemed to pause and digest her words. "Then why is he coming this morning?" he asked, his distrust still tightly threaded within the tone of his voice.

"I don't know."

"Lettie."

"I don't know!"

The stranger's stance remained taut, his features rigid. Clearly, he doubted her words, but more than that, he doubted her intentions. "Why are you helping me if this isn't some plan of your brother's?"

Lettie pulled against the restraint of his arm until he released her. She forced herself to step away, even though her heart had begun to pound.

64

"Why, Lettie?" he demanded. When she didn't answer, his voice rose. *"Why?"*

"Shh! You'll bring the whole house charging in here like a flock of sheep."

The man glanced over his shoulder as if her words could conjure someone behind him, and for a moment, Lettie saw a flash of vulnerability within his features, like an animal who felt trapped and unsure of his own ability to escape. In a moment, however, his expression once again became closed and wary.

"Why did you help me?" he repeated again through gritted teeth.

"Because I had to," she finally said, spinning away from him and marching back toward the wardrobe. Snatching a day dress from the garments that had fallen untidily onto the bottom, she slammed the door and whirled to face him. "If I hadn't helped you, you would have slept in jail."

The soft twitter of birds seeped into the silence of the room. Lettie stood up, stiffly withstanding the stranger's regard. She'd forgotten how piercing his gaze could be. Finally, when his scrutiny became almost unbearable, Lettie whispered, "Please turn around."

"Why?"

She licked her lips, then rued the gesture when his gaze zeroed in on the fullness of her mouth. "I need to change my clothes," she murmured uncomfortably. "I can't do that if you're watching."

The man's eyes narrowed, but, as if he realized he would get no more answers from her, he slowly presented his back.

She quickly stripped off the bodice and previous day's skirt and tossed them onto the foot of her bed.

The man's head seemed to jerk in the direction of her fallen clothing, then returned. His shoulders straightened, but he didn't speak.

Lettie's eyes narrowed in consideration. Her gaze slipped from the tousled dark waves of his hair to the sleep-wrinkled expanse of his shirt. Her eyes clung, then could not be pulled away. The simple chambray workshirt had come untucked at his waist on one side and the tail of fabric draped over one buttock, clearly emphasizing the way his rib cage curved in such a beguiling way into his waist. Once again, Lettie was struck by the narrow square of his hips, the firm swell of his buttocks, the lean strength of his thighs. The Beasleys would have been delighted.

"Lettie? What are you doing?"

The sound of the Highwayman's voice eased into the silence, the tone low and rich like the stroke of velvet against bare skin, but filled with suspicion.

"What?" she breathed, distracted by the fact that this man's form still seemed more fantasy than reality.

His shoulders stiffened. "What are you doing?"

He whirled suddenly, as if fully expecting her to be aiming some unknown weapon at his back. His body braced; his hands tensed. Then he paused when he realized she was unarmed. And undressed.

His eyes scorched a path from her head to her toes, returning again to linger on the flare of her hips, the narrowness of her waist, the fullness of her breasts, all lovingly encased in the soft cotton of her unmentionables and the sturdy canvas of her corset.

"I'm sorry," he murmured stiffly. "I thought . . ."

But he didn't turn around.

Lettie could only swallow against the sudden tightness of her throat. Looking into his eyes, she caught her first glimpse of masculine awareness. And although it was thrilling, it was also frightening. This man was *not* her Highwayman. This man was real. She couldn't turn him on and off at will as she did her fantasies. He had a mind of his own, a strength of his own . . . desires of his own.

Lettie clutched her dress in front of her. In matters of the heart, Lettie had little experience with *boys*, let alone grown men. Since her mother had rigidly taught her to be a "proper" young lady, and her brother guarded her like a nervous father, she could count the number of times she'd been alone with a boy on one hand—and most of those times had been far from romantic.

Yet she'd lived too long in a boardinghouse to remain

ignorant about what happened between a man and a woman. And where her own limited experience had left off, her imagination had stepped in to fill the gap. But imagination would never be enough. Some day, she wanted to know what it felt like to have a man trace her cheek with his fingers, or press his lips against her hair. But more than that, Lettie wanted to lay her own palm against a man's chest, wanted to test the texture of a beard-stubbled jaw.

The man took a step forward.

Suddenly nervous and embarrassed by her own thoughts, Lettie dragged the gray- and blue-striped day dress over her head, quickly fastened the hooks at her hip and along her waist, then shoved the buttons of the bodice into their respective holes.

By the time she'd finished, the stranger was only a few scant inches away. His eyes were burning. Aware.

Her breath seemed to snag in her chest. In her fantasies, she had never hesitated in indulging her wildest whims with the Highwayman. But this man was real.

Taking a deep gasping breath, Lettie brushed by him in a near run, intent on escape, but once again he reached out to catch her arm, forcing her to face him.

"Where are you going?" His voice was low and bittersweet, like the lap of a kitten's tongue against her bare flesh.

"Th-the baking. I have to . . . bake."

The man's grip tightened ever so slightly, and he took a step forward. His free hand lifted, and one knuckle skimmed across the delicate slope of her cheek.

Lettie reared back as if scorched. Her hand clamped around his wrist in an effort to free herself, but he refused to acknowledge her silent plea. Instead, his finger returned to touch her jaw. "You won't tell anyone that you've seen me?" His voice became silky. Hard.

"No."

His finger moved to feather across the bottom curve of her lip. She struggled to breathe when he took another step closer and the warmth of his body seeped through her clothing to her skin. Faint traces of dirt still dusted his cheeks, and the scraggly beginnings of a beard had grown even darker overnight. Somehow, his dishevelment only made him seem more unapproachable, and oh, so appealing.

"Goodbye, then."

And suddenly, Lettie wanted him to leave. This man was unpredictable. Dangerous.

His eyes dropped to where she still held him by the wrist. Unconsciously, her thumb had been brushing back and forth over the white strip of bandages.

She gasped and tried to pull away.

He glanced up, and their gazes locked.

Lettie could barely breathe. "Just go," she whispered.

He made a soft sound in the throat as if mocking her effort at control. Then he looked down and Lettie grew still. Warm. Slowly he lifted her hand, extending her fingers. For long moments, his eyes traced the angry cut across her finger. Without speaking, he peered up at her, and something within his eyes seemed to soften in disbelief.

"You cut yourself," he murmured, as if denying the evidence of his own eyes.

She attempted a nonchalant shrug. "I had to do something. Jacob kept looking at the blood on the floor."

He tugged softly at her hand, drawing her toward the abandoned tray from the night before. A small roll of cotton bandaging had dropped to the floor, and he tugged at Lettie's hand, forcing her to sit on the edge of the bed. Then he took a small cotton strip and tenderly wound it around the slash on the tip of her finger.

"You should have done this last night."

"I didn't think . . ."

He glanced up at her, his eyes dark and compellingly warm, but he didn't speak. Instead, he finished his task, his fingers brushing gently against her skin, causing her to feel things, think things, about this man that she'd never thought about any other man before.

When he'd finished, he stood up and drew her to her feet. Only a hairbreadth of space separated them, the distance so slight that Lettie could feel the friction of his trousers against her skirts as she fought to breathe.

He continued to watch her, a touch of gray entering his eyes, his mouth softening slightly. He took an infinitesimal step closer. Very slowly, his gaze shifted to trace her brow, her cheek, her mouth. "Thank you," he murmured. Then he lifted their hands. Gently, he opened her fingers and pressed his lips to her bandaged finger.

Lettie gasped at the unbelievably tender gesture. When he released her, she twisted away, feeling as if a tiny corner of her soul trembled and unfurled. Then, not knowing what more to do, she lifted her skirts and rushed past him, clattering down the steps.

Once outside the door, she leaned back against the portal for a moment to gather her scattered senses. A sweet shiver coursed through her limbs, and she closed her eyes. She was glad he was leaving. Glad.

But as she turned to walk down the steps, Lettie couldn't deny the fact that she wasn't glad. Not entirely.

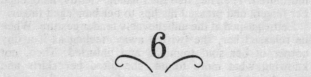

6

Jacob Grey squinted against the early morning sunlight and issued a curt set of instructions to a pair of men, then motioned for them to continue their search. Turning, he took a few steps and gathered the reins of his horse in one hand before lifting his gaze toward the boardinghouse.

His jaw tightened in frustration as he studied the simple whitewashed structure. The night before, soon after he and his men had left, his deputy had found a horse tied to an oak tree near the creek, less than three hundred yards from the house. On its back had been a valise containing a few changes of clothing and some men's toiletry articles. A faint set of bootprints led briefly west, then vanished, leaving no trace of the man. And deep in his heart, Jacob knew just who their suspect had been: Ethan McGuire.

His hand tightened into a fist. How long had he been chasing McGuire now? Seven years? Eight? As an inexperienced deputy, Jacob had been intrigued by the Gentleman Bandit—even secretly envious of the man's all-out gall. But as the Gentleman had grown more and more daring, Jacob had vowed to apprehend the man.

Within a year, he had amassed every scrap of evidence on the Gentleman Bandit. He'd become obsessed with the crimes. *And he'd nearly caught him once.*

Jacob frowned as the memory of that night five years before returned to jab him with his own stupidity. He remembered the way he'd begun to think like the Gentleman, anticipating his moves. Then one night, he'd cornered the man at the Chicago Mortgage and Thrift. The Gentleman had gazed at him in surprise from above the black bandanna tied over his mouth; his azure eyes had sparkled in something akin to admiration.

And then the safe had exploded, throwing Jacob to the ground and knocking him unconscious. He'd awakened to find himself tied and gagged, sitting in a field full of foxtails without a stitch of clothing to his name, the Gentleman's calling card tucked beneath the ropes binding his wrists.

A growl of disgust lodged in Jacob's throat. He'd vowed to find the man. Find him and hang him. But after that night, the Gentleman had ceased his thievery.

Until the last few months.

Now Jacob was more determined than ever to capture Ethan McGuire. This time, Jacob would not be so gullible. The man was out there somewhere. And Jacob intended to find him and bring him to justice.

He jammed his hat onto his head and swung into the saddle, his gaze sweeping the area. It seemed impossible to believe that the man could have disappeared so easily. Especially with nearly a dozen men on his tail. But somehow he'd managed to escape capture. Again.

Jacob stiffened slightly when the muffled clop of hooves heralded the arrival of his deputy, who had been assigned to take the horse they'd found to the corral behind the jailhouse.

Rusty Janson took one look at Jacob from beneath carrot-colored eyebrows, then spat a stream of tobacco into the dust in disgust. "You haven't slept yet, have you?"

Jacob didn't answer. He merely pulled his gloves more securely over his fingers.

"You were supposed to take a break and get some sleep."

"I'm all right."

Rusty shook his head at Jacob's stubbornness and reached for a fresh plug of tobacco from his shirt pocket. "Found anything yet?"

"No."

The deputy glanced around him as if there could be someone listening. "I was asked to give you a message," he finally murmured, handing Jacob a folded piece of paper.

Jacob stared at the note for several moments before finally reaching out to take it, sensing somehow what it would contain. Although Jacob was able to deliver messages to the Star Council of Justice by means of the lightning-blasted oak tree, the Council's replies were to be kept secret, and individual instructions were delivered only after notification had been given. This way, no man could divulge the complete workings of the Star.

After hesitating only a moment, he unfolded the missive and stared at the single symbol: an eight-pointed star surrounded by a circle. In the center of the star, the initials *SCJ* had been carefully inscribed.

Jacob stared at the note, fighting his own misgivings. After last night's robbery—and the injury of a deputy—the Star Council had evidently decided to revise their decision concerning Ethan McGuire. At dawn, a new set of instructions would await Jacob at the tree.

Taking a match from his shirt pocket, Jacob ignited the tip and touched it to the edge of the paper. After the flame had caught hold, he tossed the note to the ground and gathered the reins to his mount.

"The suspect has evidently gone. I told Cooper and Gold to take a pair of men and double check the area around the creek. Tell the rest of the men to go on home. There's no sense keeping the posse any longer. The man's probably miles away by now. Miles away."

Touching his heels to his mount, Jacob turned the animal toward the boardinghouse. He had to retrieve a few things from his office, but first he wanted to talk to Lettie. He needed to warn her about Ethan McGuire.

Moving silently across the garret, Ethan peered out the window into the sunlight. Though he couldn't see anyone near the house, he sensed the presence of the lawmen who'd stayed behind to search. Their nearness did not dissuade him from his course of action, however. He would simply have to be especially careful in leaving.

Waiting until he heard a babble of voices from the dining room, Ethan slipped into the hall and down the back stairs. Only once was he nearly caught, when an older woman bustled into the room, retrieved a pot of coffee, then left. Within moments, Ethan had slipped outside and into the barn. Unsheathing his revolver, he ducked behind the tack-room door and waited.

Barely five minutes had passed before Ned Abernathy stepped into the barn to retrieve the horse and buggy. Ethan waited until the younger man had bent down to set his sample cases on the ground, then Ethan crept up behind him and snapped an arm around his neck.

Ned jerked and grasped at the arm that held him until, without warning, Ethan released him. The younger man whirled. He froze for only a moment before he swore and snatched his hat from his head. "Dammit all to hell, Ethan! You nearly scared the life out of me!"

"Hello, Ned."

Ned regarded him stiffly, his pale gray eyes growing brittle, his jaw hardening. "What are you doing here?"

Ethan took a deep breath, but he was less than surprised by the other man's unenthusiastic welcome. After all, he and Ned had been rivals as children. And nothing much had changed in the last few years—which was the reason Ethan had journeyed to Madison: to see if his younger stepbrother had decided to enact some tardy measure of revenge.

When Ethan didn't answer him right away, Ned glanced over either shoulder, as if fearing someone might overhear their conversation, then demanded, "What do you want?"

Ethan sighed. "I certainly haven't come to argue."

Ned eyed him with disapproval. "I thought you were supposed to be in Nebraska, working on that farm."

Ethan shrugged, knowing that Ned was referring to the employment he'd taken on a potato farm in Nebraska to help pay for the fines levied against him by the governor when the man had offered him a pardon. For two years, Ethan had worked in the sun and the rain—hard, back-breaking labor—all in an attempt to earn a measure of the peace and self-respect he'd known before becoming the Gentleman. But a month earlier, to his surprise, Ethan had been approached by one of the governor's former aides to work as a private security specialist for one of the state's most prestigious banks.

Since Ned seemed far from inclined to listen to any long explanations, Ethan merely stated, "I quit. I was offered another position." When Ned didn't speak, Ethan continued: "The Wallaby bank in Chicago wants to hire me as a . . . security specialist. Ironic, isn't it?"

Ned merely stared, his expression stiff and proud.

Ethan gazed at his stepbrother for a moment. It had been years since he'd seen him. Ned was a little taller than Ethan—characteristics inherited from different parents—but he still had the same stubborn expression that Ethan saw in his own mirror each morning. And the coolness in his eyes Ethan remembered only too well.

Finally, Ethan broke away from the younger man's gaze and crossed to the door of the barn, opening it a slit, and peered outside. "How is Mama?" he asked quietly.

A beat of silence passed before Ned answered. "Worried. She's still upset with me because I left Princeton and moved to Madison to take a job drumming with Goldsmith. She still doesn't understand that I need to make my own way in the world, pay my own debts. She thinks I've sown enough wild oats." His tone grew bitter. "She wants us both back in Chicago. She wants us to be a family."

"We're not a family." A biting edge coated Ethan's words, and he sought for control.

As always, the thought of his stepfather filled Ethan with a rush of painful memories. Ethan was twelve when his father died of consumption, fifteen when his mother had married Rucker Abernathy. From the beginning, Ethan had hated the man—and his family. None of them were worthy of his mother's affections, he'd thought. And unfortunately, he'd been right. Within a few years, Rucker Abernathy had nearly driven the family mercantile into the ground. Then suddenly he'd disappeared, leaving behind the children from his first marriage and the McGuires' empty bank account.

"Things have changed at home," Ned insisted.

Ethan snorted in disbelief and closed the door.

"My father *has* changed, Ethan. And he loves Lillian. He's truly sorry for what he did. You should learn to forgive and forget."

Ethan threw Ned a hard look. "For my mother's sake, I hope he's sorry. Sorry as hell. For my sake, I don't give a damn. Mama was always more Christian than I ever was. Maybe she can forgive him, but I can't. And I can't live near them and pretend otherwise. He may be your blood father, but he's not mine."

What shimmered in the air unspoken between them was the fact that as soon as Rucker Abernathy had absconded with the family fortune, Ethan had begun to steal. First, as a means to support his mother, who had been forced to take a job as a clerk in the family business; then, as a means to show Rucker just how far Ethan was prepared to go to demonstrate his rebellion and disgust.

By the time Rucker had returned with a fortune made from mining in the West, Ethan had developed a name for himself—the Gentleman Bandit. He'd become the scourge of Illinois, robbing at least ninety percent of the banks in the state at least once, some as often as half a dozen times. And he'd refused to give up his "habit." Especially when Rucker had discovered his escapades and Ethan saw the way the man lived each day in fear that Ethan would be caught and Rucker's shaky position in society would crumble.

It wasn't until a few years later, when Rucker told Lillian what Ethan had done to support the family, that Ethan began to realize his actions had been hurting himself more than they'd ever hurt Rucker Abernathy. Before he knew she was even aware of his activities, Lillian had approached the governor, then had come to Ethan with a possible pardon. By that time, Ethan had realized he would do anything to regain his self-respect. But more than that, he would do anything to have his mother look at him again with pride.

From that moment on, he'd vowed to follow the governor's stipulations to the letter. Ethan had signed a confession of all the crimes he had committed, then promised that for five years he would stay out of trouble, work at an honest job, and repay a portion of the money he'd stolen. Each time he'd been tempted to stray, he'd remembered the look on his mother's face when she'd slipped from the shadows of the carriage house just as Ethan had returned from stealing twenty thousand dollars in greenbacks from the Chicago Mortgage and Thrift.

That memory caused Ethan to wince. Was it any wonder he hadn't been home in nearly five years? Why he'd purposely chosen to work out of state at menial jobs? When he next saw Lillian McGuire, he wanted to face her as a whole man. One with honor and self-respect. One who had served his penance, even if he hadn't gone to jail.

"Mama is happy, Ethan. She wants you to come back. To live with us."

"She wants something I can't give her," Ethan stated bitterly. "If I went back, I'd spend every waking moment hating your father. And he would always hate me for reminding him of the fact that I'm not his son—yet *I* resorted to thievery, just to feed my mother and *his* children!" Ethan paused before adding, "But that shouldn't keep you from staying at home and enjoying your father's new-found wealth." His voice took on an edge of suspicion. "What brings you here to Madison, Ned?"

Ned's gray eyes became masked and enigmatic. "I've got my reasons."

Ethan leveled a piercing gaze on his younger step-brother. "Such as masquerading as the Gentleman Bandit?"

"No!"

"You knew my methods as well as I knew them myself."

The air about them hung heavy with suspicion. Ethan had only been stealing for a few months when he'd needed an alibi and had been forced to take Ned into his confidence. Soon Ned had learned every technique Ethan had ever employed. Which was why Ethan had come to find him. If anyone could copy Ethan's methods to the letter, it would be Ned.

"Is that why you came here?" Ned parried.

"Yes."

"I'm not responsible."

"Dammit, Ned, you're the only one who could know so much!"

"I'm not responsible!"

"You always hated me when we were young."

Ned paled slightly. "I didn't hate you," he whispered. But they both knew that wasn't true. At first Ned had hated Ethan because he'd been forced to share a father. When Rucker left, Ned had hated him because Ethan refused to let "little Ned" join him during his robbing sprees. After a time, Ned had hated Ethan for reminding him of things he would rather have forgotten—like a father who had deserted him, and tainted money.

Silence cloaked the barn, disturbed by nothing more than the soft whisper of straw drifting to earth from the loft. The tension in Ned's body relaxed ever so slightly.

"Mama writes about you a lot."

Ethan tried to deny the pleasure-pain he felt at the words.

"She's tried to get hold of you, but you never re-turned her letters."

"I've been busy."

"Too busy to write to her?"

Ethan's hands clenched into fists. "I was busy breaking my back on a potato farm so that I could pay the fines the governor levied against me. It doesn't give a man too much time to write to his mother."

"You could have made the time."

Ethan pierced his brother with a proud stare. "You of all people should have known I couldn't write to Mama. Not like that."

"Not until you'd finished your penance?"

For once, Ned's voice was free from its usual bite of sibling bitterness, and Ethan was grateful. He looked away for a moment, uncomfortable with just how much he'd revealed to his stepbrother.

"Ethan . . ." Ned hesitated a moment. "She received word that the governor is threatening to rescind the offer of your pardon."

Ethan's head jerked up. "Like hell!"

"He thinks you're behind the latest rash of robberies attributed to the Gentleman Bandit."

"I have ironclad alibis for nearly every one of those robberies!"

"He thinks you've trained an accomplice."

"An accomplice?" Ethan repeated the words with a twinge of dread. If the governor thought he was training a successor, proving his innocence would be nearly impossible. Even if he had alibis for every single robbery, the governor could simply claim he'd sent his accomplice to the scene.

A searing imprecation tore from Ethan's lips when he realized his innocence would be all but impossible to prove. "Damn, I haven't even set so much as my little toe inside a bank in five years!"

"Maybe you should turn yourself in to the authorities and explain."

"Explain what?" he whispered fiercely. "Explain that I'm not responsible for the last six robberies, even though I was in the area when half of them occurred?" He shook his head. "Even with a dozen ironclad alibis, I couldn't go to the authorities now. They'd simply think I was protecting my accomplice." He heaved a rough sigh.

"There's more, Ethan."

He leveled a piercing glance on his younger step-brother. "Somehow I have a feeling I'm not going to like whatever you're about to say."

Ned shook his head. "A few months ago some of your things were stolen from the house." He took a deep breath. "Mama was notified nearly a week ago that your gold watch had been found."

"So?"

"It was found on the floor of the Eastbrook bank after the robbery. The authorities think *you* dropped it there before exploding the safe."

"Dammit!"

"The watch isn't common knowledge yet, but the authorities were notified and sent sketches of your face."

He hesitated, and Ethan sensed he still hadn't heard the last of his stepbrother's bad news.

Ned slipped his hand beneath the edge of his jacket and withdrew a tattered piece of paper from the inner pocket. "Do you remember the photograph Mama keeps on her highboy?"

Ethan nodded. It was the last picture taken of Ethan before he'd begun his career as the Gentleman.

"The night the watch was taken, she woke to find this tacked to the frame." Ned reluctantly held out the slip of paper. His eyes had grown darker, grayer, and even more inscrutable.

Ethan's fingers unfolded the paper, then paused. For a moment, he gazed at the eight-sided star in confusion. Then his eyes noted the initials in the center: *SCJ*.

"The Star Council of Justice?" he muttered slowly, already familiar with the vigilante group's method of retaliation. Though their motives might seem noble if viewed from the surface, their methods of punishment amounted to little more than cold-blooded murder. The only way to escape their wrath was to surrender to the law. But since the law was on his tail, too, Ethan couldn't even seek protection from the courts.

He took a deep breath, and the paper crumpled between his fingers. The time had come for him to cut his losses.

Ethan crossed toward his stepbrother and held out his hand. "Take care of yourself, Ned."

Ned glanced at him in surprise. "Where are you going?"

"Mexico. Canada."

"You won't solve anything by running!"

"Someone is trying to see me hanged, little brother. And I'm not about to be led like a lamb to the slaughter."

The muted clang of a pail caused both men to start. Gesturing with his head, Ethan motioned for Ned to hitch the buggy and drive into the sunshine. After Ned had gone, Ethan peered around the edge of the door. A shiver of relief slid down his spine when he realized it was Lettie who approached the barn.

Though he knew he should leave, Ethan waited in the cool shadows of the tack room as Lettie fed the chickens, then gathered her pail and stepped into the barn. "Hello, Lettie," he murmured.

She stiffened, then finally turned.

Her nut-brown eyes became wide. Her hands tightened around the handles of her pail. "I thought you'd gone."

Ethan reached to draw the door closed, then walked toward her, his boots rasping in the straw. To his surprise, she didn't seem afraid. In fact, her gaze was steady and intent.

"No. I haven't gone yet."

The silence hung between them. Thick. Warm. Then she asked bluntly, "Who are you, Ethan McGuire?"

Lettie noted the way he stiffened at the use of his name. "You've been talking to your brother."

She nodded.

"What did he tell you?"

"Nothing."

He evidently read more into her reply than she'd

intended, because he took a step forward. "But he warned you about me, didn't he?"

She watched him advance, and a curious warmth entered her veins. Her breathing became slightly irregular, causing the firm curves of her breasts to push against the pinafore bib of her apron. "Yes."

"What did he say?"

She kept her shoulders straight, her chin proud. "He said he thought you were probably a thief. Or a murderer."

Ethan drew nearer, his eyes narrowing.

"Anything else?"

"No."

"I'm surprised," he added, his voice laced with sarcasm. "Since he's deciding on a past for me, I'd have thought he would embellish things a little, come up with something a little more creative. Course, I guess *thief* and *murderer* covers just about everything, doesn't it?"

Ethan was only a few steps away now and closing the distance.

"And what do you think, Lettie?"

"I don't know."

"Do you think I've killed? Do you think I've stolen?"

He was so close now that she could smell the faint scent of soap on his skin. A trembling awareness began deep within her. Trying not to let him see his effect on her, she bent to place the pail on the ground.

"I scare you, don't I, Lettie?"

She straightened and met his gaze. "No."

He took another step, and he was so close now that she could feel the heat from his body, see the tiny beads of sweat on his upper lip. But she wasn't afraid of him. She was afraid of the way she responded to him.

As if he'd sensed a portion of her thoughts, Ethan closed the scant distance between them. His gaze grew warm and intense. "I can feel you trembling. Why? Because you think I'll hurt you?"

He stood so close now that Lettie couldn't move without brushing some part of his body in the process.

"No. I—"

"You don't think I'll hurt you?" His hand lifted to cup her cheek, forcing her to look up at him.

"No." The word was a garbled whisper.

"Why?" He took another step, and his thighs pressed against her skirts. "Because you're Jacob Grey's little sister?" His voice grew unconsciously hard, and Lettie caught a shred of bitterness deep in his eyes. "If anything, your relationship to Jacob Grey should give you more reason to fear me."

"I'm not afraid of you," she stated again—more firmly this time.

Ethan regarded her intently, evidently surprised by her refusal to cower under his harsh words.

"Then perhaps you *should* fear me, Lettie Grey." His glance flicked to the curves of her lips and seemed to linger there. "You should run a hundred miles from me, because I'm the kind of man you should never admit to knowing."

"Why?" She tried to give the word the same degree of firmness she'd used before, but the tone of her voice emerged with a breathless quality. He was standing so close to her now. So close.

His eyes grew dark and filled with shadows. "Because I'm the kind of man who could ruin a girl like you."

At the word *girl*, Lettie stiffened and wedged her hands between them, and she pushed him away. "I'm not a *girl*. I am a vibrant, mature woman! The kind any man would want to kiss. Even you!"

Silence suddenly cloaked them in a hot, sticky awareness.

Ethan's expression of shock was almost comical. "Me!"

Lettie's lips thinned. The Highwayman would never have been so rude. Nor would he have passed up such a golden opportunity. She planted her hands on her hips and glared at him in pique. "I suppose I'm not pretty enough for you."

"You're pretty."

"But not pretty enough." She brushed past him, but he caught her arm.

When she glanced over her shoulder, she found Ethan

watching her with eyes that were still and quiet, like the surface of a dark summer pond that hid tangled depths below.

After a moment he released her, and his thumbs hooked in the back of his waistband in such a way that the fabric of his trousers pulled taut across his hips. She swallowed. The man's pants were tight enough.

Her gaze bounced up and locked with his own. His features lay cloaked in shadow. Yet he seemed to know just what she'd been thinking, because he shook his head from side to side in silent reproof.

"You shouldn't be thinking those kinds of thoughts, Lettie."

"I don't know what you mean."

"I think you do," he breathed, his blue eyes gleaming, his features quiet, sensual. He edged closer.

Lettie's chin tilted at a defiant angle. "I thought you were going."

"Maybe I'll stay. Maybe I'll even kiss you."

Lettie could barely breathe.

"A man would be a fool not to kiss you," he continued, speaking almost to himself. "You're sweet. And pretty. Fresh." A flicker of nostalgic longing flashed across his features, making Lettie think that it had been a long time since Ethan had seen any of those qualities in a woman. That sliver of vulnerability touched her in strange ways.

Lettie took a step back and bumped into the stall. Ethan's hands came out to grasp the railing on either side of her. She could feel the heat of his body seeping through the layers of her clothing.

A soft, whispering "No" escaped from her lips, but Ethan smiled and shook his head.

"You asked." He leaned closer. His breath fanned against her cheek.

Lettie's head dropped back, her eyes flickered closed, and she waited. . . .

Nothing happened.

Opening one eyelash, she peered up at Ethan, only to

find him grinning at her in evident amusement. Drat and bother! He'd been toying with her all along.

Growling in anger, Lettie balled her hands into fists and slugged him in the stomach. As he doubled over with a grunt, she pushed his arm away and dodged to the opposite side of the barn.

To her surprise, Ethan chuckled aloud and turned to lean against the stall, rubbing his belly. Despite his negligent pose, his stance was still slightly wary, his blue eyes sparkling.

Lettie nearly gaped at him open-mouthed. She'd never seen him smile before—not an honest smile that entered his eyes and made them glow. It made him appear boyish and infinitely mischievous.

"Like I said, a man should never take his eyes off you. You're a dangerous girl wrapped in a pretty package."

Lettie had been about to leave the barn. She'd been all set to whirl on her toes and stomp out the door. Until she heard that word again. *Girl.* Like a thorn in her side, the word was thrown carelessly into his comment, proving to her once again that everyone saw her as a child.

She took a deep breath, a simmering frustration growing within her. She wasn't a girl, she was a woman!

As if her feet moved of their own volition, Lettie found herself stepping forward. Her shoulders pressed back, causing the rounded curves of her bosom to jut against the bib of her apron. Without stopping, she crossed toward him until her skirts brushed the tips of his boots.

Ethan straightened, his hands dropping to his sides, his eyes narrowing in disbelief at her sudden boldness.

"I told you once before: I'm not a girl, Ethan McGuire." She stepped forward again until her skirts flattened against his thighs and her breasts nearly brushed his chest. Her hands lifted to rest against his shoulders, savoring the firm musculature beneath her palms. She raised herself on tiptoe, lifting her thumbs to position his head so that they wouldn't bump noses.

He was smiling, ever so slightly, as if he thought she

were merely teasing him and would back away. But Lettie did not back away, and his smile altered.

Her own lips tilted in satisfaction, then she drew him down for a kiss, trying to remember in her mind all of the stolen embraces she'd witnessed over the years.

Wrapping her arms tightly around his neck, she drew herself tighter against his torso, until his hands wrapped around her back and he took most of her weight. Her lips parted, ever so slightly. Her lashes flickered closed.

Though Lettie feared her true inexperience would show the minute her lips met his own, she need not have worried. Ethan evidently felt no qualms in taking charge of their embrace. Within moments, he had crushed her against him, teaching her the art of blending lip to lip, chest to chest, hip to hip. One of his hands settled in the curve of her back to hold her tightly, while the other moved to tangle in the base of her thick braid to keep her head steady as his lips hungrily traced the curve of her cheek, the jut of her chin. Then he shifted slightly and followed the lower curve of her lip with his tongue.

Lettie wrenched herself free, breathing hard. She gazed up at him in disbelief, slowly backing away, her fingers pressing against her lips. Her heart pounded like a runaway locomotive and her limbs trembled, barely able to support her.

She'd never dreamed kissing could be like this!

Not really knowing what she should say to back away gracefully from a situation she didn't know how to handle, she turned and rushed toward the door. But just before escaping outside, she turned to gaze at him one last time.

His eyes were warm. Aware.

"Your horse and belongings were taken to the stables behind the jail," she stated quietly, knowing it was the last thing she could give him. Then she slipped through the door.

Ethan remained in the barn and gazed at the spot where she'd been, wondering why he couldn't ignore the sweet, heavy warmth that curled deep in his gut and spread throughout his limbs. His mind argued that their kiss had been nothing more than an experiment, a teasing game—to both of them.

But damn if his body didn't urge him to kiss her again.

Ethan waited in the barn until late afternoon. With each moment that passed, the air around him grew hot and more unbearable, until finally, he leaned against the splintered threshold of the barn, cracked open the door, and gazed out at the back porch of the house to watch Lettie iron.

She was a pretty gir—

Woman. Lettie had been right in her assertion. She was all woman, with delicate features, dark eyes, long honey-brown hair. And there was nothing girlish about her figure. She had curves in all the places a man liked best. High, firm breasts, a narrow waist, full hips. What Ethan wouldn't give to spend a little more time with her.

Grunting in disgust at his own thoughts, Ethan checked the chamber of his revolver and slipped out the door. Moving as quickly as he dared, he walked toward the far end of town, making his movements as inconspicuous as possible. With a little luck, he could reach the corral behind the jailhouse and gather his horse without anyone being the wiser. Since the deputies were scouring the area, they wouldn't expect him to have the gall to steal his horse from a corral in the middle of town.

But he only managed to make it as far as the alley butting the west wall of the jailhouse when he heard voices and flattened himself against the side of the building.

". . . paid you enough to see the man well and truly caught."

"I told you: McGuire disappeared from the area a month ago."

"Obviously not entirely. There have been three robberies since . . ."

The voices faded away, and Ethan felt only a moment's indecision before he inched toward the edge of the alleyway and peered around the corner.

". . . want him dead, do you understand?"

"On one condition."

"I've already paid you, well in advance—"

"And I'll see you get your money's worth. But I can't do a thing about your problem until you find a way to get Jeb Clark off my back. He's somehow managed to catch wind of my . . . extraneous payroll."

Straining to see around the half-dozen horses in the corral, Ethan barely managed to make out the indistinct forms of the men who spoke in such low, confidential tones. Though one man was hidden from view, Ethan was able to catch a glimpse of the silver hair of his companion. Even so, Ethan had no idea who these men could be, but he had no doubts that they meant to see him hanging from a noose at the first opportunity.

". . . and I'll take care of Clark. You see to McGuire."

Once again, the voices grew softer, some of the words fading into the dusty summer air.

"He's brought me enough grief . . . a lifetime. Just see to it that no trace . . . you or me . . . scapegoat . . ."

When Ethan heard the crunch of footsteps approaching him, he crouched low and dodged away, staying within the shadows of the alley, then blending into the traffic of the town in a way that he had learned so long before yet had hoped to some day forget.

He was slipping back into the barn behind the boardinghouse before he realized that he had even returned. As his fingers closed over the splintered wood of the door and he darted inside, he admitted to himself that he had gravitated toward the meager sense of security he had found here, a sense of security in the spontaneous trust of a young woman who had every reason to suspect him of the crimes he was supposed to have committed.

Standing silently in the shadows, he took deep drags of hot summer air to still the pounding of his heart. But as his nervous energy began to dissipate, he was filled with a firm resolve. For some time, he'd suspected that the answers to his troubles lay in Madison proper. And now he had his proof. To leave now would mean spending the rest of his life looking over his shoulder. But to stay . . .

In staying, there would be no guarantees of his safety. He was a wanted man, not only for the past crimes he'd committed, but also for the recent rash of robberies he *hadn't* committed.

And yet, Ethan trusted Lettie Grey—though he should have his head examined for even thinking such a thing. It was ironic really. The only place he felt relatively safe was with the sister of the man who had sought to convict him for so many years. But if he were caught—

Ethan closed his eyes and took a deep breath. *Sweet heaven!* Don't let anyone find him here. Because if they did . . .

He'd be a dead man.

7

Lettie clutched the edges of her wrapper more tightly against her throat and peered out into the darkness, holding a lantern above her head. "Here, kitty, kitty."

Though the moon had just begun its ascent, enough light touched the expanse of grass near the chickencoop and barn for her to see that Eloise, the boardinghouse cat, was nowhere in sight. Yet, only a moment before, Lettie had awakened to her plaintive cries.

"Kitty?" she called again, her voice just above a whisper. Something about the dark night discouraged any kind of noise, even the necessity of calling the cat.

Once again, the soft mewl of the cat melted into the blackness and Lettie lifted the hem of her wrapper free and ran through the grass in the direction of the barn. Eloise had probably managed to get herself caught in the rafters again. Though she was a brave animal on her way up, she never had the nerve to get herself down.

Slipping through the door, Lettie paused for a moment, holding the lamp above her so that its mellow light slipped into the corners and warmed the straw with a golden glow.

"Eloise?" she whispered.

Silence.

Pushing away a shiver of disquiet, Lettie padded into the barn. "Eloise, where are you, kitty?"

"Hello, Lettie."

She whirled at the sudden deep voice, a gasp lodging in her throat. She tensed when she found Ethan McGuire watching her from a few feet away. He sat in a soft pile of straw, and in his lap lay the contented form of Eloise.

Lettie gripped the handle of the lantern more tightly, then lifted her free hand to clasp the neck of her wrapper. "What are you doing here?"

"Petting the cat."

Lettie's lips thinned in irritation, but his words caused her to look down. Eloise lay in sublime contentment as Ethan's hand moved down the length of her body from head to toe. Even from her vantage point a few feet away, Lettie could hear the almost fanatical pleasure of the cat's purr.

"I thought I heard her call."

Ethan's lips lifted in a slow grin. *"Meow."*

She stiffened, realizing it had not been the cat who had drawn her out to the barn. "You told me you were leaving," she muttered stiffly.

His eyes dropped, his features becoming masked. "I came back." Once again, his hand passed down the length of Eloise's white fur, from the top of her head to the tip of her tail.

"Why?" Lettie swallowed when her voice emerged too husky, too soft. Ethan's hands were broad and firm, his touch light, yet enticing.

When he didn't answer, Lettie glanced up. She knew he'd noted her fascination with his hands. His touch.

A muted fire began to glow deep in his eyes. Gently scooping the cat from his lap, he set her in the straw beside him and stood up.

Obviously disgruntled by his actions, Eloise twined between his legs, muttering kittenish sounds of displeasure. But Ethan wasn't looking at the cat. He was watching the way Lettie clutched the neckline of her wrapper.

"It's awfully late, Lettie. Shouldn't you be in bed?"

"I was in bed." Lettie stopped, realizing she shouldn't

be talking this way with Ethan McGuire. "Why are you here?" she demanded again.

He ignored her question and took a step forward, mindful of Eloise at his feet, but his movements were determined, nonetheless.

"I never took you for the soft and frilly type." He gestured to the delicate batiste of her wrapper and the intricate white embroidery Lettie had added to the edges of the collar, sleeves, and hem. "But it suits you."

Lettie turned away, suddenly conscious of the fact that she wore nothing more than her wrapper and a threadbare nightshift beneath.

"If you've been waiting for dark to make your escape, then go now before someone sees you."

She gasped when he walked up behind her and took the lantern from her hand, setting it on an old trunk that held leather strips and old laprobes.

"What if I told you I've decided to stay?"

She whirled. "You can't stay!"

Too late, she realized he'd taken another step forward and the heat of his body seeped into her own.

But it was his eyes that made her pause. Though they were cloaked in the shadows of the barn, she thought she saw a loneliness in their depths. And a sliver of desperation.

"Do you know what I've been doing the last few years?"

She shook her head, struggling to breathe when he took another step closer. *Sweet heaven!* He was so close now, she could smell the musk of his body, feel the faint scratch of the straw clinging to his clothing.

"I've been digging potatoes in Nebraska." He took another step. "Do you know what that does to a man's hands?"

She shook her head, trying to back away, but the rough slats of the stall behind her halted any attempt at escape.

Ethan lifted a hand, and one finger touched the high curve of her cheekbone. His skin was warm, calloused.

"It makes a man's hands rough, Lettie. Rough and

scratchy." He took another step. His thighs brushed against her own, his chest grazed her breasts. "Do you know what I thought about?"

She shook her head, and her hands rose in an effort to push him away. But he was immovable.

"I thought about the velvet touch of a woman. The soft whisper of her skin against mine. The heady fragrance of soap, and lilac water, and female."

A soft moan eased from her throat when his head bent. His eyes grew dark and stormy blue. The finger at her cheek shifted, and his hand curled around the back of her neck, drawing her toward him.

"It's been so long," he whispered, just before his lips brushed against her own. "Don't push me away, Lettie. Please. Don't push me away."

Lettie's hands had braced instinctively around his rib cage, yet at his words, she hesitated, drawn by the submerged vulnerability she'd heard in his voice.

His head lifted, and her eyes stared into his own. Such a proud man, too proud to show his need of others. Until now.

Unbidden, her hands slid around his ribs to rest against his back. "I won't push you away," she whispered, just before his mouth covered her own.

Though there was more hunger than gentle entreaty in his embrace, Lettie surrendered willingly to the tumultuous emotions thundering through her. Her inexperience proved to be no impediment to Ethan. In fact, he seemed to revel in the innocent response of her mouth to his own. And when Ethan drew away, they gazed at each other.

Ethan's eyes became guarded once again. Yet Lettie had seen a flash of wonder, a flash of need. Unconsciously, she lifted a hand to brush back the dark hair spilling over his brow.

He stepped back and turned away from her, as if just now realizing how much he'd allowed her to see.

Lettie hesitated only a moment, gazing at the proud line of his back, the rigid cast of his shoulders. Then, moving toward him, she reached out and took his hand.

When he looked at her, his azure eyes dark and shuttered, she twined her fingers between his own.

"You can't spend the night in the barn. Come with me."

When she tugged at his hand, he hesitated.

"Where?"

She paused only a moment before whispering, "My room."

They crept into the sleeping house together, and Lettie once again led him up the back stairs to her room. When the door had closed behind them, she gathered a pair of quilts and a set of linens from the trunk at the foot of the bed.

"What's that for?"

"Your bed," she murmured firmly, pointing to a bare space of floor a few feet away.

His lips twitched, and he regarded her with blatant male amusement. "Come now, Lettie. The floor?"

"The floor."

He shrugged in good-natured resignation and arranged the linens on the floor. Then, when Lettie had slipped beneath her own covers and doused the lamp, she heard the rustle of clothes as Ethan removed his shirt, gun belt, socks, and shoes.

"Good night, Ethan."

At first he didn't answer her; then, finally, she heard, "Night, Lettie."

Silence slipped into the shadows, cloaking the corners in secrets. Lettie lay on her side for the longest time, pretending to be asleep, while in fact, she thought of the man only a few feet away. She wondered why he had come back. And why—though he'd never admitted as much—he'd lured her into the barn and silently asked for her help.

Lettie was about ready to sigh in frustration at her own tangled thoughts, when she heard a rustle of movement. Holding her breath, she opened her eyes just a slit. After the way Jacob had warned her about Ethan McGuire, she almost expected him to jump on her bed.

But Ethan merely stood up and moved to the window. The pale wash of moonlight stroked the strong lines of his features, highlighting the frown etched in his brow.

She heard him take a deep breath, saw the way his hand tightened into a fist next to the wall. Suddenly the room seemed to fill with his own brand of torment.

Lettie propped herself on her elbow and he stiffened, then slowly turned.

"Why did you come back?" she whispered.

"It's not important."

She waited a moment longer, then realized he wasn't going to tell her anything more.

"Who are you, Ethan McGuire?" she murmured, more to herself than to him.

To her surprise, he answered. "I'm just a man. A tired, tired man."

She opened her mouth to say something, hoping she could find the words to ease the bleak cast of his features. But he turned away to gaze out the window into the night.

"Good night, Lettie."

Realizing he'd already revealed more than he'd intended, she sank back against the pillows. The quiet seeped into the attic again, and she was nearly asleep when she heard him turn.

"Lettie?"

"Mmm?"

His voice was a mere whisper in the darkness, half dream, half reality.

"Thank you."

A sickly moon hung on the far edge of the sky, piercing the blackness like a pale, hollow bootprint that would soon fade with the arrival of the dawn. Five miles west of Madison, the dilapidated remains of the Johnston farmhouse lay nearly hidden in the shadows, partially covered by a copse of ancient oak trees.

A single figure stood on the scarred porch, breathing deeply of the cooler air lingering in the darkness. In his hand, he held the smoldering remains of a cigarette, but it lay half forgotten in his fingers as he stared into the night.

Jacob had been a member of the Star Council of Justice for only a few years, yet he felt as if he had been part of its system forever. Eight years before, as an eager deputy hungry to bring lawbreakers and sinners to their rightful ends, Jacob had discovered that Justice could indeed be blind. Over and over, he'd seen innocent men hanged for crimes they hadn't committed, while guilty men lived in pleasurable freedom. He'd ached because of that fact. Until he'd been asked to join the brotherhood of the Star.

His lips tilted in wry humor. No one really knew how the Star had begun. Perhaps over a game of cards or a drunken round of whiskey, a group of lawmen had argued about the idea of Henry VIII's Star Chamber, first introduced hundreds of years ago—if Tyler Grant of Petesville could be believed. Evidently old Henry had found a way of punishing those nobles who'd escaped justice by meting out his own form of punishment through the Star Chamber. As Tyler Grant always said, "Heads would roll when old Henry got his dander up. You betcha, heads would roll."

Jacob brought the cigarette to his lips and took a deep drag until the butt glowed crimson in the darkness. He had no interest in the Star Chamber, or Henry VIII, or anything hundreds of years old, for that matter. It was the purpose of the Council that had persuaded him to join.

Though vigilante groups were not uncommon—even in Illinois—the Star was special. Unlike most, the governing board of the Star was comprised almost entirely of lawmen who were dedicated to seeing that justice was served. Each of its members were sworn to secrecy—upon pain of death—and only a select few knew that the ruling board of the Star contained two judges, two marshals, two lawyers, a pair of deputies, and two community representatives. Jacob himself didn't know their identities, even though, two months earlier, he'd been promoted in rank to the circle of men known as "outer rings"—those who served as assistants to the board.

Though the members were known by only a few, the deeds of the Star Council of Justice were legendary, even to the community. In the past five years, the Star's reputation had grown and people lauded their efforts to rid the state of those criminals who had somehow escaped the justice system and avoided their penance.

Yet, even as the Star was praised for its efforts, it had become a symbol of fear—for once the Star had decided upon the guilt of a man, the Council served as judge, jury . . .

And executioner.

Jacob flicked the butt of his cigarette into the darkness. Tonight, the hierarchy of the Star had met to decide on the fate of Ethan McGuire, and Jacob had a burning desire to see the man caught, once and for all.

Once again, Jacob felt a tightening in his gut at the thought of the man. It was Jacob who had introduced the case to the Star. But McGuire had eluded capture, and with each month that passed, Jacob had grown more bitter and intent upon seeing McGuire pay for his activities.

Sometimes, Jacob's single-minded purpose seemed to consume him. He wanted the man punished—not just because McGuire had once bested him and dented his pride—but because Ethan McGuire had been just a little too cocky, a little too sure. Then, when things had become too hot for Ethan to handle, he'd abandoned his life of thievery.

But McGuire's penitent behavior hadn't lasted. He'd returned to his thieving ways—with a renewed fervor.

Jacob straightened, peering into the darkness, a cool determination settling in his stomach. Ethan had made a mistake by coming to Madison weeks ago. He'd made a mistake by beginning his rash of robberies again—and most of all, he'd made a mistake by injuring that deputy in Carlton.

Jacob's brow creased and he damned the fact that he'd evidently lost some of his instincts in regards to

Ethan McGuire. Jacob hadn't anticipated what had happened in Carlton. In fact, the Gentleman seemed to have grown erratic in the last few months—even careless.

Grunting in irritation at his own thoughts, Jacob straightened. Ethan McGuire *was* the Gentleman. He'd escaped capture the last time they came face-to-face and then again, when he'd abducted Lettie. But this time, Jacob had the power to stop him through the Star.

Pushing away from the porch, Jacob mounted his horse and rode toward the lightning-blasted oak. As a member of the outer circle, it was his duty to retrieve messages from the tree, then notify the other Star members assigned to his leadership. Given his length of membership, it was an honor for Jacob to have such a responsibility within the group.

Once again, Jacob removed the canister from its hiding place inside the trunk. He hesitated only a moment before withdrawing the crumpled paper that lay inside. Since dawn had not touched the sky, Jacob dug a matchstick from his shirt pocket and raked his thumbnail over the tip. The match flared to life, illuminating the scrawled words:

Proof of Ethan McGuire's guilt has been obtained. When located, notify immediately but do not apprehend through legal channels. He will be tried before the Council.

Jacob took a deep breath and squinted up at the moon, shaking out the match and tossing it to the ground. A thundering anticipation rolled through his body. Once and for all, McGuire would see that it didn't pay to toy with Jacob Grey.

Or his sister.

The thought raced through Jacob's head and his jaw clenched, his gut tightened in anger and dread. He'd never forgive the man for using his sister as a shield.

A slow, curling fury began to twine in Jacob's stomach. Touching another match to the paper, Jacob watched the licking flame as it curled around the edges of the note with a hungry glee until all but the tip he held had been consumed. Then he allowed the smoldering missive to flutter to the ground and urged his horse into a trot, reining him in the direction of the boardinghouse.

It would be dawn soon.

"Lettie!"

Her head jerked up, and she found her mother regarding her with an irritated expression. Lettie looked down to find she'd long since emptied the pan of milk gravy and had been ladling nothing but air for the last few moments.

"Sorry, Mama."

"Just stop your daydreaming and go feed the boarders."

"Yes, Mama."

Holding the heavy tureen against her stomach, Lettie hurried into the dining room, where the boarders were eagerly consuming large quantities of fried eggs, potatoes, milk, coffee, and fresh cherries.

Lettie set about seeing to the rest of the meal, refilling platters and clearing plates, moving automatically through the familiar tasks. However, when Jacob appeared— unannounced—Lettie's nerves took a turn for the worse and she nearly dropped a plate of fried eggs into Mr. Goldsmith's lap. Though she tried to act as normally as possible, she couldn't help thinking that Ethan McGuire was hidden in the garret, while the man who sought him ate breakfast just a few floors below.

After being forced to hear nearly an hour of the Beasleys' chatter, Mr. Goldsmith's slurping, and the Grubers' whispered bickering, Lettie's stomach seemed to tie into knots. Over and over again, she glanced up to find her brother staring at her with a piercing regard, and for the first time, Lettie felt a twinge of doubt. If Jacob were right, she could very well be harboring a murderer in her room. One who had robbed the bank in Carlton and left a young deputy lying gravely injured in the blaze.

But somehow . . . somehow she couldn't fit Ethan into that scenario. He was hard, yes, intense, enigmatic,

and even angry. But after last night's unwitting insights
into the man, she knew he wasn't capable of the things
Jacob thought he'd done. When she looked into Ethan's
eyes, she didn't see a killer. She saw a man who'd been
alone too long and hadn't realized yet that he needed
someone to love him.

Lettie glanced up to find Jacob peering at her as if he
could read her very thoughts. Stiffening, she tried to
affect a posture of unconcern, but to no avail.

A knock sounded at the door, and, welcoming the
excuse to leave the dining room, Lettie jumped to her
feet. Instead of a possible boarder, she found Jacob's
deputy standing impatiently on the stoop, mauling his
hat with his hands.

"Good morning, Rusty."

The bowlegged man brushed by her, ignoring her words
of greeting. "Where's your brother?"

"The dining room, but—"

Without waiting to hear what she had to say, Rusty
Janson darted into the other room. When Lettie rounded
the threshold, she found him leaning close to her brother's ear.

Jacob's eyes lifted, and a smoldering anger began to
burn in their depths. When the deputy had finished,
Jacob slowly rose to his feet, threw his napkin onto the
table, and crossed the room. Moving past Lettie without
a word, he began climbing the steps.

A cool finger of fear seemed to trace up Lettie's spine
when his deputy followed and the two men unsheathed
their revolvers, walking with catlike stealth.

"Jacob?" Picking up her skirts, Lettie hurried to follow. "Jacob! Where are you going?"

Her brother paid her no mind, his pace increasing so
that she was forced to take the stairs two at a time in
order to catch him and grasp his arm.

"Jacob, what are you doing?"

He brushed away her grip as if it were no more than
that of a fly. His hand closed around the door that led to
her garret bedroom, and he scowled when he found it
locked.

"Where's the key, Lettie?" he demanded harshly.

"I don't—"

"Where's the key!" He reached out to grip her arm, his fingers curling tightly into her skin. "Damn you, you've been lying to me for days, haven't you? He's been here all along!"

"No!"

"The key, Lettie." When she didn't budge, he reached out to pat the pockets of her apron. He was rewarded by the stiff shape of the key. Before she could grasp the key, his hand had plunged into the deep pocket and snatched it free.

"Jacob, don't!" she cried, but he brushed her aside, unlocked the latch, and flung the door wide open.

The stairwell lay bare in the bright light of the morning. Jacob and his deputy slowly began to climb the staircase. Behind them, Lettie balled her hands into fists of rage. Never before had her brother been so . . . so . . . beastly! She wanted to scream for Ethan to hide, but she couldn't—not without incriminating them both.

Long moments followed, long endless moments while she stood in the hall, waiting for a volley of shots, the scrabbling of fisticuffs. But nothing happened. Soon, no longer able to bear the tension, Lettie grasped her skirts in her hands, and crept up the staircase. Once she could see over the edge, she grew still in disbelief.

The garret was empty.

Jacob and his man continued to search the wardrobe, under the bed, and even her trunks. But Lettie knew their search would be fruitless. Ethan had left without a trace, just as her Highwayman had in so many of her fantasies.

Finally, after several minutes, her brother turned and she glared at him, the disdain she displayed aimed at inflicting the deep-rooted guilt that only a younger sibling could generate.

Jacob, however, seemed unaffected. When she waited in pointed silence, he took a step toward her. "He isn't here," he said slowly, stating the obvious but somehow making the words sound more like an accusation.

"And just who are you referring to?"

But Jacob thought she was lying. She could tell. Despite the evidence of his own eyes, Jacob's gaze flicked into the corners of the room as if he expected some secret passage to open up and reveal Ethan McGuire's hiding place. He sheathed his revolver and planted his hands on his hips, gazing at her with barely disguised suspicion.

"Rusty thought he saw someone in front of the window."

Lettie turned to glare at Rusty as well and found his face the same carrot shade as his hair.

"Both of you have more imagination than is healthy."

The two men shifted, glanced at each other, but did not admit their mistake.

"I gotta go, Lettie," Rusty mumbled, before beating a hasty retreat down the steps and out the door.

Lettie then turned her glare full-force on her brother. "Don't you have some place you need to be going as well?"

He sighed. "Look, I said I was sorry, didn't I?"

"No, you didn't. And even if you had, your apology isn't good enough. Now kindly leave my room."

He stared deep into her eyes, evidently searching for some sign of the little girl who had always adored him, no questions asked. "Yes, ma'am."

She turned toward the staircase, only to be halted by his voice.

"Lettie?"

She glanced at him over her shoulder, and something within her grew wary at the burning intensity of his gaze.

"I'll give you as long a lead as you want, little sister. But if you're thinking of tangling with Ethan McGuire, you'd better stay clear. Otherwise, you'll be opening yourself up to a world of hurt that no one can protect you from. Not even me.

A chill feathered down her spine. "What do you mean?"

"I can't tell you any more than that. Just you remember that Ethan McGuire is a man with a whole lot of enemies. Powerful enemies. And they aren't the type to be put off by pretty speeches. If they have their way, Ethan McGuire will be hanging from an oak tree soon.''

Giving her one last glance of warning, he strode toward the staircase and clattered down to the floor below.

Rubbing at the gooseflesh that had risen on her arms, Lettie slowly crossed to the window and stared out at the bright, sun-drenched yard. Ethan's absence left a hollow space within her, one that ached in a curious fashion, much like the loss of a special . . . friend. Yet, much more disconcerting than the ache was the fear she felt, wondering just who Ethan's enemies could be and why they were so all-fired up to see him hanged.

Shaking away her morbid thoughts, she slammed the window closed, threw the latch, and turned on her heel, needing the chatter of the Beasley sisters to dispel the gloom that suddenly seemed to taint the room around her.

But far from being diverted, she found that the Beasley sisters' male-oriented gossip caused her to remember the man who had so briefly interrupted the monotonous pattern of her own life.

Sighing, she slipped from the room, suddenly needing to escape the confines of the house.

A faint breeze stirred against her skin and teased the hem of her apron. Lettie breathed deeply in relief as the air caressed the perspiration dotting her brow and prickling between her shoulders. How she wished she had the time to slip out to the creek, lift the layers of skirts she wore, and paddle to her knees in the cool water.

But there were things to be done, chores to finish.

Wistfully, Lettie gazed out at the barn, remembering the fantasy that had become real, remembering Ethan's kisses. He hadn't even given her a chance to say goodbye.

Stepping from the porch, she meandered through the grass, veering toward the barn, which housed the two milk cows and horses used to pull the buggy. Her feet made soft soughing noises in the dusty grass, reminding her that summer would soon pass its zenith and she would face another fall, another winter, and another spring, each exactly the same as the other. She would rise at five each morning and retire at nine each night. In between, she would help to fix breakfast, lunch, and dinner. Mondays she would wash, Tuesdays she would bake, Wednesdays . . .

A huge sigh pushed against her corset and she turned back to gaze at the house, wondering if she'd ever escape the tedium.

Lettie glanced up and her thoughts scattered into the hot summer air. Her heart began to pound. On the outer edge of the boardinghouse roof, a dark shape clung to the gabled window of her bedroom.

Laws! She'd locked Ethan out on the ledge.

8

Grasping her skirts, Lettie raced toward the boarding-house and shot up the back staircase. Once in her room, she slammed the door and scrambled up the last flight of stairs.

"I'm coming, I'm coming," she whispered fiercely, all the while knowing he couldn't hear her but needing to say the words anyway.

She shoved the window up with such force that the panes jiggled and threatened to crack. Leaning outside, her eyes widened in delight when she found Ethan clinging to the gabled edge with a white-knuckled grip. She could only wonder why neither Rusty nor her brother had bothered to look up and find him there.

"You're still here!"

At the sound of her voice, Ethan swore, then swore again, using such a variety of curses that even Lettie was impressed by his vocabulary. "Why'd you shut the damned window?"

"I didn't know you were out here or I wouldn't have."

"Can I please—" he paused to grit his teeth, his grip becoming even more fierce—"come into the house now?"

"Well, of course. Just swing your leg over and I'll take your hand."

Ethan swallowed, and his face seemed to take on the sickly color of flour paste.

"What's wrong?"

"Nothing."

"Then come inside."

There was a moment of silence, then Ethan slowly turned his head to glare at her. "I . . . can't."

Her brow creased in confusion. "Whyever not?"

His eyes squeezed closed. "I hate heights," he whispered to himself, but Lettie caught the words.

All at once, she became conscious of his death grip on the edge of the gable and the sweat that poured down his face. The man was well and truly spooked.

Reaching out her hand, she spoke in her calmest, gentlest voice. "Give me your hand, Ethan."

"Oh, damn."

"Ethan. Give me your hand."

He opened one eye to gaze at her in stunned disbelief.

"Like hell I will! If you think I'm going to let go, you've lost your mind."

"Ethan. Please. Give me your hand." Lettie kept her gaze steady and firm, willing him to release the grasp of one hand so that she could help him.

"You're just trying to see me killed, Lettie Gray."

"Do as I say, Ethan McGuire," she repeated, using the voice she generally reserved for the recalcitrant children who occasionally visited the boardinghouse. "Take my hand."

Very slowly, he released his grasp. Even more slowly, he reached out, until finally she was able to take his hand. His palm was slick with sweat, but his fierce grip on her fingers would never give way.

With more encouraging words, Lettie talked him from the edge of the gable, around the roof, until finally he could hook his leg over the window casing and haul himself inside.

Still cursing, he leaned weakly against the wall, sliding down until he sat on the floor, his eyes closed, breathing heavily. A shudder wracked his frame.

"Damn, I hate heights," he muttered once again.

Frowning in concern, Lettie knelt beside him, her skirts spreading onto the floor and over his thighs. Though his features were still hard and uncompromising, she found herself reaching out to touch his cheek. His skin was hot beneath her touch and slick with sweat.

"Don't you ever do anything like that to me again!" he demanded, stabbing the air with a finger.

Her lips twitched slightly at his fierce expression, but she pushed her humor away and savored the texture of his beard-roughened skin. "No. I won't."

He must have sensed her amusement, however, because he growled low in his throat, then glared at her with narrowed eyes. "You think this is funny, don't you?"

"No!"

"I'll have you know it isn't!"

"I know it isn't."

"And I'll have you know I don't appreciate being laughed at."

"But I—"

"And if you ever lock that window again, I'll paddle your backside."

"Yes, sir."

His head turned slightly, and he pierced her with an azure stare. Suddenly, she became conscious of how her finger had begun to brush back and forth across the firm jut of his cheekbone.

Lettie took a deep breath. Ethan's scrutiny seemed to scorch into her very soul, singeing her with a feminine awareness she had never felt before. She knew she should go. She knew that this man could bring her nothing but trouble. But remembering last night's brief glimpse into Ethan's battered heart, she found she couldn't move.

When he didn't pull away, she shifted to cup his cheek with her palm. Her fingers delved into the silky weight of his hair. The strands were smooth as midnight, his scalp was warm and slightly damp from sweat. And though Lettie knew she should probably be repelled, she felt herself reacting in a purely elemental way to the musky heat of his body.

Ethan shifted beneath her touch, but did not back away. Instead, he watched her with eyes that were slightly narrowed and so carefully masked, she had no way of discerning his thoughts. She could only read his reaction by the slight tensing of his muscles beneath her hand and the warmth of his skin. He didn't smile, didn't frown.

But he didn't pull away, either.

Barely breathing, she slid one finger down to his jaw, then up to his lips.

His fingers snapped around her wrist, holding her away. "What kind of game are you playing with me?" he rasped.

She took a ragged breath. "I don't know."

Her honest answer seemed to shake his control. His gaze shifted, and he stared at the way his larger hand held hers immobile. When he glanced up again, she nearly backed away from the intense light that had entered his eyes. They flashed with the spark of a man who had just become conscious of a woman's proximity.

"I suppose I should thank you again for your help. For this morning, and last night."

So the soft words of thanks she'd thought Ethan had murmured just before she'd fallen asleep had not been a dream. But Lettie didn't comment on the fact that she'd heard them. She could tell by the glint in his eyes that he regretted the vulnerability she'd seen in him the night before. She tried to ease away. "I don't think it's necessary to thank me."

He tugged her back. "Yes. It is. My mother tried to teach me manners as a child, and I wasn't always an exemplary pupil, but I did learn how to say thank you. I think you should know that."

His free hand lifted to curl around her neck, pushing aside the thick braid that hung down her back and delving into the delicate hairs at her nape. His grip was firm.

Male.

"Come here."

His low tone caused a shiver to course down her spine. Once again, she realized this was not a man to fool with. The intensity of his gaze was too unnerving. The effect of his touch too disturbing.

"No, I—"

His fingers drew her irresistibly forward. "Didn't your mama teach you it was impolite to argue with your elders?" he murmured, moments before his lips covered hers.

Lettie gasped, her hands flying out to brace against his chest in support, then curling into tight fists when the warmth of his skin seeped through the chambray shirt he wore and seemed to soak into her palms.

"Ethan," she murmured against his lips.

He ignored her protests, taking advantage of the parting of her lips to deepen the caress.

"Open your mouth, Lettie," he whispered, drawing back ever so slightly.

"What?" she breathed, her lashes seeming so heavy she could barely open them to see.

"How many times have you been kissed, Lettie?"

She swallowed against the nervousness that seemed to grip her throat. "Four."

He stared at her a moment before his lips tilted in a brief smile. A smile that held only a touch of wry humor, yet seemed to echo with self-deprecation. "Only four."

"It's nothing to be ashamed of."

"No. It's not." The tone of his voice dropped. His eyes seemed to gaze at her with a strange warmth. As if he'd found something special and unique. Then the warmth was masked and the hand at the back of her neck pulled her irretrievably nearer. "But it doesn't speak well for your education, does it?" His murmured words held a taunting thread of mockery. Watching her with narrowed eyes, he used his free hand to reach out and trace the edge of her lip with his finger. Then he slipped his finger between her lips. "Open your mouth," he whispered.

Lettie hesitated. Ethan claimed she was danger in a

pretty package, but she was not half as dangerous as this man. He had the power to strip her of her idealistic fantasies and introduce her to the harsh realities of life. He had the power to capture something soft and gentle within her, something she didn't even dare name. But she also knew he had the power to hurt her.

"You don't trust me, do you?"

"No," she whispered.

His lips twitched, ever so slightly. "You shouldn't." Once again, his finger slipped between her lips. "Open your mouth."

The intensity of his gaze could not be avoided, nor could the silky temptation of his words.

"You have a beautiful mouth, Lettie. Soft, full, and quick to smile."

His finger dipped inside to trace the edge of her teeth in a featherlight touch, barely stroking the tip of her tongue.

"Let me show you," he murmured, the words so low they were barely audible. He bent toward her to replace his finger with the gentle pressure of his lips, and then his tongue.

At first she recoiled slightly, disturbed by something that seemed so . . . intimate it must surely be forbidden. But when a heavy sweetness invaded her body and settled deep within her, she closed her eyes and concentrated on the sensations that shimmered through her from that tiny point of contact.

Ethan drew back, and her eyelashes flickered open.

"Ah, Lettie girl, you're sweet." His lips tilted ever so slightly in self-deprecation. "Sweeter than honey and twice as nice." His hand moved to the hollow of her back, then slipped lower.

"Ethan, I—"

"Come here."

"No."

But his hand pulled her closer, as close as two people could be. Then he covered her lips with his own.

A moan seeped from Lettie's chest and was absorbed by his kiss. Her hands slipped around the broad expanse of his shoulders, and unconsciously, she pulled him even nearer—even though she knew she should be pushing him away.

"What are you doing to me, Ethan?" she whispered when he drew back.

He stared deep into her eyes, searching for something Lettie was almost afraid he might find. Something . . . sensual. Hungry.

Aching.

"What are you feeling, Lettie?"

She groaned, trying to ignore the heated rush that swirled through her limbs. Though she knew she shouldn't be touching a man this way—especially not a man with Ethan's reputation—she couldn't control the way her body nudged his, seeking something she didn't understand.

"E-than—"

"Tell me."

"I'm so hot, yet cold."

His hand cupped the back of her knee through the fabric of her skirts. "What else, Lettie girl?"

She blushed.

"Tell me."

"I want you to touch me. Hold me. But I shouldn't."

Ethan gently drew her knee upwards, then across his legs so that she straddled him.

"Do you want me to kiss you?"

She groaned.

He pulled her tightly against his hips.

"Do you want me to kiss you?"

"Ethan, don't."

His lips pressed against her throat. "Do you want me to touch you?"

"Yes! Please . . ."

His lips blazed a trail of fire up her throat to the underside of her chin, and then when she could bear it no longer, he kissed her. A long, heated kiss that branded her as his own.

Lettie's fingers clutched at his back, her breasts flattened against his chest. She was fire and ice. Sensation and emotion.

"Lettie?"

The shrill call echoed through the garret from the floor below.

At the sound of Natalie Gruber's voice, the two of them sprang apart, breathing heavy. Blue eyes clashed with brown.

Reality flooded through Lettie's body, leaving her stunned by her reaction to Ethan McGuire. Then she suddenly became conscious of the way she wantonly straddled his hips and clutched at his back with her hands.

Groaning in embarrassment, she scrambled to her feet and ran to the opposite side of the room. But at the steps, the low murmur of Ethan's voice brought her to a halt.

"Don't regret what happened between us, Lettie."

She turned to see him staring at her with a velvet heat. And for a moment, she thought he was as shaken as she by the sensations that had flared between them.

"It's not wrong to feel desire, Lettie. Though I'm not the man who should be teaching you that fact."

Her fingers curled around the railing until her knuckles grew white.

He took a step toward her. "But you need to know that what you felt was passion. Stark and simple."

"Maybe it wasn't quite that simple," she whispered, daring him to admit that there had been something more to their embrace than a simple animalistic urge.

Long after she'd gone, Ethan stared at the spot where she'd been, wondering why Lettie's words had somehow unsettled him.

Lettie closed the door behind her and quickly twisted the key in the lock.

"Secrets, Lettie?"

She whirled and found Natalie regarding her with curious eyes.

"Was there something you needed, Mrs. Gruber?"

Natalie's gaze bounced from Lettie's flushed features

111

to the closed door. "I wondered if I might borrow a blanket or quilt."

Lettie's brow creased in confusion. "You've been cold at night?"

Natalie smiled, a curiously smug expression crossing her features. "No," she drawled. "I'm rarely cold at night." She slid a hand down the garnet taffeta stretched across her torso. "No, I needed the quilt for a picnic."

Lettie regarded the woman in surprise. "You persuaded Mr. Gruber to step away from his duties for the afternoon?"

Natalie's lips twitched. "No."

After a moment of silence, Lettie realized Natalie was not about to explain anything more. Slightly embarrassed, Lettie strode toward the linen closet and grasped an old quilt her mother had recovered in flannel.

"There you are, Mrs. Gruber."

Natalie offered her a gracious smile. "You're such a dear." She grasped the quilt, then reached out to pat Lettie on the cheek with a glove-covered hand. "Thank you."

Lettie cringed beneath the woman's patronizing tone, but she managed to wait until Natalie's ruched train had disappeared down the staircase before she growled in irritation and set about her chores.

Natalie Gruber took her husband's horse and buggy and drove ten miles out of town to where the road took a sharp turn to the left around a thick copse of oak trees. Reining to the right, she eased the horse through the grass and scrub for another mile until the trees grew too dense to allow passage of the carriage. Then, humming softly to herself, she looped the quilt over her arm, grasped the picnic basket from the floorboards, and hurried toward the soft burbling noise of the creek.

After only a few yards, the trees opened to a thick shady knoll that sloped gently toward the banks of the creek. When Natalie saw the tall, slender gentleman who waited for her, she smiled, silently setting the quilt and basket on the grass. Then, taking slow, sultry steps forward, she murmured, "Darling."

The man turned, smiled. The dappled sunlight filtered across the blunt planes of his face.

"What took you so long?"

Natalie pouted. "I had to wait for Lettie to stop mooning in the attic and find us a quilt." She batted her lashes at him in coy invitation. "But I'm sure you'll find the afternoon well worth the wait." Her hand lifted to the pearl button at the neck of her garnet walking suit. "I brought champagne." The second button slipped free. "And cherries." The third and fourth gaped. "Not to mention a special surprise that I wore just for you."

By this time her bodice gaped open, revealing a new black silk corset trimmed in red moire and a delicate black lace camisole that seemed to have been spun by exotic spiders. Even from where she stood, Natalie noted the way his breathing became shallow and his eyes latched onto the skin and silk open to his gaze.

"But first," she murmured, stepping forward to loosen the man's tie, then reaching for the studs on his shirt, "you and I will relax, touch, love." She lifted herself on tiptoe to press a kiss against his lips. "Then we will eat." She kissed him again. "Then you and I will discuss my husband."

9

Ethan remained hidden in the garret. Though Lettie worked most of the day with her mother, she and Ethan still spent several hours together each evening. And soon, something happened between them. Something Lettie found hard to explain.

The first night, they spent most of their time together in silence. A dark brooding silence that seemed somehow more dangerous than any words could be.

Lettie sat on her bed with her books and her notepad, but she didn't write her poems. Instead, she watched the man who stood at the opposite end of the room. His thumb had slipped beneath the edge of the window shade, pulling it aside just enough for him to see into the darkness beyond.

After nearly an hour of watching him, Lettie put her books aside, wrapped her arms around her knees, and asked, "What do you see in the darkness, Ethan McGuire?"

He started as if she'd sneaked up behind him and touched him on his back. When he glanced at her over his shoulder, Lettie smiled and gestured to the window. "It's black as pitch out there, but you've been staring into the night for nearly an hour. What do you see?"

Ethan shrugged and turned away.

She took a deep breath and grimaced, wondering if she'd made a mistake by even talking to him in the first place.

But then, speaking so low she almost didn't hear it, Ethan murmured. "Stars."

Her brow creased for a moment, but she waited, until he finally continued. "My father had a telescope in his study. One of those big brass affairs. When I was small, he used to show me the constellations before sending me off to bed." He stopped, as if embarrassed.

The silence twined about them, and, wishing to put him at ease, Lettie spoke. "I don't remember much about my own pa. He died when I was little. I only remember a big pine coffin propped in the parlor, and how Mama put all of my pretty dresses away and made me wear black." She picked at a loose stitch in the quilt beneath her. "Then Jacob stopped playing with me." She smiled ruefully to herself. "He had a job putting up posters for Mr. Clark, who was marshal at the time. It used to make me so mad the way Jacob would come home all puffed out like a Christmas goose and hand Mama the few pennies he'd earned, then he'd look down his nose at me as if to say 'You're too much of a baby to even earn your own keep.' "

Ethan's lips twitched in a smile.

"Then the entire house suddenly seemed to be filled with boarders, and even though I was only five, I had my own set of chores to do." Her hands tightened around her knees and she hesitated before asking, "Do you have brothers and sisters, Ethan?"

His shoulders seemed to grow tense, but he finally nodded. "A half brother. And two half sisters."

"I bet they miss you," she whispered.

Ethan glanced at her over his shoulder. "I doubt it. They're probably glad I'm gone."

Once again, Lettie saw a flash of vulnerability in his eyes. "No," she murmured. "I'm sure they miss you. I'm sure they miss you a great deal. You should visit them."

At her words, Ethan straightened and gazed at her with a dark, inscrutable look.

"No, I can't go back."

"Soon, then."

"No."

He pushed away from the wall and moved to his pallet on the floor. Yet as he drew the sheet up to his chin and turned his back to Lettie, she wondered what he'd done to make him think he could never return to his family.

The silence cloaked them for long moments, and, thinking Ethan had drifted asleep, Lettie changed into her nightgown behind the edge of the wardrobe and dove beneath the covers of her bed. But as she reached to extinguish the lamp, she heard Ethan turn.

"I'm not the man the law is looking for," he murmured, his eyes cast in shadow.

Gazing at him over her shoulder, Lettie couldn't deny the stark sincerity etched in the strong lines of his face.

He took a deep breath. "But I have done things I'm not proud of. And I can't go back home—won't go back—until I can look my family in the eye as an honorable man."

He held her gaze for long, aching moments; then, as if embarrassed by how much he'd revealed, he muttered, "Turn off the light and let's get some sleep."

Once again he turned his back on her, but as she doused the wick and settled beneath the covers, Lettie found herself murmuring, "Sweet dreams, Ethan."

After that, Lettie learned that any mention of Ethan's family was sure to be followed by an uncomfortable silence. And nothing was more disturbing to them both than silence. With each hour they spent together, the quiet twined about them, making them realize just how alone they were in the garret.

The second night, the tension seemed to gather in the air around them as soon as Lettie entered the room. She felt Ethan's eyes upon her, and she knew he was thinking of the kisses they had shared. And the secrets.

Feeling suddenly self-conscious, she climbed the steps, then paused, clasping her hands together. Ethan had relaxed his guard somewhat. He sat on the floor with his back propped against a trunk, gazing at her with half-veiled eyes. His shirt had been unbuttoned to his waist, and beads of sweat dappled his skin.

"It's hot in here, isn't it?" Lettie murmured.

Ethan gazed at her long and hard for a moment before responding. "Um-hmm."

"I thought about doing some needlepoint tonight, but the thought of any extra cloth against my skin makes me . . ." She suddenly broke off, her eyes latching onto the dark patches of moisture beneath Ethan's arms and down his chest. The fabric of his shirt seemed to cling even more lovingly in those spots.

She took a deep breath and hurried to the wardrobe. "I suppose I'll just read."

She gathered her notepad and Natalie Gruber's book of poems and settled into the rocker. But after a moment, the silence between them became almost unbearable. "W-would you like me to read to you?" she asked, glancing up to find that Ethan was still watching her intently.

He nodded, and she began to read aloud. But soon Lettie discovered that a good portion of the poets had written about love, or longing, or desire.

Soon the garret seemed to swelter. Ethan's eyes became even more intense. And for Lettie, each moment became an exquisite torture.

The third night, the tension between them built to a fever pitch. Lettie became aware that Ethan went out of his way to avoid any chance brush of the arm or touch of the hand. To her surprise, he led Lettie into intricate arguments about philosophy and politics, unconsciously revealing to Lettie that he had come from a privileged background.

That night, Lettie's heart nearly pounded from her breast in excitement when she discovered Ethan had an extensive knowledge of literature: Milton, Thoreau, Shakespeare, and Pope. The volume of poetry Natalie Gruber had loaned her passed from hand to hand, and Ethan seemed to enjoy it when Lettie read aloud to him.

Though when she finally convinced Ethan to read a few poems to her, she could have melted on the spot from the deep melodic quality of his voice. Each word Ethan uttered fell like rain on her sun-parched soul.

Until Lettie had mentioned a poem by Whitman.

When she'd suggested reading a few pieces by a poet unfamiliar to her—Walt Whitman—their discussions had altered ever so slightly. Lettie still wasn't sure what had happened or who was responsible. She only knew that Ethan had refused to let her read Whitman. Then, within a few moments, he'd begun watching her with eyes that were dark and intense. By the end of the evening, she'd grown so aware of the man who sat across from her, it took all of her strength of will not to crawl across the bed and beg him to kiss her.

She'd never wanted anything as much as she wanted Ethan to kiss her again. And she hated herself for such wantonness. But the swirling awareness would not go away.

The following night, Lettie used her key to let herself into the garret and climbed the steps, her eyes automatically searching out the darkness until she found Ethan. As had become his custom, he stood with one palm propped against the window sill and lifted the edge of the window shade with his opposite hand.

Lettie waited in silence for a few moments, her eyes tracing the width of his shoulders and the broad expanse of his back beneath the sweat-dampened shirt he wore—one of Ned Abernathy's she'd taken from the ironing pile. There was a weary curve to his spine, as if it took most of the energy he possessed simply to remain standing.

Yet she couldn't control the slow hunger that began to rise within her.

Sweet heaven, had she abandoned every shred of decency she'd ever claimed to have?

"I brought you some cool water," Lettie murmured softly. When she'd come up to bring Ethan his lunch, the temperature in the attic had been sweltering. Though the heat had eased a little since then, Lettie knew Ethan would need the refreshment of the cold well water.

Ethan slowly turned. She couldn't see his eyes in the darkness, but she sensed their path as they traveled up the work-rumpled length of her skirts and bodice and lingered on the *vee* of flesh revealed by the buttons she'd left undone.

Becoming conscious of the way her hair hung thick and wavy around her face and clung to the dampness of her skin, Lettie lifted a hand to wipe the perspiration clinging to her brow, then dropped her head to swipe at the moisture beading her collarbone.

"Don't do that," Ethan ordered shortly.

She paused in midmotion. "Why not?"

He took a deep breath and shook his head, evidently sorry he'd made the comment at all. "I'm sorry, I just . . ."

Despite the distance between them, Lettie saw the way Ethan unconsciously swallowed. His chest swelled with another deep breath, and she felt the path his gaze made as it slipped from her face, to her neck, to her breasts. Gradually, she became aware of the way the angle of her hand pulled the worn fabric of her calico bodice taut across the contours of her body, outlining each curve that had been so intimately embraced by the restraint of her corset.

Very slowly, she lowered her arm—and because Ethan had been so free with his glances, Lettie allowed herself the same pleasure. Her eyes dipped to trace hungrily the contours of his chest visible beneath his sweat-plastered shirt—a shirt unbuttoned nearly to his navel.

Since her mother didn't permit the male boarders any latitude in regards to their attire, Lettie had seen very few men so intimately exposed. But of those she had seen, none was so pleasing to look at as Ethan. The man had a chest that was more beautiful and well-formed than any of the illustrations she'd seen of half-naked Grecian statues in the Beasleys' art books. Alma and Amelia would have had a heyday discussing this man's physique.

"Don't do that, Lettie."

"What?"

"Don't look at me that way," he growled.

"Why? You look at *me* that way."

Ethan took a deep gulp of air and closed his eyes. The energy that filled him seemed to sizzle deep inside his frame and, without warning, he turned, slamming his fist against the wall.

Both of them froze at his spontaneous action, waiting, listening. But none of the other boarders seemed to stir.

"What's wrong?" Lettie queried softly a few moments later, noting the strain that seemed to be etched around his mouth and nose.

Her words seemed to touch a fuse. He spun to face her, gesturing wildly with his hand. "I've got to get out of here!" he exclaimed in a fierce whisper. "I can't stand being penned in like this. I feel like a stud bull."

Lettie gasped. "I never—"

"Damn, I'm sorry. I didn't mean to say that."

He desired her. For a flashing instant, she could see that fact within his expression as their eyes met and clung. They'd spent too much time in the close confines of her bedroom for them not to be aware of each other. Yet until that night, Lettie had never considered that the feelings—the anticipation, desire, and temptation—that swirled inside of her tormented Ethan as well.

And suddenly, the shimmering tension hanging between them became more than Lettie could handle. She simply didn't have the experience necessary to control a man like Ethan McGuire.

Deciding to ignore his remark altogether, Lettie set the pitcher of water on the floor. "It will be over soon. Jacob has begun to turn his attention to other matters. Then it will be safe for you to leave."

Silence pounded between them.

And though Lettie knew Ethan couldn't stay in the garret indefinitely, she didn't want him to go. Not yet.

Seeking to drive her thoughts to a safer course, Lettie turned her back on Ethan. But she could feel his eyes boring into her as she crossed to the wardrobe. Feeling self-conscious, she untied her apron and slipped the pinafore straps over her head, hanging the garment on the hook inside the door. Although she'd only removed her apron, she couldn't deny the chills coursing through her body when she sensed the way Ethan watched her as if she had removed every stitch of clothing that covered her.

Jerking the lower drawer open, Lettie grasped her notebook. Perhaps if she sat in the rocking chair and worked on her poems, she would find a way to ignore the awareness crackling between them.

"If you'd rather not talk tonight, that's all right. I'll just sit here where I won't bother you."

"Bother me!" He strode across the room, grasping her arms and whirling her to face him. "You really *are* naive, aren't you?"

At the touch of his hands on her arms, the crackling tension came rushing back.

"For the past few days you've paraded through this room as if I were a eunuch. Well, I'm not."

She yanked away, putting the chair between them. Both of them were breathing hard—breathing air that hung hot and sticky and charged with words that were better left unspoken.

"I treat you as if you were a . . . what?"

Ethan groaned in frustration. "Haven't you even been listening to a word I've said?"

"I was listening." When he refused to continue, she found herself momentarily diverted. *Eunuch!* What a lovely, lovely word. Her hands rifled impatiently through the pages until she found the appropriate section. "Now tell me again. I parade in front of you as if you were a . . . what?"

Ethan gritted his teeth. "Eunuch."

"Eunuch," she repeated. "How do you spell that?"

He gazed at her in patent disbelief. "Why the hell do you want to know that?"

"Spell it, please."

"Hell, I don't know . . . e-u-nuch. Spell it any damn way you please."

121

She gave him a look of irritation but bent down to print her new word carefully in the notebook. "What does it mean?"

Ethan stared at her.

"Ethan, what does it mean?"

He shifted uncomfortably, his anger forgotten. "It's a . . . well—"

"You don't know."

"I *do* know."

"Then tell me."

Ethan hooked his thumbs into the back waist of his trousers. "It's a . . . well, a . . . man who can't . . ."

"Can't what?" She felt a tingling within her when she saw the way Ethan seemed to grow jittery and tense.

Turning away, Ethan strode toward the pitcher of cool water.

"Tell me."

Grabbing the pitcher, he spun around, retorting, "It's a guard in a harem."

"What's a harem?"

His mouth opened, then closed. Finally he muttered, "A stable of women used by a king in Persia."

Her eyes widened in astonishment, then in wicked delight. "Ohhh. How interesting." Smiling to herself, she sank into the rocker and quickly printed the word *harem* beside her latest entry.

"Lettie . . ." He moved toward her, the tone of his voice rife with warning.

"Do you mind if I ask you a few more definitions?" she asked quickly. Now that she'd begun to unravel the meanings of her words, she was loathe to put her book down, especially since her questioning seemed to push some of the tension away for a moment.

He took a deep, steadying breath. "Fine. What do you want to know?"

"*Nebbish.*"

"What the hell is a *nebbish?*"

She sighed in disappointment. "I was hoping you'd know." She flipped back a few pages. "We may as well begin at the beginning. What is the meaning of *dervish?*"

"It's some kind of a whirling priest or something."

Her brows lifted in interest.

"They spin around in circles until they go into a sort of trance."

"Ohh." She quickly scribbled a note beside the word. "How about *insatiate?*"

Ethan's eyes narrowed, wondering what she was up to, but she gazed at him in wide-eyed innocence. "Unable to be satisfied," he replied slowly.

She nodded. *"Consummate."*

Ethan took a moment to cross to the wash set on the bureau and splash some of the cool water into the bowl.

"To . . . make complete." He glanced in the mirror to see what she would make of that definition, still unsure whether or not she truly didn't know the meanings of the words she'd been asking. But her ignorance seemed genuine.

"Oh." This time her brow furrowed in disappointment. "The Beasleys seemed to talk about it as if—well, never mind."

"The Beasleys?"

"Two maiden ladies who have lived here for years."

"Maiden ladies?"

"Yes. Why?"

He dipped a hand into the cool water and swirled it around, hoping to ease the heat that generated from the inside. "What else do you want to know?"

When she didn't answer him immediately, he tensed.

"I want to know why you won't kiss me," she blurted, then rued her unruly tongue. *Drat it all! What in the world had made her say such a thing?*

The swirling motions of his hand came to a halt. His eyes lifted to snag with her own gaze in the mirror.

Groaning, he squeezed his eyes closed and dunked his head into the cool water. But the basin was shallow, and he only succeeded in sloshing half of its contents onto the bureau.

He didn't hear her moving behind him until it was too late. When her hand rested low on his back, he jerked upright, flinging water in all directions as he spun to face her.

"Dammit, Lettie, don't," he growled.

She looked at him, long and hard. "I'm sorry." For a moment, her hand poised in midair, then softly, hesitantly, she lay it against the curve of his ribs. "But you go out of your way to avoid me." Her thumb rubbed back and forth against his skin. "Why?"

His breath sucked into his chest in a harsh gulp when a bolt of sensation shot through his body. Her hand was so small, so delicate. She seemed to savor the contact between them, as if she were experiencing something special she'd never felt before.

"Ethan, couldn't you kiss me again? Just once?"

When he glanced up from her hand, he found her studying him with a steady gaze and he couldn't speak. The awareness in her eyes was clear to see. But so was her innocence.

And damned if that wasn't what had kept him from touching her for the last few nights. Ethan had wanted nothing more than to drag her onto the bed and love her until they both ached. But Lettie wasn't that kind of a girl . . . and Ethan liked to think he wasn't a total bastard.

"Lettie—" he rasped, pushing her away and striding past. He lifted his hands to rake his fingers through the dampness of his hair. "You don't know what you're asking," he stated firmly, turning to face her. "You don't know that when a man kisses a woman . . ."

She planted her hands on her hips. "For your information, Ethan McGuire, I probably know more about kissing than most people my age. I've lived too long in a boardinghouse to be ignorant of a few of the more basic facts of life."

"Lettie," he growled, deep in his throat, then strode toward her and jerked her into his arms. His mouth dipped to cover her own, tasting, plundering.

And Lettie soon discovered that she knew nothing about kissing. Nothing at all.

He pulled back, and his eyes grew hot and vibrant, a

blazing azure blue. His hand lifted toward her face . . . even as the rest of him seemed to take an emotional step back.

"Is that what you want?"

She opened her mouth to refuse, hesitated, then whispered, "Yes."

At her frank response he sighed. "Dammit, Lettie." His fingers slid across the edge of her jaw and lingered in the hollow beneath her ear. Lettie shivered in unconscious delight, her eyelids growing heavy at the sudden rush of anticipation that thundered through her body.

Ethan's hands slipped to the gentle swell of her hips, and he pulled her tightly against him.

To his amazement, she moaned low in her throat, nudging against his grip like an eager kitten, as if needing to feel the heat and strength of his body.

"Why do you have to feel so good in my arms, Lettie?" he muttered, more to himself than to her. Despite their proximity, he dragged her even closer.

Lettie could feel the heat of his body flowing into her own. She could sense the sweat-dappled texture of the hair upon his chest, the musky scent of his skin. Her hands flattened against his chest, delighting in the firm muscles beneath her palms and the tickle of chest hair between her fingers.

When he bent his knees to nudge his hips against her own, a gasp tore from Lettie's throat.

"Ethan?" she whispered.

His lips tilted ever so slightly in a self-deprecating smile, as if he'd flirted with temptation, then willingly succumbed. His head dipped, and his mouth captured anything more she might have said.

At the bold nudge of his lips, Lettie sighed in delight, slipping her hands from his chest to his shoulders and then around the back of his head, molding herself as tightly as she could to Ethan's form.

His own hands drew her against him, lifting her onto her toes and holding her weight against him so that they were pressed chest to chest, hip to hip.

Boldly, insistently, Ethan's lips nudged at her own,

until finally, her mouth opened and his caress became more demanding, and more passionate.

Swirling in a sea of intoxicating sensations, Lettie clung tightly to his shoulders, reveling in the pressure of his arms, the persuasion of his lips. But Ethan was not one to take all of the initiative himself. Lifting his head, he murmured, "Now you try it."

"What?"

"Taste me, Lettie."

Her pulse began to throb, low and sweet, seeming to center deep within her stomach.

"No, I can't."

"Taste me, Lettie."

Needing no further bidding, Lettie hesitantly drew him close. When their lips pressed together, she paused, eyes half closed, wondering if she dared to be so bold. But the teasing of Ethan's tongue against the curve of her lip seemed to bid her to follow suit.

Her lashes drifted shut and Lettie surrendered to temptation herself. Softly, tentatively, she flicked her tongue against the curve of Ethan's lip.

"I like this," she murmured against his mouth. Then she tangled her hands in his damp hair and kissed him with all the fervor and passion of her youth.

After several long moments, Ethan groaned and broke away, whispering, "This is dangerous, Lettie girl." He pulled back and gazed at her with eyes that were hotter than a summer sun and filled with a tinge of regret, as if he hated to act as the voice of caution. "You don't know where all this is leading."

"No!" She framed his face in her hands. "They're just kisses, Ethan."

"I'm wrong for you, Lettie."

"You aren't wrong for me, Ethan. Something that feels this good couldn't be wrong."

"But it can't last."

"It can!"

"One day soon, I'll walk out of Madison and never come back. I won't be taking you with me."

She grew still in his arms.

Ethan sighed and pulled away, crossing to the opposite side of the room. Lettie wrapped her arms around her waist, feeling suddenly bereft.

"Ethan?"

"I don't want kisses, Lettie." His voice was tight and a little rough around the edges.

"But you—"

"Dammit, Lettie, I *want* you," Ethan finally rasped. "I want to *make love* to you. Now. I want to drag you onto the floor, and in the mood I'm in, I wouldn't be gentle."

Lettie felt the air whoosh from her lungs. Her heart slammed against the wall of her chest.

Suddenly she knew just why Ethan had avoided touching her for days. In his eyes, she saw the hunger of a man for a woman. She saw the raw heat of desire. The unbridled light of passion.

The sultry air grew thick and heavy between them, rife with their own unspoken thoughts and fantasies. Awareness became a living thing that twined between them with wicked glee.

"I *want* you, Lettie," he whispered again, the velvet-and-smoke texture of his voice brushing against her.

For a fleeting moment, Lettie saw a flash of vulnerability in his expression. And loneliness. Dear heaven, this man was as lonely as she. He needed her touch, her gentleness, just as surely as she needed his strength, his humor.

His love.

But they were two people who should never have met. She could never allow herself to grow attached to Ethan McGuire. Just as he could never allow himself to care for her. Because feelings like that would destroy them both.

"Are you willing to take me as I am, Lettie? Are you willing to make love to a man who will never offer you commitment or promises, who will only use your body as he'd use any other convenience?"

"Don't be crude."

"I'm being honest. Now it's your turn." He held out

a hand, palm up. "Are you willing to make love to a man like that? Now?"

Silence pounded between them, thick with regrets.

But Lettie couldn't speak. Try as she might, though the silken whispers of temptation weaved through her head, she couldn't take a step forward to take his hand.

"I'm going to check some things in the center of town after dark tomorrow," Ethan finally muttered, turning away. "I may not come back."

Lettie fought to keep from reaching out a hand to touch him and draw him back into her arms. Because she knew that to do so would mean admitting to herself that she just might accept this man and what dregs of affection he could offer her. Under any conditions.

10

Lettie held the hem of her apron in front of her so that it formed a scoop of fabric large enough to hold several large handfuls of chicken feed, then unlatched the gate to their enclosure and stepped inside. Immediately, a flurry of hens scattered about the pen, squawking and flapping their wings while the rooster grumbled to himself and paraded from one end to the other in a preening manner.

Murmuring softly to the skittish fowl, Lettie took a handful of dried corn and scattered it on the ground, chuckling to herself when the chickens stampeded toward the yellow nuggets, abandoning their reticence.

Once she'd littered the chicken feed throughout the enclosure, Lettie threaded her way through the pen to the coop. Taking a wire egg basket from a peg on the inside door, she spent several minutes gathering eggs and carefully setting them one on top of the other in the basket. Finally, after she was sure she'd found all of the eggs, including those carefully hidden below the straw, she slipped out of the pen and fastened the gate behind her.

"Morning, Lettie."

Lettie whirled, then smiled when she found Ned Abernathy standing behind her.

"Good morning, Ned. Are you and Mr. Goldsmith drumming again today?" she asked, noting the way Ned had carefully dressed in a brown suit, starched shirt, and dark bowler.

Ned nodded, quickly reaching up to yank his hat from his head. "Yes, ma'am."

"Where are you going?"

"Petesville."

"You're taking the train?"

"Yes."

"I suppose it must be exciting, traveling all over the countryside, visiting with storekeepers and processing orders."

He grimaced. "There are other things I'd rather do."

Her brow creased. "Then why are you apprenticing with Mr. Goldsmith?"

He opened his mouth, hesitated a moment, then stated slowly, "I have some debts to pay. Some debts that are long overdue." Suddenly he looked at her, and she was shocked by the intensity of his gaze, but then he smiled and his features lightened. He finally said, "I haven't seen you as much as I usually do."

She fidgeted slightly, bending to pay a great deal of attention to her eggs. "I've been a little busy."

"I see."

"Lettie!" Lettie started at her mother's call from the back porch. "Lettie, I need you this instant!"

Lettie flashed Ned an apologetic smile. "I'm sorry. I'd better go."

Ned's eyes seemed to flash with impatience for a moment, then he nodded. "I understand. I only wanted to tell you . . . how pretty you look today."

Lettie smiled ruefully at the compliment. She'd worn one of her best navy calico skirts and bodices—an unconscious bid for Ethan's admiring glance—but it seemed she'd attracted Ned's attention instead.

"Thank you."

"Lettie!"

"Coming, Mama!" She once again flashed Ned a regretful smile, then hurried toward the house, where her mother stood on the back porch, her arms crossed, her lips tight with disapproval.

"Lettie, how many times have I told you not to become familiar with the boarders?"

"But I—"

"Ned Abernathy is a pleasant man, but he is without funds and without station. I will not condone your becoming involved with a man like that."

"But Mama, he only wanted to talk for a minute."

"I've seen the way he looks at you, Lettie. Ned has a bad case of cow-eyes every time you walk into the room, and I won't have you encouraging him. Now come into the house and wash those eggs. We've got butter to make and milk to strain, and it's already nine o'clock."

"Yes, Mama," Lettie answered, a little more subdued. As the screen door slammed behind her mother, she sighed. Between her mother's worries that Lettie would marry a man with no money—or, worse yet, a boarder—and Jacob's fears that she'd marry a man who wasn't purer than God, she supposed she was lucky they didn't just hang a sign around her neck that said "No males allowed within a fifty-yard vicinity." She could only imagine what her guardian protectors would say if they knew she had a wanted man hidden in her bedroom.

Sighing again, Lettie bent to lift her skirts into her hands so that she could climb the steps into the house and wash the eggs. She was about to straighten, when her movements were arrested by a flutter of white caught beneath the lattice work surrounding the porch.

Thinking it must be a handkerchief or napkin blown free from the line during the dust storm, Lettie set the basket of eggs on the top step and marched around the porch to the side of the house where the lattice had been pulled free by the wind.

Knowing her mother would chide her for carelessly allowing the laundry to be left outside in a storm, she shimmied under the porch, awkwardly crawling on her hands and knees toward the bright patch in the shadows. When she reached out to grasp it, she groaned to herself when she discovered it was not a handkerchief, but a scrap of half-singed paper.

Still muttering, Lettie backed out from under the porch and dusted her skirts off. Knowing her mother would be irritated by her less-than-tidy appearance, Lettie cursed herself even more for having wriggled under the porch for a single piece of paper. Her thumb ran over the burnt edge and she idly unfolded the crumpled sheet. What she found made her pause for a moment, a slow chill beginning to seep through her veins. Despite the burned portions of the page, there was no disguising the eight-sided star that had once been drawn in the center. Though the flame had eaten a portion of the star, the initials *S* and *C* were clearly visible, as was a part of a *J*.

The Star Council of Justice.

Lettie felt her fingers begin to tremble and she crushed the paper into a ball, shoving it into her apron pocket. She whirled to face the wide expanse of land behind her, and, despite the early morning heat, she shivered.

The Star Council was a fierce, determined lot, and their modes of justice were fatal.

The chill within Lettie seemed to settle deep in her bones. It was her fault that Ethan had stayed as long as he had. She'd been the one to make him feel safe in her room. She'd wanted him to stay, just a little longer. He'd filled her days with such adventure and awareness—things she'd never felt before—that she hadn't wanted him to leave a moment sooner than he had to.

Now she'd waited too long.

Her hand plunged into the pocket of her apron and clenched around the half-burned note. She must see to it that Ethan left Madison. Tonight. He'd have to catch a train out of the state and never return.

Otherwise, if he were captured and killed, his blood would be on her hands.

Perhaps it was only Lettie's imagination, but from that moment on, everything seemed to go wrong. Her mother came down with a migraine and had to remain in bed until the doctor arrived. When Dr. Matz ordered Celeste to remain in her room for the next few hours and prescribed another vial of sleeping powder, Lettie naturally assumed her duties, even as she chafed under the restrictions.

Within hours, the boardinghouse seemed to close in upon her like a jail cell, while the boarders became children who needed to be endlessly entertained and kept out of trouble. Despite her care to keep things organized and tidy, the Grubers had a bitter argument, supper burned in the oven, and Mr. Goldsmith spilled ink in the parlor. Because of all that happened, Lettie had no time to join Ethan, no time to even take him some fresh water or a sandwich to tide him over until dark.

As the day wore on, Lettie began to peer at each boarder, each visitor, each neighbor, wondering who was watching her on behalf of the Council. And Lettie had no doubts that someone *was* watching, since rumor had it that the Council was based somewhere within a thirty-mile radius of Madison. The Council must surely suspect Ethan was in the vicinity of the boardinghouse, otherwise why would a note be found so close?

As Lettie scrubbed the last of the supper dishes, she was struck by another chilling thought: What if they suspected her own involvement as well? The Star wouldn't believe her innocence, nor her innate trust in Ethan's goodness. Just for harboring the man, she could be punished. She could be found dead in an alley with a star pinned to her chest like all the other Council victims.

Her hands trembled as she swiped the beads of water from the last pan and hung it on a metal rack beside the stove. She'd never admired the Star—not like some people in town. The whole idea of their organization had always seemed a little frightening.

Now she was beginning to believe that the men involved were savage bounty hunters who killed without first proving the guilt of those they executed.

Lettie stood for long moments gazing out of the kitchen window, staring at the whipping of the grass beneath the gusts of the hot June wind. Though she hated to see the moment when Ethan would really go, she knew he would have to leave Madison within the next few hours.

Her arms wound about her torso and she hugged her chest, fearing the inevitable. She probably wouldn't see him again. Not for a very long time. Not for the rest of her life.

Squaring her shoulders, she took a deep breath and turned to march up the back steps. There were a few things she needed to gather. Then Ethan would have to be told.

Just as he had a hundred times before, Ethan crossed to the garret window and reached out to lift the edge of the shade enough for him to peer outside. Although evening had come, the temperature of the bedroom was sultry, sapping his strength and his ability to think.

His hands closed into slow fists and he shook his head. As if he could think clearly. For nights, Ethan had endured the soft murmur of Lettie's voice, the heat of her glances. In the dim lamplight, he'd watched the way the fiery highlights of her hair seemed to shimmer and dance. Removed of their restricting plait, the long, silky tresses had waved about her shoulders and down her back in braid-crimped strands, reaching beyond her hips to puddle on the bed beside her. Every time he looked at her a tingling excitement seemed to ripple within him like spring water. More than once, Ethan had found himself wondering what her hair would feel like sliding against his skin, or what her hands would feel like clutching his shoulders.

But Lettie was not a girl to be dallied with.

Not without hurting her spirit. Not without destroying her trusting nature.

And although it was ironic, Ethan found himself putting those simple homespun values high above his own pleasure. Because he didn't deserve her.

Taking a deep breath of the hot, muggy air, Ethan consciously opened his fist, forcing himself to relax. He needed to leave. He'd already lingered far too long in the garret.

And yet . . .

Ethan closed his eyes, but the action only seemed to provide him with a clearer image of Lettie. For the past two nights, she'd gone to bed in a nightgown more severe and modest than his ancient Aunt Minnie's. She'd forced Ethan to turn around while she'd climbed beneath the covers, the whole time unaware that he'd watched her progress in the mirror above her bureau. Despite the havoc to his own system, he'd noted the way the worn fabric of her nightdress draped against the curves of her breasts and tangled between her legs as she moved.

Ethan's hand tightened into a fist. She was so inexperienced—too inexperienced, dammit! She didn't even know the extent of her power over him. She didn't realize that, because of her, he'd begun to hesitate in his course of action. He'd begun to . . . feel.

Groaning low in his throat at his inability to control his self-destructive tendencies, Ethan strode across the room toward the newspaper articles and daily reports he'd strewn across the bureau. Each day, Ethan had slipped out of the room long enough to steal the boarders' newspapers and periodicals to apprise himself of the latest efforts to capture the thief. As the true Gentleman Bandit, Ethan had thought he would be able to find some clue, some tiny piece of information that would help him unravel the riddle of who was responsible.

So far, none of his information had managed to help.

So far, all he'd discovered was the heat of the garret and the restlessness of his own soul.

Unconsciously, Ethan found himself turning to stare at the garret door and wondering when Lettie would return. Damned if he knew why he found the little minx so fascinating. Perhaps it was her passion for life. Perhaps it was her wholesome, fresh-scrubbed features, or the sensuality that lingered deep in her nut-brown eyes.

Or maybe it was simply that, for the first time in nearly ten years, someone trusted him explicitly, without need of excuses or explanations.

Lettie took a deep breath and stepped through her bedroom door. Keeping her expression firm and void of all emotion, she climbed the steps and waited for Ethan to turn and look at her before saying, "You've got to go away. Now."

Ethan's eyes narrowed and he straightened from where he'd been peering out the side of the window. "Why?"

"I can't hide you anymore. I'm tired of lying to my family."

He advanced toward her, clearly not believing her reasons. "What happened?"

"Nothing."

"Lettie!"

"Just go! Get out of here. I don't want you around anymore."

He took another step.

"I don't want to see you in my room every night. I don't want to hear you sleeping just a few feet away. I don't want to be worrying that you'll be idiot enough to climb out on the roof"—her voice faltered—"o-or that you'll be hurt, even killed. I won't be responsible for that. I won't!"

When her last cry emerged more like a sob, Ethan hesitated only a moment before drawing her into his arms. He wrapped his arms tightly around her, rocking her, comforting her. He'd never had anyone care for him this much before. Not in a long, long time.

Drawing back, he slipped a finger under her chin, forcing her to look at him. He noted the misery in her eyes, the tear-streaked features, and something cracked within him, melted.

"Aw, Lettie," he whispered, more to himself than to her. His palms framed her face and he brushed his lips against her own, savoring their sweetness.

She sighed against him, nudging closer, and suddenly, what had begun as a simple expression of concern became a hungry embrace. Her arms slipped around his waist to hold him tightly, even as his own hands dipped and lifted her against him.

Damn, how he was beginning to want this woman. Need her. Her kindness was an addiction to him. Her spontaneity a delight. And when she kissed him, he felt reality spinning away, so that he almost believed in a future.

Pulling her tightly against him, he reveled in her embrace. When she moved closer still, he braced his feet apart, making room for her legs between his own. He gasped when her arms slipped up the contours of his back, her fingers seeming to search for something. There was a hungry desperation to her touch—almost as if she never thought she would see him again.

That thought finally pierced the sensual fog surrounding Ethan's brain, and he grasped her wrists and tore free.

Their gazes met and clung.

"What happened?" Ethan said after a long moment of silence.

She shook her head and tried to draw away, but Ethan pulled her tightly against his hips. Vaguely, he heard a crackle of paper, and when she froze in his arms, he wondered what could have caused such an immediate reaction. Slowly, he drew back and slid his hand into the deep pockets of her apron.

"No!"

He grasped the paper and twisted away from her, striding to the opposite side of the room. Quickly, he flattened the paper.

Despite the singed portion of the note, the eight-sided

star glared up at him with stark finality. Once again, Ethan didn't need to be told what it meant.

"Where did you find this?" He turned to find her gazing at him with eyes that were huge and nut-brown in the dim light of the loft.

"Under the back porch, jammed into the latticework. The wind must have blown it there within the last few days."

Ethan's chest swelled as he dragged a deep measure of air into his lungs in an attempt to push his own fear at bay. Despite his efforts, he felt his stomach grow heavy and tense, as if a cold weight had been dropped inside.

Once more he glanced down at the letter. A deputy had been injured during the last robbery.

A deputy who wore an eight-pointed star.

"You realize what this is, don't you?" he murmured, partly to himself. With the wounding of a deputy, the Council would be out for blood.

He glanced up to find Lettie staring at him with anguished eyes. "Yes," she whispered.

His expression grew bitter, his voice low. "This is my death warrant." His words seemed to echo in the room, the calm tone giving his statement more credence than if he had ranted and raved.

Lettie regarded him with blatant pain. "I'm so sorry. So sorry."

His shoulders drew back, and he took another deep breath. "If you don't mind, I'll wait and leave tonight when it's dark."

Though she ached to see him go, she nodded. "I'll see to it that you have some food and supplies. After sundown, I'll take you to a whistle stop north of town. You can get a train to Chicago that way."

He nodded, then stepped toward her, his hand lifting and cupping her cheek. She nudged against the simple gesture, and his thumb lifted to brush across her lips. "I'll miss you, Lettie Gray," he whispered. "You've been very kind. More than you had to be."

"I haven't been kind." Her arms lifted to rest against

his chest. Her fingers splayed wide, her thumbs brushed idly against the sensitive skin bared by the placket of his shirt. "I care for you, Ethan."

"Don't say that." He drew her hands away from his chest. "I'm leaving, Lettie, and I won't come back. Don't bind yourself to me. Don't say things best left unsaid. Don't wish for things that could never be." A bitter sound tore from his throat. "You know nothing about me, Lettie. I've spent a third of my life on the run, and now I'll spend the rest of it looking over my shoulder."

"I don't care about that."

He moved away from her, his eyes blazing. "You *should* care. Dammit, you should care a lot! I'm wrong for you, Lettie. I'm the kind of man you should never admit to knowing. I'm the kind of man who ruins little girls like you, then leaves them to pick up the pieces. I'm the kind—"

"Stop it!"

"What's the matter, Lettie? Can't you bear to hear the truth? I'm dishonest. I'm ruthless."

"Stop!" She strode toward him, her own eyes blazing. "You aren't any of those things. You may have made mistakes in the past, but the man I've seen in this garret is tender and gentle."

He grasped her wrist, yanking her toward him. His features grew fierce in the dim light of the garret. His other hand clasped around her neck and he bent to kiss her with all the hunger and desperation that burned within him. But, to his surprise, she didn't shrink away. Instead, she returned his kiss, measure for measure.

Drawing on what little control he had left, Ethan wrenched free and framed her face in his hands, forcing her to look at him. "Dammit, Lettie. Don't paint pretty pictures around me. I'm not one of your poems that can be neatly pieced together. I'm flesh and blood." His hands wrapped around her back, pulling her tightly against the cradle of his hips. "I take what I want and I give no quarter."

"You didn't take me."

Her murmured words hung in the air, shivering, quiet. Neither of them moved. Neither dared breathe.

Then Ethan's chest lifted in a shuddering sigh. "Dammit, Lettie. Don't do this. Just let me go."

Her hands lifted, forcing him to look at her. "I care for you, Ethan McGuire." When he tried to interrupt, she broke in: "No, I do, and whether or not you hear the words, the feelings inside of me aren't going to disappear." Her hands pushed the hair away from his brow. The dark strands spilled like rain through her fingers, soft and smooth.

After long minutes of silence, Ethan looked up. Lettie's heart ached at the expressions mirrored in his eyes: pride, determination.

And loneliness. Always the loneliness.

Perhaps Lettie was starved for some sort of companionship. Perhaps, as her mother was wont to say, she couldn't resist siding with an underdog or nurturing strays, but suddenly she couldn't let Ethan leave like this. Not alone.

She grasped his wrist, her grip almost desperate. "Let me come with you, at least part of the way. I know all of the back roads."

"No."

"But I could help you!"

He tensed. "No, Lettie," he repeated more firmly.

"Why not?"

His shoulders drew back in a proud line. "Because you're wholesome and good."

"You make me sound like a loaf of bread," she retorted in disgust.

"Dammit, Lettie, I'm a wanted man!"

"And I already know that fact." Her gaze grew earnest. "Please. Let me come with you."

After a moment's hesitation, he drew away. Lettie knew by the stiffness that eased into his shoulders what Ethan's answer would be. He thought she was painting rainbows again, believing things that were more fantasy than truth.

"No."

Her hands dropped to her sides. A heavy mantle of sadness cloaked her so that she could barely breathe.

"I'll miss you, Lettie Gray." And she knew his admission cost him a great deal.

Her throat grew tight. "I'll miss you, too, Ethan McGuire."

The boardinghouse lay dark and sleeping, heavy with the night, as Lettie and Ethan crept down the back stairs. Lettie glanced back at him and her eyes stroked Ethan's form with regret. He'd changed from his chambray shirt to one of Mr. Goldsmith's dark workshirts, and the fabric billowed around him in ghostly excess, giving him the appearance of some pirate or—

Or the Highwayman.

She felt a twinge of nostalgia at the idea and resisted the urge to drink in his appearance like a person condemned to a lifetime without fresh spring water.

Once at the kitchen door, she touched his arm.

"You remember the directions I gave you?"

He nodded. "Follow the creek north until I reach the fourth bend, then head due west until I reach the tracks. Move northeast along the tracks for about five miles to the first whistle stop."

She nodded. "Make sure you raise the red flag. Two passenger trains will pass through before dawn. If you don't arrive in time for one of those, wait until tomorrow morning, otherwise you'll be boarding a train that stopped in Madison, and someone may recognize your description."

He nodded, slipping his revolver into the holster of the gun belt that was once again strapped to his hips.

"You have the food I gave you?"

"Yes."

"And the water?"

"Yes."

Her hand lingered just above his elbow, absorbing the warmth of his skin, the firm muscles of his arm.

"You'll be careful?"

He nodded, his eyes gleaming in the darkness. Though they still held a hard cast, there was a certain tenderness in their depths that made their goodbyes seem that much more difficult.

He seemed to hesitate, battling with some inner demon before he said, "And you, Lettie? Will you be careful?"

Her head cocked. "Of what?"

His hand reached out to cup her cheek. "Of helping strange men and hiding them in your bedroom."

She tried to smile—she really did—but the task was near to impossible with the way her heart seemed to lie within her chest like a crushed piece of china, brittle and aching.

"You'd better go."

His thumb rubbed against her cheek. "I won't forget you, Lettie girl."

Her smile grew sad. "You will. You'll go back to your home and discover yourself littered with beautiful women with jet-black hair and glittering black eyes. And you'll forget me. Plain little Lettie."

He shook his head. "You're wrong—I won't forget you." For once, she saw the enigmatic mask crack, and his expression grew gentle. "And you're not plain. When you smile, no other woman could hold a candle to you."

His large hand reached out to stroke her hair. The soft strands caught against his calloused palms with a delicious friction. "You're the prettiest woman I know, Lettie. You have hair the color of rich earth, eyes the color of a new fawn's . . ." He paused, reaching to lay his palm over her chest just below her left collarbone. "And you're pretty inside, where it counts. You have a heart bigger than life itself, but, more importantly, you're not afraid to show it."

He leaned close, brushing his lips against her own.

"Goodbye, Lettie," he murmured against her mouth.

"Bye."

He hesitated, then drew her close, wrapping his arms around her waist and burying his head into the hollow of her shoulder.

Lettie embraced him as tightly as she could, trying to imprint the last possible ounce of sensation into her head forever so that she would never forget this moment, never forget the brush of his beard-roughened jaw against her neck, never forget the strength of his arms, the scent of his skin.

Slowly, ever so slowly, he set her back on her feet. He tipped her chin with a crooked finger and pressed a single kiss against her lips, a kiss so gentle and exquisite that Lettie thought she might shatter into a thousand pieces when he drew away.

"Goodbye, Lettie."

She couldn't trust herself to answer, so she nodded instead.

Ethan reached to open the door, and a taunting breeze teased at her skirts. Slowly drawing away from her, he slipped outside with the decisiveness of a man who knew just what he had to do and shut the door behind him.

Lettie stepped forward, pressing her hands against the glass. Numbly, she watched as Ethan crept down the back porch, heading in the direction of the creek. Within moments, he had melted into the darkness.

A heaving sigh shuddered through her body, and with it came the pain she had tried to push away. She'd only known him a little while, yet he had filled her days and nights with wild imaginings, chasing away the tedium and allowing herself to believe she could be anything she wanted to be: a great poet, a *grande dame* of literature . . .

A woman loved.

But as the house echoed dully about her, Lettie realized that her dreams were as far removed from reality as her dreams of the Highwayman. She was locked into her present pattern of work and duty as surely as if she were a part of the property. Her mother could not run the boardinghouse alone, and it was up to Lettie to help her. And Lettie had lived too long with the word *responsibility* hanging over her head to treat her duties lightly now.

Yet it was Ethan who had recognized that fact and forced her to stay.

Pressing more tightly against the window, Lettie tried to shield the glass from the faint light of the lamp in the hall, hoping she could catch one glimpse—just one more peek—of the man she'd once mistaken for her Highwayman.

But, like his namesake, he'd vanished into the darkness taking everything but her memories . . . and leaving no trace that he had ever really been there at all.

Ethan moved as noiselessly as he could through the darkness. Not long after he'd slipped away from the house, his heart began to pound so hard in his chest he could scarcely breathe. He'd felt this way before. Years before, after he'd become embroiled in crime in order to survive, he'd learned to love the exhilaration of the chase, the match of wits. Yet now, there was a difference. Now his stomach churned and his breathing rasped in his throat. Despite all he'd done—and the hell he deserved for doing it—Ethan didn't want to die.

Without warning, the thunder of hooves split the heavy night air and Ethan dove to his stomach, trying to find cover in the brush. Distantly he heard voices.

". . . meet up with the posse riding out of Harrisburg. We'll need every man available, but leave Rusty and a few men on duty in case the thief doubles back toward Madison."

Ethan grew still; his hands curled into the dust. Another set of hooves pounded on the ground, coming within yards of where he lay, then rumbling by. The unknown horseman drew to a halt, and Ethan chanced a quick look, lifting his head so that he could see through the brush.

"What's all the ruckus, Jacob?"

For the first time Ethan noted the man in the center who firmly held the reins of his gelding as it skittishly danced from side to side.

"Another robbery. This time on a gold shipment bound for Harrisburg. The railroad has telegraphed for men to join a posse. Someone head into town and ring the bell . . ."

The words faded in the fitful breeze, then were drowned

144

completely by the sound of galloping hooves, as part of the posse rode north toward Harrisburg and another part rode toward town for more men.

Ethan's heart nearly burst from his chest and his breathing became strident in the sudden silence of the night. Every able-bodied male within a twenty-mile radius would be on the lookout for anyone they considered suspicious. And nothing would arouse more suspicion than a lone man on foot heading north along the creek line, where his only possible destination could be the next whistle stop between Madison and Harrisburg.

Grimacing to himself, Ethan slapped the ground with an outstretched hand. Damn, damn, damn! He'd be lucky if he could even manage to return to the boardinghouse.

11

Lettie heard the men on horseback long before they ever appeared at the house. Her hands curled into tight fists and her breathing became labored. They'd caught him!

Dodging to the front porch, she flung open the door, ready to lash out at Jacob and his men for their injustices, but she hesitated when she found that the men rode toward the boardinghouse without the cumbersome addition of a prisoner.

When her brother guided his mount toward the front stoop, she took a hesitant step forward, trying to keep her features calm. She didn't know how the posse had been informed of Ethan's escape, but she wasn't about to give anything away to them if they hadn't found him yet.

"What's happened?" she finally shouted, having to raise her voice to be heard above the din of the horses. As soon as the words had escaped from her mouth, the clamor of the warning bell could be heard in town.

Jacob edged his horse toward the portico. "Another robbery. This time on a freight train five miles out of town."

A cold fist seemed to tighten around Lettie's stomach. "And another man was hurt?" she asked, almost fearfully.

"Yeah. Jeb Clark. He was working as a guard on one of the gold shipments." A fierce expression crossed his face. "He died, Lettie."

Lettie gasped, feeling the color drain from her face. The Clarks lived just a few blocks away from the boardinghouse. Many years earlier, before he'd taken a job with the railroad security forces, Jeb Clark had been a marshal in Madison. It was Jeb who had introduced Jacob to the life of a lawman.

"This time we're going to hang the bastard!" someone shouted from the back of the group.

Jacob turned to pin Lettie with a powerful stare that was rife with his own turbulent emotions, but when he spoke, his words were directed toward her safety. "Get into the house and bolt the doors and windows. I don't want you or any of the other boarders outside until this is—"

"But the Grubers and Beasleys are in town, and Mr. Goldsmith and Ned haven't come home."

"Get in the house, Lettie! The other boarders can take care of themselves." When she hesitated, he shouted, "Now!"

Whirling on her toes, Lettie ran into the house and slammed the door behind her, breathing heavily, her mind whirling. *Ethan!* She had to find him and bring him back to the boardinghouse. It was the only way to ensure his safety. If he stayed out in the dark in this manhunt, he'd be shot down like a dog in the street.

Pushing herself away from the door, Lettie ran up the stairs, quickly gathering a pillowslip and a few articles of clothing from the Beasleys' rooms and ignoring the little voice within her that scolded her for entering without permission.

Darting back down the steps, she grasped a dark cloak from the closet under the stairs and raced through the kitchen.

The clamor of the bell in town had aroused many of the farmers from the outlying areas, and Lettie could hear the men's curses in the darkness and the muffled stamp of their horses. Praying she could slip by them unnoticed, Lettie darted down the porch steps and ran into the night.

She didn't know how she would find Ethan—she wasn't sure she *could* find him. With all the noise, he wasn't likely to approach anyone, especially someone who was stumbling through the bushes along the creek.

Despite all of the rational reasons why she should remain at the house, Lettie ran through the grass and dodged toward the tree line that marked the path of the creek. Judging by the amount of time that had passed, Ethan couldn't have gone much more than a few hundred yards north—unless he'd veered away from the creek. If he'd headed away from the directions she'd outlined, Lettie would never find him.

Lettie firmly thrust her fears aside. She wouldn't think of that right now. She had to pray that Ethan was safe and that she could find him before the men from town began riding in his direction. Judging from the noise being made, another posse was being formed and the men would begin sweeping the area around the rail lines, working their way toward the men who would join them from Harrisburg.

There wasn't much time. There wasn't much time.

Lettie's heart pounded so hard in her throat she could barely hear, but slowly, steadily, she moved through the brush, following the directions she had given Ethan. Once or twice she paused, cocking her head to listen to the night. Although the shouts of the men from town grew closer, she heard nothing that could account for Ethan's whereabouts. There was nothing but the gurgle of the creek.

A hand whipped around her mouth, stifling her instinctive scream, even as another arm snapped around her waist and drew her back into a copse of trees.

Lettie relaxed against the man who held her, recognizing that it was Ethan who had approached so noiselessly. When he released her, she uttered a soft cry, turning and throwing her arms around his neck.

"You're safe!" she whispered into his neck. "I was so sure they'd found you, that somehow the Star knew you were escaping. Then I heard about the robbery just out of town."

"Shh." His fingers pressed against her mouth and he flashed her a quick smile of relief. He paused long enough to peer at her in welcome, then his gaze lifted to dart from shadow to shadow, searching for shapes that did not belong.

"We've got to get you back to the house," Lettie whispered.

He nodded. "We'll have to wait until most of the furor has passed."

"A man was murdered tonight. His family lives here in Madison."

He turned his head to gaze at her with solemn eyes.

"I don't think the furor will die down this time," she stated slowly.

Ethan's hands tightened into rigid balls and he swung his arm, striking the tree behind him with the edge of his fist. "Dammit! Who is trying to do this to me?" he whispered fiercely.

Long moments passed before Lettie reluctantly added, "It appears you have more enemies on your list than just the Star Council of Justice."

He shook his head in confusion. "I don't understand it. This . . . person has copied my methods completely. Every move, every detail, is exactly the way I would have done it." His expression grew fierce. "But I would never have killed anyone. Never!"

"I know." She lay a calming hand on his sleeve and was not surprised when the muscles beneath her palm were tense with frustration and anger. "Someone is obviously trying to hurt you."

"But who?"

She shook her head in mute commiseration.

The thunder of horses grew near and Ethan pulled her into the shadows against the tree as a trio of horses bolted across the opposite side of the creek and galloped toward Harrisburg.

As soon as the horsemen had gone, Lettie drew back, quickly reaching for the bundle that had dropped to the ground. "We've got to get you back to the boardinghouse."

Ethan shook his head. "There's no way possible. At least not until things die down."

She shoved the bundle she'd formed of a pillowcase into his arms. "Change into these. They'll disguise you long enough for us to get back. Now hurry!"

His brow furrowed in confusion, but he worked the knot loose until he could peer inside. "Lettie, these are—"

"Hurry, Ethan!"

Turning around, she presented her back to him, keeping a careful eye out for anyone who might come.

Behind her, she heard the soft rustle of bushes as Ethan began to change his clothing. When the noises stopped, she slowly turned to survey his new appearance. Inch by inch, her eyes regarded the heavy gabardine cape that covered him from ankle to chin, disguising the masculine square of his hips and the breadth of his chest and shoulders.

"They're going to know I'm a stranger in Madison."

"Nonsense. If you play your cards right, they'll think you're Alma Beasley. Everyone always remarks on her height."

Reaching down, Lettie grasped the bonnet in the bottom of the pillowslip and jammed it over the top of his head before reaching to pull the mourning veil over his face. "As long as you let me do the talking and walk like a female, we can at least make it as far as the boardinghouse."

"Yes, ma'am," he muttered.

With a curt nod of approval, Lettie turned and led the way back to the house.

Jacob reined his horse to a stop beside the blasted hole in the back of the railroad car and grimaced against the rank smells of fire and death. Quickly, his eyes scanned the area, taking in the shards of wood that littered the area, as well as the twisted remains of the safe, which now lay on the side of the track.

This time the scene of the robbery held a much more personal impact, because a friend had died here. It was Jeb Clark who had introduced Jacob to his current position. In fact, Jeb had been his first employer. As a boy of ten, Jacob had been hired to post wanted signs about the town. Jeb could have done the job himself, but he'd understood the fact that Jacob had needed the job after the loss of his father—as much for his own sense of dignity as to provide more money for those at home.

Damn, Jeb, why did it have to be you?

The stench of powder and singed grass became almost overpowering, and Jacob felt a sting in his eyes that he quickly blinked away. His gaze swung to the gaping hole in the boxcar. Though the body of his friend had been taken away, he couldn't seem to pull his eyes away from the dark stains on the floor of the railway compartment. Some of the patches were still dark. Fresh.

"Quite a mess, isn't it?"

Jacob started when Gerald Stone, deputy of Harrisburg, stopped his horse in front of him and watched Jacob with enigmatic eyes.

"Yeah." The word was little more than a whisper.

"He was a friend of yours, wasn't he?"

Jacob nodded. "Jeb . . . where—"

"They've taken his body into town to the funeral parlor. We figured it'd be better to take him to Harrisburg and let Mortie pretty him up a bit before his wife gets a look at him."

Jacob swallowed, remembering the plump, boisterous woman who had been Jeb's companion for as long as Jacob could remember. Abby Clark had been like an aunt through the years. And damn, if she didn't think the world revolved around her husband's shadow. What was she going to do?

"How . . ." Unable to continue without embarrassing himself in front of the other man, Jacob gestured in the direction of the railroad car.

Stone seemed to understand and said slowly, "Shot

through the hip. Might'a made it if the explosion hadn't finished the rest of the work.''

Once again, Jacob swallowed against the bile that rose within him, trying to keep his features outwardly unaffected and calm. Taking a deep breath, he forced himself to remember that he was in charge of his own group of men. ''What was taken?''

''Five hundred dollars in gold and another thousand in bond certificates.''

Jacob peered at his companion in confusion. ''Nothing else?''

Gerald Stone shook his head.

''But I thought the shipment contained another thousand in paper.''

''It did.'' Gerald Stone shrugged. '' 'Bout eight hundred survived the blast; the rest was blown to bits. My men have been gathering scraps of it all night.''

Jacob's brow creased. ''He took the bonds, too?''

''Must have. We haven't found any evidence of them in the rubble. They were in the same compartment as the gold. The bills were in a separate safe.''

Jacob glanced around Stone, surveying the scene with careful intent. A niggling sense of unease caused him to shift slightly in the saddle. In the past, the Gentleman had never taken stock and bond certificates. He always took the paper.

Gerald glanced around him, then edged his horse a little closer so that his mount stood nose to tail with Jacob's horse. When he spoke again, his voice had grown low and harsh. ''We're going to get the bastard this time,'' he rasped, then dug into his pocket and withdrew something that appeared to be a coin. He held it tightly in his hand a moment, studying Jacob with a careful regard. Then, as if satisfied with what he saw, he reached for Jacob's hand and pressed the coin into his palm. ''The old abandoned mill. Tonight—or, rather, this morning. Three o'clock.''

With that said, he grasped the reins of his horse and, issuing orders to his men, turned into the night.

Jacob watched him disappear around the rear of the

train, a cold tension beginning to grip his body until he could barely move. Then, slowly, cautiously, he opened his fingers to stare at the object in his hand. It was not a coin, as he had first expected, but a brass token engraved with an eight-sided star.

His fingers began to shake so hard that he had to tighten his hand into a fist to keep the token from falling to the ground. He darted a quick glance around the area, but Gerald Stone had disappeared.

Jacob stiffened in his saddle, taking deep breaths to still the sudden pounding of his heart. For months he'd worked on the periphery of the Star Council, but his only contacts had been Rusty Janson, Jeb Clark, and the lightning-blasted oak tree. Now, however, he suspected he'd just been introduced to one of the governors of the Star.

But if that were true . . .

Then it meant the Star was about to open its ranks to Jacob Grey and he could become privy to all its secrets.

Jacob took a deep breath of the smoke-tainted air and swallowed against the tightness that once again gripped his throat. His fist grew more fierce until the brass token bit into his palm, and Jacob was sure that if he opened his fingers he would find an impression embedded in his hand. The impression of an eight-sided star.

Gerald Stone rode his mount into the screen of trees toward the pair of men who waited for him there.

"You gave him the message?" Judge Harry Krupp asked, staring through the network of branches at the men who scurried about the rubble like overprotective ants.

Gerald glanced at the tall, white-haired man who had served with him on the Star Council since the group's conception. "Yep."

"Think he'll come?"

"Yep."

"And will he join the governors of the Star?"

Gerald made a sound in his throat that was half laugh, half snort. "After Clark got killed in the blast? You know Grey. He would've walked barefoot through fire for that man when he was alive. He'll walk barefoot through hell now the man's dead."

Pulling on the reins of his horse, Gerald guided his mount through the trees, leaving Judge Harry Krupp alone in the darkness with his portly companion.

"It seems you keep your promises," Krupp told his companion, gesturing toward the rubble with a negligent thumb before nodding in satisfaction.

Silas Gruber barely glanced at the remains of the boxcar and the litter of singed boards. "I told you I'd see to it that Clark didn't have a chance to tell anyone that you've been taking bribes as one of the governors of the Star. Or that for a thousand dollars, you'll throw a case out of court. And for ten thousand, you'll see to it that the Star executes the suspect—whether or not he is guilty. Now it's your turn. I've already paid you nearly eight thousand dollars to execute Ethan McGuire for robbing my bank five years ago. And since I killed Jeb Clark for you tonight, I consider the balance paid in full. This should bring Ethan McGuire out of hiding."

Krupp shrugged. "Maybe. Maybe not. If I were him, I'd hightail it out of the area as fast as I could go."

Silas shook his head. "Not McGuire. He's led a charmed life in the past. No doubt he thinks he's incapable of getting caught." He turned to fix a steady look of determination on the judge. "Just remember, Judge. I've done your dirty work, and I've paid your fee. See to it that you apprehend the man and hang him, once and for all."

The judge smiled in the darkness. "Have no fear, Gruber. No one ever escapes the Star Council. Especially if the price is right."

Silas Gruber threw his companion a look of contempt. "For the past three months you've been unable even to find the man, let alone execute him. Forgive me if I seem a little doubtful now."

The judge stiffened. "I told you that once you'd killed Clark, I would take care of McGuire."

"Just see to it that I get what I've paid for," Silas

interrupted heatedly. "Otherwise I'll make sure you sorely regret having cheated me," he muttered. "And I won't turn you in to the law. I'll turn you in to the so-called men of honor who constitute the Star Council of Justice. Somehow, I think they'd be very interested in knowing that, for the last four years, the head of their group has been taking bribes to assassinate innocent men. And he's been using the Star Council of Justice to do it." With that parting remark, Silas threw Judge Krupp a look of mocking disdain, then drew back on the reins, maneuvered his horse from the trees, and disappeared into the night.

As Krupp stared at the spot where Silas had been, his jaw tightened in anger and his hands clenched around the reins. Gruber was getting far too cocky. *And the man knew too much. Far too much.*

Krupp's expression tightened and his jaw grew hard. "I'll see to McGuire. Then I'll see to you, old man."

Though his return seemed to take twice as much time as his escape, Ethan and Lettie were able to slip through the trees and across the back yard with little more than a passing glance in their direction. Once inside, Ethan hurried up the stairs while Lettie darted to the front of the house to delay Natalie Gruber, who had just arrived from town.

Heaving a deep breath of relief, Ethan slipped through the door to Lettie's bedroom and closed it behind him. Then, as the panicked energy he'd felt began to subside, he wearily climbed the steps and moved across the broad expanse of floor in the middle of the garret. Lifting a hand to his brow, he winced when he saw that his fingers shook slightly.

Damn. He'd nearly been caught that time.

Impatient with his own outward show of weakness, Ethan drew the bonnet from his head and walked to the center of the room, gazing around him at the familiar domain. In the last few days, he'd grown to hate this garret, grown to hate its hot confines, its sloping ceilings, its profusion of windows.

Yet, now, he couldn't think of any place he would rather be.

Dropping the hat onto the bed, he reached to unfasten the collar of the mantle, stripping the heavy garment from his arms and tossing it in the direction of the bonnet, until he stood once again in his black trousers and Goldsmith's voluminous shirt.

When the door opened, Ethan jerked, his arm automatically whipping to hold his revolver at a ready aim, even though, deep down, he knew Lettie was the only person with a key.

She topped the stairs and eyed the revolver with startled concern. But her concern was tempered with the dregs of her own fear.

Something sober and just a little frightening shivered through Ethan's system when he realized this girl cared for him. She truly cared for him. Not as a thief to be captured, not as a McGuire to be respected, but as a man.

Lettie slowly smiled, and to Ethan, her smile seemed more welcoming than the sanctuary of the garret. Somehow, though he didn't know why, her smile represented hope. Hope that he could find a way out of this mess and make a future for himself. An honorable future.

When he didn't speak, Lettie gestured to the revolver he still held pointed at her chest.

"Jumpy?"

"A little," he admitted grudgingly after a slight hesitation. Taking a deep breath to still his hammering heart, he lowered the weapon to his side.

Lettie placed a pail of water at the top of the steps and gazed at him consideringly for a moment before saying, "You'll be safe here."

"For how long?" he inquired bitterly. "It's only a matter of time before someone in this house discovers I'm here."

She didn't have any answers for him, and he finally turned away, slipping his revolver back into its holster. Outside, the sound of the manhunt had subsided somewhat. The cursing of men and thunder of hooves had become more distant, but no less disturbing.

"I think it's time I stopped this," Ethan muttered, turning toward the window but knowing he couldn't even look out for fear someone outside would see him. A bubbling frustration built within him and he swore, then swore again. "Dammit! Who's doing this to me? What have I done to deserve being hunted like a rabid dog for someone else's crimes?"

He heard Lettie move closer in an attempt to placate him, but he spun away, striding to the opposite side of the garret. "I've spent enough time cooped up in this damned attic! Even now, I feel the walls closing in on me." He turned again, stabbing the air with an out-stretched finger. "I want to get even. Hell! I want the person responsible for this to pay. In spades!"

Lettie opened her mouth, then hesitated before finally saying, "I think I have a couple of ideas."

Ethan regarded her with sudden interest, feeling the embers of hope within him beginning to take spark. "Well?" he prompted, when she didn't speak right away.

"I could go to my brother and provide you with an alibi."

Ethan shook his head. "They think I'm training an accomplice. Besides which, the moment the Star got wind of my whereabouts, I'd be a dead man." His eyes narrowed. "What's your other idea?"

Lettie smoothed her hands down her skirts. "I don't think you're going to like it."

He waved her objections aside. "Now's not the time to get shy on me, Lettie."

"Someone is evidently trying to trap you, copying your methods as the Gentleman and—" She stopped when he regarded her in sudden suspicion. "I've known you're the true Gentleman Bandit for some time."

"You know?" he echoed in confusion. "How?"

"I may be young, but I'm not stupid." She stepped toward him. "As a little girl, I remember hiding on the stairs and hearing my brother rant and rave about the Gentleman. I am not so scatterbrained that I'm unable to put two and two together. My brother has begun looking for the Gentleman, and you are going to a great deal of effort to avoid him. *You* are the Gentleman Bandit—or at least you were years ago. But you weren't the man who stole that gold in Carlton two weeks ago, or in Petesville, or Dewey, or Eastbrook months before that. And you didn't injure that deputy, or murder Jeb Clark.''

He took a deep breath, shaking his head in amazement —yet why he was so surprised by her insight, he didn't know. From the beginning, Lettie had seemed to sense more about his past and his character than anyone else he'd ever known. He took a deep breath, and the anger and frustration within him subsided somewhat beneath a slow blossoming of purpose. ''My apologies if I insulted your intelligence. So, what do you suggest I do to get out of this?''

She plucked at the edge of the pocket of her apron, staring at it as if it held the secrets of the world, then glanced up, her expression determined. ''I think it's time you went out into the community to do a little sniffing around. Since the robberies are occurring within a twenty-mile radius of Madison, I think the culprit has to be here, in this town, don't you?''

Ethan's eyes narrowed, realizing that he hadn't been the only person who'd noted that fact in the recent months. He watched as a slow, mischievous smile slipped across her features and seeped into her eyes. At once, Ethan was reminded of Lettie's youth and the impulsiveness she'd displayed more than once on his behalf.

''I just checked an Agnes Magillicuddy into room five—last door on the women's wing, next to the back stairs landing. If anyone happened to see us return, they'll believe it was our new . . . reclusive boarder.''

She lifted a key from her apron pocket and tossed it to Ethan. He caught it easily and peered at the tip, discovering that an elaborate numeral five had been engraved in the brass.

''Mrs. Magillicuddy has recently suffered the loss of a loved one and wishes to be alone,'' Lettie continued.

"All alone. She will not be dining with the rest of the boarders and has agreed to pay a substantial sum in order to have her meals brought to her on a tray." The tilt of her lips lifted even more in a slow, self-satisfied smile. "A stroke of brilliance, wouldn't you say?" she asked, referring to her attempt at subterfuge.

"I have a feeling we haven't reached the part I'm not going to like yet."

"Well . . . no."

Ethan took a step forward. "Am I right in assuming that your plan has something to do with the mysterious Mrs. Magillicuddy?"

"Well, yes."

A slow wave of suspicion began to seep into his mind, but Ethan pushed it away. No. Lettie couldn't possibly think that he would . . . that he could . . .

"Lettie, I won't do it," he growled.

"You don't even know what I'm going to say."

Ethan's eyes narrowed in suspicion. "No, but I have a feeling you're going to suggest I—"

Lettie's smile became an audacious grin and her eyes sparkled in the lamplight. "I think Mrs. Magillicuddy should be seen on occasion in town, don't you? Just to keep people from suspecting . . ." Her words trailed away, and she reached into the deep pocket of her apron to remove two switches of thick black hair.

Ethan shook his head from side to side in fierce refusal. "No. I won't do it."

She continued as if he hadn't spoken. "I've also obtained a corset and a pair of . . . um . . . false bosoms for your use."

"I will not dress up like—"

"Your equipment was supplied by none other than Mrs. Silas Gruber, Grey Boardinghouse's infamous Lady of the Manor. Be careful what you reach for when you're with Natalie. It's not all real."

"Lettie."

"Of course, we'll have to find you a few changes of clothing, but there aren't that many more days until wash day. I'm sure something will manage to get lost between the pot, the line, and the boarders' armoires.''

"Lettie, I am not dressing up like a woman!" Ethan muttered fiercely, then quickly lowered his voice to a mere whisper. "I won't."

"Yes, you will. Just once or twice," Lettie coaxed. "Just enough to give the ruse some credibility."

When she advanced toward him, Ethan began to back away, wary of the spark of humor that still gleamed in her eyes.

"I won't," he insisted again.

"It's the only way you'll get into town unnoticed."

He regarded her with stubborn refusal. "No."

She huffed in irritation. "Then you'll spend the rest of your life in this garret—unless Jacob finds you first."

Ethan swore, lifting his head to glare at the ceiling as if searching for any other alternative.

Lettie dropped her teasing facade and moved across the room to lay her hand on his arm. "It's the only way, Ethan."

Ethan knew it was not the only way. He'd managed to slip away from the boardinghouse several times before. But Lettie was correct in the fact that he would not obtain much information that way. He needed to get into Madison proper. He needed to be free to visit the robbery site in Carlton—as well as the site of the robbery that had occurred only hours before.

He glanced down at her, his expression gradually changing from stubborn refusal, to disbelief, to acceptance. "No one is going to believe I'm a woman," he muttered one last time.

"They'd better," she warned. When he sighed, she pressed her point. "Tonight proved that these robberies aren't going to stop even if you manage to leave the area. The Star Council suspects *you*. No matter where you go—unless we find a way to clear your name—you'll spend the rest of your life waiting for the Star to catch up to you."

He knew she was right, but something within him still resisted. "But . . . a woman?"

"In the next few days Madison will be in an uproar. With two robberies so close to one another . . ." Her voice trailed away as she realized just how serious Ethan's position had become now that Jeb Clark had been killed. "With two robberies and Jeb Clark's death, there'll be enough strangers coming into town for the funeral services for you to slip unnoticed through the crowd."

"Why couldn't I dress up as an old man?"

"They'll be looking for a man, Ethan. They'd never look for a woman."

Ethan cringed away from the idea, trying to imagine himself cavorting around town in skirts and a bonnet. *Hell.*

"It's the only way, Ethan."

He studied her, his brow furrowed.

"You said yourself that you've got to do something."

He sighed.

"My brother's not stupid, Ethan. He's suspected that you've been hiding nearby for some time. One of these days, he'll burst through that door without any warning and you won't have time to get to the roof. You've got to do something before that happens."

"As Mrs. Magillicuddy," he added slowly.

"As Mrs. Magillicuddy." Her fingers tightened on his arm. When he still hesitated, she pressed her advantage, sensing that he was weakening to the idea. "Someone on the Star Council knows who you are and probably what you look like. Even if we tried to disguise you as an old man, there's a chance they could recognize you. But they won't look twice at a woman. It's the only way."

Ethan took a deep breath, considering the plan from all sides. Although he hated the idea of flouncing through town in women's clothing, he had to admit Lettie's thinking was sound. By dressing in skirts, a bonnet, and veil, he could walk through Madison, listen to the theories being bandied about, visit the sites of the latest robberies. And maybe, just maybe, he could begin tracking the person responsible for putting him in this mess. But . . . *dress as a woman?*

"I won't see you killed, Ethan McGuire."

He looked down to find Lettie staring at him with sober eyes. Desperate eyes.

Not for the first time, Ethan realized that this woman cared about him. Perhaps just a little too much.

With a sigh of acceptance, he reached to draw her into his arms, pulling her tightly against him. She wrapped her arms about his neck, clinging to him as if she feared he could be discovered at that very moment.

And Ethan found himself wondering what it was about this woman that made him consider abandoning his masculine dignity . . . just so that he could prove himself honorable in her eyes.

12

Darkness hung about Jacob's shoulders like an inky mantle, pressing in upon him with a relentlessness he found difficult to withstand. A few moments before, he'd met Gerald Stone at the old mill. But rather than lead Jacob directly to the Star's whereabouts, Gerald had pulled an old flour sack over Jacob's head and led his horse into the night.

Within minutes, Jacob's stomach had become a knot of apprehension. Within a quarter of an hour, his hands were icy, filmed with a clammy layer of sweat that even the leather of his gloves could not absorb. The horses moved at an achingly slow gait. If it weren't for the gentle rock of the saddle, Jacob would have wondered if they were moving at all.

For a few miles, he had tried to map in his head exactly where they were going. He'd been able to trace their path back to the main road, and then south, but Gerald Stone began to lead their mounts in a tangled maze of directions, until Jacob had no idea where they were or where they were headed. His only comfort was the occasional gurgle of the creek and the lazy *grup-crup* of the frogs. But soon even that comfort seemed hazy and far removed.

Without warning, the gait of his horse grew even slower, then came to a complete stop. Drawing a deep breath of air that was tainted slightly with the powdery smell of flour and the stench of his own sweat, Jacob reached to lift the hood from his head but was stopped by the metal of Stone's revolver pressing none too gently against his throat.

"No. Leave it on."

Jacob's hands spread wide and drifted back to his sides.

"Dismount."

Grasping the pommel of his saddle, Jacob swung from his horse, stumbling slightly when he stepped onto rocky soil. He found himself adrift in confusion when someone led his horse away, and Jacob was left alone and defenseless in a world of black shadows and hazy imaginings. Sweat began to trickle between his shoulder blades with a prickling unease. He wondered how much longer this would go on before someone explained what this was all about.

Suddenly, his revolver was whipped from his holster. Jacob whirled, reaching out to grasp the person responsible, but his hands encountered nothing but empty air.

Gerald's voice floated to him through the darkness. "No use reaching for ghosts," he said. Jacob heard the crunch of footsteps against the rocky ground. Then he was taken by the elbow and led forward.

"Step up."

Lifting his foot, Jacob hesitated a moment before his boot tip encountered the edge of a step and he climbed up.

"Again."

Jacob complied, a little more easily this time.

"Now move forward."

Resisting the urge to feel his way with his hands, Jacob allowed himself to be led through a splintered doorway and into what he assumed was some type of meeting room. The moment he crossed inside, something within him tightened, warning him that he was not alone but was being watched by a group of people. He sensed their gazes boring heavily into him from all sides, and Jacob felt the sweat began to bead his face and pool beneath his shirt.

The butt of Gerald's revolver against his ribs urged him to continue walking. After a few steps, a pull upon his arm drew him to a stop.

"Sit."

The scrape of a chair being dragged along the floor came from behind, and Jacob stumbled when it bumped into the back of his knees. He thumped heavily into the chair, then straightened. Unconsciously, he moved his hands to his sides, keeping them slightly away from his body should it prove necessary for him to drag the hood from his face and dodge out the door.

"Jacob Grey?"

Jacob stiffened at the sound of a deep raspy voice, one that seemed vaguely familiar—yet he couldn't pinpoint where he had heard it before.

When he didn't answer, the voice came again.

"You are Jacob Grey, are you not?"

"Yes."

"Marshall of Madison City?"

"Yes."

"For how long?"

"Three months."

There was a murmur of voices, and Jacob sensed their disapproval of his lack of experience.

"And how did you obtain that position?"

A surge of fury cut through Jacob's fear. "Now, see here!"

"Answer the question!"

The tip of a revolver was pressed none too subtly against his temple.

Stiffening, Jacob muttered, "I was appointed after the death of Morely Shipton."

"That's enough."

The murmuring came again, but too softly for Jacob to hear beyond his own panting breaths.

"Jacob Grey," the raspy voice began again, "are you familiar with the spurt of robberies that have been occurring in this vicinity for the last three months and those that occurred in this area of the state nearly five years ago?''

Jacob slowly straightened, gritting his teeth. "Yes."

"Are you familiar with the methods used by the thief?"
"Yes."

"You believe these methods to be the work of whom?"
Jacob hesitated.

"Do you believe these robberies to be the work of the Gentleman Bandit?''

Once again, Jacob hesitated, unsure why he felt it would be better to remain silent, but keeping his own counsel all the same.

"Jacob Grey, are you aware that two lawmen have been hurt while trying to apprehend this man?"

Anger and frustration shuddered through Jacob's system at the other man's words. Jeb Clark had *died* tonight.

"Are you aware—''
"Yes!''

Someone grasped Jacob's hand and he jerked free, but the unknown person caught his wrist and held it with an iron grip, pushing it down. Jacob tried to wrench away, wondering what he was being forced to do. When his fingers encountered a nubby flat surface, his brow creased in confusion, and his eyes strained to see through the tough weave of the flour sack. Although a faint light seeped through the cloth, it came from behind, offering him nothing of value—no blocks of shape, no hazy shadows.

"Jacob Grey, you now have your hand upon the cover of the Holy Bible. Do you swear to tell the truth, the whole truth, and nothing but the truth, so help you God?''

Jacob felt a rush of confusion at the familiar oath. "Yes."

"Are you aware that in breaking your oath, you will be held accountable with your very life?"

The variation of the oath caused Jacob to pause before answering. "Yes."

"Do you know who is responsible for these robberies?"

"Yes."

"Who?"

Once more he hesitated before answering. "Ethan McGuire."

"Jacob Grey, have you ever been associated with a group known as the Star Council of Justice?"

A sickness swirled in Jacob's stomach and he began to shake. How should he answer? If he weren't in the presence of the Star, admitting his involvement would mean death. If he *were* in the presence of the Star Council, the penalty for breaking the code of silence . . . would also mean death.

"Answer."

Jacob remained stubbornly silent. He jerked when the barrel of a revolver was placed against the side of his temple.

"Answer!"

Growling deep in his throat, Jacob lashed out, jabbing his captor in the groin and grasping the revolver in one hand while ripping the flour sack from his head with the other. In one instinctive motion, he was on his feet, the revolver aimed and ready.

Then his eyes adjusted to the light and he grew still when he found himself in the company of seven exhausted, dusty men who had crowded into the cramped keeping room of the abandoned Johnston farmhouse.

"Sit down, Jacob." The voice came again, much more warmly this time.

His gaze swerved across the room to connect with that of Judge Harry Krupp, the man who had been interrogating him.

Very slowly, Jacob sank into the chair, but he did not relinquish his hold on the revolver.

Judge Krupp pushed himself to his feet and crossed toward Jacob. His white hair gleamed in the dim lamplight, making him appear more of an elderly grandfather than the "hanging judge" he was reported to be.

"Gerald, take a seat," the judge ordered.

Behind Jacob, Gerald Stone gasped for air, bending his body at an awkward angle and swearing. "Dammit all to hell, Jacob,'' he muttered, hobbling toward the nearest chair. "Why'd you have to hit me?"

Jacob's gaze once again swept across the room. He recognized each of the men present: Walt Moore, a lawyer from Petesville; Slim Garson, a deputy from Dewey; Tony Lambert, Lincoln's only attorney; Judge Garson Miller, from the circuit; Thaad Cusper, marshal from Libbyville; and Judge Harry Krupp, also from the circuit. And the community men: Silas Gruber and Ned Abernathy.

"We apologize for the theatrics, Grey. But not many people are allowed an introduction to the governors of the Star. We have to make sure those who do are honorable enough to keep our identities a secret"—he leveled a piercing gaze in Jacob's direction—"but not so honorable as to reveal our identities to a United States marshal."

Since the judge waited, Jacob nodded his head in confirmation of the warning.

"Getting back to our original purposes: A message was left for you at the old oak explaining that Ethan McGuire had been found guilty and should pay for his crimes." Krupp continued in an almost negligent manner, his voice calm and low, "Judging by what you've just said, you agree that Ethan McGuire is responsible for the robberies."

Though Jacob felt a twinge of uneasiness, he stated, "Yes."

"And Jeb's death?"

Jacob paused. "Yes."

The judge took a deep breath and nodded in approval. "You've been a devoted member of the Star for what— five years now?"

"Six."

Once again, the judge paused and turned to his companions. "Gentlemen, your decisions. All in favor."

The room echoed with a chorus of resounding "Ayes."

"All opposed."

Silence.

The judge turned.

"Jacob Grey, would you willingly defend the secrets of the Star with your life?"

A slight chill seemed to feather down Jacob's spine, then a slow realization. "Yes."

"Would you take a blood oath to that effect?"

"Yes," he stated firmly, thinking of Jeb. It was Jeb Clark who had introduced him to the Star Council, who had taught him the secrets of the lightning-blasted oak.

"Jacob Grey, you have been nominated to replace Jeb Clark on the Star Council of Justice. Do you accept?"

Jacob straightened ever so slightly in his chair, and his eyes slipped over each member of the group. A powerful combination of anger and revenge began to tumble through his veins.

"Yes. I accept."

Only then did Jacob taste the metallic bitterness of foreboding lingering on his own tongue.

Dawn streaked across the sky, scarlet and heavy, with thick sultry clouds. Feeling the first insistent fingers of light pressing against her eyelids, Lettie blinked and snuggled a little more deeply into her pillow, regretting the fact that another dawn meant another day at the boardinghouse: cooking, cleaning, washing, milking. Once again, the chickens would have to be fed and the eggs washed. There was bacon to fry in the morning, sandwiches to make in the afternoon, and vegetables to scrub in the evening.

A heavy sigh pushed against her chest and escaped in a slow puff of air. As always, morning was the worst time of day for Lettie. She buried her nose into the pillow in regret, wishing that she could have the time, just once, to lie in bed and linger until the sun had completely risen.

"Lettie?"

From the door below, she heard her mother's soft tap and she jerked completely awake. "Coming!" she called. Despite her efforts, the lack of enthusiasm in her response was evident.

Rolling onto her back, Lettie pushed her hair away

from her face and rose to a sitting position. Almost immediately, as had become her habit, her eyes swung to the man who slept in a nest of blankets and sheets on the opposite side of the room.

Her arms wrapped around her legs and she rested her chin on her knees. She had delayed moving Ethan into his room until she could prepare him for his new role. A smile flitted across her features when she noted the way Ethan's neatly trimmed hair lay closely cropped around his ears and neck and a little longer on top, emphasizing the bold bone structure of his face. Although a night's growth of beard darkened his jaw, the strong lines were free of the darker whiskers, which had been there until last night.

Yes indeed, her Ethan was a handsome man.

Lettie's smile flickered and disappeared beneath a warm wave of awareness. Last night her fingers had been allowed some small measure of freedom as she'd wrapped a bath sheet around his shoulders and trimmed his hair to a more fashionable length. Time had seemed to pass as slowly as an inchworm measuring a stalk. With each moment that moved by, something warm and infinitely sensual had begun to simmer between them in the hot summer night until the very air seemed heavy and static, like the tangible beginnings of a lightning storm. Soon, Lettie had barely been able to maintain her grip on the shears. And when Ethan drew her between his legs to hold her tightly against his chest, she hadn't demurred. She'd simply threaded her fingers through his hair and bowed to hold him tightly against her.

For long moments, they'd remained that way, remembering their fear when the posse had come and pushing aside their fear for the days ahead. Somehow, without really intending it, the bond between them had strengthened, becoming an almost tangible thing that drew them together as surely as a spider's web. Then Ethan had drawn back and looked into her eyes. Despite the dim lamplight, despite the gloom of evening, Lettie had felt something open and blossom inside of her at the expressions she found there: strength, desire . . . hunger. And she'd known, deep in her heart, that it would be only a matter of time before she and Ethan became joined in the most intimate manner possible.

Now Lettie blinked, allowing her eyes to slip from Ethan's jaw to the breadth of his shoulders. He'd flung an arm above his head during his sleep, and her eyes lovingly traced the firm contour made by his ribs as they swept in a beguiling arc to the narrowness of his stomach.

Her breath paused, then quickened. The sheet had slipped low upon his hips. So very low.

Lettie straightened, her chin lifting from her knees without her really being aware of it. Her eyes widened ever so slightly, and she found herself tracing the dark hair that feathered down his stomach from his chest, swirling around the slight indentation of his navel before slipping lower.

Lettie felt herself growing warm. Though the sheet covered Ethan where it counted, there was no denying the washboard honing of his stomach, the flat scoop of his pelvis, and the masculine jut of his hips beneath the sheet.

Lettie's eyes grew wider still. Her heart began a slow, methodic pounding at the base of her throat and the pit of her stomach. Impulsively, she pushed aside the covers and slipped from the bed.

Her bare feet made no sound on the hooked rug in the center of the floor as she padded across the garret to where Ethan lay beside the wardrobe. Slowly, silently, she knelt beside him, her nightgown puddling onto the floor beside them. Her hair became a curtain of honey-brown waves as she bent toward him.

"Ethan?" she whispered, so softly that he probably would not have heard her had he been awake.

Trying to breathe against the warmth flooding her body and the heavy beat of her own heart, Lettie leaned forward and brushed a light kiss against his mouth. His skin was warm and still smelled of soap.

Once again, she bent to brush the opposite corner of his mouth, then moved to trace the tip of her tongue against the lower swell of his lips.

Ethan awakened with a start and she drew back, ever so slightly, smiling at his expression of confusion.

"Good morning, Ethan."

He blinked at her, still obviously disoriented from his heavy slumber. The events of the previous night had evidently taken their toll, and he'd slept without stirring most of the night.

"You seemed to sleep well," she commented softly.

Ethan's eyes narrowed, becoming azure hot as they slipped over her features and the hair that spilled over her shoulders and surrounded them like an intimate set of bedcurtains.

"At least you *must* have slept well," she continued. "I didn't hear you stirring."

In fact, she was very aware that he had spent part of the evening watching her. She'd felt the warm heat of his gaze long into the night until, finally, he'd succumbed to his own exhaustion.

"You're up early," he murmured, his voice sleep-gruff and endearing.

"Boardinghouse rules," she teased. "Late to bed, early to rise."

His eyes dipped, and Lettie became acutely aware of the way her unfettered breasts swayed provocatively above him. She tried to draw back, but he grasped a strand of her hair and wound it around his wrist, drawing her irresistibly forward. Once again, she found the intense heat of his gaze directed toward her. And there was no denying that he wanted her. Now.

Lettie balked slightly. "I guess I'd better get dressed."

"No." He drew her closer, so close she could feel his breath whispering against her cheek. "I haven't thanked you for helping me last night." His voice was low, husky. Firm.

"There's no need."

"Oh, but there is. My mother tried to teach me—"

"Manners," she supplied, laughing softly.

"As I said once before, I wasn't an exemplary pupil."

"But you try."

"I try."

With an insistent tug of her hair, he drew her to him and their lips brushed, then met again for a kiss that revealed their mutual hunger and the desire that had been growing steadily between them for days.

Placing her hands on his shoulders for balance, Lettie allowed herself to be drawn tightly against his chest. She moaned deep in her throat when the heat of his body seemed to seep through her nightgown with the intensity of a burning brand—branding her as Ethan's woman. When his hand slowly moved from her waist, to her back, then around the curve of her ribs to rest beneath her breast, she jerked slightly in an unconscious reflex, her heart beginning to pound, her breath locking in her throat. Without being aware of it, she nudged her chest against his own, unconsciously bidding his hand to cover her breast.

"Do you suppose we'll have flapcakes or cornbread this morning, Sister?"

They sprang apart when the Beasleys' voices drifted up from the floor below.

"What do you think, Alma?"

"I'm putting my money on the cornbread."

"I have to go," Lettie breathed. "Otherwise Mama will come looking for me." She turned back to Ethan, knowing her eyes must mirror some of her own passion and regret. He was watching her, and, for a moment, she thought she saw a hint of softening within his features, before they settled into their usual blunt-hewn lines.

"I'm sorry."

He pressed a finger over her lips, then drew her down for a soft kiss. "I'll miss you."

Her smile was shy, despite their intimate position.

"I'll miss you, too."

Reluctantly, regretfully, she untangled herself from Ethan's embrace and moved toward the wardrobe to retrieve something to wear for the day.

When she turned to find Ethan watching her, she gave him the all-too-familiar swirling gesture of her hand to signify that he should turn his back.

"And no peeking in the mirror this time," she scolded, then blushed when she realized she'd given away the fact that she'd known he'd seen her undressing on occasion by watching her reflection in the mirror.

To her surprise, Ethan chuckled. A low, rusty sound, but a chuckle nonetheless. Following her command, he pushed himself into a sitting position and swiveled so that his back was presented to her.

Lettie swallowed against the sudden tightness of her throat when her gaze slipped across the width of his shoulders. His skin was smooth and dappled with a light beading of sweat. Broad shoulders tapered to the firm span of his ribs, delineated by the curving length of his spine. A slim masculine waist tapered into narrow hips and the bare curves of his buttocks.

"Why, Ethan McGuire, you aren't wearing any drawers!" she blurted, then slapped a hand over her mouth at the impropriety of her hasty words.

Ethan peered at her over his shoulder, his eyes hot and blue. "No, Lettie Grey, I'm not."

After that, it became harder than ever to slip into a gingham day dress and fasten the tiny hooks along her hip and waist, let alone fasten the tiny mother-of-pearl buttons that marched up the front of the bodice.

When she announced that she'd finished dressing, Ethan wrapped a sheet around his hips and pushed himself to his feet.

"You look pretty in that color," he murmured softly, moving toward her.

His compliment flustered her slightly, and she glanced down at the tiny Wedgwood-blue squares amid their field of winter white.

"Thank you."

He stopped only inches away. "I like the way it fits, too." His finger lifted to feather across her chest. "It's nice and tight here—" his fingers slipped down the side of her ribs and she gasped—"and here." His hand slid around her waist. "It's fitted here, then flares here." His hand moved from the tight tailored bodice to the gentle gathering of her skirt, slipping down the curve of her derrière.

"What the—" The pressure of his hand grew a little firmer and she tried to bat his hand away, but he insistently kept it where it was, grasping a fistful of skirt. "That isn't all you, is it?"

She grunted in outrage. "I'll have you know I'm wearing a bustle pad under there."

"So Natalie Gruber isn't the only one padded to her eyeteeth?"

"Well, I never!"

Ethan chuckled and his hand flattened, drawing her firmly against the cradle of his hips. "Never mind," he murmured next to her mouth. "I like a woman who can fill my hand like a luscious peach."

"Ethan!"

He silenced her shocked outburst with his mouth, immediately coaxing a response from her that she found she could not willingly deny him. As he explored the tempting sweetness of her mouth, one of his hands reached to take her own and lay it against the firmly toned muscles of his stomach.

Moaning in delight, she moved closer still, her fingers curling slightly to test the resilience of his skin before slipping around the side of his waist to the hollow of his back. For a moment, her fingers ran up and down the crease of his spine in a tantalizing motion before pausing and dipping.

"Lettie?"

Once again they separated at the sound of Alma Beasley's voice.

"Your mother asked me to come get you."

"Coming!" she called, then turned back to Ethan. "I have to go now or she'll wake the whole house. I'll come up again as soon as I can."

"When?"

She reluctantly backed away, ignoring the way his hand lingered on the curve of her ribs before finally dropping away. Something had changed within him since the night before, Lettie realized. Somehow he'd softened, though ever so slightly. His features were a little less bitter. His eyes a little less grim.

"Soon," she answered, taking a ragged breath. "We have to get Mrs. Magillicuddy into town."

"Lettie, I've been giving it some more thought and I don't think it's such a good idea for me to dress up like a woman."

"Be brave, Ethan," she teased, then turned and clattered down the steps. At the bottom, she hesitated, looking up to see him peering at her over the edge of the railing. "Bye," she mouthed, then slipped into the hall.

She shut the door behind her and glanced up to find Alma and Amelia regarding her with curious gazes. Afraid of what they would see in her features, Lettie mumbled a good morning, then hurried down the staircase.

Alma watched her with a considering look. "That girl's up to something, wouldn't you say, Sister?"

Amelia glanced at Lettie's retreating figure, then back at her sister. "She did seem a trifle flushed."

"I'd say she's in love."

Amelia gasped. "Really? How can you tell?"

"When a woman starts acting daft, it's usually one of two things: love or senility." Alma glanced at her sister, and her eyes twinkled. "Course, in our case, one can never tell, can they?"

13

Breakfast at the boardinghouse was served at seven o'clock without deviation. Because of this, Lettie and her mother rose at dawn in order to prepare for the first meal of the day. On most occasions, the boarders arrived a little early. They would chatter and gather around the table, eat quickly, then disperse, intent upon their own daily tasks.

But there was a difference today. Lettie could feel it. Jeb Clark's death had cast a mood of mourning over the assembly. The boarders talked less frequently and their appetites were slightly off—all except for Natalie Gruber's. She swept into the dining room, her features wreathed in smiles.

"Good morning, all!" she called, then proceeded to settle herself on one of the far chairs, her spine at least three inches from the back of her chair, a snowy napkin carefully covering the peach dimity morning gown she wore. As the other boarders spoke of Jeb Clark in regretful murmurs, she began to dine upon one cup of tea, one slice of bacon, and one piece of nonbuttered bread, with her usual delicate enthusiasm.

"It's a shame, that's what it is," Alma Beasley stated with a sad shake of her head. "A man cut down in his prime. The person responsible should be shot!"

At her words, Dorothy Rupert suddenly jumped from her chair, causing it to clatter behind her. "I'm sorry, I—" Holding a trembling hand to her mouth, she darted from the room.

Amelia made a *tsk*-ing noise of concern. "Oh, dear. It must have been something you said, Sister."

Despite the embarrassment she felt at her own wayward tongue, Alma rolled her eyes.

Lettie sighed and moved to right the chair, sliding it under the table. When she turned back, Mr. Goldsmith was stuffing a bright yellow napkin into the collar of his shirt and reaching for a helping of fried eggs. "I hear tell they'll have the funeral tomorrow." He scooped three eggs onto his plate, then a healthy portion of fried potatoes. "Ned, see to it that you exchange our train tickets to Chicago for a later time in the day so that we can attend." He fixed Ned with a stern glance.

"Yes, sir."

Mr. Goldsmith stuffed a forkful of dripping egg yolk into his mouth and chewed with eager enthusiasm. "I also hear tell there's a hefty reward for the culprit," he added, after swallowing and scooping another bite of food.

Lettie stiffened and reached out to brush an imaginary crease from the tablecloth.

"More than a thousand dollars, if I remember correctly. And they'll take him dead or alive. Personally, I'd see to it I brought him in dead. I wouldn't want to rastle with a no-account weasel like that."

Lettie's heart began to pound, and her breathing became short. The Star had done this. The Star was to blame. If they had been doing their job correctly, they would have known Ethan wasn't responsible.

She looked up to find Alma regarding her in concern, Amelia in surprise, and Natalie with a piercing stare. Glancing down at her hand, Lettie saw that she had unconsciously grasped a thick fistful of the tablecloth and seemed ready to yank it free from the table.

As casually as she could, Lettie released her grip and smoothed the wrinkles she'd caused. "I'll just get some more coffee,'' she muttered, then turned and strode from the room. Once in the hall, she leaned her back against the wall, taking deep, gulping breaths. She had to be more careful. The Star could be watching her even now, and the first wrong move could mean Ethan's death.

She glanced up, starting when she saw a man's shadow stretching across the parlor floor. Pushing herself away from the wall, she crept toward the threshold until she could peer around the edge. Her fingers curled tightly around the woodwork when she found her brother standing at the far window, staring out at something in front of the house.

"Good morning, Jacob," Lettie remarked softly, stepping forward.

Her brother jerked away from his intense study of the front yard. He'd seemed so deep in thought, she'd been hesitant to disturb him. But the expression on his face had not been one caused by pleasant thoughts.

When he didn't speak, Lettie moved farther into the room, gesturing behind her at the dining-room doors. "Did you come for breakfast?"

"Yeah."

Despite the fact that he'd spoken in the affirmative, he turned to stare out of the window once again.

"Is something wrong?"

Her brother stiffened, then turned. 'No. Nothing.''

"You look tired. Did you sleep at all last night?"

He gave a jerky nod, but Lettie knew he was lying. His features were pinched in exhaustion, and dark hollow circles punctuated his eyes.

Lettie hesitantly took a step forward. "I'm sorry about Jeb," she whispered, knowing how close her brother had been to the older man.

His jaw hardened and he glanced away from her, seeming to blink against the sun streaming through the windows.

"Has Abby been told?" she asked, referring to Jeb's wife.

Jacob clenched the brim of his hat in his hand, then

slapped it against his thigh. "Yes. I—" He swallowed. "I told her."

"I'm so sorry, Jacob." Impulsively, she moved to embrace him, lifting herself on tiptoe to slip her arms about his neck.

He remained stiff for a moment, then something inside of him seemed to crumble and he hugged her back. "Damn, Lettie, why did it have to be him? He wasn't supposed to be on that shipment. He was supposed to be home. . . ."

Lettie held him even tighter, feeling his pain as her own. It had been a long, long time since she'd seen her proud brother this vulnerable.

"He didn't have to die," Jacob continued. "He was shot in the hip. Hell! Men have lived from worse than that."

"Then how did it happen?"

"The explosion. He must have died in the explosion."

Without warning, he jerked free of Lettie's embrace. His arm swiped at his eyes, then he moved to brush by her, but Lettie reached out to grasp his arm.

"Jacob, I—"

At his harshly indrawn breath, she gazed at him in concern. Then she glanced down. A small patch of blood was beginning to seep through the white cotton of his shirt from a spot on the inside of his forearm.

Lettie gasped. "You've hurt yourself! How in the world—"

Jacob wrenched his hand away. "Don't touch me. It's none of your concern. I don't need your coddling, Lettie. I'm not another of your wounded sparrows. *I'm* in control of this one."

Lettie took an involuntary step backward as if he'd slapped her. "I see," she murmured stiffly.

"Lettie!" he called, reaching out to stop her. "I didn't mean that the way it sounded."

"Then just what *did* you mean, Jacob?"

"I . . ." He sighed. "I'm just tired. Don't pay me any mind. I'm sorry."

"Let me take a look at that." She gestured to his arm. "If I don't, you'll get an infection."

"No." His voice became firm. "I just came for breakfast."

"Jacob, you can't leave a bleeding wound untended. At least let me bandage it."

But her brother wouldn't listen to her; he merely stepped around her and refused to answer.

Sighing in disgust at Jacob's pig-headed stubbornness, Lettie marched into the dining room. Before he left, she'd see to it that his arm was washed and bandaged. Even if she had to hog-tie him to the chair in order to do it.

In the end, she accomplished the feat by "accidentally" spilling coffee down the front of his shirt. Jacob swore and darted into the kitchen to strip his shirt away and splash cold water over his chest. When he turned, Lettie stood behind him with her mother's basket of bandages and ointments.

"Sit down."

His eyes narrowed in dawning anger. "Lettie, that was a low-down, rotten, sneaky trick."

"Sit down."

When Celeste Grey entered the room, Jacob reluctantly took a seat on the far end of one of the trestle benches lining the kitchen table.

Lettie stood at the head of the table, motioning for Jacob to stretch out his arm. She gasped at the horizontal cut made across the upper portion of his forearm. "How in the world did you get this?"

Jacob glanced at his mother, then mumbled, "I cut myself shaving."

Lettie shot him a look of sibling disgust at his sarcastic comment, but, sensing he would not say more in her mother's presence, she set the basket on the table and moved to pump fresh water into a basin.

After Celeste Grey had examined Jacob's arm and chided him for not taking better care of himself, she returned to the dining room, instructing Lettie to care for the wound.

The moment she'd gone, Lettie walked back to the table and set the basin next to Jacob's arm. Taking a scrap of flannel, she began to swipe away the blood. As the wound was wiped bare, she noted that the cut was cleanly made—as if it had, indeed, been made with a straight-edged razor.

Lettie glanced at the door between the kitchen and dining room to ensure her mother was truly gone, then commanded in a low voice, "Now tell me what really happened."

Jacob winced beneath her ministrations. "I told you: I cut myself."

"Don't lie to me, Jacob Grey."

"Why not, Lettie? You've been lying to me."

A chill feathered through her body and she looked up, but Jacob didn't press the issue. He was staring at his arm and the collection of ointments in the basket.

"I think that's fine now, Lettie. You don't have to use that—"

Ignoring his words, Lettie chose a jar of ointment and quickly unsnapped the iron wires that held it shut.

"Lettie, I told you that was enough! You don't have to—"

Without compunction, she slapped a healthy measure of ointment into the cut, despite the fact that she knew it would sting on the open wound like the fires of hell.

"Dammit, Lettie! You didn't have to use so much!"

"This cut hasn't been bandaged. You're lucky your arm didn't turn green and fall off." Taking a roll of bandages from the basket, she began to bind the wound in quick, no-nonsense motions. "How did you get it, Jacob?"

He refused to speak.

Her fingers tightened for a moment on his arm, before she quickly tied a knot in the ends of the bandages. "It's a clean cut. Looks almost as if you made it yourself."

At her words, Jacob wrenched free. "Keep out of this, Lettie."

"You're my brother!"

He regarded her with dark eyes. "Then it's about time

182

you remembered that fact. I've been good to you, Lettie. I've taken care of you and protected you."

"And smothered me!" she blurted, then slapped a hand over her mouth in regret. But it was far too late to retrieve the hasty words.

Jacob looked as if he'd been struck.

"I'm sorry, Jacob. I shouldn't have said that."

"But you meant it, didn't you?" When she didn't speak, he added more forcefully, "Didn't you?"

"Yes!" She took a calming breath. "I'm sorry, but it's true. I'm not a little girl, Jacob. I'm a woman. And I can't have an overprotective brother hovering over me every minute."

"Well, I'm sorry I ever inconvenienced you," Jacob growled, snatching his hat and shirt from the table and striding from the room.

"Jacob!" She lifted her skirts and darted after him. "Jacob, I'm sorry. You know I didn't mean that the way it sounded. Jacob!"

But he didn't listen, didn't pause. He simply stormed from the house and slammed the door behind him. Lettie stood in the front hall, in full view of the boarders, feeling that she'd failed some sort of a test.

And lost her very best friend in the process.

Jacob paused a few yards away from the house and turned to glance over his shoulder. For weeks now, he'd been fighting the gut instinct that something was out of place at the Grey Boardinghouse. And though he'd fought his suspicions, Jacob was beginning to believe that it was not the house itself that had somehow changed.

But his sister.

Nearly an hour later, Celeste Grey strode into the kitchen, where Lettie was finishing the last of the breakfast dishes. "Lettie, I need you to take the buggy into town and pick up supplies at the dry goods."

Lettie straightened slightly, eyeing her mother in surprise. Celeste usually made the trips to the dry goods, since she and Mr. Schmidt had a long-time routine of haggling for the best prices and arguing over the choicest goods.

"I meant to go myself," Celeste continued without pause, "but because of Mr. Clark's funeral, the ladies' auxiliary has asked me to do some baking for the supper afterward."

"Yes, Mama."

As if her mother already had her mind on the task ahead, she took a voluminous apron from the hook on the inside of the pantry and wrapped it around her waist.

"I put a list on the hutch by the back door. Take the Beasleys if they wish to go. Or perhaps our new boarder, Mrs. Magillicuddy, would like a chance to ride into town. You could show her the area, help her get acquainted. That is, if you can find her," Celeste muttered. "I knocked on her door, hoping to introduce myself, and the woman didn't even answer."

"Sh-she's a little hard of hearing," Lettie blurted.

Her mother sighed. "I suppose that explains it. Though I had hoped to get her first week's fee ahead of time. If she decides to go into town with you, get her money for the room first, understand?"

"Yes, Mama."

Lettie quickly dropped her gaze to the last plate she'd been scrubbing so that her mother wouldn't see the sudden delight that leapt through her body. This was just the opening she'd been waiting for. She and Ethan could hurry into town, then hurry back.

"I've also fixed a basket of jams and a loaf of bread for Mrs. Clark, if you'd please stop by for a condolence call. Assure her that the church has made all of the arrangements for the meal after the services, and she isn't to trouble herself."

"Yes, Mama." Lettie placed the plate atop the stack on the hutch and untied her apron. "I'll just change into something more suitable," she added quickly.

"Yes, of course, dear."

Not waiting another moment, for fear her mother would change her mind, Lettie lifted her skirts and rushed up the back stairs, stripping her apron from her waist as she went. After carefully knocking on the Beasleys' bedroom door, she gathered a few supplies, then hurried upstairs. At the garret door, she paused to glance behind her, then unlocked the door and slipped inside.

"Ethan?" she whispered, tiptoeing upstairs.

She'd only taken a few steps before she heard his soft curse, and Ethan stepped from behind the edge of the armoire and released the hammer to his revolver.

"Sorry,' she murmured, climbing the staircase.

"It's all right."

A sweet, sticky silence settled between them for a moment, before Ethan strode across the room and slid his revolver beneath the pillows of the bed.

"You seem a little tense," Lettie remarked, noting the way his shoulders seemed to be pressed back in a rigid line against the fabric of his shirt.

"No. I'm fine."

"Ethan—"

"I'm fine, Lettie," he bit out. Then he sighed and shook his head. "I'm sorry. I don't mean to snap at you."

"What's happened?" she whispered.

He shrugged. "Some of your boarders have simply become a little too inquisitive. I hear their footsteps stopping outside the door."

"Has anyone tried to come in?" she asked in concern.

"No."

Though his features remained bland, Lettie knew Ethan was lying. But as if a tacit command had been given, neither of them voiced their newest concern. Instead, they avoided looking at each other and gazed about the room instead.

"Any luck?" Lettie finally asked, gesturing to the periodicals strewn about on the opposite end of the bed.

Ethan shook his head. He bent to lift one of the crumpled newspapers he'd managed to retrieve from Goldsmith's room. "No. None of it makes any sense."

"I'm sorry," she murmured again, sensing his frustration and his mounting tension, but knowing no way of easing it.

"Damn!" he suddenly exclaimed. "Who would possibly do this to me? Who would hate me so much that they would go to such extremes to see me hanged for crimes I haven't committed?" He threw the newspaper onto the bed and strode across the room to the window.

Lettie crossed to retrieve the periodical, reading the article he had just abandoned. In a florid, journalistic style, the excerpt outlined one of the first robberies to hit the area.

"You couldn't possibly have robbed the railway offices in Eastbrook. It says here that the thief climbed in through a third-story window after jumping onto the roof from a nearby hotel balcony." She issued a short snort of humor. "*You* wouldn't have made it outside of the window."

"But no one else knows about my . . . problem except you."

"Oh."

"So you see, there's no way to prove *I* didn't do it, until I can find the man who did."

"Perhaps once you get into town . . ." Remembering why she'd come upstairs in the first place, Lettie dropped the bundle of clothing she'd taken from the Beasleys onto the bed beside her, then hurried toward the wardrobe and flung open the door. Swiftly thumbing through her dresses, she chose a black grosgrain skirt and bodice to wear into town, since she would be paying a call on Mrs. Clark.

"Mama has asked me to go into town for supplies." She threw a meaningful glance over her shoulder. "She told me I could take Mrs. Magillicuddy, if she wanted to go. Does she want to go?"

Ethan made a face of masculine discomfort. "Lettie, this isn't such a good idea."

"It's the only way you're going to get in and out of town. Mr. Goldsmith told me that they've issued a reward for your capture."

Ethan grew still. "How much?"

"One thousand dollars."

He swore. "How much time do I have to get dressed?"

"Ten minutes."

"That's more than enough."

Lettie laughed. "You have a lot to learn about being a woman, Ethan McGuire."

In the end, Lettie dressed first, forcing Ethan to turn his back while she slipped out of her day dress and into the more appropriate suit of mourning. Then she strode toward the clothing she'd placed on the bed.

"You're going to have to strip down to your drawers."

"I have to what?"

"Strip to your drawers."

"Why?"

"Because no one is going to believe you're a woman if you have on a pair of men's trousers beneath your skirts."

"Who's going to know?"

"Ethan, you'll be climbing in and out of a buggy all day. The first thing a man watches for in a woman is a glimpse of stocking."

Ethan opened his mouth to refute her statement, then closed it again. "Well, maybe not the first." His eyes took on a heated glow, and he stepped toward her. "That wasn't the first thing I saw with you."

Lettie damned the warmth that flooded her cheeks when she realized she'd first confronted him with her bodice half undone.

"Nevertheless," she inserted firmly, holding out a hand to stop his advance, "you will need to strip."

"You just want to see me without my clothes."

"I've seen you without—" Once again she snapped her mouth shut.

"Not entirely."

"Ethan!"

Ethan only chuckled.

The sound was music to Lettie's ears.

"Strip."

"Yes, ma'am."

When he didn't move, she cocked an inquiring eyebrow. "Well?"

He made a swirling motion of his hand, much as she did every morning. "Turn around."

Hurrumphing to herself, Lettie turned, grasping the clothing to her chest and marching toward the bureau.

"The mirror, Lettie."

Feeling another tide of warmth flood her cheeks, Lettie turned and marched toward the window. "Hurry it up, will you?"

"Yes, ma'am."

From behind, Lettie heard the rustle of clothing and she forced herself not to think about what part of his anatomy he was uncovering with each subtle sound. Each night he had undressed in the dark, and Lettie's imagination had run wild. The image was so clear and fresh in her mind that she could nearly see the suspenders dropping to each hip. Soon the shirt he wore would slip from wide shoulders to reveal a leanly contoured chest and flat stomach. Then he would unbutton his trousers.

"Now what?"

The temptation to turn was nearly unbearable.

Lettie strode to the bed, keeping her eyes carefully averted from the man in the center of the room, even as she wondered if he'd notice if she took one peek—just a quick one—in the mirror over the bureau.

Opening the pillowslip she'd used as a sack the night before, Lettie removed a pair of black cotton stockings and a pair of frilly women's underdrawers, then threw them over her shoulder. "Put these on."

There was a moment of silence, then Ethan blurted, "These are women's!"

"I know."

"I'm not wearing these women's . . . things."

"They're underdrawers, Ethan."

"Lettie—"

"Put them on."

"They're . . . lacy."

"Put them on."

"Lettie, these are women's underclothes!"

"I know, Ethan. There wouldn't be much point in giving you men's, would there?"

"But—"

"You're wasting time."

"I don't like this, Lettie. It's bad enough dressing like a woman, but you didn't tell me I had to wear . . . *these*."

"Ethan, just put them on and stop arguing about it."

"Lettie—"

"Put them on."

"Damn."

She heard the squeak of the bed as he sat on the side, and within moments she heard his muttered, "Now what?"

Turning, she bit back a snort of amusement when she saw Ethan standing in the middle of the garret, wearing his own drawers and a pair of Alma Beasley's black cotton stockings and lace-edged underdrawers.

At the sound of her laughter, Ethan scowled, planting his hands on his hips. "Lettie," he growled.

"I'm sorry." She grasped the corset from the pile of things on the bed and marched toward him.

Ethan took one look at the contraption and backed away. "Oh, no you don't. It's bad enough wearing"—he waved to the underdrawers—"but I won't wear that."

"Yes you will, Ethan McGuire. No one is going to believe you're a woman if you have a thirty-two-inch waist. Now turn around."

After much fussing and cajoling, Lettie finally managed to dress Ethan in a corset, a pair of false bosoms, two petticoats, and a bustle pad. Then, before he could complain again that he couldn't breathe and she had to loosen his corset strings for the umpteenth time, she quickly dropped the skirt over his head and handed him a bodice and a waist-length mantle.

She returned and gestured for him to sit on the side of the bed. He strode across the room, swearing at the tangling of his skirts, then whirled and sank onto the ticking, swearing again when his brusque motions caused the corset to jab into his ribs.

189

Lettie only laughed.

"Damn, how do you stand this thing?" he muttered, gesturing to the boned corset beneath his borrowed bodice.

"The only other alternative is flopping around like a two-bit floo—" Lettie clapped a hand to her mouth at her own unguarded words. A well-bred woman did not even discuss the unmentionables she wore beneath her clothing, let alone the effects of going without them.

Ethan's eyes blazed and he whipped an arm around her waist and drew her between his wide-spread legs, so that Lettie's skirts tangled between them. One broad hand rested low on her back, pressing her tightly against him, while the other reached to cup the indentation of her waist just below her ribs.

"I guess I never thought about it much," he murmured, staring at his hand as if fascinated by the firm line of her torso. His thumb rubbed against her bodice, discovering the faint ribbing caused by the boning of her corset. "I suppose you'd get used to it after a while."

His hand began to move up, and Lettie fought to breathe when his thumb continued its brushing foray, finally coming to rest at the bottom of the gusset that cupped her breast.

"Still," he murmured, "I don't think I'd make a very good woman. I'd rather go without."

His thumb continued its insistent brushing, back and forth, and of their own volition, Lettie's hands lifted to rest on his forearms, grasping the firm musculature beneath in support when her limbs seemed to grow weak.

"That's because you're too lean. There's no soft flesh to mold with the corset. You're too hard. . . ."

Her words trailed off and she swallowed past the tightness of her throat when Ethan's thumb lifted to press against the flesh of her breast where it had been pushed above the restriction of her corset. A tingling burst of sensation seemed to shoot through her body, so that she jerked slightly. Her breathing became labored.

"Ah, Lettie, this is madness." Ethan sighed, drawing

her even closer. 'I swore I wouldn't touch you again," he mumbled as if to himself.

She couldn't speak; she could only nod, staring at him wide-eyed as his gaze became piercing and sweet. Azure-hot.

"This is dangerous, Lettie girl," he murmured.

"I know."

"I shouldn't be doing this."

"I know."

"You're too young."

At the word *young*, Lettie tangled her fingers through the hair at the back of his head and tipped his head up.

"I'm not young," she insisted, then covered his mouth with her own.

Their lips met in a hungry melding of mutual desire. Lettie moaned in satisfaction and delight as Ethan pulled her closer, pressing her tightly against him, his arms winding about her waist until she was sure she would be absorbed into his flesh.

Sighing, her hands slipped beneath his arms and around his shoulders. Her knees bent, and she settled onto one of his thighs.

"Lettie," he muttered, breaking away. "We've got to stop this."

Lettie barely heard him. She was inundated by a flood of hunger. A hunger to taste him, smell him, touch him. Her head dipped to place feverish kisses along the line of his jaw. When his head arched back, her tongue swirled around the shape of his Adam's apple.

"Lettie," he moaned, then reached for her, lifting her chin so that he could kiss her again. A hungry, demanding kiss that left no holds barred.

Lettie eagerly matched his ardor, quickly following the pattern of his caresses with those of her own, showing him without words that, although she lacked experience, she was eager to learn.

Ethan groaned and his hand dropped, reaching past her thigh to tug at her skirts until he managed to bunch them at her hips. Then his strong, calloused palm slipped down the worn cotton covering her thigh to cup the back of her knee, lifting her leg so that her hips pressed intimately against his stomach and her thigh brushed against his ribs.

She moaned at the intimate contact of his hard flesh, damning the skirts that bunched between them in an awkward way. She wanted to feel him.

The rattling of a doorknob echoed through the room like a gunshot, followed by a muffled *"Lettie? I've got the basket ready. My lands, what's keeping you?"*

They drew apart, acknowledging the faint call from the hall below.

"I'll be right there, Mama," Lettie answered, hoping the distance would disguise the strained quality of her voice.

"Well, be as quick as you can. Though I'll fix a cold luncheon, we'll still have supper to prepare, you know."

"Yes, Mama."

When the muffled sound of her mother's footsteps faded away, Lettie sagged in relief, dropping her head against Ethan's shoulder.

His chest shuddered in a jagged breath. His hand lifted to brush back the hair that had come loose from her braid and tangled about her face. Though Lettie fought against the realization, she felt him taking an emotional step back.

"I'm sorry."

She drew back, her hand lifting to cup his cheek. "No. I don't want to hear that. You're not sorry."

His brow creased and his jaw grew firm.

"Neither of us is sorry."

Then she framed his face in her hands and kissed him with the fervor penned up inside her, a fervor she knew he could stoke into a raging blaze, knowing deep in her heart that her time with this man would be brief.

And her memories would have to last a lifetime.

14

A few minutes later, Ethan had dressed completely. While Lettie recombed her hair and pinned it to the back of her head in a swirling knot, Ethan had donned a short wing-backed mantle and buttoned it to his chin, swearing at the added covering in the heat of the day. But neither of them suggested leaving the extra layer behind. Too much depended upon the success of their subterfuge.

As soon as he'd finished, Lettie forced him to sit on the side of the bed while she carefully pinned the switches to his head. Despite her efforts to appear casual, Lettie's movements were tender and her hands lingered over each pin, each silky lock of Ethan's hair. His own hand lifted to rest in the hollow of her back, as if he too sensed the tension, the apprehension. But neither of them voiced their fears. Instead, they spoke of trivial matters.

Ethan lifted a hand to the plait coiled at the base of Lettie's neck. "You've pinned your hair up."

She nodded. "I only wear it down when I'm working around the boardinghouse. It's become so long and heavy in the last few years that it makes my head ache to wear it up for very long. I've thought of cutting it but—"

"No," he inserted firmly, lifting a hand to the swirling knot at the back of her head. "Don't cut it."

The memory of the way her hair had hung about them earlier that morning sifted between them like the soft echo of music.

"We'd better go," Lettie murmured finally.

She handed Ethan an old crocheted reticule, then stepped back. When he stood up, she took a deep breath to still the nervousness galloping in her stomach and ran a critical eye over his appearance.

Since he was completely covered from the tip of his chin to his ankles, there was not much of him to reveal his true gender, save his face. The veiling of his bonnet would cover that last detail while the switches she'd pinned to his head would provide him with just enough of a feminine outline to give credence to his masquerade.

"Well?" Ethan prompted.

Lettie frowned in indecision. Below his chin, the wing-back mantle completely covered Ethan's torso, and although his shoulders strained against the garment, the light corseting gave him enough of a feminine shape to get by. The shirt she'd chosen was simple, and Lettie regretted the fact that it was pleated and not gathered, since Ethan's hips were too narrow to be fashionable. She'd been forced to use the longest skirt she could find, however, and this one would have to do. Even so, it only reached his ankles, revealing a pair of Ned Abernathy's old black high-tops.

"The shoes are wrong," she muttered.

Ethan grabbed his skirts, lifted them to his knees, and peered down at his feet, revealing hopelessly masculine calves covered in women's black cotton stockings.

"What's wrong with them?"

"Nothing, compared to your legs."

"What's wrong with my legs?"

"Just keep them covered, Ethan."

He dropped his skirts and lifted his chin, batting his eyes at her in a gesture of coy femininity. "Just what kind of a girl do you think I am, Letitia Grey? I'll have you know I don't lift my skirts for anyone who asks."

Her lips twitched, but the thought of the possible risks their excursion might incur muted her usual humor. She was beginning to regret ever making her foolish suggestion to Ethan. Now she wished he would remain in the garret, where he would be safe.

Ethan seemed to read her thoughts because he murmured, "I have to do this, Lettie."

His voice held an edge of the fierce determination she'd grown to expect from him.

She took a breath, held it a moment, then nodded. Once again, her eyes scanned his appearance. Although Ethan did not look completely like a middle-aged woman, he could at least pass inspection, as long as no one caught a really good look at his face.

"Well?" he asked a second time.

"You look—"

"Like an ass."

This time her lips lifted in a ghost of a smile. "As a matter of fact . . ."

The silence of the garret echoed between them.

"Ready?" she finally asked.

"As ready as I'll ever be in this get up."

She handed him the bonnet and a satchel filled with his own clothes, in case they should meet with an emergency and he should need to change. But one look at his blunt-edged hands had her scurrying toward her bureau again. Retrieving a pair of old gloves she used for gardening, she gave them to Ethan.

"Here, put these on."

He took one look at the dainty-sized gloves and held up his hands. His palms alone were nearly as large as her whole hand. "You've got to be joking."

Lettie took one look and bit her lip in frustration. "We'll simply have to buy you some today. Keep your hands hidden until then. They're a bit too hairy to be a woman's."

"Yes, ma'am."

"And don't talk so low."

"Yes—" He cleared his throat and raise his voice to a high falsetto. "Yes, ma'am."

Lettie shook her head. "You don't make a very good woman, Ethan."

He jammed the black bonnet onto the top of his head and stabbed a hatpin into one of the switches to keep it in place. "Thank you. I'll take that as a compliment."

With a sweeping gesture, Lettie motioned for him to precede her down the steps. "After you."

He'd taken only a few ground-eating steps before she called, "Oh, and Ethan?"

He turned, and their eyes met.

"Please try to walk like a woman." Though her words were light and matter-of-fact, she knew he saw the concern in her eyes.

"Nothing will happen, Lettie," he murmured, and in his voice she heard the slightly bitter edge that told her more clearly than words that he'd been in tight spots before and somehow he'd managed to survive. "We'll slip into town, ask a few questions, then slip back out again."

"I hope so," she whispered.

He crooked a finger and used it to tilt her chin so that he could offer her a reassuring glance. "Hey, I used to do this kind of thing all the time, remember?"

"Yeah, and that's what got you into this mess."

He offered her a wry smile, then pulled the waist-length veiling over his head and moved in tiny mincing steps toward the staircase.

Watching the all too masculine shape of his hips as he descended the stairs, Lettie shook her head and murmured to herself, "Ethan McGuire, you make a sorry, sorry woman . . . but you're some kind of man."

Once out in the hall, Lettie whispered, "Make sure you're as quiet as can be. I think the Beasleys are home from their committee meeting." Gesturing for Ethan to follow her, she led him toward the back staircase.

They had nearly reached the landing, when Lettie looked down to find the Beasleys on their way up. She quickly stepped in front of Ethan to shield his body as much as she could with her own, but the Beasleys stood on the staircase in such a way that they barred anyone else from slipping past.

"Why, Lettie, is this our new boarder?" Alma inquired, coming to a halt. Her crystal-blue eyes snapped with curiosity as she leaned from side to side, trying to catch a good glimpse of Ethan's form.

"Is this the one?" Amelia echoed, standing on tiptoe to peek over Lettie's shoulder.

Lettie's eyes darted from the Beasleys to the landing beyond, searching for an avenue of escape. If anyone were to uncover their subterfuge, it would be the Beasleys. And the Beasleys were not well known for keeping a tantalizing secret to themselves. "Yes," she answered vaguely. "She just joined us last night."

"Why Alma, this is our new boarder!" Amelia repeated in delight.

"Oh. Yes, of course," said Alma.

Alma took a step closer, and Ethan bent his head to shield his face even more beneath the brim of the bonnet. Although the veiling was thick enough to disguise his features, it was not completely opaque in the sunlight that streamed through the windows around the landing.

"I'm Alma Beasley, and this is my sister."

After a beat of silence, her younger sibling supplied, "Amelia."

"This is Mrs. Magillicuddy," Lettie offered reluctantly. When the two sisters waited for something more, she added, "Agnes Magillicuddy."

"Oh?" Alma's brow creased in thought.

The two sisters glanced at each other, then peered in Ethan's direction.

"Any relation to the Beaver Rapids Magillicuddys?"

"No!" Lettie smiled when her answer burst out much too forcefully. "No, I . . ." She drew the ladies aside as if imparting a confidential secret. When she returned, the Beasleys were filled with clucking concern and sympathy.

"We are so sorry to hear about your unfortunate . . . condition," Alma murmured, gesturing with her hand that her lips would remain sealed in regards to that secret. "We were just about to gather our wraps and walk into town for a cup of tea at the hotel. Would you care to join us?"

"No!" Once again Lettie paused to control her tongue. "No, Mrs. Magillicuddy and I were just on our way to the mercantile. Mrs. Magillicuddy wished to pick up a few things before returning for a quick nap."

"Yes, of course." Alma nodded her head in sage agreement. "Best thing for . . . what ails you."

Ethan's snort of confusion was drowned by Amelia's echoing, "Best thing."

"Well . . ." Lettie sighed after a long moment of silence, in which the Beasleys made no move to leave and stood trying to catch a glimpse of Ethan's features through the veiling of his bonnet. "We don't want to keep you ladies from your stroll. Good afternoon," Lettie murmured, taking Ethan by the hand and pulling him after her down the staircase.

Alma and Amelia Beasley turned to watch them with evident interest.

"Amelia?" Alma queried softly. "Isn't that your bonnet?"

"Mmm?" Her sister turned to gaze vaguely down the steps after the retreating duo.

"Isn't that your bonnet?"

"Oh, I don't think—well, yes, it does look like—surely it couldn't be—"

"That's my skirt," Alma interrupted with much more certainty.

"Really?" Her sister glanced at her in confusion.

Both of them quickly dug into the pockets of their skirts to withdraw the spectacles they were too vain to wear in public. They wrapped the handles over their ears just in time to see Lettie and her companion slip into the kitchen.

"You don't think—"

"Surely not."

"But—"

"It is."

"Well, I'll be jiggered," Alma breathed.

"It seems our little Lettie has a beau," Amelia whispered in amazement.

"And despite that ridiculous getup . . . he's got a set of buttocks that could stop a train," Alma added.

After hitching one of the horses to the boardinghouse's buggy, Lettie motioned for Ethan to climb in beside her, carefully watching the yard for anyone who might be studying them a little too intently. Most of the boarders had already gone for the day, however, and her mother was up to her elbows in baking ingredients. Celeste had done little more than glance up at Lettie and "Mrs. Magillicuddy" as they'd placed a stack of coins on the counter and slipped out of the door.

Lettie regarded Ethan's grip of the reins, then sighed and took them from his grasp. At his questioning look, she merely said, "You hold them like a man."

Lightly slapping the reins onto the horse's rump, she guided the buggy to the front of the house, where the boardinghouse butted against one of the side streets a few blocks from the commercial center of town.

"Mother will need me back to help with the evening meal, so we have four or five hours before she'll expect me home. I'll need to go to the dry goods and Mrs. Clark's before we return. I can't delay much, but Mama will understand if I'm a few minutes late. She'll think I've spent the time at Mrs. Clark's. I could drop you in town if you wanted, while I make the condolence call."

Ethan glanced at her, and, despite the thick veiling attached to his bonnet, Lettie saw the fierce determination burning in his azure eyes. "I'll go with you to the Clarks'. I'll need you to ask as many questions about her husband's death as you can."

Lettie nodded, understanding Ethan's frustration and

his impatience to begin investigating the most recent rash of crimes that had been pinned to his name.

"Then I'd like to go to the robbery site," he added.

"Fine." Her voice was low and filled with her own concern. She could only pray that their ruse would work. If not, and Ethan were caught, his actions would simply damn him even more in the eyes of the Star and everyone else.

The boardinghouse was situated within blocks of the railroad station and business district, yet was still tucked far enough away that it remained removed from the usual noise and bustle of town. However, within a hundred yards, Lettie found herself competing for space on the narrow roads with other carriages and wagons intent on reaching the commercial center of town.

Guiding the horse and buggy with practiced ease, Lettie crossed from Main Street onto one of the less traveled side streets west of the railroad tracks, drawing the conveyance to a stop beside a simple whitewashed house.

"You're sure you want to do this? I could leave the basket with Mrs. Clark and you could stay inside the buggy."

Ethan shook his head and firmly stated, "I'll go with you."

"Fine." Despite her calm acceptance, Lettie felt a twinge of nervousness. Mrs. Clark would be the first person other than herself to see Ethan close up in his disguise. If Abby were to suspect he were a man . . .

"Just remember to talk like and walk like a woman."

"Yes, Lettie," he muttered dryly.

"Secure the buggy while I get the basket."

"Yes, Lettie. Oh, and Lettie?"

"Yes?"

"Stop being such a nag."

Lettie climbed from the seat, hiding a smile when she heard Ethan gasp and swear at the unaccustomed restriction of the corset when he tried to follow suit. He still hadn't grown used to the fact that one did not slouch, bend sideways, or breathe deeply in a corset.

Taking the basket of jams and breads from the back of the buggy, Lettie motioned for Ethan to walk beside her instead of slightly behind, then nodded in approval at his tiny footsteps and erect posture.

Climbing the steps to the front door, Lettie dropped the brass knocker against its base, averting her eyes from the solemn black wreath that had been nailed to the lintel.

After a moment, the door creaked open, and a plump matronly woman with ginger-colored hair peeped outside. Her lips lifted into a shaky smile when she saw Lettie on the doorstep, and for a moment, there was a glimpse of her usual good cheer in her silver eyes.

"Hello, Mrs. Clark," Lettie murmured.

"Lettie, how nice of you to call."

"We don't mean to impose on you at a time like this, but . . ."

"Nonsense. Come in." There was a slight edge of desperation to Mrs. Clark's invitation, as if she'd spent too much time alone as it was. "I've got some hot tea on the stove. Please say you'll stay and have a cup."

Lettie glanced at Ethan and saw his slight nod from beneath the veiling.

"If it's not too much trouble."

"No trouble at all. Come in, come in."

Lettie and Ethan stepped through the doorway, and Lettie handed Mrs. Clark the basket.

"Mama asked me to bring this by and to tell you that the church auxiliary has everything arranged for the meal after the services tomorrow. She also asked me to convey her condolences."

Abby Clark reached for the basket. Her lips trembled for a moment before she pressed them together and tried to smile. "How kind. The bread smells delicious. Your mother is such a fine cook." She glanced up, and there was an echo of a familiar twinkle in her eyes. "I'm glad you brought it over. It will give us something to have with our tea."

She gestured for Lettie to precede her down the hall.

"We'll just sit and visit in the kitchen, if you don't mind, Lettie—and of course your guest."

"This is one of our boarders: Mrs. Magillicuddy. Agnes Magillicuddy."

Abby nodded and smiled, but when Ethan did not offer his hand in greeting, she politely refrained from forcing the familiarity. "Pleased to meet you, I'm sure. Come and have some tea."

Abby Clark led them into the kitchen, where she poured tea, sliced bread, and opened a jar of jam. Lettie felt a moment of panic when the portions were placed in front of Ethan, but he calmly lifted the veiling of his bonnet—just enough to eat without revealing his features —then placed the cup back on his saucer. If Abby noticed the dusting of dark hair on his hands, she gave no indication. Instead, she chattered and talked, while Ethan listened patiently, nodding now and again to show he was attending each word.

Lettie tried to tactfully probe for any information that might be helpful to Ethan, but it wasn't until they were leaving and Mrs. Clark was leading them toward the front door that her expression became suddenly bleak. She seemed to sag. Her skin grew pale and white against the deep mourning of her woolen gown. "He wasn't supposed to go last night, you know," she whispered, turning to Lettie. "But he received a message at the last minute. One of the other boys . . . got sick . . . and Silas Gruber asked if he would guard the shipment." Her last words were uttered in a choked voice.

Without speaking, Lettie drew the woman into her arms and rubbed her back, blinking fiercely against the moisture that sprang to her own eyes.

A few moments later, when she and Ethan had stepped into the sunshine and the door had shut behind them, she turned to him, sensing that Ethan had been as affected as she by the echoing sadness that had pervaded Mrs. Clark's home.

"Five years ago, I prided myself on the fact that I never hurt anyone," Ethan muttered. "I started stealing because my mother had been abandoned and we needed to eat." He gazed at Lettie. "But I never thought I'd hurt anyone—only myself."

He took a ragged breath. "But I'm partially responsible for that woman's pain. The man who did this copied *my* methods." His shoulders squared and his hands balled into fists. "But once I find him, he'll pay, Lettie," Ethan muttered. "Whoever did this will pay."

After leaving Mrs. Clark's, they drove out of town, following the road north to where the rail lines from Harrisburg ran parallel to the creek. A huge water tower had been constructed for the freight trains a few years before, when the Petesville line had circumvented the stop in Madison. It was here—while the train had stopped for water—that the latest robbery had occurred.

Long before they'd reached the area, Lettie and Ethan encountered several other buggies headed in the same direction, as well as a few that were evidently leaving the scene. By the time the train had come into sight, they could smell the faint odor of charred wood and could see that the grassway on either side was dotted with at least a dozen onlookers.

Lettie maneuvered the buggy onto a shoulder a few yards away from the train and separate from the other townspeople who had come to see. A chill coursed through her when she saw such blatant destruction for the first time. She turned to find Ethan peering at the shattered boxcar from his vantage point within the buggy.

"Can you get any closer?"

She gestured toward the men a few feet away who were poking through the rubble. "Not without calling attention to ourselves. Some of them are members of Jacob's posse."

He nodded and settled back against the tufted seat, then lapsed into a brooding silence. Lettie glanced at him, and, because of the angle of the sun, she was able to see a shadow of his features through the veiling. A thoughtful intensity had settled over his face.

"He must have panicked last night," he said after several long moments of silence.

"What do you mean?"

'Something must have disturbed his routine, forcing him to make a mistake, the most obvious of which was shooting his witness in the hip. If you want to ensure a man won't talk, you don't shoot him in the hip. You aim for the stomach, or the chest, or the head."

Lettie shivered beneath the obvious intent of Ethan's words.

"Why would the thief want to kill him?"

Ethan's head turned and she grew still, sensing a part of him that she found hard to accept: a harder, more calculating side, one that was infinitely more dangerous than the man she'd come to know over the past few weeks.

"If not for the blast, Clark could have been a witness if he'd survived."

"But he was killed in the blast."

"The thief didn't know that. He was gone by the time the blast occurred, otherwise he would have been killed or injured as well." Ethan gestured to the rubble. "Look at that."

Lettie gazed at the boxcar but didn't know what she was supposed to see. For the most part, very little of the railroad car remained. Most of it lay littered about the charred grass around her.

"He obviously used too much dynamite. He blasted a hole out of the boxcar and destroyed too much of the safe."

"So?"

"That blast shouldn't have happened," Ethan continued. "Not like that." He gestured to the rubble strewn away from the car. "There's too much damage. Any idiot would have known better than to set something like that on purpose. If he'd been within twenty yards of the explosion, he would've caught a piece of debris in the back of the head. Look at the way the force of the charge knocked the other cars off the rails."

"Then why did he do it?"

"I don't think it was done this way on purpose. Not for a simple robbery. I'd say something surprised him, *someone* surprised him. Maybe Clark shot at him or there was a scuffle and the man accidentally shot Clark. Regardless, our man panicked and set the charge incorrectly. He probably high-tailed it out of here and never knew he'd murdered Jeb Clark."

When Ethan grew quiet, Lettie sensed there was more. "Ethan?" she prompted. "What is it?"

Ethan took a deep breath. "It doesn't make sense."

"What doesn't?"

"Up until now, he's been copying the methods of . . ." He paused, then continued: "Copying my methods. But last night, he broke the routine."

"Why?"

"You told me earlier that five hundred in gold was taken."

"And the stocks and bond certificates."

"And he left the paper money." Ethan gestured to the ground, which was covered with shreds of singed paper that had obviously once been part of a stack of dollar bills. "He didn't take the money."

"So?"

"I always took paper over gold. If I was forced to leave something for a quick retreat, it was the gold— gold is heavier and harder to conceal, especially if you're in a hurry and on the run. This man took the gold but not the paper." His hands tightened into fists on top of his thighs. "And yet, he took the bonds. That's stupid. Those bonds can be traced."

"So?"

"So I think our thief is beginning to get nervous. Scared." His voice grew hard. "If that fear takes hold, he'll make more mistakes in the future, dangerous mistakes." Ethan turned to pin her with an intense stare. "Since the authorities think I've trained the man as an accomplice, we've got to find him before one of those errors puts him in his grave and destroys any chance I have to see my name cleared and this bastard hanged for his own crimes.''

Once again, his eyes swept across the area, and then Ethan frowned. Not more than a hundred feet away, his stepbrother, Ned, and another man stood beside their mounts, gazing at the wreckage. There was something vaguely . . . familiar about Ned's companion.

"Lettie, who's that?" he asked, making certain his voice emerged with nothing more than casual curiosity.

Lettie glanced in the direction of Ethan's nod and answered, "That's Mr. Gruber. Natalie's husband. Why?"

"Nothing. He just seems . . . familiar." When the man in question turned toward him, Ethan looked away, then glanced back, realizing Gruber could never see his features through the veiling from that distance.

"What does Gruber do?"

Lettie shifted the reins in her hands. "He's the director of the Thrift and Loan. He and his wife moved here from Chicago a few years ago."

Ethan's eyes narrowed and he motioned for Lettie to head back into town. Although the buggy soon disappeared from the area, Ethan couldn't push away the nagging thought that he'd seen Gruber somewhere before.

The drive back to the dry-goods store was made in silence. Lettie carefully threaded the buggy through the morning traffic that clogged the dusty streets of Madison. Nevertheless, she kept a careful eye for anyone who might be overtly curious about her passenger.

"I'll only be a minute or two," she told Ethan as she brought the buggy to a stop. "You may as well stay here until I'm done."

Ethan nodded and reached for the reins while she backed out of the buggy.

Since Schmidt's Dry Goods was accustomed to her mother's business, it only took a few moments to gather the supplies and arrange for the bill to be sent to the boardinghouse. Then, counting out a few of her own precious coins, Lettie bought a pair of large gloves for Ethan.

"Aren't these a little big for your hands, Lettie?"

Lettie glanced up, startled, when Irma Schmidt, one of the clerks, carefully handed her the parcel wrapped in brown paper.

"They're . . . a gift," Lettie explained quickly, then grasped the package and strode out the door. Irma Schmidt's ten-year-old son scurried after her, carrying the box of supplies.

"If you'll just put the crate in the back, Arnie."

The little boy nodded and hurried to do as he'd been told. "There you are, Miss Lettie."

Lettie smiled and handed him a penny. "Thank you for your help."

The boy took one look at the shiny penny and flashed her a wide grin. "Yes, ma'am!"

"Lettie?"

Lettie stiffened when she recognized her brother's deep voice. Turning, she found him gazing at her from the boardwalk.

"Jacob," she acknowledged formally, fighting the urge to look in Ethan's direction, fearing that even a single glance could betray his masquerade.

Jacob pushed off the boardwalk and strode toward her. "Will you give this to Mama, please?" he asked, his voice slightly cool.

Lettie straightened her shoulders even more. Jacob was evidently still a little peeved about her earlier remarks. "Of course."

Jacob handed her a folded piece of paper. "See to it that she hangs it in a place where everyone can see it."

"Yes, I'll do that."

"Thanks." Jacob turned and tipped his hat in Ethan's direction. "Afternoon, ma'am." Without glancing back, Jacob walked away.

Lettie took a deep breath and climbed into the buggy.

"You two have a fight?" Ethan asked softly.

"I guess so."

"About me?"

Lettie didn't answer. She grasped the reins and quickly maneuvered the buggy into the street.

From the far end of the boardwalk, Rusty Janson stepped from the barbershop and ambled toward the tall, gangly form of Ned Abernathy, who had just ridden into town.

"Goldsmith is just about done," Rusty announced, tucking a hammer beneath his arm and reaching for one of the nails in his shirt pocket. He'd been nailing wanted posters all over town and still had a dozen to post.

"Mmm?" Ned turned to stare at him as if just noting that Rusty had reached his side.

"I said, Goldsmith's about done," Rusty repeated. "Though if you ask me, when he takes off that sorry-lookin' hairpiece he wears, he hasn't got all that much of his own hair to worry about. Certainly not enough to make it worth paying a barber to trim it."

Shaking his head in amazement at the other man's lack of frugality, Rusty struggled to juggle the posters, the hammer, and the nails while attempting to press a wanted notice against one of the roof supports to the barber shop. Seeing his predicament, Ned reached to hold the poster. With a nod of thanks, Rusty grasped his hammer and positioned a square-tipped nail on one corner of the rumpled placard. He hammered the nail into the weathered wood, then repeated the process on each of the remaining corners.

Once the poster was secure, he stood back to eye his handiwork, but Ned continued to hold the paper, not even noticing that Rusty had finished.

Seeing Ned's preoccupation, Rusty followed the line of his gaze, squinting against the glaring light. "Who's that with Lettie?"

When Ned continued to stare, Rusty forcibly removed the man's hand from the poster.

Ned glanced at Rusty in embarrassment, then slipped a finger beneath the muggy restriction of his collar and tie. "Must be Mrs. Magillicuddy. New boarder. Came in last night."

Rusty stared again and his brow creased. "Damn. Have you ever seen a woman that size before?" He shook his head. "Look at her! She must've been raised by some of them African gee-raffes. She's gotta be nearly six feet tall."

Ned didn't speak. He only nodded, his gray eyes following the buggy as it left town in a spray of dust. But he cared little about the larger figure in black. His gaze existed solely for the petite, brown-haired girl driving.

"She's pretty, isn't she?"

"The old crow in black?"

"No. Lettie."

Rusty shook his head and tucked his hammer beneath his arm. "You'd better not let Jacob hear you say that. Hell, I'd sooner take the biddy in black."

15

"What did Jacob give you?" Ethan asked once the buggy had pulled away from the dry-goods store, gesturing to the paper in her hand.

"I don't know." Since she had given Ethan the gloves and they had passed through the main flow of traffic, Lettie handed the reins to Ethan and glanced down, nimbly unfolding the paper with one hand. Her voice became trapped in her throat when the word *WANTED* seemed to leap from the page. Beneath it lay a crude sketch of Ethan McGuire.

Her hands trembled and she gasped, looking up at Ethan. His head had already lifted, and she sensed the way his gaze scanned the buildings and townspeople as they moved through town.

"It seems I'll have more than the Star on my trail, doesn't it?"

"It isn't fair, Ethan. You haven't done anything."

"Life is rarely fair, Lettie girl."

He turned the buggy down the side street that led to the boardinghouse, and Lettie glanced at him with worried eyes, wishing there were something she could do. She felt so helpless and alone in her plight. *She* knew Ethan was innocent. But no one else would ever believe her, and with each moment that passed, the evidence was stacked higher and higher in an appearance of Ethan's guilt.

"Maybe if we could contact someone and tell them."

"Tell them what? That I've been holed up in your bedroom?" He shook his head. "It wouldn't do any good. In the first place, that makes me look even more guilty—hiding behind the skirts of a woman." He glanced down at the somber fabric covering his legs. "Literally. In the second place, we have no proof that what you say is true. You're the only person who knew I was there." Through the veiling, she caught his quick glance in her direction. "And in the third place"—his voice grew husky—"Jacob would see me hanged for something he would consider to be far worse."

"What?"

"Compromising his young sister."

"I haven't been compromised."

"Haven't you?" Through the veiling, she saw his lips tilt in a shallow smile, one she'd come to know so well because it mixed humor with pain. "Admit it, Lettie. You and I have . . . crossed the lines of respectability more than once. Your mother would have a fit of apoplexy if she knew I'd even been *inside* your bedroom, let alone that I've shared that garret with you for nearly two weeks. And now . . ."

Lettie noted the way he glanced down at his hands. Despite the lace edging on the cuffs of his bodice and the new white gloves, they still gave the impression of being masculine hands. Broad, masculine hands. Lettie could remember the first time one of those hands had touched her on the shoulder. It seemed like eons had passed since Lettie had mistaken Ethan for her Highwayman . . . but it hadn't been that long at all.

When he looked up again, Lettie sensed Ethan taking an emotional step backward, as if he believed his own words and thought he had, indeed, compromised her situation. He had no idea that, in Lettie's eyes, he had accomplished just the opposite. He had brought her a memory that would last a lifetime. One she could look back upon with a secret smile and a tingle of pleasure when reality once again became just a little too dull, a little too harsh.

Ethan swung the buggy onto the drive leading to the boardinghouse, then brought the conveyance to a halt next to the barn. The buggy rolled to a stop, and for a moment, there was nothing to break the stillness of the afternoon but the impatient snuffle of the horse.

"I'm glad you came into my life, Ethan McGuire," she murmured.

Ethan shook his head. "You shouldn't be." He paused, then added, "You know I'll have to go, don't you? Once this is over." His voice was low, almost impossible to hear.

"I know." In fact, she'd known for some time. Ethan McGuire could never make a life for himself in her world. She'd been aware of that reality long before his face had become the artwork for a wanted poster. She couldn't imagine his staying in a sleepy Illinois town. She doubted he would ever make a good farmer, and she certainly couldn't see Ethan behind the counter of a mercantile or china shop. He belonged in a world apart from her own: a big city where his innate energy would blend into the hustle and beat of hired carriages, theaters, and restaurants. And even if those obstacles could be surmounted, Madison was a small, straight-laced community. Ethan's drive and tainted past would be as out of place here as a banana plant in clover.

Ethan handed Lettie the reins and stepped from the buggy, then took a few steps before halting and asking, "When I'm gone, will you tell people what happened?"

Lettie didn't like the sound of that question. It sounded much too much like talking about a person after they'd died, but she couldn't tell Ethan that. Instead, she wrapped the reins around the buggy rail and stepped to the ground. "I don't know. I don't know if anyone would believe me if I did." She walked around the back of the buggy, studying Ethan and trying to see beyond the veiling of his bonnet.

The crackle of paper reminded her that she still carried the wanted poster. Crumpling it into a ball, she shoved it deep into the recesses of her skirt pocket. But the pressure of the wadded paper against her hip only served to remind her of just how tenuous her relationship with this man had grown. If they weren't careful, Lettie would probably be forced to tell her story one day . . . and she could indeed be talking about the dead.

She walked around the back of the buggy, studying Ethan's rigid posture. "Like you said before, I haven't any proof that you were ever here. Since I have a reputation for . . . having an overactive imagination, people might not believe me."

She stopped a few feet away from him, and her breathing quickened slightly. "Sometimes *I'm* not sure if this is really happening. Every now and then, I wonder to myself if I'm just dreaming all this." She glanced away from his profile to stare out at the grass and the trees crowding next to the creek line. "I don't think I could bear it if you were to leave without—"

"Lettie . . ."

His voice was filled with warning, but she ignored him and continued as if he had not spoken.

"—without leaving me with some proof of my own."

"Lettie, no."

"I'm not asking you to—" she began quickly, but he turned.

"Yes you are," he interrupted firmly. "Though you aren't saying the words, you want me to make love to you, give you the ultimate proof of my existence." A shade of his usual bitterness coated his words.

She took a deep breath, then finally admitted the truth to herself, despite the way she trembled slightly in fear and shame at her own wantonness. "Yes. I guess I do want you to love me."

"I want you too, Lettie."

"Then—"

"No."

She regarded him in hurt confusion, laying her own turbulent emotions bare within her gaze. "Why?"

"Lettie . . ."

From deep within, she felt the first unfurling bud of an emotion she had tried to ignore, then tried to deny. And knowing they had so little time together somehow gave her the courage to whisper, "I love you, Ethan."

"You don't love me," he denied fiercely.

Her shoulders stiffened beneath an inexplicable pang of hurt. "How can you be so sure?"

"Love doesn't happen in such a short space of time. Not to men like me."

"And are you some expert on the subject?" she bristled. "Are you telling me you've been in love dozens of times and know all about it?"

"No."

She paused. "Then are you saying . . ." Hesitating, she rephrased her question. "Do you love me, Ethan?"

"No."

"You could never love me?"

"Lettie, there's no sense in going over this. As you so eloquently put it, I don't belong here in Madison and you can never escape. Let's just leave it at that." He strode away, moving toward the glider swing that stood a few yards beyond the chicken coop.

Lettie waited a moment, then followed him. He seemed to stiffen at her approach but did not move away. Instead, he reached out idly to push the glider back and forth.

"Could you ever love me, Ethan?" she whispered.

His body grew tense, even as his hand continued to push the glider. Instead of answering her question, he said, "When I leave, you'll have a whole lifetime ahead of you."

"A lifetime in Madison."

"A lifetime with another man."

"Another man who won't be you."

His hand grew still. "I can't tell you that I love you, Lettie. I can't tell you that I care."

"Can't? Or won't?"

There was a long space of silence that was punctuated by the weary squeak of the glider and soft luff of the grass.

"Won't."

"Then you *do* feel something for me?"

Once again, the silence stretched between them. Then Ethan turned. Even as she watched, something within the hard facade he'd built around his feelings seemed to crack. She felt an almost physical pain at the depth of loneliness she saw mirrored in his eyes. He fought to cover his emotions, but the wall he'd built around his heart had grown a little less impenetrable, and his true feelings were still evident.

"Yes. God help me, but I do."

When the reverent silence of the Madison City Thrift and Loan altered slightly, Silas Gruber looked up from his account books and found his wife standing in the doorway to his office—or, rather, preening in the doorway. She was leaning against the molding in such a way that the tight cinching of her waist could not be mistaken. Nor could the lush swell of her bosom and the full sweep of her hips.

When she saw that she had his attention, Natalie threw him a brilliant smile and straightened.

"Busy?"

He hesitated a moment before answering. "As a matter of fact, I am."

"Good. Then I won't keep you."

Lifting her skirts, she glided forward amid a wealth of rustling indigo taffeta and perched one hip on the corner of his desk before leaning toward him. Silas could barely breathe when a soft whisper of lilac water wafted his way, its subtle scent combining with that of sweet feminine skin. His eyes dipped to latch onto the fullness of her breasts, their swells made even more enticing by the extra padding Natalie used, and the taut stretch of taffeta that seemed ready to split from the pressure of the firm mounds.

"Well?" Natalie prompted when he didn't speak.

Silas glanced up at her face. "Well what?"

She laughed and whirled away from the desk, once

again affecting a sophisticated pose. "What do you think of my new hat?"

Silas pressed his lips together, wondering why she'd been brushing up against him like a hungry cat if she'd wanted him to look at her head all this time.

"It's very nice," he muttered. "But now I have other things to do."

She pouted at him in mock disappointment. "Really, Silas, don't get all grumpy and grouchy on me. Aren't you going to ask me about it? Why, you haven't even taken a good look."

Silas's fingers tightened around the pen in his hand, but he obediently looked up at his wife's hat, even though he knew she was simply goading him into asking her where she'd bought it and how she'd obtained the money to buy it.

"It's very nice," he muttered again, barely glancing at the tiny blue bonnet with its swirl of scarlet veiling and spray of ebony feathers.

He glanced pointedly at his account books again. "Now, if you'll excuse me."

Natalie frowned in displeasure and glided toward him, stepping behind his chair and bending low over his shoulder so that he was forced to look at her.

"I think this color does marvelous things for me, don't you?"

"Mmm."

"It makes my eyes seem darker, my skin paler."

Silas cleared his throat, darting a glance out of the windows that surrounded his office above the forest-green wainscoting. A few of his tellers were surreptitiously watching their exchange. "I suppose."

Natalie straightened, then bent over his opposite shoulder. "Aren't you going to ask me where I bought it?"

Once again, Silas's jaw tightened. "No, but I'm sure you'll tell me."

Natalie frowned again in displeasure when he refused to surrender to her baiting. Pulling herself upright, she moved across the room to the door in such a way that her bustle swayed enticingly from beneath the elaborate swags of fabric draped below her tiny waist.

"For your information, the hat was shipped to me on the eight o'clock train from Chicago"—she paused dramatically, glancing at Silas over her shoulder—"along with a shipment containing an entire wardrobe selected from the finest *couturiers* of Europe." Her dark eyes sparkled with silent derision. "*You* could never do that for me, could you, Silas?"

"Natalie, I told you to stop this nonsense," he growled in warning.

"But someone else obviously can," she taunted, barely heeding his words, her chin tilting at a defiant angle. "Someone who is more of a man than you could ever be, Silas Gruber."

Silas rose from his seat with such force that his chair crashed against the back wall. Despite the startled glances of those within the bank, he strode toward his wife and grasped her by the elbows, shaking her. The hat she'd been so proud of threatened to topple from her head.

"Who is he, Natalie? Who have you been seeing?"

Her face twisted in an ugly expression of disgust and triumph. "As if I'd tell you! You're nothing but an old lecherous coward, Silas. You couldn't even stand up to the board of inquiry in Chicago. Instead, you let them send you whimpering and whining to this po-dunk town in the middle of nowhere."

"I *told* you! There was nothing else I could have done."

"Save your excuses for the board, Silas. I don't want to hear them. Since you've been unable to . . . satisfy my needs for quite some time, I've gone elsewhere."

Silas felt his whole body tighten in rage and jealousy. "Damn you, who is he!" he ground out between clenched teeth, his hands tightening around her arms until he could feel the bones beneath his fingers like fragile twigs. He shook her once more for emphasis. "*Who is he!* No one has the kind of money you've been flaunting around. No one here in Madison. No one honest."

She wedged her hands against his chest and wrenched

free. Flinging open the door to Silas's office, she shouted, "I've found myself a man who can be a *gentleman*, Silas. Something *you* would know nothing about."

With that remark, she reached behind her to whip the fabric of her train aside and strode out the door in a rustle of taffeta and lace.

Slowly becoming aware of his surroundings, Silas tugged at the hem of his vest, his skin flushing with a ruddy heat when he met the aghast looks of his employees and one of the local matrons.

Taking a deep breath for control, Silas closed the door with calm deliberation, then turned away from prying eyes. His hands tightened into rigid fists as his wife's parting words seemed to echo about him.

I've found myself a man who can be a gentleman, *Silas. Something* you *would know nothing about.*

Once again Silas felt a burning certainty settling inside of him. For some time, he'd suspected Natalie had been seeing another man. The *Gentleman* Bandit had been his prime suspect. Now he'd heard a confession from her own lips—or at least the closest thing to a confession he was likely to get.

But Natalie would soon see just what kind of a man she'd married. He'd see Ethan McGuire hanged for his crimes. Once and for all.

Striding to the glass partition, Silas threw open the door and bellowed for his assistant to come forward, then returned to his desk.

Supporting a clipboard and a harried expression, Harold Beechum scrambled inside and gently closed the door behind him. When he turned, his lanky frame tensed, as if he expected a physical blow after all that had occurred in his employer's office. "You called, Mr. Gruber?"

"Hell yes, I called! Don't be an ass."

"Y-yes, sir. I mean, no, sir."

"I want you to go to the telegraph office and send a telegram to the effect that since the Madison City Thrift and Loan has received the replacement shipment of gold, it should tighten its security accordingly."

Beechum hesitated, his stubby pencil poised over his clipboard. "Sir?" he asked in confusion.

"Just write it down."

"But we didn't receive a shipment of gold."

"Just write it down."

Beechum cringed and scrambled to do as he was told. "May I ask why, sir?"

"No, you may not ask!" Silas took a deep breath to calm himself and jerked the hem of his vest back into place.

"Who—" Beechum cleared his throat and began again. "Where shall I send the telegram?"

"To myself, at my home address."

"Sir?"

"Just do it, Beechum."

Harold Beechum's normally sallow features grew even more pale beneath his green canvas visor. "But I don't understand."

"Just do it!"

"Yes, sir."

Getting up and crossing toward the safe in the back of his office, Silas reached out to run his hand over its painted surface, already formulating his plans. He allowed a small smile of self-satisfaction to crease his lips. By leaking news of a mythical shipment of gold to his wife, Natalie would take the news straight to the Gentleman Bandit. When Ethan McGuire arrived that night at the Madison Thrift and Loan, Silas would be waiting inside the office to "apprehend" the thief at gunpoint. Then he would turn the man over to Judge Krupp—and the Star Council of Justice. That way, Silas would not only see his wife's lover swing at the end of a rope, but he would probably earn himself a promotion as well.

"Sir, was there anything else?" Harold whispered, obviously wondering if his employer had lost his senses.

"Ever read *Hamlet*, Beechum?" Silas turned to find his assistant regarding him in alarm. "Well?"

"No, sir."

"To paraphrase the old bard: 'The gold's the thing to

catch the conscience of a thief.' " He paused, and his brow furrowed. "That doesn't rhyme, does it?"

His assistant opened his mouth, floundered for a moment, then replied, "No, sir."

Silas merely shrugged and turned back to trace his finger over the swirling floral design painted on the top lip of the safe. "No matter. When the Gentleman Bandit is caught trying to rob *my* bank, the whole state will hear sweet, sweet music."

He glanced over his shoulder, and Beechum offered him a placating grimace that was meant to be a smile. "Yes, sir."

"Well, don't just stand there, man! Go send that telegram."

"Yes, sir."

"And see if you can round up Judge Krupp. I need to talk to him." This time Gruber wanted no mistakes. He would notify Krupp himself of his plans. Then the moment Ethan McGuire stepped into the bank, he would be surrounded by Krupp's men.

Silas glanced up to see his assistant still staring at him with wide eyes. "Go get him, man!"

"Yes, sir!"

Beechum fled from the room with evident relief, and Silas turned back to his safe, running his palms over the cool upper edge. He'd show Natalie just what kind of a man he was. Once she read his telegram—and he had no doubts she would—he'd capture her lover and see him hanged. Then, when she tried to become all pouty and perverse, Silas would shower her in the gold he'd taken from Jeb Clark's train. Cool, heavy, lovely gold.

A few moments later, Judge Krupp entered the bank. While he conversed with Gruber, Stone waited in the shade by the far wall. He smiled and tipped his hat to a pair of pretty women, then glanced up and met the gaze of a fellow member of the Star, Ned Abernathy. The man stood a few yards away, his hand propped against the newel support of the barber shop. Gerald acknowledged the man with a barely perceptible nod of his head, then looked away.

Within moments, Krupp emerged.

"Well?" Stone asked.

"Gruber has set a trap for Ethan McGuire and he wants the Star to dance attendance." His eyes narrowed.

"Do you want me to arrange for some men to guard the bank?"

Krupp's lips thinned. "No. I'll take care of it." He turned to pierce Gerald Stone with a meaningful gaze. "But I think it's time to test the faithfulness of our newest governor. Arrange for Jacob and a few of his men to meet me at the farmhouse just before dawn."

"Yes, sir." He eyed Krupp's rigid jaw and asked, "You're sure you don't want some men at the bank tonight?"

Krupp took a deep breath, and his voice became hard. "No. I think it's time we taught Silas Gruber that he shouldn't take the Star for granted." He settled his hat on his head. "Once he's squirmed a bit, I'll come to his aid."

Gerald grinned. "Yes, sir."

Krupp strode away, heading toward the hotel down the street. After a moment, Stone walked in the opposite direction.

From the alley beside the bank, Ned Abernathy straightened. After the Star had broken into his mother's room, stolen Ethan's watch, and left their calling card on Lillian's bureau, Ned had wormed his way into the secret vigilante group. He'd hoped they could help him learn just how much was known about the Gentleman and when the law intended to strike.

He smiled slightly to himself and ambled back toward the barber shop. It seemed he'd just hit pay dirt.

When Ethan hesitated in front of her, Lettie paused. He stood on the back path, gazing at the boardinghouse door and shaking his head. "I can't go in just yet." He shrugged his shoulders as if already feeling the confines of the garret. His fingers tugged the gloves from his hands and stuffed them into the valise they'd packed with his clothes. "I think I'll take a walk or something."

"Letitia, my dear girl!"

Lettie froze, her fingers digging into Ethan's arm when she recognized Mr. Goldsmith's voice coming from the direction of the barn.

She turned very slowly, motioning for Ethan to move on without her.

"Good afternoon, Mr. Goldsmith."

Though she tried to block as much of Ethan's bustled and beribboned frame as she could, Randolph Goldsmith hurried to greet them, darting his head from side to side in an effort to catch a glimpse of the elusive Mrs. McGillicuddy.

"And who might this charming creature be?" he boomed.

Ethan froze.

Lettie reached out to dig her fingers into his shoulder in a tacit command for his retreat.

"You've met Mrs. McGillicuddy, of course. Everyone knows Mrs. McGillicuddy."

Mr. Goldsmith smiled, refusing to admit he had not received the honor. "Yes, of course, of course. I sat by her last night in the parlor, did I not?"

"Mmm. I believe so. Now, we really must be going."

"Ah, Lettie!" Mr. Goldsmith reached out to snag her arm, forcing her to pause. "Let me give my regards to the lady first."

"Mr. Goldsmith, I really don't—"

He ignored her, brushing past her to stand on the step beside Ethan.

Ethan carefully averted his head so that Goldsmith could not see around the brim of his bonnet, let alone through the veiling.

"She's very shy," Lettie murmured when Mr. Goldsmith glanced back at her for guidance.

Randolph beamed, as if he alone were aware of that sterling quality, and he took personal pleasure in the fact. Clearing his throat, he reached for Ethan's hand.

"My dearest lady." He paused, waiting for some sort of a response. When Mrs. McGillicuddy didn't answer, he once again turned to Lettie.

"She's also hard of hearing," she murmured, trying hard not to laugh.

"My dearest lady!" Mr. Goldsmith boomed. "May I offer you my most humble services and assure you that if there is anything—*anything*—you need of me, please do not hesitate to ask!"

When Ethan didn't answer, Lettie dug her nails into his shoulder. A muffled *youch!* burst from his throat, then a quick, "You are too kind." Lettie rolled her eyes, certain Ethan's high falsetto had given him away. But Randolph Goldsmith merely smiled in delight, reaching up to tug at his hairpiece when it threatened to slip.

Holding one of his hands to his head, Mr. Goldsmith made a deep courtly bow that threatened to split his pants in two and reached for Ethan's hand. When he lifted it to his lips, there was a brief tug-of-war before Mr. Goldsmith won and planted a moist kiss on the back of Ethan's hand.

"Until we meet again, fair maiden!" he shouted, then climbed the steps and backed into the house, smiling and waving as he went.

As soon as he had disappeared behind the screen, Lettie grasped Ethan's wrist and pulled him down the stairs and across the back yard. Racing as fast as she could, she led him to the creek, then dodged behind a screen of trees. Unable to hold her mirth any longer, she collapsed against a tree, giggling uncontrollably, while Ethan glared at her with his hands on his hips.

"You'd best beware, Ethan. He's the Lothario of the Grey Boardinghouse," she gasped.

Ethan whipped his veil over his head and scowled at her. "Dammit, it isn't funny. That man kissed me!"

Lettie merely burst into another fit of giggles.

Deciding she was hopeless, Ethan strode toward the creek, then squatted with legs spread wide to furiously scrub at the back of his hand.

Lettie wrapped her arms around her waist and slowly slid down the trunk of the tree, still laughing.

16

Natalie Gruber waited in the shadows of the Lilac Suite at the Starlight Hotel for nearly an hour before the door opened and her lover appeared. Though they had been using the room for nearly a week, she felt certain that no one had seen either of them come. And when the time came, no one would see them leave.

"Where have you been?" she demanded, still feeling a remnant of pique from her encounter with Silas.

The man's tall form seemed to grow a little more intimidating as he paused and shut the door behind him. The late-afternoon shadows of the room stroked his firm jaw and the blunt features of his face.

"I've been taking care of a little business."

When he refused to elaborate any further, Natalie's hands balled into fists and she whirled to look out the window. "And would that business have anything to do with my husband's bank?" She shot a glance over her shoulder, but the man's features remained neutral, giving nothing away.

Realizing that her anger would get her nowhere, Natalie took a deep breath, forced herself to relax, and offered him a coquettish smile. "Forgive me for being so beastly, darling." She turned and sauntered toward him, ensuring that the sway of her hips was just exaggerated enough to draw attention to the artful swags of her gown, but not so blatant that the man before her knew she was about to begin wending her wiles. "It's just that I've had a frightful day. And to top it all off, I've had another row with Silas."

"Oh?"

She slipped her hands around his neck and toyed with his string tie. "I swear, that man will be the death of me!" Despite her attempt at calm, some of her frustration and anger seeped through. "If Silas had been a little smarter, I would still be a woman of society in Chicago. As wife to the director of the Chicago Mortgage and Thrift, I would have power and prestige." Her voice became low and intense. "And money."

The man's hands moved to grasp her hips and draw her tightly against him. "You have money now."

"Thanks to you." She chuckled at that thought and shot him a look filled with a self-congratulatory smile. She wriggled slightly beneath his hands. "Perhaps I should thank Silas for being such a fool in that respect. If he hadn't been stupid enough to tell me all about the Gentleman Bandit and his robberies, we wouldn't be where we are today." She sidled closer still. "I wouldn't have had such intimate knowledge of the Star. Told you everything I knew." Her voice became low and husky. "Made you mine." Her fingers slipped through his hair, and she lifted herself on tiptoe to press a kiss against the corner of his mouth, his chin, his neck.

Her lover's response was instantaneous. His arms wound more fiercely about her waist until she was pressed so tightly against him that she couldn't fail to read the measure of his passion.

"My lusty stallion," she growled low in her throat. Her arms slid across his chest, then inched up the placket of his shirt. "Why did you wait so long to get word to me if you needed me so?"

Without warning, she grasped the edges of his shirt and ripped it open. Buttons flew, spattering to the ground. Then a silence settled about them, broken only by their strident breathing. The stark flare of passion Natalie saw in his eyes was all she had been waiting to see. She finally had this man right where she wanted him. He *wanted* her. He *needed* her.

He would do anything for her.

When he bent to kiss her, she stopped him with a firm hand on his chest. "I think it's time we did something about my husband."

The man's arms tightened around her, and his eyes flashed in annoyance. "Later."

Studying him a moment from beneath heavy lashes, Natalie placed a kiss in the hollow of his throat. Then, smiling against his skin, she traced a moist line down the center of his breast with her tongue. He shuddered beneath her, his hands clenching into the fabric of her gown. And when Natalie glanced up at him, she knew she would have her way.

Her hands lifted to the buttons of her bodice, and he allowed her just enough space to complete the task, even as his hands roamed her back and his eyes traced the sliver of skin she exposed.

"What do you want?"

She waited until she had unbuttoned the bodice and it hung poised on her shoulders so that he could see she had foregone the use of a camisole and stood bare before him, save for her corset. Then, as her bodice slithered to the floor, she murmured, "I want him dead."

The man before her didn't even pause. Instead, his hands wrapped tightly around her and he bent to place a kiss on the mounding flesh of her bosom.

"I'm sure something can be arranged." His tongue trailed across the exposed skin of her breast and teased the edge of a nipple half hidden by the tatted lace of her corset. "Soon."

"Mind if I get a bite to eat?"

Jacob glanced up from the papers spread over the top of his desk and found Rusty Janson standing at the bottom of the steps that led up to the jail cells on the second story.

"No, go ahead."

"Want anything?"

Jacob absently shook his head. "Nah, I've got some of the pie my mother sent over the first of the week. When I get a minute I'll take a break, read the *Gazette*, maybe have a drink. Right now, I'm trying to sift through the reports the railroad sent over after Jeb's . . ." His voice grew husky, and he cleared his throat. "After the last robbery."

Rusty nodded and straightened, obviously uncomfortable at the reminder of Clark's death. "If you're sure you don't want anything?"

"I'm sure. Thanks."

After snatching his hat from the coat tree by the door, Rusty slipped outside and closed the door behind him. The bell overhead issued a muffled jangle, then grew silent.

Jacob looked up again and watched his deputy stride out of sight down the boardwalk, then bent back over the reports on his desk. A frown creased his brow. For hours now, he'd been studying the reports from the railway theft: printed accounts of physical damages, monetary losses, witnesses' statements. But there was something unsettling about the whole affair. Something more than the death of a friend.

First of all, why hadn't any of the railroad employees seen anyone approach the train once it had stopped? Except for a few trees and some bushes, the water stop was in a virtually clear area. And why hadn't anyone heard Jeb's cries for help, or a shot in the night? Though the Gentleman had never been known to rob a train before, the security for the gold shipment had been amazingly lax. Yet no one had stepped forward to point a finger of blame toward the railroad. The officials were too concerned about placing blame upon an outside influence.

Damn! It just didn't make sense. If was almost as if someone had planned for the robbery to occur. And for Jeb Clark to die.

Sliding open the drawer to his desk, Jacob withdrew

the file of clippings he'd collected over the years. One by one, he lifted the articles from the folder and placed them on the desk until the top was littered with yellowed squares of newsprint. Then he began to place the clippings into one of two piles: Those that had occurred five years before were placed on the left; those that had occurred in the last few months were placed on the right.

For several long moments, Jacob sifted through the information he'd gathered over the past few years, but it was not until the articles had been sorted into separate piles that he began to notice a slight deviation in pattern.

Those on the left were almost identical. Five years before, the Gentleman Bandit had displayed a tendency to steal paper first, then gold—never taking more than he could carry in order to get cleanly away. Once he'd gathered his booty, the man would explode the safe, tack a vellum calling card to the inside of the front door, and disappear into the night before help could arrive.

Jacob's finger nudged the smaller pile of clippings on the right, spreading them onto the desk. In the last few months, the robberies followed basically the same pattern. In most cases, the bills were taken first, then the gold. But the quantities were larger, heavier, as if the man had become greedy in his tasks. And there were slight deviations from form. In Eastbrook, some jewelry had been taken; in Dewey, a bag of coins; the train to Harrisburg, stock certificates. Yet the rest of the pattern remained intact: the destroyed safe, the vellum card, the lack of tangible evidence—but then there had been *one* piece of evidence. The watch at Eastbrook. A watch that reportedly belonged to Ethan McGuire. It was that one piece of damning evidence that had forced the Star to show its hand.

And then there were the murders.

Jacob's hand suddenly stilled over the pile of newsclippings. Five years before, the Gentleman had never hurt anyone. In fact, he had put himself in danger of being caught once or twice rather than see a person injured. Even that night Jacob had nearly caught him in

Chicago, the Gentleman had seen him safely out of the bank.

So why would a man who had shown such respect for life five years earlier suddenly become a cold-blooded killer?

For the first time, Jacob found his instincts balking against what he knew to be true. He couldn't help thinking that Ethan McGuire was not behaving true to form. And although the passage of years between the two sets of crimes could explain the discrepancies, Jacob still felt a tension in his gut—as if he were missing something. Something important that would cause all of the pieces of the puzzle to fall neatly into place.

Shaking off his own doubts, Jacob took a deep breath and scooped the clippings together before dropping them back into the folder. Ethan McGuire was merely slipping in his old age. It was the only logical explanation. After all, it had been five years since the man had supposedly "retired."

The bell to his office door jingled, and Jacob glanced up to find Gerald Stone standing just inside the threshold.

"Got a minute?"

Jacob nodded and casually replaced the folder in his desk drawer.

Gerald closed the door behind him and stepped into the room. There was a certain caution about the other man's manner that put Jacob immediately on his guard.

Gerald glanced behind him. "Anyone but Rusty here?" he asked, with overt casualness.

Jacob eyed the man, sensing he'd come on behalf of the Star. "No. Did you need Janson for something? He's gone to the Mercury for a drink and a bite to eat. I could send for him if you'd like."

"No. No, that's fine." Gerald sat on the edge of the desk and picked up a cast-iron plaque that Jacob kept on his desk as a paperweight. "We're alone, then?" he asked again.

Jacob nodded, keeping his features expressionless, while all the time his heart had begun to beat in his chest with a powerful insistence.

"I just had a chat with Krupp."

Jacob regarded his friend with narrowed eyes. "Oh?"

"We're setting a trap for Ethan McGuire tonight. Gruber has leaked word that a mythical shipment of gold has already arrived in town . . . unannounced. Krupp's planning on having his men guard the place in case someone might be planning to take it during the night. He wants us to be ready to back him should he need us."

"Us?" Jacob repeated.

"You. Me. Our men." He threw Jacob a meaningful glance. "Krupp has this feeling that the Gentleman will take the bait and make an appearance."

"The thief would be a fool to try anything so soon after Clark's death."

"Nevertheless, we're to be there, just in case."

Jacob waited a moment before adding, "On behalf of the Star."

"On behalf of the Star," Gerald repeated, reaching into the inside pocket of his vest. "Since you're now a part of the governing board, you're to memorize this list of members who are subject to your orders. Once you've committed the names to memory—"

"Burn the paper."

"That's right."

Jacob hesitated only a moment before reaching for the list. Skimming the names, he found himself slightly shaken by the number of men involved, men who would be subject to his orders and would follow them to the letter, whatever those orders might be. There was Mason Whitby, the blacksmith; Adolph Schmidt, the owner of the dry goods—even Randolph Goldsmith.

"There are a lot of names here," he commented needlessly.

Gerald shrugged. "Not really. Old Krupp's got the major portion of the group. His battalion's about twice what you've got."

Jacob glanced at him in surprise, then looked at the list again. Each man's name had been written beneath that of the contact from the outer circle of assistants and the location of his communication station. The Johnston farm serviced only a fraction of Jacob's group of men.

"Come dawn, Krupp wants you and a few of your men to meet him at the Johnston farmhouse—you won't need the entire battalion tomorrow; three or four men should do it. You're to tell Rusty which men you wish to employ. He'll notify them all tonight."

"Rusty knows the identity of the governors?"

Gerald nodded. "He was Clark's lieutenant. We figured you wouldn't mind if he kept his position."

"No," Jacob answered quickly. "No, I don't mind. What if Krupp needs our help before dawn?"

"We'll let you know."

Jacob nodded. "And if we apprehend the Gentleman, we execute?"

"No."

Jacob looked up in surprise.

"Not immediately. If the man is caught, the Star wants McGuire's guilt to be fully exposed to the public before his execution—just so things appear nice and tidy when he winds up dead. We'll have you keep the Gentleman under guard at the Johnston farmhouse so that it appears he's escaped again. That will create a stir in the town, what with Clark's death and all. By the time we actually execute him, the townspeople will be singing the praises of the Star."

"But—"

"Are you questioning orders?"

Jacob took a deep breath, then finally murmured, "No."

"Good," Gerald replied firmly. Then he stood up and stepped toward the door, settling his hat over his head. "Tell your sister I said hello, will you? She's a pretty thing. Smart."

Jacob felt his blood turn to tiny shards of ice.

"Yep, she's a right pretty girl. It'd be a pity if anything had to happen to her, especially with the two of you being so close. Course, nothing could go wrong if you follow your instructions and see to it that Ethan McGuire doesn't escape you again." Throwing Jacob a deceptively congenial smile, Gerald opened the door and lifted a finger to the brim of his hat. "Night, Jacob. Let me know if there's anything I can do to help."

The door closed and shuddered slightly within its frame, but Jacob barely noticed. He was staring instead at the place where Stone had been, while a cold fist seemed to close around his heart.

The Highwayman joined me by the side of the old beaver dam. The afternoon fairly dripped with heat. The sky hung low and stormy, filling the air with its heavy hand. I had escaped from the house and come to the water, hoping for a breath of air, a whisper of a breeze. But the stagnant weight of the approaching storm seemed to smother all motion, save for the rhythmic lapping of the creek.

My eyes closed, my neck arched, and I lifted a hand to wipe away the perspiration that gathered beneath the thick weight of my hair. Thinking I'd heard a whisper of sound—like a breath of air ruffling through the grass—I let my hand slip around my neck and unfastened the first button of my bodice. Then the second. And the third. Soon my blouse gaped, ready to catch the slightest breeze, the first stirring of air.

Still standing with my eyes closed, I reached for the satin ribbon beading the edge of my chemise. Slowly, ever so slowly, I drew the ribbon free from its bow.

It was at that moment I heard him gasp.

My eyes flew open, and I whirled toward the stand of trees beside me. Fear shuddered through my veins as I sought to pierce the darkness for the source of that single betraying sound. Then a shadow stepped away from the gnarled cottonwood not five yards away.

My Highwayman.

For some reason I have been unable to fathom to this day, the fear seeped from my body and, with it, my resistance to his charm. As he moved closer, my breathing quickened, my heart began to pound. But not with fear. No, something else began to throb in my veins. Something hot, and urgent, and aching. With each step

*he took toward me I grew more restless, more wanton.
Until, stopping only a few inches away—so close that I
could feel the heat of his body, smell the musk of his
skin—he reached out to touch me.*

*One single finger, clad in black leather, slipped be-
neath the edge of my bodice and slid the garment from
the curve of my shoulder, all without touching my skin,
so that I felt only a whisper of warmth, a shiver of need.*

*He looked up at me just once, his eyes glittering
darkly before he glanced down at the firm curves of my
breasts. They thrust above the tight lacing of my corset
and threatened to spill from the edge of my chemise. He
gazed at them, long and hard, for several moments.
Until they ached. I ached. Then he smiled and reached
out to touch me. . . .*

Lettie moaned sleepily, opening her eyes. As if she
had conjured his image, she found Ethan squatting beside her. The late-afternoon sunlight stroked the dark
waves of his hair and haloed his features until he appeared more fantasy than reality. He'd changed into the
clothing he'd had in the valise, clothing that only seemed
to emphasize his strength, his masculinity.

His finger reached out, grazing the curve of her cheek,
before dipping down to circle her lips. His eyes were
dark, intense, as if he had been able to sense a portion
of her fantasies.

"You fell asleep for a few minutes. Perhaps you should
go to bed for an hour or two," he murmured.

She smiled, wondering if he had intended the double
interpretation that could be attached to his words.

"Tired?" he asked softly.

She nodded. "I never seem to get enough rest."

His eyes seemed to grow serious. "That's because
you spend too much time with me."

She shook her head. "No. Not enough time."

A shuttered look slipped over his features, and, not
for the first time, Lettie knew that her words had caused
a silent battle within him. For years, Ethan had convinced himself that he was somehow unworthy of life's

gentler emotions. And her own joy at being with him seemed to fill him with distrust.

"You don't know what you're saying," Ethan murmured after a few moments of silence.

But Lettie found it hard to concentrate on what he was saying. His finger had begun to stroke back and forth across the fullness of her lower lip, scattering all possibility of coherent thought.

Her lips parted and her tongue darted out to tease his finger before disappearing again.

Ethan groaned.

She smiled, feeling a delicious thrill at becoming the temptress for once.

He reluctantly pulled his finger away, closing it into his fist, as if Lettie would come looking for it unless he hid it. His gaze flicked away, then returned to lock with her own. "You're playing with fire, Lettie girl," he whispered huskily, his jaw tightening.

Her chin tilted and her smile filled even more with womanly seduction. "I've told you, Ethan: I'm not a *girl*."

Her hands reached out to twine behind his neck, pulling him forward. Knocked off balance, Ethan fell to his knees, bumping his chest to hers before he could push himself upright. He tried to draw back. Lettie followed.

"Lettie," he sighed, reaching up to try and unclasp her hands.

Inexplicably hurt by his actions, she allowed herself to be pushed away.

He stood up and walked a few feet away.

"Why, Ethan?" she asked after the silence seemed to become smothering. "Why are you always pushing me away?"

He sighed, shoving his hands into the pockets of his trousers. "I told you my conditions. There can be nothing more between us than a few stray nights. And for once in my life, I'm trying to do the right thing. I'm no good for you, Lettie."

She waited, sensing there was more.

"I haven't always been honest, Lettie. You know

234

that." He turned, and his eyes gleamed with self-disgust. "After the death of my father, my mother remarried. Her second husband was a bastard. He wasted my mother's inheritance, then left her when the money was gone. We had to eat." His head dipped and his shoulders lifted ever so slightly in a self-deprecating shrug. "And do you know what? I liked it. Damn, my heart used to race so hard! I never felt so alive. When I was stealing, I felt vindicated. My stepfather had never been able to support my mother. But *I* could. I could support her and *his* children as well. And no one ever knew where the money came from. No one but me and my stepbrother."

He moved slowly toward the creek. "I developed quite a reputation for myself. No one could catch me. And except for your brother's half-formed suspicions, no one had the slightest idea who I was." He laughed, but the sound was bitter. "Then one morning, my stepfather returned with a fortune that made my efforts look puny. And I woke up and realized I couldn't look at myself in the mirror. I didn't like that feeling."

He turned to gaze at her with eyes that had grown dark and fierce. "I swear, Lettie, I haven't done anything illegal in the last five years and—damn, I was so close to that pardon! So close. Because I'd never killed anyone, I was granted leniency. All I had to do was restore a bulk of the money I'd stolen. The money had to be earned in honest labor, and I had to stay out of trouble with the law for five years. Now they'll never believe me. They'll never believe that I've been honest or that I'm not responsible for the latest robberies."

She walked toward him, reaching out to slip her arms around his neck and hold him close. He grew stiff at first, then, bit by bit, he relaxed until his arms wrapped around her and he held her to him as if he would wither and die if she let go.

"They'll believe you, Ethan. When the true criminal is found, they'll believe you."

He shuddered against her in evident disbelief.

"*I* believed you with much less than that."

He twisted his head to bury his mouth into the hair

spilling around her nape. "I'm not quite the hero you think I am. In fact, I'm the worse kind of bas—"

"No." She forcefully stopped his words with her fingers. "The true criminal will be found and you'll be given your pardon. Then we'll find some way of being together. You have to believe in that."

When he gently disengaged himself from her embrace and turned away, Lettie glared at him in frustration. "Damn you, Ethan McGuire! Don't turn away from me as if I were some child painting rainbows for you."

"Then what are you doing?" he demanded, facing her. "Even if I were to gain my pardon by some miracle of chance, what good would it do me? Do you actually think your brother is going to allow you to become involved with a man like me? Pardon or not?" He issued a short bark of sarcastic humor. "Jacob isn't going to take lightly to your being involved with a man who has any kind of a blemish on his past, let alone a criminal record, like mine."

"I am not living my life for my brother!"

"Well, maybe you should!" he shouted, then quickly lowered his voice. "I'm bad for you, Lettie."

"In what way?"

"No woman should be shackled to a man like me."

"Stop waltzing around what you're really thinking. The only person concerned about your past is you!"

"All right then." He scowled and advanced toward her, stabbing the air with his index finger. "I am incapable of the emotions you want from me, Lettie. The years have bled me dry of anything but disappointment." His head dropped and he seemed to suddenly become aware of the fact that she was advancing toward him. "Lettie, what the hell are you doing?"

"Even if I believed you, I have love enough for both of us, Ethan McGuire." She was within mere feet of him now, and she closed the distance. "But I happen to know you're lying. The years may have bruised you a little, but a gentle, loving man still exists within you," she murmured, lifting her hands to the spot low on his chest where the placket of his shirt gaped open.

"Lettie—"

Her fingers began to nimbly unbutton his shirt.

"Did I ever tell you that I used to dream of a man like you, long before you came?"

"The Highwayman," he breathed, revealing that he'd read the fantasies recorded in her notebook.

"The Highwayman," she confirmed.

"Lettie—"

As her fingers uncovered a swath of flesh down his chest, he tried to fasten the buttons behind her.

"I think you'll admit that my dreams were rather detailed . . . and just a little risqué," she whispered, glancing up at him. When her lips tilted in a mischievous smile, he seemed to forget the fact that he'd been trying to button his shirt.

Savoring each second as if it were a delicate wine, she unfastened the last button, looked up to gauge Ethan's expression, then lay her hands flat against the flesh of his chest.

Ethan took a shuddering breath.

"Dammit, Lettie, this isn't a good—"

"This is a fine idea, a wonderful idea," she interrupted smoothly, her thumbs extending to rub against the soft brown patches of his nipples. His skin was warm and firm beneath her palms.

"Oh, hell," he muttered in surrender, before reaching out to cup his hand behind her neck and drawing her toward him for his kiss.

Their lips met in hungry anticipation, made all the more sweet by the fact that it had seemed so long—too long—since they had held each other this way and touched, embraced. Hungrily stepping closer, Lettie's hands slipped around Ethan's neck to hold him tightly against her, until the combined heat of their flesh seemed to meld together in a tantalizing manner.

He broke away once, his lips eagerly tracing her chin, her eyes, her ears, moving across the delicate contours of her face in scattered abandon.

"Damn you, Lettie, why can't you leave well enough

alone?'' he whispered, more to himself than to her, his voice thick with his own desire.

"Because I can't bear to see you aching."

He drew away, ever so slightly, and clasped his hands around her hips, pulling her against him in such a way that she could not deny the evidence of his arousal. "I'm aching now."

She shuddered beneath the stark passion she saw in his eyes. "Ethan." Her hands curled around the gaping placket of his shirt in support when her knees threatened to give way. "I want you to love me."

"Nothing has changed, Lettie. I can't give you anything more than this," he muttered, before pulling her tightly against him, taking her weight and lifting her so that his lips could hungrily take her own.

Her arms wound around his back, feeling the power of his shoulders and the strength of his arms. She felt no fears being so close to him, no inhibitions. It was as if the two of them had been fashioned for each other—two halves to a whole. She knew his thoughts, his desires, as if they were her own, and she knew just how to please him with soft caresses of her hands and hungry kisses. The effect of his passion was heady, the depth of his desire exhilarating, because he wanted her—her! Not some black-haired, dark-eyed temptress with natural curl in her hair and a wanton swing to her hips. Ethan wanted her! Plain, ordinary, brown-haired, brown-eyed Lettie Grey.

Gasping slightly, Lettie broke away. Ethan regarded her in confusion, obviously taken aback by her sudden retreat, until he saw the mischievous glint in her eyes.

"What are you up to?"

"Not a thing," she retorted, but her hands were lifting to the back of her head to remove the pins still holding the coils in a tight knot against her nape. With utter disregard to their value, she flung the hairpins into the grass, backing away.

Ethan obligingly followed, his eyes burning with his own desire.

"You are a sinful, wanton creature, Lettie Grey."

"Yes, I am, aren't I?" Tunneling her fingers through her hair, she pulled it free, then shook her head so that her hair rippled down her back in a wealth of braid-crimped waves.

"Your mother would be shocked and appalled if she knew."

"Mmm. No doubt."

"Your brother would lock you away."

"No doubt at all." She offered him a smile rich with her own delight and desire. "But if you can catch me, I'll give you a kiss."

When he dodged toward her, she issued a muffled shriek and grasped her skirts, running down the creek bank. Within seconds it became apparent that Ethan could catch her any time he wished and she was only delaying something they both wanted to happen.

Giggling and breathing hard, she jumped onto the trunk of a fallen tree that stretched over the water and dammed the flow, creating a shady pool. When Ethan jumped up behind her, she backed away, still laughing and trying to catch her breath.

"You are an evil, evil man, Ethan McGuire," she murmured, giggling. Her hands dropped to her bodice and she began to unfasten the hooks at her neck, shoulders, and sides. "Compromising a young, innocent girl."

Ethan stopped, regarding her with a scaldingly thorough look when she stripped the garment from her shoulders and threw it onto the bank. She could almost feel the touch of his gaze as it slipped from her shoulders to the tatting of her camisole, to the firm mounds of her breasts. "You're the one taking your clothes off," he retorted, lifting his eyes, but his voice was slightly husky.

She only smiled. "I am, aren't I?"

Though she knew he tried not to look again, Ethan's eyes dipped to trace the soft skin of her shoulders. Once more, he studied the handmade lace edging her camisole, the thrusting mounds of her breasts, the tight shape of her torso, and the small span of her waist within the sturdy black corset she wore.

When his gaze lifted once again to the swells of her

breasts, Lettie could barely manage to breathe as she felt them tighten beneath his gaze, thrusting wantonly against the worn fabric of her camisole.

"I've told you before that I'm not a girl, Ethan McGuire. I'm a woman."

He didn't speak; he merely moved toward her and pulled her to him, crushing her against his chest and covering her mouth with his own. Willingly surrendering to his embrace, her own arms wound about his chest and she lifted herself on tiptoe, nudging her hips against his.

Ethan gasped, wavered.

Too late, they both realized they were balanced upon the slippery bark of the tree. Flailing for something to hold on to, Lettie felt her feet slip and grasped Ethan around the neck, then squealed as they both tumbled sideways into the water.

They emerged, sputtering and laughing, the cool delicious water lapping against their waists as they scrambled to their feet, holding each other for support. Then, without warning, a stillness settled around them when Ethan glanced down at the wet fabric plastered against the curves of Lettie's breasts.

"Lettie," he moaned, his hands rubbing up and down her arms.

"Don't leave me aching this way, Ethan."

He closed his eyes and clenched his teeth. "You're making this very difficult."

"I'm trying to make things easy. Love me."

His hands curled around her arms and he finally opened his eyes, but he did not meet her gaze. Instead, he stared over her head, an expression crossing his face that warned her he was seeing things better left in the past.

"I wish things could be different, Lettie," he stated slowly.

"I know."

His broad hands cupped her shoulders and his thumbs moved in a slow, sweeping motion across the delicate ridges of her collarbone.

"You're some kind of woman, Lettie."

Her lips tilted in a sweet smile. *Woman*.

"I wish I deserved you."

"You do."

"I can't be what you want me to be, Lettie."

"You *are* what I want you to be, Ethan. You're noble, and strong, and brave. And you're real."

He shuddered slightly, then drew her tightly against him and murmured against her nape, "I'm sorry I dragged you into all this."

"I'm glad."

He drew back, and one hand lifted to push the wet hair away from her cheek. "I wish I could give you more."

Very tenderly, she took his hand and laid it upon her breast, then drew close to his body so that she could rest her head upon his chest. "Then give me all you can . . . and let tomorrow take care of itself."

He shuddered against her.

"Love me, Ethan McGuire."

He drew away, then stepped out of her embrace. She shivered in disappointment, thinking she'd said too much, her arms wrapping around her waist and bereft of his warmth.

At the edge of the bank, he stopped.

"Think about it, Lettie." He turned to pierce her with a dark azure stare. "Think about the consequences and think about the price. Then, if you ask me again . . . I won't say no."

From the trees several yards away, the soft, almost imperceptible rustle of leaves whispered a warning that was never heard. Ned set the heavy sample cases of buttons and lace on the ground and leaned against a tree for a moment to catch his breath. It seemed the valises grew heavier and heavier each day. He'd cool off for a moment at the creek.

Glancing up, Ned felt his heart pound deep within him when he saw the couple a few yards away. Drawing back into the shadows, he watched, barely breathing as Lettie's arms slipped around the man's waist. The dark male head was bent, but Ned had no doubts about the man's identity.

Ethan.

Ned's fingers curled into the rough bark of the tree, and he fought against the rush of anger and jealousy. Once again, his brother had bested him. Ethan had told Ned he was leaving the country, but he'd apparently stayed to woo Lettie Grey.

A slow burning pain began to eat at his heart. "No," Ned whispered softly to himself, something crumbling deep inside. "No . . ."

17

In order to avoid as much suspicion as possible, "Mrs. Magillicuddy" dressed in her afternoon finery and crept up the back stairs once Lettie had ascertained that no one was using the kitchen. After what Lettie thought would be a safe interval, she also ducked through the back door and headed toward the stairs. However, she'd only taken a few steps before she looked up to find her mother on her way down.

Celeste's gaze lifted disapprovingly from the muddy toes that peeked beneath Lettie's skirts to the sodden skirts and then the shoes and stockings Lettie held in her hand. "May I ask where you have been?"

"I went wading."

Her mother eyed her soaking skirt and dry bodice but merely shook her head and muttered, "Saints preserve us," before she edged around Lettie's sodden form and bustled into the kitchen. "Ten minutes," she called behind her. "Then I'll need you to help with supper."

"Yes, Mama."

More calmly, Lettie climbed the rest of the stairs. Once at the top, she nearly bumped head-on into Natalie Gruber.

Natalie eyed the condition of Lettie's clothing in the

same manner a schoolmarm might eye a disruptive student. "Wading?" she asked, the tone of her voice expressing her doubts about Lettie's choice of activities.

"Mmm," Lettie answered noncommittally.

Natalie's eyes once more slipped from head to toe. "It's a shame you don't have the money to do something with your appearance. Still, I suppose there are some men in the world who find that quality . . . intriguing."

Lettie clamped her jaw shut to keep from saying something rude.

Giving the younger woman a wide berth, Natalie held her skirts against her body and stepped around her toward the stairs. She'd taken only a few of the steps before she turned and asked, "Do *you* like my hat, Lettie?"

Lettie glanced at the tiny flirtatious bonnet poised on the top of Natalie's black curls.

"It's very nice," she answered, keeping her voice as bland as possible.

"Yes. It is, isn't it?" Throwing her a quick smile, Natalie turned and descended the steps in a rustle of indigo taffeta and lace. Once in the kitchen, she was stopped by Celeste Grey, who handed her a telegram.

"This just arrived for your husband. Will you see he gets it?"

Natalie took the piece of paper, and, without respect for the fact that her name had not been included on the front, she slit it open and read the contents. A tiny smile tugged at her lips. "Yes, thank you, Mrs. Grey. I'll see to it that it falls into the . . . proper hands."

Within moments, Natalie had ridden through town and tied Silas's buggy to a tree behind the Mercury Saloon. Then, moving quickly through the back alley, she made her way down the block to the Starlight Hotel.

Waiting until she was sure that no one had followed her, she slipped through one of the side doors and hurried toward the Lilac Suite. Twisting the key in the lock, she stepped into the false twilight caused by the drawn drapes. Regardless of the lack of light, her gaze moved toward the bed, and she smiled.

Sauntering forward, she tossed the telegram toward the man lying within the twisted sheets. Then her hands began the task of ripping her buttons from their holes with unrestrained eagerness. "It was delivered to the boardinghouse, just like you thought." She pouted. "But if you knew what it contained, why did you make me interrupt our afternoon to retrieve it?"

She watched as he scanned the telegram, then tossed it to the ground.

"I had an errand of my own to run. I thought it best to insure the information I'd been given was correct." His eyes slipped over her figure. "Even you should know that a good criminal always double checks every contingency. This time it was almost worth having you dress."

She smiled and dropped the bodice to the floor. "Almost?"

His eyes became hot and intense as he watched her slip the button free to her skirts and petticoats, unbuckle her bustle, then push the layers to the floor.

"Almost." She could hear his breathing become ragged in the quiet of the room. "You do know how a man likes to see his woman wearing a hat."

She smiled, moving toward him wearing nothing but the flirtatious hat, corset, and stockings. At the edge of the bed, she lifted one foot and began to roll the silk hosiery down to her ankles. She tossed first one stocking to the floor, then the other, then lifted her hands to the busc of her corset.

"Well? What about Silas?" One by one, she snapped the metal hooks to her corset free. When the garment fell to the ground, she paused and waited for his answer.

He rose from the bed and knelt on the ticking, drawing her close. "It appears he won't live to see daylight." His hands lifted to frame her face and his fingers dug into the skin of her cheek ever so slightly. "Tomorrow, I want you to reserve a ticket on the first train to New York. I'll meet you at the Empire Hotel Sunday at noon in a room reserved for Mr. and Mrs. Smith."

She chuckled softly. "Mrs. Smith?"

"By the end of the month, you and I will be bound on a steamer for Paris, where we'll live like royalty."

Natalie smiled and took a deep breath of self-satisfaction. She liked the sound of that word. *Royalty*. After all she'd suffered in the last five years because of her husband's stupidity, she deserved to live like a queen.

Her hands slipped around his shoulders and she leaned toward him, forcing him flat upon the mattress. As she ran her fingers through his hair, then down the planes of his chest, she purred in delight. "Does this mean that you have a plan?"

He smiled and slipped the diamond hatpin free, then tossed it and the bonnet to the floor.

"I have a plan." He gazed up at her, his eyes sparkling with a hidden pleasure. "And when we're done, everyone will believe that Silas Gruber and the Gentleman Bandit perished at each other's hands at the Madison City Thrift and Loan."

Lettie wearily slammed the door to the cellar shut and dragged the rug back into place. Although all of the windows and doors had been thrown open to catch the slightest breeze, there was none to be caught. The night settled about the house like a thick, sultry blanket, making all but the most necessary tasks too insurmountable to even consider attempting.

"Lettie?"

At the deep tone of her brother's voice, Lettie turned. Jacob stood in the threshold leading into the hall, his hat in his hand.

Lettie felt a pang of concern when she saw the exhausted set to his features. He looked so tired and alone, as if the pressures of his job were almost more than he could bear.

A strained silence seemed to stretch between them, underscoring the fact that the two of them had not parted on the best of terms. Finally, needing to show some semblance of normality, Lettie tried to smile.

"Good evening, Jacob. How have you been?"

He stepped into the kitchen from the hall, idly slapping the brim of his hat against his thigh. When he didn't speak immediately, Lettie's smile faded and she murmured, "I think Mama's upstairs. I can get her for you."

"No. No, I didn't come to see her."

Lettie waited for Jacob to explain why he'd come, but when he still didn't speak, she asked, "Have you had supper yet? There's some greens left, and a few potatoes."

"No." Jacob lifted his head to regard her with watchful eyes. "I just came to . . ." He hesitated, stiffened, then continued more forcefully: "Tell me the truth, Lettie: Have you seen Ethan McGuire since that morning in the barn?"

Lettie grew cold, still. Her heart began to pound fiercely in her breast. "No."

Jacob stared at her, his eyes dark and cloaked. Then he placed his hat on his head and turned to leave.

"Jacob!" she called when he was nearly out of the room.

He twisted his head to glance at her over his shoulder.

"Why—" She halted and tried to appear as casual as possible. "I told you before that I hadn't seen him. Why would you ask me again?"

"A secret shipment of gold has been delivered into town."

Lettie felt a cold lump settle in her stomach.

"Oh?"

"Mr. Gruber's afraid that the Gentleman might make an appearance."

He turned to leave, hesitated, then glanced over his shoulder and said, "I'm sorry if I wasn't the brother I should have been, Lettie. I only wanted to see to it that you weren't hurt."

She gazed at her brother with sad eyes, realizing that things could never be the same between them. Even if they could patch up the strain that existed between them now, Jacob would never be able to return to his former role as an overprotective dictator. Because Lettie could never return to her role as a child.

"I don't say it often enough, Lettie, but . . ." He

glanced down at his hat, then looked up at her again. "I love you, little sister. I'm so proud of you. I'd do anything to see you happy."

Lettie's throat seemed to tighten in surprise and unexpected tears. For a moment, Jacob seemed to be looking at her as if he'd never seen her before. His eyes were dark and inscrutable. His brow furrowed as if he were debating some weighty problem. Before she could speak, however, Jacob had turned and walked from the room.

"Jacob?" She took a step forward, then picked up her skirts and ran after him. "Jacob!"

By the time she reached the porch, Jacob had already mounted his horse and ridden from the yard. Grasping the porch support, Lettie watched him go, the cold heavy sensation still lingering in her stomach. Something had upset her brother, something more than the recent tension between them. It was almost as if . . .

He'd come to warn her.

Lettie's breathing came quick and sharp and her limbs began to tremble. But had Jacob come to warn *her*? Or had his warning been intended for Ethan?

Jacob brought his mount to a slow halt and glanced over his shoulder. His sister had returned to the house.

Taking a deep drag of the heavy air, Jacob prayed that his suspicions would prove unfounded. He prayed that Lettie was indeed ignorant of McGuire's whereabouts.

But if Ethan McGuire appeared that night at the Madison Thrift and Loan, Jacob would have to believe that tiny voice within him that whispered Lettie was not as innocent in this affair as she appeared.

And all this time, she'd known just where to find Ethan McGuire.

Lettie moved back into the kitchen, her movements slow and automatic. Sighing, she clasped her skirts in one hand and bent to grasp the handle of the huge copper laundry tub she'd dragged into the middle of the floor only moments before. Just as it did every week, wash day had once again approached. Tomorrow morning, Lettie would be relieved of helping with meals so that she could attack the pile of linens, dishcloths, and boarders' clothing in need of washing.

Pulling the tub outside and across the back porch, Lettie left it lying next to the railing where no one would trip over it, but in a spot where it would be safe until the next day. Since the copper pot was kept in the cellar between laundry days, it was easier to remove the tub the day before she needed it, rather than fight the morning rush.

Turning toward the creek, Lettie rested her hands on her hips and gazed out toward the golden ball of sunlight hovering high above the treetops beyond the creekline. Lands, it was hot! Despite the fact that the day was finally beginning to wane, the muggy air seemed to cloak her in a lethargic haze until it was all she could do to draw breath into her lungs and let it out again. Most of the boarders had abandoned the house for the thick shade to be found on the front porch. There they could sit and talk about the activity they could see in town or the neighbors that strolled by on their way home to supper.

Lettie could only wonder how Ethan was faring in the sultry heat of room five, where he'd spent the afternoon. She'd been able to see him just once—briefly—when she'd brought him his lunch tray. Since she'd also brought more maps and periodicals, she assumed he'd spent most of the afternoon poring over the diagrams and dated newspapers that held articles on the latest raids of the Gentleman Bandit.

"It's hot today, isn't it?"

Lettie started at the low voice behind her and turned to find Ned Abernathy staring at her from within the doorway to the kitchen.

"Hello, Ned." When his stare became intense and a little uncomfortable, she turned away, ostensibly to study the dusty grass baking in the late-afternoon sun. "Yes. Yes, it is hot."

She heard the clump of his boots across the weathered wood of the porch and knew the moment Ned stopped, directly behind her. There was a space of silence, then she heard him take a breath.

"Lettie?"

She turned, but only enough so that she could see him without looking him directly in the eyes, since he seemed to be studying her so intently. "Yes?"

"Lettie, I've been trying for days now . . . I mean . . ." He dropped his head and studied the tips of his boots for a moment, then glanced up, his eyes dark and filled with untold secrets.

"What is it, Ned?"

He took another gulp of air. "Remember that time by the chicken coop, when I told you I thought your dress was pretty?"

"Yes."

"I actually wanted to tell you . . ."

"What, Ned?"

"That I liked you."

"I like you, too, Ned."

"No—" He looked up. "I—I mean, I *really* like you." He swallowed, and his eyes became slightly desperate. "I'd do anything for you. Anything. If I could, I'd see to it that all those poems you write came true."

Lettie grew still when she realized Ned was trying to tell her that he had grown fond of her.

"I know your brother's real protective of you—and your mama's got her standards. . . ." His voice became strangled with evident nerves. "But do you suppose you could ever . . . like me, too?"

Lettie felt a prick of guilt and compassion for the quiet man beside her who was trying so hard. "Well, I don't know, Ned. Of course, I already like you . . . quite a bit."

His features seemed to lighten in hope, and Lettie knew then that she couldn't deceive him. She reached out to touch his arm. Though he started, she did not back away.

Taking a breath, she continued: "But I don't know if I could ever . . . *like* you the way you want me to, Ned."

He seemed to sag a little beneath the slight weight of

her hand. Then he backed away, a look of quiet dignity spreading across his features. Without saying anything more, he turned and escaped into the kitchen.

Lettie watched him go with sad eyes, her hand slowly dropping to her side.

"It's just as well, Lettie."

She glanced over her shoulder to find her mother watching her from the grass by the side of the house. Celeste moved forward, cradling a cache of carrots in the scooped-up folds of her apron.

Lettie stiffened at her mother's words. "Why? Because he's just a boarder?" she asked defiantly.

Celeste shook her head and climbed the back steps, her movements slow and somehow weary. "No. Because he's just a boy." She reached out to touch Lettie's cheek with a single finger, her skin slightly rough from the dirt of the garden and the calluses of her daily chores.

"You *have* grown up, haven't you, Lettie?" Her voice grew soft, almost indistinguishable in the night air. "It's happened all of a sudden, I think. Either that, or I haven't been paying you much mind lately."

Turning, she disappeared into the house. Through the windows, Lettie watched as her mother dumped the carrots onto the counter next to the pump, then unhooked a pail from the rack beside the stove. She pumped it full of water and began to scrub the baby vegetables.

Somehow, Lettie found herself shivering slightly in the sultry heat. Her mother seemed so frail in the harsh light of the afternoon, so . . . alone. Yet things had been different when Lettie's father had been alive. So different.

Turning away, Lettie leaned against the railing, uncomfortable with her own unwitting insights. Although she might try to push happier thoughts into her mind, she couldn't help wondering if she, too, would become a hollow shell once Ethan left Madison for parts unknown.

Lettie's hands curled around the weathered wood of the railing, and she took a deep breath. Ethan had asked her to consider the consequences. The price. Yet, as the hot air settled around her, Lettie couldn't help wondering if the price might be even more dear if she were to let him leave her without loving him. Just once.

Silence settled over Ethan with the same heavy weight as the muggy summer air. Soon after returning from the creek, he'd moved into Mrs. Magillicuddy's room near the back staircase, so that the boarders would believe "Agnes" was in residence. He'd spent the afternoon poring over the information he'd gathered from the boarders' rooms as well as his trip into town.

As the afternoon became evening, Ethan became drawn into the maps and periodicals spread across the bed. He barely noticed the way the ribbons of sunlight spilling around the window shade slipped across the floor, then extended across the coverlet. It was late when he finally surfaced from his own deep thoughts. A warm certainty began to seep into his mind as he stared at the grainy picture on the front page of a *Madison Gazette* dated nearly two months earlier. Though he couldn't be sure, he thought that he'd just discovered the identity of one of the men he'd heard discussing his fate near the jailhouse corral.

Stepping toward the light around the window shade, he studied the photograph with great care, taking in the tall, lean build of the man. Although the picture was an imperfect shade of sienna brown and cream, Ethan thought that the man's hair would probably be silver.

There was a rattling of the doorknob, and Ethan dropped the paper onto the bed and retrieved his revolver from beneath the pillow. Standing behind the edge of the armoire, he waited as a key was slowly turned in the lock and the knob turned. When he saw Lettie entering with a tray, he automatically relaxed.

"Supper," she stated. "Sorry I'm late, but I finished cleaning up the rest of the dishes first."

He pulled a face at the bland fare prepared for him by Celeste Grey, but since Lettie had told her mother he was suffering from a bad case of "dietary distress"—which prevented him from joining the other boarders—

252

there wasn't much hope in being offered a piece of beef steak or even a hearty stew.

"Looks good," he commented nonetheless, taking in the rich smells of homemade custard, fresh fruit, greens, and bread.

Automatically, Lettie took the glass of bicarbonate from the tray, dumped it out of the open window, then returned. As she neared the bed, she glanced at the paper on top of the cover.

Reaching for a radish, Ethan waited until she had seen the picture before asking, "Do you know him?"

"Judge Krupp? Of course. He's served Madison for years."

"Judge?" he repeated.

"Mmm. Jacob knows him better than I. Judge Krupp seems to be nice enough, but he has a reputation for being a bit of a hanging judge."

The radish lay forgotten in Ethan's hand. "He's a judge?" he asked again.

Lettie glanced up at him curiously. "Yes. Why?"

"Nothing." Ethan bit into the radish. "The name seemed familiar."

"He's been in the news quite a bit lately." She threw the paper back onto the bed. "Judge Krupp presided over a case involving the Willie gang in Dewey a few months back. Before the trial could end, there was an attempted escape and the men were executed by the Star before—Ethan?"

He jerked his mind back with great difficulty.

"What's wrong?"

He shook his head. "Nothing, I . . ." His words trailed away, and once again, his thoughts began to whirl within him like grappling hounds. There was something that he should be noting, something that would connect.

"I've got to go. Mama will be suspicious if I don't spend some time in the parlor."

Once again, he yanked his thoughts back. "Yeah. Thanks for the food."

"Ethan?"

She waited expectantly, and Ethan knew she waited

for a kiss, a touch, some show of affection. But he made no move toward her. He couldn't. If he touched her again, he knew his control would shatter. Though he would have laughed at any man for telling him so a month ago, Ethan found himself ensnared by a mere slip of a girl. A young, innocent girl. And he would do anything to keep from hurting her more than he had already.

"My brother came by," Lettie stated softly. "A secret gold shipment has arrived in town. They're worried the Gentleman will show up." She hesitated. "I think he was trying to warn me."

Ethan regarded her carefully after that statement. "Of what?"

"I don't know. He seemed . . . jumpy."

"Where's the shipment?"

"Madison City Thrift and Loan—Mr. Gruber's bank."

Once again, the name teased something on the fringes of Ethan's memory. "Gruber," he repeated softly, more to himself than to Lettie.

"Silas Gruber—the man we saw today by the train. You know, Natalie's husband. I told you about Natalie. The two of them don't get along too well."

Ethan took a step toward her, his eyes narrowing. "How long have the Grubers lived here?"

"I don't know . . . five years. They came from Chicago, where Mr. Gruber managed a bank. Natalie's always complaining about the fact that they were sent here as some sort of demotion. She was bitter about that for a while, but lately she seems to have adapted to—Ethan?"

His head jerked up, and he pushed aside his whirling thoughts to give her his full attention.

"Ethan, I . . ."

Her words trailed away, and she took a step toward him. One delicate finger lifted to push aside a lock of hair that had fallen to his forehead, and he jerked slightly. Her skin was warm, soft. She smelled of sunlight and lilac water.

Heaven help him, he wanted her. And her love.

"Don't back away from me. Please."

He closed his eyes against her plea. "Lettie." He sighed. "I'll have to go soon."

"I know. Just don't leave me before you actually go."

He opened his eyes to gaze at her, his face once again masked, and she reached out to touch his heart.

"You're leaving me here"—she touched his temple—"and here." She stepped forward until her skirts brushed his thighs. And her breasts—dear heaven, her breasts feathered across his chest, filling him with a pounding hunger that grew sharper each time she stepped into the same room with him.

"I know what you're trying to do, Ethan. You think I'll hurt less if you stay as far away from me as possible in the next few days. But I'll hurt more, Ethan. I need your strength, your passion, your tenderness. They're the memories I'll treasure forever. Please don't leave me with memories of your distance."

Closing his eyes to her earnest expression, Ethan slipped his arms around her waist and drew her tightly against him, holding her next to his heart as if he had the right to keep her there for all time. Her arms clutched his shoulders, and he felt her shaking. There was nothing he could deny her if only she were to ask.

"Can I come to you tonight?"

He froze, realizing that she was asking him to make love to her.

"Please?" she whispered next to his ear.

Ethan squeezed his eyes shut and held her even tighter, fighting the emotions roiling within him, before finally whispering, "I'll come to you. After everyone is asleep."

18

I eased deeper into the warm, fragrant water of my bath and rested my head against the porcelain rim. Dipping one idle finger into the petal-strewn water, I closed my eyes and allowed the scented liquid to lap over my breasts.

He would be here. Soon.

Slowly, sensually, I smiled. As if he were already there, I breathed deeply of the pungent scent of the candles and the musky odor of the roses. My finger drew idle circles across the surface of the water, and I imagined the touch of his fingers against my ribs, the warmth of his breath against my nape.

The soft snick of a key in the lock split the silence, and I knew he had come. Just as he'd promised. Standing up, I reached for the bath sheet draped across my bed and turned, holding the cloth to my body and stepping from the bath.

I stood rooted as the door to my bedchamber opened, letting in a soft swirl of air. Around me, a forest of candles sputtered. Light shivered, danced. The pungent odor of smoke grew sharper, then disappeared as the musky scent of roses drifted through the garden windows.

He took a single step forward, his muscles moving

sinuously beneath the tight fabric of his breeches and the fullness of his shirt. Then the door snapped closed behind him, shutting out the blackness of the hall and sealing us in the whispered light of the candles. Silence shimmered like silk in the air. An eloquent silence filled with intimate words of the heart.

My lips tilted in a rich, provocative smile. Slowly, sensually, my hands lifted to the pins that held my hair. My fingers paused.

He barely seemed to breathe.

One by one, I drew the gold hairpins from the dark twists of my hair, allowing the pins to drop to the floor with a delicate metallic patter. Then I arched my head back so that my hair fell from its intricate coils in a thick swath that swung to a point just below my hips.

When I lifted my head and opened my eyes, he seemed to watch me more intently than before. A shimmering excitement filled my veins like the effervescent bubbles of champagne.

He wanted me. He needed me. And I was the only woman who could satisfy him.

The low purr of thunder overhead echoed my latent satisfaction as I moved slowly, gracefully, across the room. My hands lifted to touch him.

No words were spoken.

None were needed.

My towel dropped, and I lifted my hands to the buttons of his shirt and drew him irretrievably toward the scented water behind me.

"Love me," I whispered, as I drew him backward. . . .

At the soft rattle of the doorknob, Lettie turned and waited. The door opened, inch by inch, and finally, Ethan stepped inside and shut the door behind him.

For a moment, he stood at the bottom of the staircase, gazing up at her. As his eyes slipped from her shining hair to her freshly scrubbed face to the simple lawn wrapper belted about her waist, something quiet within Lettie's soul blossomed and warmed. Because she felt pretty. Loved.

"What took you so long?" she murmured.

He climbed the steps before speaking. "I wanted to make sure everyone was asleep."

When he continued to study her with eyes that had grown dark and heated, she nodded and watched him with an intensity that she hoped would convey just a few of the emotions twining within her.

"I also brought us some refreshments."

She glanced up to see him brandishing a jar of her mother's currant wine and two tin cups.

"How did you know where to find it?"

"I was a thief, Lettie," he answered with a quick grin. "Everyone was asleep, so it was a simple enough matter to slip through the house and gather what I thought we might need."

She smiled in delight. Her heart was already pounding in eager anticipation and her skin seemed to tingle. But Ethan's romantic gesture enhanced those emotions even more.

She turned to wave a hand toward the tin hipbath in the middle of the room. "I—I arranged for a bath for myself, then thought you might like one."

He turned toward the tub. "I don't think so."

"I won't look."

He hesitated.

"The water's cool and refreshing. It would wash off some of the grit from the creek."

He glanced up at her.

"Please." After a slight hesitation, she added, "It would make me happy, help me to feel like I've done something special for you."

He glanced at the tub again, then at Lettie, before finally conceding. "All right. But first we drink."

She smiled and took the jar from his hands. Taking it to the bureau, she uncapped the wine and poured a small measure into each of the cups.

Padding toward him, she offered one of the cups to Ethan. "Shall we make a toast?"

He nodded his head.

"To us."

She drank from her cup, but he turned away, walking toward the window and pulling aside the shade to stare out at the moon-drenched yard. Seeming restless, he set his cup on the sill and rubbed the back of his neck with his hand.

"You know there can be no 'us,' Lettie," he finally murmured.

Moving toward him, she slipped an arm around his waist and kissed his shoulder. "Please. Not tonight."

His hand reached out to cover her own and they stood together for long moments, absorbing the silence of the house and the shivering awareness growing between them with each breath they took.

Finally, he turned. "I guess I'd better take that bath."

Lettie smiled to herself in secret pleasure when his voice emerged just a little too low and a little too ragged.

"Take all the time you want." She crossed to the bed and sat with her back to the tub, her shoulders resting against the footboard. "I'll just sit right here and entertain us with a few poems." Taking Natalie's poetry book from the foot of the bed, she bent her knees and rested the book on top.

She paused for a moment, waiting for some sign that Ethan had begun to undress. When she heard no noises, she prompted, "Well? Aren't you going to bathe?"

There was a pause, then: "Yeah. I suppose."

She heard his bootstrides, then looked up when he approached the bureau, refilled her cup with currant wine, then handed it to her.

"Why, Ethan McGuire, are you trying to get me drunk?"

"It's an idea."

"It won't work."

"Then maybe *I'll* get drunk."

She grinned. "That's an idea."

Smiling at her impudent humor, he moved toward the hipbath. "Don't turn around."

"Afraid of what I'll see?"

"No. But *you* should be."

She giggled and took another sip of her wine. Behind

her, she heard the soft rustling of Ethan's clothing and she closed her eyes, savoring the sound. In her imagination, she could see him slipping the suspenders from his shoulders, one by one. Then he unbuttoned his shirt, tugged it free, and dropped it to the floor.

The noises stopped.

"What are you doing?" he demanded lowly.

"Imagining."

"Imagining what?"

She smiled, though she knew he couldn't see her. "I'm imagining each stitch of clothing as it falls from your body."

"Oh, hell," he muttered softly.

"Go on, Ethan."

"With what?"

"Undressing."

There was a pause, then she once again heard the rustle of cloth.

"One button."

"What?"

"You're unbuttoning your pants."

"Lettie."

"Two."

"You're incorrigible."

"Three. Take your trousers off, Ethan."

"Lettie!"

She chuckled. "All right, I won't listen anymore."

She heard the thump of his boots, the whisper of his socks, and the rustle of his pants. Taking a deep breath, Lettie held tightly to the image in her head: the image of Ethan, lean and naked, standing in front of the tub.

A soft moan of delight melted from her throat.

"Dammit, Lettie, stop that."

She chuckled. "What poet do you want to hear?"

"Anything. Just wipe that smirk off your face and let a man wash up."

"Yes, sir." She took another sip of the wine in her cup and yawned deliciously, grasping the book and stretching her legs out before her.

As she heard the lap of water from behind, she turned

to one of the last sections in the anthology of poetry. Walt Whitman. Months before, there had been a ruckus in the boardinghouse when Celeste Grey had discovered poems by Whitman in one of her subscriptions. Even the Beasleys had been atwitter. Before Lettie had been able to get a copy of the periodical, her mother had canceled her subscription and burned the magazine. When Ethan had forbidden her to read the poet several nights before, Lettie had read all of Walt Whitman's poems in Natalie's book, then read them again.

"Are you ready?" she asked, finding the appropriate page.

There was a pause, then Ethan muttered, "Just read."

She giggled, then took another sip of her wine before settling back against the pillows she'd mounded against the footboard. The wine was evidently relaxing her, just a titch, because she felt all tingly and warm.

" 'From Pent-Up Aching Rivers,' " she slowly read. "By Walt Whitman."

She heard a splash behind her. "Lettie," Ethan growled in warning.

"Oh, hush up and listen," she muttered, then took another sip of her wine. "From pent-up aching rivers, /From that of myself without which I were nothing, /From what I am determin'd to make illustrious, even if I stand sole among men/From my own voice resonant, singing the phallus—"

"Lettie—"

His protests were a little less forceful this time, and Lettie smiled. "Singing the song of procreation,/Singing the need of superb children and therein superb grown people."

Turning onto her stomach, Lettie dropped her empty cup to the floor and stared at Ethan through the iron rungs of her bed. His chest rose from the barrier of the tub, strong and broad, dappled in moisture. His eyes met hers, heated and filled with passion.

The book dropped to the floor beside the cup and Lettie continued by memory: "Singing the muscular urge and the blending,/Singing the bedfellow's song . . ."

Ethan's eyes closed as if he were fighting for control, and Lettie smiled, a slow sultry smile. Standing up, she took a bath sheet from the foot of the bed and walked toward him, slowly, wantonly.

"O resistless yearning!/O for any and each the body correlative attracting!/O for you whoever you are your correlative body! O it, more than all else, you delighting!"

She knelt beside the tub and reached out to place her hand against his breast, absorbing the heat of his skin, the water-dappled texture, the swirl of hair.

"From the hungry gnaw that eats me night and day,/From native moments, from bashful pains, singing them,/Seeking something yet unfound though I have diligently sought it many a long year."

She bent close, pressing her lips against his own, and Ethan moaned, grasping her behind the head and pulling her so close that her breasts were crushed against the wet expanse of his chest.

She hungrily met his need with one of her own, seemingly intent upon absorbing his essence into hers until there was no separating the two of them and they ceased to be two separate souls and became one. Her hand slipped down the muscled contours of his breast, tracing the hair that grew there, circling his navel with her nail, then moving farther down.

Her hand was captured by his own, and he forced her palm to a safer location higher on his chest, even as he held her tightly against him, his lips slanted against her own. His kiss was hungry and filled with a desperation that this time they might once again be forced to back away.

But Lettie wasn't about to let that happen. She had given Ethan McGuire her heart and her soul. As surely as if she had spoken marriage vows, she knew she belonged to this man. For now. And for all time.

She drew back, her lips leaving his own in tender regret, then bent to brush another butterfly-light kiss against his mouth, as if leaving the caress were too much to bear.

Ethan shuddered, knowing that he had never felt such

passion with a woman, such delight. It stretched far beyond the physical pleasures, blending heart and body and soul.

Smiling at him with the smile of Eve, she took his hand and stood up. Grasping the bath sheet in front of him, he allowed her to pull him upright in a rush of water. His skin burned as he felt her gaze sweeping over him in open curiosity.

Tugging gently on his wrist, she tried to draw him forward, but he slipped his hand free and wrapped the bath sheet tightly around his hips.

"Shy?" she murmured.

A shaky chuckle eased from his throat. "I guess so."

She giggled in delight and took a step backward, her hands closed around the tie of her wrapper. "Make love to me, Ethan."

Ethan swallowed hard against the tightness building within him, trying to tamp down the fire stoking within his own blood. The sultry heat of the garret closed about him, filling him with a tension, a yearning, that he knew he could no longer deny. Yet he still hesitated, all of the reasons he shouldn't touch her tumbling into his head.

Lettie gazed at him with dark, slumberous heat. "Make love to me, Ethan. Please."

If not for that last whispered plea, Ethan could have resisted. He could have gathered his clothes and slipped from the room.

Sensing his hesitation, Lettie continued her recital, and, being familiar with the poem himself, Ethan knew just what she was about to say.

"Hark close and still what I now whisper to you,/I love you, O you entirely possess me."

"Lettie," he moaned, trying to cling to the last vestiges of control within him, but Lettie merely smiled with the awareness of a temptress. Gone was the child, gone was the delicate girl in need of protection. And in her place was a woman. A woman of passion and grace.

Yet she offered him no relief, continuing with her poetry. "From exultation, victory and relief, from the bed-fellow's embrace in the night,/From the act-poems of eyes,

263

hands, hips and bosoms,/From the cling of the trembling arm,/From the bending curve and the clinch,/From side by side the pliant coverlet off-throwing—"

He moved toward her, interrupting Lettie with the line he knew followed her own: "From the one so unwilling to have me leave, and me just as unwilling to leave."

He pushed her hair away from her face, absorbing the silky texture of the well-brushed strands against his calloused palms. Her eyes flickered closed in delight, and he watched as her entire body seemed to soak in the sensation of his touch. He had never known a woman who reveled in him so much. He had never known a woman who cared for him so much.

And he ached to be the man she wanted him to be.

Dipping his head, he kissed her, allowing his mouth and hands and body to tell her all of the things that he knew he could never say. That he cared for her. That he wished they could have a future together.

Finally, he pulled away, squeezing his eyes shut and muttering one last time, "Your husband should be the first."

Her hands tunneled through his hair, forcing him to look at her. "Don't say that, Ethan. You're the only man I'll ever love."

"Lettie." His voice was husky, filled with raw emotion.

"Love me."

"You'll be hurt. It's wrong to take you like this."

"It's not wrong. It's beautiful."

"You aren't thinking right now."

"Maybe not. But I'm feeling. And what I'm feeling for you is special."

He looked at her, and he found his strength of will weakening beneath the firm intensity of his gaze.

She frowned. "You think I'm too young, don't you?"

He shook his head and held tightly to her hand when she tried to lay it on his chest. "I think you're too special." His thumb brushed against her palm. "You don't know yet what it means to make love."

"I *do* know."

"I'm not talking about the mechanics, Lettie. I'm talking about the emotions, the feelings, the responsibilities. No one ever forgets the first time, Lettie. Especially a woman. It should be special. Something that can be remembered without regret. I won't take that from you."

"The only way you can take the memory is by not giving it to me tonight. In my heart, you will always be the first." Her arms wound about his neck. "And the last."

She hesitated, then drew him toward her for her kiss. Ethan moaned when he realized that he had taught her too well the art of seduction, because even now he felt himself weakening. He wanted to abandon his conscience. He wanted to delight in the fervor of her embrace and the simple passion of her caresses.

Lettie drew back, and her eyes lifted to study him. She smiled as if she saw just how much she had affected him. And just how fragile his control remained. Then she placed her hands upon his breast. Her touch was tender, almost reverent. "I love you," she whispered, then bent to place a kiss upon his chest. "I love you." She kissed one brown male nipple, then the other, then glanced up. "I love you."

He swallowed against the pure emotions that shone from her eyes. Desire and passion. Pure adoration. And something more. Something that could only be the light of her love.

His hands lifted to frame her face.

She purred, nudging into the pressure of his hands.

And he was lost.

"Just promise me you won't ever regret this night," he whispered, closing his eyes and crushing his mouth against her own before she could reply, or before he could see any flickerings of doubt that might flash across her features.

But her hands slid up his chest, and she melted into his embrace as if she were coming home after a long journey. Her arms, strong and supple from her work at the boardinghouse, held him with a strength he never would have imagined. Ethan could feel her breasts flattening against his chest. The fabric of her wrapper was cool and damp with the moisture it had absorbed from his own skin.

His arms swept down her back, grasping at her hips and pulling her closer still, and Ethan was shaken to the core. Dear heaven, how he wanted her. Needed her. Not just physically but emotionally as well. He needed her laughter, her passion, and her hope. And he didn't know what he was going to do when he was forced to leave her.

Breaking free, he gazed down at her flushed features. "If I had my way, you and I would be together forever."

"I know."

He lifted his hand and pushed the hair away from her features. "You'd live with me in Chicago in a big white house, and—"

She covered his lips with her fingers, knowing that neither of them were ready to hear might-have-beens. "I know," she whispered. "But right now, we have tonight. And we have each other." Her hands lifted to caress his face and the features she had grown to love so much. "Love me, Ethan," she murmured. "Love me tonight as if you and I were man and wife with a whole future spreading out before us." She raised herself on tiptoe to press her lips against his own, whispering again, "Love me."

The shadows of the garret cloaked them both in the warm velvet heat of summer, and Ethan scooped her into his arms and gently placed her on the bed. He then lay beside her, his head propped in one palm.

In the shadows, his eyes seemed even more blue and intent. For long, heart-stopping moments, he didn't move, didn't touch her. Then, just when she thought that she would die from wanting his touch, he reached out. One single finger dipped toward her face, tracing the jut of her cheekbone, the smooth shape of her jaw, her lips.

When she moved impatiently to wind her arms about his waist, he drew away and whispered, "Shh. My way."

His lips lifted in a tender smile. "We're going to savor each moment."

Lettie shivered as Ethan's finger once again began a tingling journey, slipping to her chin, then plunging down the line of her throat. He hesitated a moment at the hollow between her collarbones, then skimmed lightly down.

Her breathing became ragged as starbursts of sensation rushed through her veins from that single inquisitive finger. As Ethan began to nudge beneath the delicate boundaries of her wrapper, she shuddered and tried to draw air into her lungs.

Needing something, anything, to ground her, she grasped his arm, just above his elbow. But she didn't push him away. Instead, she uttered a husky moan and tacitly bade him to continue his explorations.

Ethan hesitated, his gaze lifting to tangle with her own. Then his finger lifted to caress her stomach, her ribs, then finally touched the underside of her breast.

She jerked, a jolt of pleasure racing through her veins. When he smiled at her reaction, she fought to breathe. When he hesitated, her hands slid down his arm to take his hand, forcing him to abandon the foray of his finger.

"Touch me," she whispered.

His head dipped, and his mouth took her own in a hungry kiss even as his hand closed over her breast.

She moaned, rolling into the pressure, her own arms slipping around his shoulders and pulling him tightly against her.

As if they had tried to douse a fire with kerosene, the passion suddenly ignited between them. Lettie's arms wrapped tighter around his shoulders, drawing him over her torso. The weight of his body against her own filled her with a delicious flood of sensation. Her pulse pounded, her body strained.

Ethan drew back suddenly. "Not so fast," he whispered thickly, but she clutched at his shoulders, forcing him to look at her.

In his eyes she saw an echo of the raging emotions that must surely be seen in her own. Her hands dropped from his shoulders and slipped down the curve of his ribs, then burrowed between them to tug at the tie of her wrapper. When she would have torn it free, he stopped her hands, rolling away slightly so that he could gaze down at her.

Softly, tenderly, he drew the edges of her wrapper apart, then gasped. "You are so beautiful," he murmured. His hand hesitated, then skimmed from her neck to her navel.

She moaned and grasped his wrist. "Love me," she begged.

His eyes met her own, as if searching for last-minute doubts. But she knew that he would find no doubt there. Only a hungry passion for his touch.

Her hands reached to tug at the towel still wrapped around his waist.

"No." His fingers clasped her wrist. At her questioning gaze, he reluctantly added, "I don't want to scare you."

Her lips tilted in a smile. "How gallant. But how very, very unnecessary." She rolled him onto his back, and, before he could prevent her actions, she had tugged the fabric of the bath sheet free.

She held her breath and gazed at him, and for a moment, Ethan felt an unfamiliar flush of embarrassment rise into his cheeks. Sure that he had scared her to death with the evidence of his passion, he tried to tug the sheet over his hips.

"No."

Lettie caught his hand and looked up at him. But it wasn't fear that he found in her eyes; it was passion.

"Love me," she whispered once again. Releasing his hand, she trailed the pad of her thumb down the ridges caused by his ribs, then caressed the line of his hips to the top of his thighs. There she paused, her thumb making soft, sweeping half circles that caused him to shudder in delight.

"You are a witch," he murmured, his hands tangling into the hair on her nape and bringing her close for a hungry kiss. He had thought to slow down the pace of their lovemaking, at least until she was ready for him. But at the sensation of her bare flesh pressed so tightly against his own, he felt the last dregs of his control slipping away.

When he would have paused, however, Lettie made a soft purr of denial and returned his passion, measure for measure. Her hips pressed against his own, already mimicking a rhythm she had yet to learn.

Ethan's hand swept down her back, holding her tightly against him. He knew now that he couldn't stop, couldn't wait. And Lettie was ready for him.

Awash in pleasure, Lettie barely noted when Ethan pressed her back into the pillows. Her hands clutched at his waist, then at the firm slopes of his buttocks, urging him nearer.

He broke away from their kiss and gazed down at her with eyes that blazed with his desire. "I'll try not to hurt you," he whispered.

She shook her head. "You could never hurt me."

Bending, he tenderly kissed her cheek, her chin. His hand caressed her breast, then moved down her body to slip beneath her knee, drawing it up against her hip as he settled over her.

Lettie's head arched back and her eyes closed as she absorbed the delicious weight of the man above her. Then her eyes flickered open and her arms clutched at his shoulders.

"Now," she whispered.

When he would have hesitated one last time, she grasped his hips and gazed deeply into his eyes.

"Now."

Thrusting the fingers of one hand into her hair, he gazed at her, long and hard. She felt him shift, the muscles of his legs tensing ever so slightly. Then, slowly, sensuously, he entered her.

Lettie gasped, and her gaze darted down to watch their bodies become one. She shuddered beneath a storm of sensations that she had never known could exist. Fullness and heat. Beauty and tenderness. "I love you," she whispered, before her eyes closed and she surrendered to the storming passions within her.

Ethan paused for only a moment, then thrust through her last final barrier, covering her lips with his own and absorbing her cry.

Lettie's hands dug into the muscles of his shoulders, waiting until the pain had died to a reluctant throb. Only then did she realize that Ethan had grown still. Her lashes flickered open, and she looked up at him with wide eyes, absorbing the tense set to his features and the heat of his gaze.

"Is that all?" she murmured.

She saw the way he fought the urge to smile. When he spoke, his voice was strained.

"No, sweetheart, that's not all."

Her brow creased when he reached down to lift her knee a little more securely against his hip. Then he began to move within her and she gasped, pressing closer. Her eyes closed in delight as Ethan began to teach her a sensual rhythm as old as time itself.

She moaned as a swelling pleasure built within her. Her eyes closed, and her pulse raced. Wrapping her arms around Ethan's shoulders, she held on to the one thing that seemed to ground her to the earth. But she didn't know how the pleasure could possibly grow more intense until it suddenly seemed to burst within her like a fiery implosion of sparks.

Mere moments followed before she felt Ethan stiffen and join her in the culmination of their passion. Long minutes of shimmering delight seemed to pass between them, trapping their bodies in a silken web of pleasure, until slowly, ever so slowly, the sensations melted into the darkness. Then, in the final moments of pleasure, they both closed their eyes and fought to breathe.

Folding her arms more tightly about Ethan's shoulders, Lettie drew him against her as muscles trembled and released their exquisite tension. She took a slow, shuddering breath as reality finally returned to the fringes of her consciousness. Her body filled with a delicious warmth, and her lips curled in the barest ghost of a smile. Without a doubt, she had crossed the final boundary into womanhood.

Dredging the last bit of strength she could muster, she lifted her head and pressed a soft kiss against the hollow of his neck, then another on his shoulder. Slowly, her hands lifted and her fingers sifted through the damp strands of Ethan's hair. How she loved this man.

His head lifted, and he gazed down at her with eyes the color of a hot summer sky. Though he didn't speak, she sensed his concern. But more than that, she sensed his pleasure.

She shifted and pressed a kiss against his brow. He answered by dipping his head and placing a soft kiss against her shoulder.

"I love you, Ethan," she murmured.

Once again, she felt a kiss against her shoulder. Then she smiled as the night closed about them, warm and dark, and filled with the silent echoes of their passion. And for once, she knew without a shadow of a doubt that Ethan loved her with his heart and soul, just as she loved him.

Even though he couldn't seem to find a way to say the words.

Much, much later, Lettie awoke to see Ethan standing in his customary place by the window. She smiled, stretching and delighting in the weary ache of her body.

"Ethan?" she murmured, and rolled onto her side.

Her brow creased when he stiffened slightly but did not immediately turn.

"Is something wrong?"

He turned then, and the expression on his features banished her fears. He didn't regret what had happened. His eyes still glowed with a smoldering warmth.

He took a step toward her. "How do you feel?"

She felt a heat rise into her cheeks and prayed the darkness concealed her blush. "Fine."

"Sore?"

"Yes."

He sighed and padded toward her, slipping beneath the sheets and drawing her against his chest. "I'm sorry."

"Really?" she asked after a moment, slightly hurt and wondering how she could have misinterpreted the expression she'd seen in his eyes only moments before.

At her disappointed tone, he chuckled. "I'm sorry you're sore, not sorry we made love."

"Oh." Her lips curled into a smile, and her arms wrapped around his waist. After the silence had settled around them with a silken heat, she asked, "What time is it?"

Once again, she felt Ethan hesitate. "Almost midnight," he finally said. His arms tightened around her shoulders, holding her close, and she thought she felt him place a brushing kiss across the top of her head. Then he sighed and reached out to hand her more currant wine.

"Drink this."

She regarded the cup in surprise, wondering when Ethan had retrieved the cup from the floor and filled it again.

"It will ease some of the aches," he murmured when she hesitated.

Lettie obediently swallowed the contents, frowning slightly when the drink didn't seem nearly as palatable as it had only hours before.

She handed Ethan the cup, and he returned it to the bedside table. Then she lay her head on his shoulder, her hand brushing idly against his stomach.

Once again, she felt a kiss against the top of her head. Looking up, she found Ethan watching her with a curious regard.

"What's wrong?" she whispered, noting the serious set of his jaw.

He shook his head. "Nothing." He crooked a finger and reached to skim his knuckle over her cheek. The caress so closely imitated the way Ethan had touched her in prelude to their lovemaking that Lettie's fingers curled into his waist and her breathing came a little quicker.

Fighting against the delicious lassitude that seemed to seep through her veins, she rolled onto her back, pulling him with her.

"What makes you look so serious?" she murmured, running her hand up his torso to his shoulder, delighting in each curve and hollow she found along the way.

Silence pulsed between them for a moment, then Ethan said, "You know I care for you, Lettie."

She nodded, her eyes growing heavy and slumberous. "Of course I know."

"I would never hurt you."

"I know."

He bent to kiss her, once, twice. The pressure of his lips was poignantly gentle, almost worshiping. Yet there was a hint of sadness to the caress, one that tugged at Lettie's consciousness.

Her arms wrapped around his shoulders and she drew him closer, hungrily seeking the passion she had felt only moments before in his arms. But she felt so tired.

Ethan broke away, noting the dark luster of her eyes and the velvet texture of her skin. She nudged against him like a hungry kitten and he bent, crushing his mouth to her own and pressing her so tightly against him that they were nearly melded into one flesh. Once again, awareness flared between them. Hot and insistent. And Ethan surrendered to the sensations, wanting to commit them to his memory for all time.

When Lettie's fingers slipped down weakly to curl into the muscles of his shoulders, he moaned, holding her tightly against him.

But she broke away and whispered, "I love you . . . Ethan." Her nails dug into his skin, and she uttered a sound that was half sigh, half groan. Then her fingers slipped from his back, inch by inch, and she became lax in his arms.

Setting her against the pillows, Ethan tenderly pushed the hair back from her face, his motions gentle, yet filled with an untold regret.

A tightness gathered in his throat as he gazed down at

her innocent features. His heart seemed to have wedged in an aching lump in the center of his chest.

"Sleep now, Lettie girl," he whispered. He brushed her lips once again with his own, knowing that it would probably be the last time for them both. Then he got up from the bed and retrieved the currant wine that he'd laced with a healthy dose of Celeste Grey's sleeping powder only moments before. Dumping it into the chamber pot, he stepped into his trousers and moved to the stairwell. At the top, he paused and turned.

Despite his own pain in deceiving her this way, Ethan knew it was for the best. "I really do love you, Lettie," he whispered. "Some day you'll understand." Then he padded down the steps and slipped into the hall.

19

Once back in his own room, Ethan quickly finished dressing and gathered what few belongings he could claim as his own. Glancing at his watch, he swore when he realized he was late. Much too late.

Taking one last look, Ethan strapped his gun belt around his hips and stepped toward the bed. Lifting one of the periodicals, he gazed at it in the dim light of the lamp on the bureau.

Only moments before joining Lettie, some of the pieces of the puzzle had begun to slip into place. Looking through the assorted magazines, Ethan had been able to discern a pattern in Judge Krupp's career. Whenever hope seemed dim and a suspect seemed about to slip through the judicial system, the Star appeared to execute the man. And seven times out of ten, the men involved were being tried in Judge Krupp's court.

Ethan's eyes dropped to the article that had merely intensified his suspicions. Though small and easily overlooked, the piece had named Judge Krupp as one of the new owners of the Hamilton Mississippi Railroad. Jeb Clark had been killed while guarding a shipment for the same line. And somehow, though he didn't have any proof, Ethan suspected that Clark had also been a member of the Star.

Although Ethan was nearly certain that Krupp was the man behind the Star's sudden interest in the activities of the Gentleman Bandit, Ethan still had no clues as to who was attempting to copy his own methods. But if all went well tonight, he would know for sure. One way or the other.

Dropping the paper onto the bed, Ethan extinguished the lamp and slipped into the hall. Silence pressed down around his shoulders, reminding him of all the nights he'd spent with Lettie. Talking. Touching.

Pushing back the regret that taunted him with all the might-have-beens he'd been battling for some time now, Ethan hurried down the staircase, let himself out through the back door, and disappeared into the night.

But even as he moved silently through the darkness, away from the boardinghouse and all it entailed . . . he knew that the feelings he had for Lettie Grey would never be so easy to abandon.

Jacob jerked awake and blinked, staring down at the reports on his desk. Somehow he'd fallen asleep amid the wealth of tasks awaiting him. Yet, now that he was awake, the thoughts that had drummed through his head returned to haunt him.

Why had the Star decided to trap Ethan McGuire with the mythical gold shipment? It would be much more logical for Jacob and his men to guard the bank. If Ethan were caught red-handed, there would be no need for a vigilante execution. The courts would see to it that Ethan was shot or hanged, without any possible repercussions.

So why all the attempts at subterfuge?

A soft knock broke the quiet, and Jacob rubbed a hand across his face, realizing it was the same noise that had awakened him.

"Coming!" he called, reaching for a match and quickly igniting the wick of the lamp kept on the corner of his desk. Setting the chimney back in place, he moved to open the door a crack and peer outside. When he found

Abby Clark waiting on the boardwalk, he gazed at her for a moment in surprise, then quickly opened the door.

"Abby! Is something wrong?"

"No, no. Nothing like that." She took a step into the room, then stopped, halfway through. "They brought Jeb's body in from Harrisburg tonight . . . and I . . ." She took a deep breath, then continued in a rush. "I was on my way home from the funeral parlor when I came to a decision."

She held out a tattered box, which had been bound by a worn piece of string.

"These were Jeb's." She pressed her lips together, then continued. "I know you'll do the right thing by them." She looked up, and her eyes were filled with worry. "Keep them someplace safe, and don't let anyone know what they contain. I think Jeb would have wanted you to have them." Her head bobbed in a curt nod. "Yes, I know he would have wanted it this way." Her hand reached out, and she squeezed his arm. "You take care."

"Let me take you home."

"No," she answered brightly, then added again, "No, I'd rather take the time to walk back. Alone. Besides" —she gestured to the box—"you've got a little reading to do tonight, and I don't want to keep you."

Moving back outside, she turned and walked away from the house at a slow gait, until finally, the black of her clothing blended into the night.

Taking a breath, Jacob closed the door, set the box on the table, and pulled on the string. When he lifted the lid, his brow creased in confusion at the scraps of note-scribbled paper, newspaper clippings, and letters. Lifting one of the dog-eared pages from the pile, Jacob scanned the angular writing that belonged unmistakably to his dead friend.

At first, the words darted through his mind in a scattered volley of images, but soon the images began to coalesce, then burn with the intensity of a brand. Dropping the page, Jacob picked up another, and another, reading quickly, haphazardly. Then his hand dropped into the box, curling around a handful of Jeb Clark's carefully documented notes concerning the governing board of the Star.

"Dear God," he whispered softly to himself, his voice filled with the sound of his own dread . . . and his own epiphany.

Dropping the papers, he jammed the lid over the box. Then he grasped his hat, rifle, and a box of shells, and he strode out into the black of the night.

Ethan crouched low in the shadows around the bank, listening for the slightest noise that might be out of place in the darkness. When only the lazy chirp of the crickets punctuated the silence, he moved around the back of the bank to the side alley. Taking a long metal file from his pocket, he inserted it into the keyhole, nudging slightly until he managed to twist the lock and open the door.

Glancing over his shoulder, Ethan slipped inside and closed the door behind him, then stood to full height. For a moment he paused, waiting for his eyes to adjust to the blackness of the interior. His heart raced in a heady combination of exhilaration and dread as he was rushed by the familiar scents and shadows of a night-cloaked bank office. Not for the first time, he found himself grateful that he'd given up this kind of a life. And if his hunches were correct and the man imitating him appeared tonight, he could give up this kind of life for good.

Slipping his revolver from its holster, Ethan crept into the bank, looking for a place to hide until the thief made his own appearance. He was nearly halfway through the front lobby when he halted and became still. He thought he'd heard something: a mere whisper of a sound that was out of place.

Changing directions, Ethan crept toward the door of the office, crouching low so that his shadow would not be seen from the windows surrounding the cubicle. Slowly, cautiously, his hand closed around the doorknob and he opened the door a crack, wincing at the slight creaking noise.

A split second later, Ethan realized that the thief had already been there. The doors to the safe hung open, the shelves lay bare, and the overpowering stench of kerosene cloaked the tiny office and rose to assault Ethan's lungs.

Standing up, Ethan took only a moment to gaze into the office. Through eyes that watered and stung, he glanced down, seeing the shape of Silas Gruber's blood-soaked body. A searing curse rose in Ethan's mind, but he bit it back, realizing he'd just walked into a trap.

A burst of panic shot through his body and he whirled to race from the room, but before he could take three steps, something heavy crashed over the top of his head and he felt himself crumpling to the ground.

For a moment, the bank was silent.

Then a figure in black stepped forward and gazed down at Ethan's body. "Krupp said you would come," the thief murmured, then dropped an iron bar to the ground and grasped Ethan McGuire by the heels. "I guess you weren't as smart as everyone thought."

Once Ethan's body had been positioned by the front door, the thief grunted in relief, then stepped outside to retrieve another container of kerosene and a white vellum calling card.

The thief smiled in secret pleasure. Tonight, Ethan McGuire and the Gentleman Bandit would die forever in the blaze of the Madison City Thrift and Loan.

The stench of kerosene clawed at the back of Silas Gruber's throat, causing him to struggle to consciousness. Blackness surrounded him. A grasping, heavy blackness filled with the stark odors of sweat and fear.

He gasped and coughed. Biting back the whimper that rose in his throat, Silas reared his cheek away from the splintered wood of the floor. A searing pain shot from a point behind his ear to the center of his skull, threatening to plunge him once again into unconsciousness. If only he had waited for the Gentleman outside. But no, like a fool, he'd waited in his own office, thinking the darkness would conceal him.

Clenching his jaw to still the unmanly sobs that seemed to tumble loose from his throat, Silas squeezed his eyes shut, trying to focus his mind on something other than the pain: the accolade he would receive for apprehending the Gentleman and his wife.

Natalie.

After tonight, she'd never let him live down the debacles of his career. She'd never believe that he had done it all for her. For Natalie . . .

With her name filling his head like a tangled litany, Silas's eyes opened and he reached out, sliding his left hand across the rough floorboards. Even in the pitch black of the night, he could see the oily sheen of his own blood, could sense the rasping grate of the crushed ribs in his chest. But he was a desperate man. Desperate and frightened.

Clawing at the floor, he slid his body forward, inch by agonizing inch, praying all the while that the black-garbed figure would not return. An almost hysterical bark of laughter burst from between his clenched teeth. How many times had he assured himself that he would know just what to do if the Gentleman returned? How many times had he contemplated the beating he'd give the thief responsible for his loss of position and wealth and his wife's disfavor? Yet when the moment had come, Silas had seen nothing, heard nothing, done nothing.

Silas's laughter became a jagged sob. His head sank to rest on the floor, and he panted for breath. The fingers of Silas's left hand once again moved to claw a path forward, while those of his right clenched miserably around his prize: the black neckerchief of the figure who had caught him unawares. He had no doubts that the thief had been the Gentleman, and he had to get outside . . . had to warn Krupp . . . had to . . .

Silas's hand reached out again, then froze. His fingers had not encountered the rough boards of the floor, but a smoothly polished boot. He fearfully raised his head. In the darkness, he saw nothing but a solid ebony shape within the blackness of the bank office. Then the figure took a step back, opening the door that led to the side alley bordering the bank and the Mercury Saloon. A weak, blue-gray wash of starlight slipped over the figure's unguarded features.

"Goodbye, Gruber," the shadow whispered.

Silas's eyes squinted in the darkness. That voice. That—

The shadow moved again. A match rasped against the doorframe and flared to life. Silas's head reared, and he tried to push himself upright. Recognition and panic shuddered through him, along with the pain.

Then the figure flicked the match from gloved fingers.

Silas watched in horror as the tiny whisper of light arced through the blackened building toward the puddle of kerosene in the corner by the safe. The door closed. The match fell.

"Nooo!"

The night filled with the whooshing breath of fire.

At the rush of heat and smoke, Ethan coughed and struggled to consciousness. "Lettie?" he rasped, then winced at the pain thundering at the back of his head. Opening his eyes, he came face-to-face with a licking trail of flame eating its way toward him.

Ignoring the searing pain of his own body, Ethan lifted himself, intent upon reaching the door. But when he saw the dark shape of another body, he crawled toward the man, reaching out to turn him onto his back.

A shudder of recognition raced through Ethan's body when he found himself staring into Silas Gruber's wild eyes. Memories came pounding to the fore, and with them a shimmering realization. Five years before, Ethan's last heist had been in Chicago, where Gruber had served as director to the Chicago Mortgage and Thrift. And although Ethan had never personally seen the man, he'd followed the publicity, heard about the scandal that had ensued. Because of his lackadaisical security, Gruber had been demoted and sent to another bank in . . .

Madison.

Silas Gruber's eyes widened in mutual recognition. His face suddenly became fierce, and he reached out to grasp Ethan's shirt with a bloody hand. "Damn you," he growled. "You did this to me. You—" His words suddenly stopped and his brow creased in confusion. "You aren't . . . the one . . ." he muttered, almost to himself.

Ethan grew still at the man's words. "Who did this, Gruber?" he demanded. "Who's responsible?"

But the man didn't seem to hear him. Instead, his eyes grew dull, seeming to look in upon himself. "I paid Krupp to kill you . . . hated you." His fingers tightened, pulling Ethan toward him. "After what you did to me . . . I would have done anything. Anything!" He gasped and squeezed his eyes shut against the pain. The fire roared closer and hotter, but Ethan found himself unable to move until he knew the truth. "Krupp . . . Star. For a price, he will arrange . . . murder."

Ethan glanced beyond Gruber at the licking flames. From the moment he'd seen Silas's face, he'd guessed that Gruber was the man he'd overheard talking to Krupp weeks before. Now he had his proof. But that didn't explain who had been impersonating the Gentleman Bandit. It was obvious that Gruber had thought it was Ethan McGuire.

Gruber cried out, and his fingers grew lax. Bending toward him, Ethan demanded over the hiss and crack of the fire, "Who did this? You realize they meant to kill us both tonight. Who?"

Gruber's eyes flicked open, but Ethan knew his mind was in the past. "I killed . . . Jeb . . . for Krupp." A gurgling chuckle bubbled from his throat. "Discovered I didn't have the . . . nerve to kill a man . . . I meant to wound him . . ." His fingers clenched. "Just . . . wound him . . ." His lips twitched. "But the blast . . . set it wrong . . . it finished the job . . ."

"Damn you, who—" Ethan's words died and he straightened, realizing he was talking to a dead man.

He coughed. The flames licked closer, filling the air with a cloying smoke and the rushing crackle of timber being consumed. Knowing that he, too, would be a dead man if he didn't get out of the bank immediately, Ethan reached out and belly-crawled toward the front door. He lifted a hand to the doorknob, only then realizing he couldn't get out without a key. The fire roared behind him, growing hotter and searing his skin. There was no time to pick the lock.

Swearing to himself, Ethan growled and pushed himself to his feet. Grasping a chair from beside the door, he threw it through the plate-glass window, then, holding a hand over his face, lunged into the night.

The impetus of his movements threw him forward, and he stumbled and fell to the ground. He moaned when sharp bits of glass dug into his clothes and skin, but the relief from the scalding heat of the flames overshadowed his pain. Trying to gather his strength, Ethan dragged sweet, gulping lungfuls of air into his chest, then straightened, intent upon escaping before the law rode hell-bent toward him.

The snap of a rifle being cocked split the night and Ethan froze, slowly lifting his head. When he found himself pinned beneath the sights of Jacob Grey's weapon, he took a deep breath, coughed, then reluctantly lifted his hands in surrender.

Jacob didn't speak. He merely walked toward him and clamped a set of irons around his wrists, then gestured for Ethan to follow him in the direction of the jail. Behind him, the bank shrieked in a sudden explosion of fire.

The figure in black rode toward the outskirts of town. As if already certain of the way, the horse followed the commands of its master and veered away from the road. Slowly, quietly, the animal threaded through the trees before coming to a stop at the end of the weed-infested drive leading up the abandoned Johnston farmhouse.

After only a moment, the thief was joined by another figure. Moonlight glinted off Judge Krupp's silver hair, giving him the appearance of a jovial grandfather or an ancient sage.

"Well?" he asked quietly.

The thief smiled. "I did everything just as you told me, then emptied the safe, just for the hell of it."

"What about—"

"McGuire? Dead."

"And Gruber?"

"Dead."

Krupp lifted a brow in surprise. "I'm impressed."

"You should be."

His own lips twitched in a suggestion of a smile. "You'd best head back into town."

"In a minute." The thief turned in the saddle and gazed back at the yellow glow beginning to tinge the edge of the horizon. "It's really too bad, you know— about the bank, I mean."

"Why's that?"

"They'll never find my calling card in the rubble."

Krupp snorted in ironic humor. "They'll find two bodies and assume the thief was caught in his own blast. Don't you think that's calling card enough?"

"I suppose it will have to be."

The clamor of the town bell rose eerily from the distance, and the judge stiffened. "Damn," he muttered, almost to himself.

"It's just because of the fire."

"The bell's too fast, too regular. Almost as if—" He twisted in his saddle to glare at the thief. "As if a murderer had been caught." His eyes narrowed. "Or a thief."

"No! He was dead. I know he was!"

"Dammit, you'd better hope so! Otherwise both of us could be in a hell of a lot of trouble."

Jacob whirled to face Gerald Stone, slamming his fist onto his desk in emphasis. "The man is within *my* jurisdiction and he will be held within *my* jail until he can be brought to speedy trial!"

"You had your orders, Jacob. If you managed to apprehend Ethan McGuire, you were supposed to take him to the farmhouse."

"I caught the man crashing through the plate-glass

window of the Madison Thrift and Loan. Since Krupp's men evidently left before the appointed hour, I was alone and found myself forced to apprehend him without help.''

"Dammit! You've created an awkward situation, Grey. This man was supposed to be turned over to the Star.''

"The Star, hell! Where was the Star when I needed someone to cover my ass?''

"Nevertheless—''

"The Star blew their chance to execute McGuire without drawing suspicion to themselves. Now it's a matter for the courts.''

"Courts!''

"No jury in the world would acquit him. It's simply a matter of linking him to the other crimes. Then Ethan McGuire will be punished through due process.''

"Due process?'' Stone repeated in disbelief. "The man is guilty! You know that, I know that—hell, the whole town knows that. If you weren't able to take him to the farmhouse, why didn't you plant a bullet through his head?''

"If I'd done that, the whole town would have known within an hour that I was a member of the Star.''

"There are ways to cover up your involvement.''

"I wasn't about to undermine my own authority here by exposing myself in that way.''

"This is the same man who murdered your friend!''

"Jeb Clark would have backed me in my actions.''

"Clark was a member of the Star. He would have followed orders.'' Stone strode toward the front window and gestured toward the crowd lining the opposite boardwalk. "Do you see them, Grey? Those men have lost everything in that bank—some of which will never be recovered. They aren't looking for law and order, they're looking for—''

"Justice?''

"Damn right. And the only justice they'll see will be found in McGuire's death. Those men are out for blood.''

Jacob regarded his friend through narrowed eyes. "And

so, it seems, is the Star. Why are you so all fired up to see the man shot? He'll meet his just deserts in time."

"The man is guilty. You said that yourself. You're simply tying up time and money that will end with a bullet in his head anyway. What would it have mattered if you'd shot the man?"

"I would have been taking the law into my own hands."

"You're a member of the Star."

"That doesn't make it lawful."

"We *are* the law, dammit!"

"Then why can't you see that I had to bring him into custody? If I'd shot the man without at least making an effort to bring him to trial, my authority would have been in jeopardy in this town. *This time* the lawful order of things had to be obeyed."

Stone pointed to the crowd. "Those men aren't going to care whether the court damns him first or if he just ends up dead."

"I say it matters. And I'm the one who is responsible and ultimately to blame," Jacob repeated stubbornly.

"Don't be a fool, Jacob. The Star—"

"The Star is not responsible for upholding the law in this town. *I* am."

"Then turn the man over to me."

A heavy beat of silence pounded in the crowded office. "What?" Jacob asked in disbelief.

"Turn the man over to me. Notify the town that McGuire can't get a fair trial in Madison. Once the man is in my custody, the Star can take care of matters without endangering your position here."

Jacob hesitated.

"It will work," Stone added smoothly. "And no one will ever know you're turning the man over to the Star for execution."

Jacob stared at the man before him, taking in his earnest expression and the cajoling cast of his features. His stomach churned sickeningly as he studied Stone's eager expression. "I'll think about it," he finally conceded.

Stone's features hardened for a moment in displeasure. He threw Jacob a stern glance and swept his hat onto his head. "It's the only way, Jacob. The Star has already made a decision on McGuire's guilt. To buck its authority would only prove to be a mistake."

"Maybe. But I'm the one who has to decide if it's a mistake I can live with."

"Just don't take too long in deciding, Grey. An awful lot of things can happen to a man when—"

"Don't threaten me, Stone," Jacob inserted in a low voice. "And don't you dare threaten my family." He leaned forward on the desk in emphasis. "I'm not as stupid or trusting as some of your other members—and you should have known that long before now. I'll act within my own conscience. And if anything should happen to me or my kin, arrangements have already been made that will uncover the entire network of the Star."

Stone seemed to pale. "You took a blood oath."

"That was before you started making threats."

Stone's face settled into a mask of fury, but he knew he would get no farther with Jacob. "Make your decision, Jacob. I'll be back at nightfall." Jamming his hat onto his head, he threw one last hard glance in the other man's direction, then stormed out of the office.

Stone wove his way through the crowd of onlookers, then swung across the street and climbed onto the boardwalk just in front of the china shop. Taking a quick glance around him, he joined Judge Krupp.

"Well?"

"Grey is balking at the idea of releasing McGuire."

Krupp scowled and tipped his head to glare at the harsh summer haze coating the sky. He had to see to it that McGuire was executed. Soon. Otherwise, there was too much of a risk that the true circumstances surrounding Gruber's murder could be exposed. "Exert a little pressure."

"He's not taking too kindly to threats."

"If Grey won't release the man, we'll simply have to arrange another 'escape' like we did in Dewey and kill the man when he tries to run."

"When?"

"We'll wait until tomorrow morning, when everyone will be distracted with Clark's funeral."

"What do you suggest?"

"Go ahead with the original plan. At dawn, we'll escort McGuire to the farmhouse and shoot him." He turned to spear Stone with a stern glance. "Then see to it that Grey meets with the same fate—some unfortunate accident occurring in the line of duty. I don't want someone on the Star Council who won't take orders from his betters."

Stone grinned and touched a finger to his hat in a mocking salute. "Yes, sir."

Jacob took a set of keys from his top desk drawer and held them tightly in his hand for a moment.

"Rusty, I'm going up to the cells for a minute. Once I come down, why don't you go grab yourself a bite to eat? I'll go later."

"Sure thing, Jacob."

Stepping to the back of the office, Jacob unlocked the heavy oak door at the foot of the staircase, then climbed the worn stone steps to the top floor.

As jailhouses went, Madison's was one of the securest in the area. Built entirely of stone, the two-story dwelling had no full-length windows except those on the main floor. Above, in the portion containing the prisoners' cells, smaller windows had been cut into the rock high above eye level, allowing light and ventilation but no view of the street below.

Pausing to open the door at the top of the steps, Jacob stepped inside. A large open area led into two separate cells, each big enough to hold a pair of men comfortably— four uncomfortably.

Crossing the room to the last cell, Jacob found Ethan sitting upon one of the bunks, his back propped against the wall. Though he'd no doubt heard Jacob arrive, the other man waited a moment before turning his head to meet Jacob's gaze.

McGuire's eyes were dark, his expression calm but

wary. Finally, he said, "You're on the Star, aren't you, Grey?"

Jacob didn't speak. He measured the man before him, wondering if Ethan McGuire were aware of all the forces that had brought the two of them face-to-face after so many years.

"Have you come to kill me?"

"Not yet."

Jacob stared at his long-time nemesis through the iron slats of the jail cell, his body filling with a thousand conflicting emotions: triumph, frustration, self-righteousness—even a little pity.

Ethan endured his gaze for a moment before slowly stating, "I didn't kill Gruber or empty his safe."

Jacob gave a snort of sarcastic humor. "And you expect me to believe that fact just because you say so?"

Ethan scowled. "No. I expect you to believe me because it's true. Gruber was all but dead long before I ever stepped into the bank."

"And what were you doing in the bank?"

"Waiting for the thief."

"Why?"

"*Why?* Because I'm tired of running for something *I* haven't done."

"So the rumors of a pardon were true?"

"Yeah."

"And what were the conditions?"

"Other than restoration of property, five years within the law."

Jacob became quiet, and some of the pieces of the puzzle in his head began to shift into place.

"You've been with my sister, haven't you?"

Ethan opened his mouth to deny it, then met the other man's quiet gaze. "Yeah."

"You were at the boardinghouse all this time."

Though it wasn't a question, Ethan nodded.

"And you were there that day we broke into the garret?"

"On the roof."

"My sister is responsible, isn't she?"

"Don't blame her for this!"

"I don't blame her for anything." Jacob's eyes grew quiet and dark. "She's in love with you, isn't she?"

Ethan turned away, denying the heavy regret that settled in his own stomach. "Yeah."

"And you? Do you love her?"

Ethan swiveled his head to glare at the other man. "I don't see how it's any of your business. You're going to make sure I swing for the crimes I may or may not have committed."

Jacob's hand tightened into angry fists. "Dammit! She's my sister. I have a right to know whether or not you really love her, or whether you're merely playing her for the fool!"

The stone walls echoed his words, and Ethan sighed, plunging his fingers through his hair.

"I love her," he admitted, though it seemed a crime to be saying the words to anyone but Lettie. "If I knew a way, I'd show her just how much. I'd take her away from here, see to it that she had the kind of life she deserves." His voice betrayed him by becoming slightly husky. "But that's not going to happen, is it? You're going to see to it that I never touch her again. Aren't you?"

"I love my sister. I won't see her hurt."

"And you think I've hurt her." Ethan sighed, rubbing a hand over his face. "I suppose you're right. But I never meant to hurt her at all. She's so sweet and kind." He swallowed past the tightness gathering in his throat. "She was the first person who accepted me—flaws and all—and believed me when I told her the truth. I never thought I'd meet a woman like that." He glanced at Jacob, and his lips quirked in an unwilling smile. "I certainly never thought I'd fall in love with *your* little sister." His eyes met Jacob's. "But I did. And now I suppose you're going to have to decide whether to believe in your sister's judgment or continue a five-year vendetta."

Jacob didn't speak. He merely studied Ethan with narrowed eyes, then backed away. He was nearly to the doorway that led to the staircase before Ethan's voice stopped him.

"Will you do me a favor? For old times' sake?"

Jacob turned to find Ethan watching him through the iron slats.

"Old times? We were never friends."

"You've been after my tail for so long, Grey, we're more than mere acquaintances."

Jacob hesitated, then nodded, realizing he knew as much about Ethan as he did about some of his oldest friends. "What do you want?" he asked, less than graciously.

"I need to talk to Lettie."

"No."

Ethan's jaw became hard, but other than that he didn't react. "Then can I talk with the Beasleys and a preacher?"

"The Beasleys?" Jacob repeated in disbelief.

"Surely two old harmless women wouldn't jeopardize your reputation as a strict upholder of the law. I'll need someone to send word to my family. I'd rather it were the Beasleys who did it."

Jacob opened his mouth to refuse, then finally shrugged. "Fine. I'll see if Rusty can't round 'em up somewhere."

"Thanks."

Once again he turned to walk away but was halted by Ethan's voice.

"Oh, and Jacob?"

He glanced behind him in impatience. "What?"

"Take care of Lettie for me, will you?"

"She's my little sister."

"Yeah. But she's my woman."

Although it seemed like hours to Ethan, in reality it was only a few minutes before the door at the top of the steps opened and the Beasley sisters peeked around the edge. They stepped hesitantly inside, and Jacob trailed behind them. He gave Ethan a stern look, then offered one to the ladies that was a little kinder but forbidding nonetheless.

"Five minutes," he stated bluntly. "And I don't want any talk passing between you except for a message to his folks." He turned and closed the door behind him and walked down the steps.

Ethan waited until the heavy thump of the other man's boots disappeared before standing up and walking toward the door to his cell. His fingers curled around the iron slats and he smiled in what he hoped was a congenial manner, knowing that if he were to set things to rights, he would need the help of these two women.

"Ladies," he began. "I know you don't know me, but—"

"We know you," Alma inserted.

"You're Lettie's beau," Amelia added.

"You know?"

"We've known for days," Alma retorted.

Ethan frowned, amazed that the women had kept such a secret. "And you didn't tell anyone?"

"Indeed not!" both women exclaimed at once.

Ethan took a step forward, and his voice dropped to a confidential murmur. His palms grew slightly sweaty, knowing that the next few minutes would probably prove to be some of the most important in his life. "Ladies, since you know about . . . us, can I trust you to do a favor for me?"

Both Alma and Amelia moved closer, glancing over their shoulders as if someone were listening.

"Do you want us to break you out?" Amelia whispered.

Despite his predicament, Ethan's lips twitched ever so slightly. "No. That won't be necessary. I need you to send some messages to my family."

Amelia's features creased in distress. "Oh, Alma!" she breathed, turning toward her sister. "He has family."

"Well of course he has family! Did you think he sprouted from a cabbage patch?"

"Alma, I never—"

"Ladies, please," Ethan interrupted quickly, knowing that if the women got too deep into their argument, his time with them would run out.

At the sound of his voice, both women turned toward

him, their faces settling into apple-withered masks of contrition.

"Do you have a scrap of paper? I need to send a telegram to my family and another note to my brother, Ned. Ned Abernathy."

"Ned? I never would have thought it," Amelia muttered as she scrambled in her reticule and removed her diary and a pencil. "If you would simply be so kind as to skip some of the more . . . personal pages in the front, Mr.—"

"McGuire. Ethan McGuire."

Ethan grinned at her and selected a page in the back. He quickly wrote the necessary information, then ripped the page free. "This will inform my mother what has happened and notify her that I'll need a lawyer. It also instructs her to change my will, naming Lettie as my beneficiary should anything . . . happen. At the bottom, there's a personal item that I'd like my mother to send as soon as possible. When the package arrives, I'd appreciate it if you'd see to it that Lettie gets it right away."

Amelia reached for the notes, but Alma slapped her hand and took them instead. "We'll send this immediately. Don't you worry about a thing."

"Thank you." He cleared his throat and glanced down at his feet. "There's one last thing I'd like you to arrange, if you don't mind. Before long, it will be common knowledge to everyone that Lettie has hidden me in the boardinghouse for two weeks."

"Oh my, yes," Amelia inserted. "Her reputation will be in shreds after staying in the garret with a man for over—*ouch!*" She glared at her older sister, who had reached out and pinched her arm.

"Amelia, hush up!"

"No, she's right. And that's exactly what I'm afraid will happen." Ethan allowed his facade of calm control to drop for a moment and a small measure of his frustration and fear—not so much for himself, but for Lettie—to show through. He'd opened her up to a situation worse

293

than any he'd ever dreamed of, and all because he'd thought he could resolve things himself.

"I've arranged for a minister to visit me at two. I need you to see that Lettie is here as well. Can you do that for me? I'd like to see us married before the day is out."

The two women gasped in delight, but when they looked at Ethan, they suddenly seemed to realize the seriousness of their errand, and their pleasure faded.

"We'll do whatever we can," Amelia whispered when they heard the thump of Jacob's feet on the stairs.

Alma quickly folded the note in half and slipped it down the front of her bodice, then patted the voluminous expanse of her bosom. "You can count on us, Mr. McGuire."

"Ethan."

The two elderly women straightened a little after being granted the unexpected pleasure of using his first name upon such a short acquaintance. However, when Amelia opened her mouth, Alma held her sister's arm to keep her from speaking. "Yes, Ethan. We'll see to it that all of the arrangements are made. Don't you worry about a thing."

The door opened, and Jacob stepped inside. His eyes darted from Ethan to the Beasleys, but he obviously couldn't tell much by their expressions.

"Your time is up."

The Beasleys nodded, glared at him, and brushed past, carefully holding their skirts so they wouldn't lap against Jacob's boots.

"What did you tell them?" Jacob asked, turning toward Ethan.

"Nothing you need to know. Just tying up some personal business."

"You know I'll have them followed."

"I figured that."

"It won't do you any good to try and escape. There's a crowd of men waiting to catch a glimpse of you. They'd fill you full of holes the minute you stepped out the door."

"Like I said before, Grey, I'm not about to run from

something I didn't do. And if you shoot me, my blood will be on your hands.''

Jacob's jaw remained hard, his eyes dark. Without another word, he turned and closed the door behind him. Once in his office again, he stood for a moment, battling the feelings swarming within him. So much had happened in the last few hours: reading Jeb's clippings, then coming face-to-face with Ethan McGuire after all these years.

And now I suppose you're going to have to decide whether to believe in your sister's judgment or continue a five-year vendetta.

But his conscience wouldn't let him rest.

Very deliberately, Jacob turned to Rusty Janson and said, "Find Gerald Stone and tell him that the prisoner will be delivered into his custody at nine tomorrow morning."

Rusty evidently understood the import of the message, because he nodded and strode from the office, slamming the front door behind him.

Stepping to the window, Jacob watched his deputy disappear down the boardwalk. Although he tried to control the tension seeping into his body, he could not control the heavy sickness that seemed to settle into his stomach for the duration.

Jacob moved back to his desk and sank into his chair, grasping the long iron key to Ethan's jail cell. He stared at the front door, waiting for his deputy to return. His only company was the pounding of his heart and the restless *tic, tic, tic* of the key as he tapped it against the desk and formulated his plans.

20

Before going in search of Lettie, the Beasley sisters made a slight detour down the alley beside the jailhouse. They waited in the shadows of the alley until Rusty had returned and Jacob slipped outside, intent upon reaching the small house behind the marshal's office, where Jacob's living quarters were situated.

Alma had earlier outlined a plan of action—one that would keep Jacob out of the office for at least a few hours. Now they could only hope it would work.

"Ready, Sister?"

"Of course, Alma."

The two of them glanced at each other, half in fear, half in worry, then stepped out of the alley and moved through the grass toward Jacob's house. They stopped at the door, took a deep breath, and then Amelia began to gasp and cry as if she were on the verge of hysterics. Alma knocked, waited for Jacob's response, then flung open the door, helping her sister inside.

Jacob glanced up from the plate of food in front of him, rising in concern.

"Ladies, what's wrong?"

"It's Amelia. You know how susceptible to a shock she can be."

Immediately concerned, Jacob rushed to take Amelia by the shoulders and guide her into the room. "You sit down here and tell me what's happened."

"If . . . if you could just fetch me a g-glass of water first."

Jacob nodded, clearly uncomfortable with a near-hysterical woman on his hands, and dodged outside to the pump. As soon as he'd disappeared, the Beasleys took their positions on either side of the doorway.

"Now remember, Sister," Alma whispered, "when he comes through the door, hit him over the head enough to stun him. Then we'll tie him up until morning."

Amelia nodded in understanding and took her place.

"Ladies, I hope you don't—"

Jacob stepped through the door, and Alma crashed him over the top of the head with her book-laden purse.

"What the—"

"Hit him, Amelia. Mine didn't take!"

Before Jacob knew what was happening, Amelia had struck him on the top of his head with her purse. There was a muffled clang, then Jacob's eyes widened in surprise, rolled back in his head, and he crashed to the floor. Amelia's bag fell onto the floor beside him with a loud clank.

Alma gazed in surprise at the fallen man, then at her sister. "Well done, Amelia!"

"Why thank you, Sister."

"I didn't know you had it in you."

Amelia straightened with pride.

Alma moved to grasp her sister's voluminous reticule then frowned when she picked it up. "What in the world have you got in here?"

Amelia's features creased into a network of worried lines. "I couldn't find any books that would fit in my bag."

"So what did you use?"

"Jacob's cast-iron paperweight."

Alma gazed in amazement at her sister, then at the figure spread-eagled at their feet. "Somehow I don't think it will prove necessary to tie the man up."

* * *

Lettie stormed through the jailhouse door, and when Rusty Janson tried to escort her outside again, she dodged his grip and whirled away. She immediately rued the action when her head pounded and her stomach churned. Though she'd awakened nearly an hour before, the effects of the drug Ethan had given her the night before still clouded her mind—but not her purpose.

"I need to see Ethan McGuire."

"He's not being allowed any visitors."

"It's important that I see him."

"Not important enough."

"Jacob would let me see him."

"No, Miss Lettie. He wouldn't."

Lettie tried to keep her voice calm, but a small measure of her desperation seeped through. "You've got to let me in, Rusty."

"No, Miss Lettie, I don't."

Lettie resisted the urge to stamp her foot in frustration, whirling instead to glare out the window. A few clumps of men still stared at the jailhouse with hollow eyes, or argued and gestured toward each other in evident fury.

Lettie wrapped her arms around her waist in an effort to still the panic that welled within her. But she kept butting head-on with the certainty that something was brewing in Madison. Something more than a simple arrest and trial. Somehow, she knew other forces were at work. Forces that wouldn't rest until Ethan McGuire was dead.

Turning, she tried again. "Rusty, you don't understand. I have to see him." Her voice grew husky, and she cleared her throat, despising the telltale weakness. "I have to see him, talk to him. Please."

Rusty shifted his weight and glanced down at his hands. At the first sign that she might be making headway, Lettie pushed her pride aside and begged, "Please, please let me in."

Once again, Rusty straightened. "No."

"If you don't, I'll tell Jacob about that night you fell asleep on duty. Or the time you came in out of the rain and—"

"Aw, Lettie, you know I can't let you in. You know what your brother would do to me."

"He'll never know."

Rusty clenched his jaw and stared at a point beyond her shoulder. "No."

Lettie closed her eyes and allowed the mask of control she'd worn up to date to fall. "They're going to kill him, Rusty. Please . . ." Her voice cracked.

"Lettie?"

"Lettie!"

The Beasleys burst through the jailhouse door, but Lettie ignored them. "You have to let me in, Rusty. I love that man in there, and I couldn't bear it if time were to slip away without my being with him any minute possible."

"Aw, Lettie," Rusty moaned.

Alma and Amelia Beasley bustled up beside her, taking her by the arms as if Lettie were going to faint and needed their support. "Rusty Janson, what in the world are you thinking of, being this heartless to a woman in her condition? Can't you see she's—"

"In the family way," Amelia whispered.

Both Lettie and Rusty glanced at the women in surprise, but Alma plunged on. "The last thing she needs right now is a shock. Landsakes! Haven't you got the brains God gave a piss ant?"

Rusty's eyes darted from Lettie's face, to her stomach, to her face, then a point above her shoulder.

"I—I didn't know."

"Well of course you didn't. You're only a man."

"But I—"

"A heartless man, keeping this girl away from—well, I can't even say it. It's simply too cruel."

"Too, too cruel," Amelia echoed.

"Never in all my born days have I seen anyone so wicked."

"And heartless!"

"I said that, Amelia."

"It deserves saying again."

"How true." Alma threw a fulminating glare in his

direction. "This girl carries that man's child, Rusty. Don't you think a man deserves to know about a thing like that before he's taken away?"

"You . . . you . . ." Amelia balled her hands into fists, unable to come up with a suitable insult. "You *man!*"

Alma's head bobbed in a fierce nod of approval.

Rusty swallowed nervously. "But if someone should see—"

"No one will see. Landsakes, this is a jailhouse, not a hotel. Surely you can keep any unwanted intruders away."

"But Jacob—"

"You leave Jacob to us."

"Yes, to us."

"We'll see he stays put right where he is."

"Yes, we'll see."

"Well . . ."

"You just keep everyone out and give these young-sters some privacy."

"Privacy."

"No one needs to come in, except for the clergy."

"Clergy!" Rusty shouted. "What in the hell for?"

"We've got to give that child a legal name! Even if its father is a criminal—not that I'm saying he is."

Rusty finally threw his hands up in defeat. "Fine. Fine! Have one of them *soi-rees* up there, for all I care. Just keep it quiet so's Jacob doesn't find out."

Spinning on his toes, Rusty stamped toward the door that led up to the cells. Lettie threw a thankful glance at the sisters and followed him with shaking limbs.

"We'll be up in a few minutes with the preacher, Lettie."

"Don't you worry!"

"You've got a visitor, McGuire." With a gesture of his hand, Rusty motioned for Lettie to step inside the cell block.

Lettie moved into the stone antechamber, surprised by the fact that it was smaller then she'd imagined, but pleasantly cool.

"Hello, Ethan."

At the soft sound of her voice, Ethan lifted the arm that had lain across his eyes.

"Lettie?" he breathed in disbelief.

"Ten minutes. Then if the preacher isn't here, I'm sending you home," Rusty muttered, then backed from the room and slammed the main door shut behind him.

Both Lettie and Ethan remained rooted where they were until the shuffle of Rusty's feet had disappeared down the stone steps and the ground floor door had been shut.

Ethan rose from the bunk and moved slowly toward his cell door, his eyes trained hungrily upon her face. "I didn't think they would let you in here."

"The Beasleys are very resourceful."

An awkward silence settled between them for only a minute. Then Lettie rushed toward him, thrusting her arms through the iron bars and framing his face in her hands so that she could reassure herself that Ethan was real and unharmed. "I was so scared," she whispered.

Ethan's hand slipped through the slats to wrap around her waist, pulling her as close as the bars allowed.

"Why did you drug me that way?" she asked, her voice filled with the panic she'd felt those first few moments after she'd struggled to consciousness.

"I had to."

"Am I that horrible to make love to?"

"No! But I knew you'd try to follow me to the bank."

"I wouldn't have done any such thing!"

"You would."

She rubbed her thumbs across the contours of his jaw; the stubble of a beard rasped against her skin, and she frowned at the remnants of smoke and grime. Her brow creased in concern when she found several shallow cuts still caked with dried blood and dirt. "Yes, you're right. I would have come with you."

"You're too impulsive."

"Yes."

"You're too impetuous."

She nodded.

"But . . ." His hand lifted and slipped through a higher bar so that his thumb could lightly skim across her cheek. His expression became sad and just a little wistful. "But, even though I shouldn't be telling you at a time like this, I love you, Lettie Grey."

A slow burning warmth began in her chest and radiated outward. Lettie tipped his head down with her hands so that she could look deep into his eyes.

"I'll never tire of hearing you say that."

His lips twitched in a self-conscious smile. "I love you."

Lettie wrapped her arms more tightly around his neck and pulled him close. "Why?"

"Because you're you, Lettie Grey." He drew back, and his expression became at once serious and tender. "Letitia Grey, will you marry me?"

Lettie drew back ever so slightly and lifted her fingers to her lips in an attempt to still the shakiness of her smile. But despite her efforts to appear calm, her eyes sparkled with joyful tears. "I would be honored," she replied with warm sincerity.

The thump of Rusty's boots on the steps warned them of his approach.

"You're sure, Lettie," Ethan asked quickly. "Nothing has really been solved, you know. I'm still up to my ass in alligators."

"We'll see it through."

"I want you to stay in Chicago with my mother during all of this mess. She'll want to meet you—and your mother. Promise me you'll go there."

"I promise. I'd love to meet her."

"Promise me you'll live with all the advantages my family can give you. I ignored the money my mother set aside for my use, but that doesn't mean you have to."

"Ethan, you'll be there with me," she insisted.

But the silence that settled between them was filled with the tacit haze of their own desperation.

The second door rasped open.

"Promise me, Lettie," Ethan said quickly, his grip tightening.

"I promise."

Rusty stepped into the room and glared in their direction. A moment later, the Beasleys rushed past him, carrying a huge parcel wrapped in brown paper and a basket covered with a gingham cloth.

"Pastor Phillips will be here in five minutes, Rusty."

Rusty only glared at them. "I still don't know about this. You're going to get us all into a hell—heck of a lot of trouble."

"Nonsense."

"Jacob's going to come."

"Oh, he's not going to come," Amelia blurted.

Alma pinched her sister in warning, shot her a desperate look, and offered Rusty a quick smile. "What Amelia means is that we just saw Jacob, and he's all . . . tied up with affairs in town."

"Yes, all tied up."

"He told us to tell you that he won't be back until late."

"Very, very late."

Rusty eyed them in suspicion. "You'd better hope so."

"Oh, we're sure about that."

"Absolutely positive."

Rusty's gaze slipped to the paraphernalia the Beasleys held in their hands. "What the hell—heck is all that?"

"Supplies."

"There's to be a wedding, you know."

Rusty growled.

"If you would be so kind as to open the cells for us—"

"*What?*"

"—we have a few things to prepare," Alma continued as if he had not spoken.

"Shee-it! Why don't I just escort the man all pretty like down to the church?"

"No, that would be asking too much of you."

"Far too much."

Rusty turned to stab an incriminating finger in Lettie's direction. "*You* go downstairs."

"Well of course she will," Alma retorted.

"It's bad luck to see the groom before the wedding," Amelia added.

Muttering softly to himself, Rusty grasped Lettie's arm and dragged her toward the outer door. "After you," he stated sarcastically.

But the Beasleys paid no heed to his mood. Alma hurried to hand Lettie the brown paper parcel and whispered, "Go on and change into this. I'm sorry it's not a real wedding gown, but it was the best I could do in a pinch."

Rusty swore. "Miss Beasley!"

"Move along, Rusty."

Picking up her skirts, Lettie preceded the harried deputy. Then, left alone in the office, Lettie took a deep, calming breath, set the cumbersome packages on the desk, and untied the string. A soft gasp of delight escaped from her lips when she found a store-bought dress and a set of delicate unmentionables lying within a bed of tissue paper.

Quickly scooping the package into her arms, Lettie hurried into the back storage room and closed the door. In a moment, she had stripped off her own clothes and reached for those in the package.

On top of the pile lay a delicate batiste camisole trimmed with insertion and a matching pair of underdrawers. Sliding them over her limbs, Lettie delighted in the texture and fresh scents of the undergarments. It had been so long since she'd had any new clothes. Especially new undergarments.

Breathing deeply in anticipation, she pulled aside the next layer of tissue to uncover a delicate corset made of grosgrain ribbons and lace. The kind worn only to bed . . . or on a wedding night.

Slipping it around her torso, she quickly cinched the garment around her ribs, tightening the laces as much as they would allow. Then she slipped on a dimity-flounced petticoat with an attached bustle and buttoned the foundation garment around her waist.

Unsure of what the Beasleys had chosen as a gown,

yet knowing it would become her wedding dress, Lettie
drew aside that last layer of tissue and gasped. Lettie
had seen the gown before in Mrs. Goddard's dress-shop
window, and she had never hoped to own something so
beautiful herself.

Lifting it free from its wrapping, Lettie first donned the
gray cashmere skirt and buttoned it around her waist.
The front tablier of the skirt was formed by tiers of
puffed and gathered fabric, falling to a gathered ruffle
along the bottom and decorated with a knee sash that
swooped in a graceful arc, knotting in the center of the
skirt. The back portion had been draped and tucked with
yards of cashmere that fell into a demi-train in the back.

After fluffing the skirt to see that it lay properly over
the bustled petticoat, Lettie slipped into the hip-length
bodice of garnet velvet, fastening the hooks that edged
the mock vest of smocked gray cashmere from neck to
hip. Her hands trembled as she smoothed the full-cut
bodice over her bust and hips, then reached to hook a
matching cashmere capelet over her shoulders.

For a moment, Lettie stood trembling in her unaccustomed finery, blinking back a slight sheen of tears. There
would be no family at her wedding, no guests, no flowers, no music. Instead, it would be a rushed affair that
would appear unseemly to even her most liberal neighbors and friends.

And yet . . . there could be no choice. Lettie loved
Ethan McGuire with all her heart. She wanted his name.
She wanted his love. She wanted . . .

Him.

A soft knock interrupted her thoughts, and she opened
the door to find Alma Beasley waiting for her.

"It fits!" Alma breathed in solemn pleasure. "I thought
you'd be delicate enough to wear it—though why Mrs.
Goddard makes all of her models in such an ungodly
size, I'll never know," she added, in an attempt at
lightness. But her humor seemed flat in the tension
settling around them.

"Thank you, Miss Beasley. I don't think you know
how much this means to me. I love Ethan so much. I—"

Alma Beasley reached out to squeeze Lettie's hand, and, for a moment, something vulnerable and aching lingered in her own eyes. "I know, Lettie. I know."

"You've been so kind to me. And to Ethan."

"A kindness you richly deserve." Alma reached out to cup Lettie's cheek with a soft, wrinkled hand. "You don't know what a joy you've been to Amelia and me. We've watched you grow from a child into a woman." Her voice grew whisper soft. "And we've seen our own youth in your eyes. My, what wonderful memories you've brought back to us." Her lips wobbled slightly, and she tried to force a smile. "You're a good daughter, Lettie. And a fine sister to Jacob. But just keep in mind that there comes a time when a young girl has to break free from the ties that bind her. Then it's time to be a woman. Time to fly from the nest and find your own little niche in the world."

Alma took her hand and patted it gently. "But now's not the time for such speeches. We've got a wedding to attend." She drew away, and Lettie followed, trying to accustom herself to the weight of the train behind her and the added boning in the bodice of the gown.

"Here's your bouquet," Alma murmured, handing her a nosegay of yellow summer roses that had been inserted into the center of a lacy handkerchief and tied with ribbons. "And your veil." She took a square of tulle that she'd obviously obtained from the dressmaker and tenderly draped it over Lettie's head. "Ready?"

Lettie nodded, tamping down her own nerves and her regrets that her marriage had to be so rushed and secret. "Yes. I'm ready."

"Good."

Taking her hand, Alma led her toward the door and helped her up the steps. Lettie carefully held her skirts and stepped through the top door, then looked up. A tightness gripped her throat when she saw that the Beasleys had taken a few minutes to decorate the iron bars of the jail cells with pink and white ribbons and yellow roses.

Her smile wobbled a little, and a tightness gripped her

throat at the thoughtful gesture. But her pleasure was overshadowed by a much warmer emotion when she looked beyond them to find Ethan waiting beside Pastor Phillips. Though Ethan wore the same soot-stained clothing, he was freshly scrubbed and shaved, and his hair had been neatly combed back from his face.

"If you'll step this way, Miss Grey," the pastor intoned. Although he obviously felt pleased about saving her soul from eternal damnation, his eyes flicked to her stomach and he frowned disapprovingly.

But Lettie only had eyes for Ethan. Offering him a shaky smile, she took his side, then reached out to take his hand. Only then did she feel the irons encircling his wrists. Glancing up, she realized that, although he was free from his cell, he was shackled nonetheless.

"Let's get on with this," Rusty blurted.

"Yes, of course." Pastor Phillips slipped his spectacles around his ears, then folded his hands around his prayerbook and eyed Ethan and Lettie with serious regard.

"The prospect of matrimony is not one to be entered into lightly. . . ."

As the pastor continued, Lettie glanced up at Ethan and soon found herself lost in the watchful, tender emotions she saw shining from his eyes. In all of her imaginings, in all of her fantasies, she had never dreamed that love could truly be like this. She never dreamed that it could be filled with such a measure of passion and pleasure . . . and pain. And yet, though she knew the future was far from settled between them, she also knew that she would have no regrets, regardless of what might happen.

So when the pastor asked her to repeat her vows, her words were strong, and sure, and sweet. And when Ethan spoke, she absorbed each word into her hungry soul, knowing that she would never forget this moment. Ever.

"The ring?"

Ethan lifted his hands, and his shackles clanked as he drew the ruby signet ring from his finger and slipped it over Lettie's finger. Since it was far too big, she closed her hand to keep it in place.

"By the power invested in me by the Church and the state of Illinois, I now pronounce you man and wife. You may kiss the bride."

Ethan lifted a hand to her shoulder, turning her toward him. His eyes blazed with love and just a hint of buried desperation. "Never forget I love you," he murmured for her ears alone, before folding the veil away from her face. "No matter what happens." Then he tipped her chin with his finger and pressed his lips against her own.

Though the kiss was brief and tender, Lettie swayed toward him automatically, drawing back only when Ethan lifted his head. Time hung suspended for a fraction of a moment, filled with an unequaled sweetness made all the more precious by the uncertainty of their futures.

"Congratulations!" Amelia blurted, tossing a handful of rose petals into the air.

Alma beamed through a sheen of tears.

The pastor regarded them all in stern disapproval.

"Now all of you get out of here," Rusty growled. "This is a jailhouse, dammit!"

Pastor Phillips needed no further urgings. "Sign this, please," he stated, thrusting a set of marriage licenses in Ethan's direction. Taking Lettie's hand, Ethan drew her toward the wall and signed the papers against the rough stones, then handed the pen to Lettie. She hastily signed the licenses with the last bit of ink, then handed them to the pastor.

Affixing his final signature, the man handed Ethan one copy, then gazed at the newly married couple over his spectacles. "You've done the right thing. Come to me for the christening when the time comes."

"Christening?" Ethan muttered, but Lettie silenced him with a glance.

"Now—all of you—get the hell out of this jail!"

The pastor *hurrumphed* deep in his throat and strode out. He was followed by the Beasleys.

"Her too," Rusty snapped, gesturing to Lettie.

"Lettie?" Amelia gasped. "But she's just been married."

"I don't care. Out!"

The Beasleys erupted into a storm of protest, while

Ethan grasped Lettie's waist and pulled her tightly against him.

A shrieking whistle pierced the air, and all turned in surprise as Alma lowered her fingers from her mouth.

"Rusty, a word please," she murmured in a genteel manner, gesturing to the staircase. Walking ahead of him, she forced him to follow her by her very silence, while Amelia took up the rear.

Once at the bottom of the steps, Alma gathered the basket that contained their reticules. Turning, she flashed Rusty a disarming smile. "Be reasonable, Rusty. They've just married."

"I don't care."

"They need some time together."

"I don't care."

"Can't we persuade you to reconsider?"

"No."

Alma sighed. "Then I'll go fetch her."

Brushing past him, Alma took one step, then turned. "You really won't reconsider?"

"No."

Sighing again, Alma withdrew her sister's reticule from the basket. "Then I fear I simply must take matters into my own hands."

With a smile of apology, she brought the concealed paperweight crashing down onto Rusty's head.

He issued a garbled yelp and stared at them a moment in incredulity. Then he crumpled to the floor.

Alma slipped the reticule back into the basket and turned to regard her sister. A blaze of determination shone from her eyes. "Those two are going to have a wedding night if I have to crack open the skull of every lawman from here to Kansas. Now find the key to Ethan's shackles, so we can get the honeymoon started upstairs."

A few moments later, Alma and Amelia returned to the cells and smiled blandly in the newlyweds' direction. "All set. You can stay."

They walked toward the couple, and Alma removed a key from the hidden pocket of her skirts and inserted it into Ethan's shackles. "You have until dawn, Lettie.

We'll cover for you until then. I wish there were some way to see to Ethan's escape, but with the crowd outside, I don't see how—even if Ethan dressed up like a woman."

Ethan flushed, but Lettie smiled in gratitude. "Thank you. Thank you both."

"Our pleasure, dear," Amelia responded, her eyes blinking against a sheen of unshed tears. "I've never seen a more beautiful bride, or such a handsome groom. I know you two will be happy together. So happy."

"Come along, Amelia. We have work to do."

"Yes, Alma. Congratulations, you two."

Once downstairs, the two sisters each took a heel and dragged Rusty's inert body toward the cellar door. They tied him with a piece of rope, shoved a gag into his mouth, and rolled him onto the top step leading down into the storage space below.

"Now what, Alma?" Amelia asked, gasping for breath. Just for safekeeping, they locked the door, then dragged a heavy crate in front of the threshold.

"We take care of this jailhouse and see to it that no one disturbs our newlyweds."

Alma strode into the outer office and Amelia followed more slowly, gazing at her sister in confusion. "How are we going to do that?"

Alma crossed behind the desk and threw open the door to the gun cabinet. "Grab yourself one of these rifles and load up, Amelia."

21

Ethan twisted his wrists free of the shackles and threw them onto the floor by the wall. They hit the stone with a loud clatter, then settled into a puddle of iron.

"You should go," Ethan stated quietly, staring at the dark shackles lying against the rough stone floor.

"No."

"Despite the roses and ribbons, this isn't a pretty place." He looked up, spearing her with his glance. "This is a jail, and I'm a prisoner. No amount of fantasizing is going to change that fact or make it any prettier."

"I know that."

"I don't want you here, Lettie. Not like this."

"I'm here, and I'm not going."

He stepped away from her, moving back into his cell. When Lettie turned to follow him, she ached at the rigid set of the shoulders.

"Ethan, we're married. Why are you pushing me away?"

He didn't turn, but she heard his harshly indrawn breath. "Don't you understand! I only married you to protect you. I only married you to see that you had some means of support. It was my way of saying thank you before I left you to deal with the mess I'd left behind."

Lettie gasped, feeling as if he'd slapped her.

"I see." Stinging beneath his cruel remark, she gathered her tattered dignity around her with some difficulty and turned to escape the close confines of the cellblock. But at the door, something stopped her.

Turning, she moved slowly, silently, toward him. She gave no warning of her approach. Yet she knew the moment he sensed her presence behind him.

Reaching out a hand, she tried to turn him to face her, but he resisted. Filled with a burning determination, Lettie moved around him and looked up into his face.

"Oh, Ethan," she murmured, her own voice echoing the pain she saw etched upon his features.

He tried to turn away, but she reached up to hold his face, forcing him to look at her and share a part of his soul that he had never shared with anyone before.

"Tell me," she whispered.

Ethan shook his head, but she tightened her grasp, forcing him to meet the love shining from her eyes.

"Tell me what's wrong."

The cell shuddered in silence for a moment, and then some of the tension seemed to falter within him.

"I would have wished better for you than this." He reached up and twined his fingers around Lettie's wrist, drawing her hand to a vicinity just above his heart. His throat moved as he swallowed. "You deserve better than this. You deserve flowers, and poetry, and a man of honor."

Lettie stood on tiptoe and wrapped her arms around Ethan's shoulders. "You *are* an honorable man, Ethan McGuire," she murmured against his neck. "You've met your mistakes head-on and changed them for the better."

"Things should have been different between us."

"None of that matters. Nothing matters . . . as long as I'm with you."

His arms slid around her waist, and he clung silently

to her for a moment, his embrace fierce. "They're going to kill me, Lettie."

"No!"

He forced her to look at him. "This isn't one of your fantasies, Lettie. Not everyone lives happily ever after in this world."

"Ethan, don't—"

"They're going to kill me, Lettie," he repeated bluntly. "And heaven help me, I should send you marching out that door. I've already hurt you more than I ever dreamed I would. But I won't lie to you. I won't paint pretty pictures about what will happen, because, by lying, I'd only hurt you more in the long run."

He took a deep breath, and one broad hand reached out to caress her cheek. "But right now, I can't bring myself to force you to leave." His voice deepened, growing husky and low. "Because I need you, Lettie Grey. I need your softness, your sweetness, your hope."

Lettie tried to smile, tried to lighten the moment; she really did. But her attempt was unsuccessful. Instead, she felt something within her letting loose of childhood for the very last time, and she knew she could never again be that young girl who fantasized of the Highwayman and recited Poe by lamplight. Instead, she had to trust a man enough to give him a piece of her soul.

"I'm not leaving. I want to make love to you again tonight, Ethan McGuire," she whispered. "I want to know you—heart, and mind, and body. And if this is all there can ever be, then this is all there can ever be."

Slowly, ever so slowly, Ethan's head dipped, and she rose on tiptoe to meet him halfway. Yet when their lips touched, Lettie noted there was a sense of wonder to the caress, a worshiping.

Knowing that their time together would be limited at best, Lettie basked in each soft brush of his mouth, each tender stroke of his fingers. When Ethan pulled back, burying his mouth in the softness of her hair, she sighed, taking a shuddering breath as her heart began to beat with slow, heavy strokes. She wanted this man. She needed him.

"If I had my way, our wedding night would have been spent in a luxurious hotel."

She smiled, and her arms reached to cling to the firm muscles of his back.

"I love you, Ethan McGuire, no matter where we are."

Her hands slipped from his nape, to his shoulders, to the buttons of his shirt. When Ethan lifted his head, she gazed at him in rapt adoration and slipped the first button free. Her thumb brushed across the exposed flesh, then moved to release the second button. Then the third. Softly tracing the vee of skin she'd exposed, she bent to place a kiss against his throat.

He groaned, and, smiling, she continued.

Soon the garment gaped about his chest and she slid her hands inside, placing her palms flat upon the firm span of his waist. Her thumbs brushed back and forth against the firm flesh. When he gasped, she bent to place a kiss in the crease of his stomach, just above his navel. Then, inch by tantalizing inch, she trailed a path of kisses up his ribs, to his breastbone, to the hollow at the base of his throat. Finally, her tongue flicked out to tease the tender spot, and she felt Ethan shudder.

"Let me love you, Ethan McGuire," she murmured.

His hands reached out to curl around her waist, then spread across her back. "Just promise you'll leave in the morning. Before Jacob can find you."

The tension seeped from her body in a willing breath. "I promise."

He wrapped his arms more tightly around her, attempting to draw her close, but she slipped free, moving to the opposite side of the cell. Turning her back, she lifted her hands and began to pluck the pins free from her hair, her motions smooth, graceful . . . poetic.

When all of the pins had been freed from the glossy strands, she arched her head back, allowing the thick waves to tumble down to her hips, shimmering like a thick honey-brown curtain. Then she turned and reached for the hook of her capelet. In one smooth flick of her hand, the clasp lay open and the capelet dropped from her fingers to the floor.

Ethan swallowed convulsively. "Lettie," he murmured, his voice filled with aching desire.

"I love you, Ethan," she whispered, then began to unhook the bodice of her gown. Ethan took a deep breath, evidently striving for control. Though his eyes did not dip to follow her movements, she could sense a silken tension beginning to fill his body as, inch by inch, the bodice gaped open and the delicate unmentionables she wore beneath came into view.

"You can't say I'm too young anymore, Ethan," she whispered, slipping her hands under the edge of her bodice and sliding it from her shoulders.

Ethan's eyes burned a trail from the delicate insertion of her camisole to the grosgrain ribbons of her corset and back up again. "Hell no."

She smiled and reached behind her to flick open the button to her skirt, then that to her petticoat. In one lithe movement, she pushed the garments to her ankles.

Then she moved toward him and slipped the shirt from his shoulders. The muscles beneath her hands were warm and firm, slick from the sheen of sweat caused by the heat of the cell.

"Love me."

"Yes."

Ethan bent to kiss her cheek, his lips skimming down the line of her jaw to the tender skin of her neck. His hands cupped her shoulders, then moved in a sweeping gesture down to her hips. He shifted his weight, parting his feet ever so slightly before reaching out to clasp her buttocks and pulling her into the space he had provided.

Lettie gasped, feeling the urgent proof of his arousal against her. Her body was flooded with the remembrance of the pleasure she'd experienced in his arms once before, and she wanted that pleasure again and again. She clung to him even as the warmth of his hands seeped through the delicate fabric of her drawers. The sweat beading his chest teased the taut mounds of her breasts.

"Show me what to do, Ethan," she muttered through a throat grown tight with a delicious tension she could not explain. "I want to please you."

He drew back, and one hand lifted to cup her cheek. "You already please me. More than you could ever know."

He tunneled his fingers into the hair at her nape and kissed her, long and slow and deep. Then, still engaging her tongue in an erotic duel, his palms slipped to push the edges of her camisole over her shoulders. Bending, he greedily explored the slopes of her shoulders, the swelling mounds of her breasts.

Lettie moaned low in her throat, feeling a heaviness settling within her and a burning tension. She couldn't seem to get close enough, couldn't seem to touch him enough. Gasping for breath, she reached to tug at the busc of her corset, dropping the garment to the ground.

Almost immediately, Ethan's palm closed over one breast. She groaned in relief, but her relief was short-lived. Rather than easing the ache within her, his touch only stoked the fires, causing her to strain against him. Instinctively, her fingers moved to the buttons of his trousers, fumbling with the unfamiliar fastenings.

Ethan broke away, arching his head back and gasping for breath. "Slow down, Lettie girl."

"But I want you."

Despite the drugging effects of their passion, he grinned. "And you'll have me. Soon."

Slipping his arms around her waist and beneath her knees, Ethan lifted her against him and carried her to the bunk on the far wall. After setting her on the fresh sheets and quilts the Beasleys had so thoughtfully provided, he stepped back and unfastened the buttons to his trousers. Then, turning to sit on the bed, he removed his boots and his socks.

Needing to touch him, Lettie pushed herself onto her knees, slipping her arms down his chest and bending low to place a string of kisses along his shoulders.

He reached up to wrap his arms around her neck, holding her there for one long, aching moment. But when Lettie arched backward to press her hips against his back, he groaned and twisted free.

Lettie shuddered at the unleashed passion she found deep in his eyes. Yet, for a moment, neither of them moved, neither of them breathed. Desire hung thick and tense about them like the heavy air just before a storm.

If Lettie had ever doubted that Ethan loved her, those doubts would have disappeared at that moment. He watched her now with a gaze that was dark and filled with a need that could only come from love. Not just a physical need, but a spiritual need as well.

Smiling, Lettie slowly lifted her hand and tugged on the satin ribbon of her camisole. The ribbons slipped free, bit by bit, then dropped between her breasts. The delicate cotton shifted against the firm swells of her breasts, and, since there was no fastening to the garment save the ribbon and a button at her waist, a creamy expanse of flesh lay bare to his gaze, nearly to her waist.

She saw the way he shuddered, the way he watched her every move. Then she fought to breathe herself as he reached out and, with a single questing finger, traced the flesh open to his gaze.

Her eyes flickered closed and she reached out to grasp his wrist, needing something to hold on to when, with a single touch, he sent her senses reeling. Then, as his hand paused, then slipped beneath the fabric of her camisole to cup her breast, she gasped, her fingers clenching around his wrist in support.

Ethan moved toward her, slipping the camisole from her shoulders. A sigh of delight escaped from his lips. "You are so beautiful," he whispered, his voice rough from the labored quality of his breathing.

Basking in the adoration she saw in his eyes, Lettie released him and reached behind her to unfasten the button at the waist of her drawers. Beneath the power of his gaze, she twisted her hips, and her drawers dropped to her knees in a puddle of fabric.

Ethan moaned and pulled her tightly against him.

She wrapped her arms around his back and slid her hands beneath the waist of his trousers, filling her palms momentarily with the firm swells of his buttocks, then pushing the pants from his hips.

Obviously impatient and on the brink of losing any aspect of control, Ethan broke free and stepped from the last remaining barrier of clothing and drew Lettie tightly against him.

She reveled in the sensation of flesh against flesh, hardness to softness, rough to smooth. When Ethan took her weight and pressed her down upon the bunk, she willingly surrendered, her arms wrapping tightly around his shoulders.

His hand swept down her body from shoulder to thigh, then back again before he leaned toward her for a hungry kiss. Though they had only been separated for a handful of hours, the passion flared between them as if they hadn't touched in years.

Straddling her hips, Ethan knelt above her, gazing down at the uneven rise and fall of her chest and the hectic flush of her skin. Slipping his hands beneath her shoulders, he drew her toward him and placed a kiss on the corner of her mouth, then the hollow of her ear. Her head arched back as his lips continued their tender torment down the line of her throat to the hollow of her collarbone. When his tongue flicked out to graze the tender skin, she clutched at his arms as he slowly lowered her against the ticking, trailing a moist path down to the hollow between her ribs.

For long, aching moments, he explored her with loving hands and gentle kisses. Each inch of her body seemed to pulse to life as he savored the softness of her skin and the womanly strength of her body. Soon her flesh seemed on fire and her hands clenched into the muscles of his shoulders, sifting through the damp curls of his hair.

Then she forced him to look up at her.

He must have read the overwhelming need within her, because he finally heeded the insistent urgings of her hands and settled between her legs.

Her knees bent and she shifted against him, showing him how ready she'd become for his ultimate possession.

318

His eyes flared and his hips nudged against her own in a tormenting fashion, but he refused to take her.

She made soft mewling sounds deep within her throat. Her pulse pounded. But still he hesitated.

She felt him shift more completely above her. With one lithe movement, he could enter her. But he paused instead and framed her head with his palms, his fingers tangling into her hair. "I love you, Lettie McGuire," he whispered fiercely. "No matter what happens, never forget how much I loved you."

She frowned at his use of the past tense, but then he was moving against her, preparing her.

Covering her mouth with his own, Ethan thrust within her, filling her completely with his strength, his warmth. Lettie arched against him, gasping at the instantaneous pleasure that began to swell within her as he withdrew, then moved within her again.

When his hands slipped beneath her hips, tipping her slightly, she moaned, her arms wrapping around his shoulders, holding him tightly against her as if she could absorb him into every pore of her being. Her legs moved to hold him close as she and Ethan strove for release.

This time there was a difference to their embrace—a shimmering expectancy—as if, now that her body knew of the pleasure that would follow, it waited for something more. Something wonderful. Her muscles seemed to grow tight and the aching became almost unbearable. Then, without warning, her very soul seemed to shatter into a million pieces.

Squeezing her eyes shut, Lettie thought she saw every color of the rainbow, a shower of sparks. Pleasure flooded her with a swiftness that was nearly unbearable. Then her body shuddered, and she tightly grasped the man who held her.

Wrapping her arms around his back, Lettie whispered, "I love you, Ethan. I love you."

As if her words were his undoing, he thrust against her, and she felt his warmth spilling into her womb.

Lettie held Ethan as the storm of sensation roiled within them, then slowly dissipated into the velvet darkness. Though it seemed impossible, her love for this man blossomed even more, warming her like a deep-seated fire in her breast. He had become a part of her heart. A part of her soul. And she didn't know how she could ever learn to live without him.

His head lifted. His eyes burned into her own. When he lifted a hand to touch her, she shivered beneath the exquisite gentleness he displayed.

"I love you, Lettie McGuire," he whispered.

She swallowed beneath the tightness that gathered in her throat, and because there had been a glint of sadness deep in his eyes, the almost imperceptible sheen of desperation, she hugged him closer to her warmth.

They made love again in the ruby glow of sunset. And this time, their caresses were long and slow, each moment savored and held to its last possible moment. Then, as they caught their breath, Ethan drew Lettie more securely into the circle of his arms and pressed a kiss against the top of her head. As the last bars of color slipped across the floor and gave way to darkness, the two of them talked, laughed, made plans.

Lettie knew that each word spoken was for her benefit alone. She knew Ethan was simply trying to reassure her, trying to take her mind away from his present predicament.

But as they spoke of wishes, and dreams, and promises of the future, her fingers curled tighter around the solid flesh at his waist, and inside, she became more desperate and unsure.

Ethan reached for her again as the rosy light of dusk filtered through the windows high above them. There was a sadness to their caresses and a note of panic. And afterward, Lettie found herself making promises she knew she could never keep.

"You could live with my mother in Chicago," Ethan murmured in the darkness, his hand moving back and forth across the curve of her shoulder. "You'd like it there. You could see the theater and the opera. The lending library is just a short ride away. And you could write your poems and publish them under your real name, so everyone will be shocked by your audacity."

Lettie nodded, afraid to speak for fear he would hear the thick tears clogging her throat.

"Take your mother with you. She doesn't belong in a boardinghouse. She should have someone waiting on *her* rather than the other way around."

Once again, Lettie nodded.

"There will be plenty of money set aside for you."

"No, Ethan."

"Yes," he stated firmly, his grip tightening. "It's honest money. Some inherited, some earned. Promise me you'll use it."

"Ethan, I—"

"Promise."

"I promise."

Silence sifted between them for a moment, filled with the distant creak of the crickets. Ethan's hand stilled. When he spoke, his voice was low and firm.

"When they come for me, I don't want you to be here."

"Ethan, no."

"I want you to go home. And I want you to stay there."

"I can't leave you."

"Promise me, Lettie."

"No."

She glanced up to see his eyes squeezed closed in the darkness. "Please, Lettie. When they come to take me away, I need to know you're safe. Let me go knowing you're with people who care for you and who will protect you."

Lettie's heart nearly cracked in her chest when she heard the way Ethan's voice faltered.

"I lived part of my life like a fool, Lettie. At least let me do something with dignity."

When his eyes blinked open, Lettie saw the faint shimmer of tears, and she realized this quiet, fierce man was just as terrified of the future as she. Knowing that the only thing she could offer him was peace of mind, she whispered, "I promise."

Gerald Stone moved through the smoky warmth of the Mercury Saloon and sat in the empty chair next to Judge Krupp. "The files weren't there." As he spoke, he kept his voice low, his manner casual, so that he would melt into the crowd. Otherwise, someone was bound to notice that he'd been spending a great deal of time outside his own jurisdiction.

Judge Krupp glanced up from his game of solitaire and stabbed him with a disbelieving gaze. "What do you mean, they weren't there?"

"I broke into Jeb Clark's office and rifled his desk, went through all of the files, every box, every envelope. His personal records weren't there."

The judge swore fiercely to himself. "Where could he have put them?"

"I don't know, but if they fall into the wrong hands, we're all in deep trouble."

Once again, the judge swore. "Jeb had records on nearly all of us. Not only documented lists of Star business, but notes on some of our illegal activities as well. If that information leaks into the community, they'll have a lynch mob chasing us with blood in their eyes."

"So what do you want me to do? "

"Just let me think a minute!" The judge frowned in concentration, a slow, dawning certainty spreading over his features. "Damn, it's been staring at us all this time."

Stone's eyes narrowed in confusion. "What?"

"Grey. Who else would Clark have entrusted with the papers?"

Stone shook his head. "If Jacob Grey had known you were taking bribes and using the Star as your highly paid assassination team, he wouldn't have joined the board of governors."

Krupp turned to face him. "Unless he didn't receive the information until later."

"You're stretching with that theory."

"What did Jacob say to you when you made a few well-phrased threats if he didn't follow orders?"

"Only that he'd reveal the network of the Star to . . ." Stone's words trailed off. "Damn," he whispered to himself. "We haven't given him that information yet. He only has a list of his own battalion."

Krupp's jaw hardened, and his eyes narrowed against the sting of smoke hanging low over the tables.

"Kill him."

"When?"

"Just before dawn. We still have some dynamite left from the train robbery. Set the charge around the foundation of the jailhouse. Use enough to level the whole building. I don't want any corpses reviving from the dead this time."

Gerald Stone's lips eased into a smile. "Yes, sir."

"Then I want you to watch his family. If those papers aren't in Grey's office, his family will lead you to their hiding place."

Stone nodded and reached over to take a card from the pile. With a soft chuckle of delight, he threw it onto the table.

It was the ace of spades.

22

Dawn had not yet arrived when Gerald Stone eased his horse toward the trees along the creek line. As he drew nearer, Krupp straightened in his saddle.

"Well?"

"There's enough dynamite set against the foundations at the back of the jailhouse to blow the whole building to kingdom come."

"And the crowd of men?"

"Most of them went home about an hour or two ago. I had one of my men lure the rest of them into the Mercury Saloon for a commiserating drink.

"You're sure? I don't want any witnesses cropping up. From now on, I won't tolerate any mistakes."

"Now see here, Krupp!" Stone snapped. "I wasn't the one who created this mess in the first place. But I'll clean it up, just like I always do."

Krupp settled into a seething silence. "I want the charge detonated within the hour."

Stone rubbed the side of his nose with his finger. "We've got a little problem there."

"What do you mean?"

"Jacob Grey hasn't been to the office since early this morning."

Krupp swore. "Dammit! Where's he been?"

"How the hell should I know? I couldn't go storming in and ask, now could I?"

Krupp's features settled into a scowl of impatience and fury. "Keep a watch on the jailhouse. As soon as he makes an appearance, I want that charge exploded."

Stone touched his fingers to the brim of his hat. "Yes, sir," he murmured sarcastically, before urging his horse back toward town.

Jacob struggled against the ropes that bound him and finally pulled free. For hours, he'd been straining at the bindings, a fury building within him with each passing minute. He had no doubts why the Beasleys had done this to him. And he had no doubts as to who had put them up to it, either.

Damn, damn, damn. They had no idea what they'd done.

Swearing again, he threw the cords aside and quickly untied the bindings around his feet. Then, lunging toward the other room, he gathered his revolver and rifle and stormed into the weak light of dawn.

When Jacob stepped through the alley onto the empty boardwalk, he felt a shiver of unease. Only hours before, there had been a dozen or so men watching the jail with haunted eyes. Now the street was empty. Still.

Taking a deep breath of the heavy air, Jacob fought the tension rising within him. Now was the time to make his move. If nothing else, his frustrating night had forced him to think and filled him with a calm certainty about what needed to be done.

Taking another ragged breath, he forced the tense set of his jaw to ease. By nightfall, this would all be over. One way or another.

That thought seemed to fill him with a certain amount of calm; yet when he opened the door and found his office being guarded by two elderly women armed with rifles, he growled in fury and ordered them to return to the boardinghouse.

"Jacob!"

"Ladies, if you don't leave, here and now, I will arrest you on the spot!"

Alma and Amelia glanced at each other, then at Jacob's furious scowl, and surrendered their weapons.

"Where's Rusty?" he snapped.

Amelia shot Alma a guilty glance, then sidled toward the door to the cellar, pushed aside the crate, and slowly pulled it open.

"Dammit all to hell!" Jacob blurted when he saw his deputy lying on the steps. He was trussed up like a Christmas goose, his face as red as his hair.

"Ladies, I would advise you to leave." When they opened their mouths, he shouted, "Now! Before I forget that my mama taught me how to treat my elders."

Gathering their things, they reluctantly began to walk home. Within moments, Jacob had released his deputy and was storming into the cellblock.

Lettie started, pulling the quilt tightly against her breasts when the door slammed open. Pushing away from Ethan's chest, she whirled to confront the intruder.

"Jacob!"

Her brother didn't speak. He merely stared at her with eyes that were dark and furious.

"Go home, Lettie," he stated slowly.

"No."

"Go home!"

His voice was so harsh and angry that Lettie didn't know how to react for a moment. Before she could speak, Jacob continued. "Ethan McGuire, you're to come with me. I have orders to transfer you to Petesville, where you will die at dusk by firing squad."

Lettie gasped, regarding her brother in horror and barely comprehending what he was saying. But when Ethan's arms stiffened instinctively around her waist, she lashed out. "You can't do that! He hasn't done anything. He's been with me all this time. He hasn't done anything wrong!"

"Rusty!"

The carrot-haired deputy stepped forward.

"See to it that my sister is taken home. Now."

When the deputy moved to take her, Lettie tried to fight him, although she was covered by nothing but a blanket. But Ethan grasped her arms and forced her to look at him. His eyes were warm and clear. Like an azure sky.

"You promised me, Lettie," he whispered, so that only she could hear.

Her eyes filled with tears. "Nooo."

"Lettie, you promised."

She tried to control the emotions raging inside of her.

"I love you, Lettie. Please—please—don't make this harder for me."

She gazed up at his features, and her heart seemed to twist inside. Ethan had given up hope.

"Ethan," she moaned.

"We knew this was coming. We knew this would happen."

Her fingers tightened, digging into his skin. "There has to be something we can do."

But Ethan shook his head. "It's over, Lettie." His hands slipped deeper into her hair, holding her steady so that she couldn't escape the stark finality of his expression. "It's over."

She shivered and slowly wrapped her arms around his shoulders, needing to absorb the vitality of the man she had grown to love so much. His arms wrapped around her waist, but his embrace was that of a friend and not a lover.

He was already beginning to distance himself in an effort to make the parting easier to bear.

"I love you, Ethan," she whispered, pressing her lips against the underside of his jaw.

She felt him take a shuddering breath. When he spoke, his voice was slightly husky. "Remember your promises, Lettie. You're to become a great poet some day."

She nodded against his shoulder.

"You'll stay with my family for a while. You and your mother. You'll see all the theater and opera and poetry readings any human being can stand."

She sniffed.

He drew back and tipped her chin up. "And you'll be happy. Please promise me you'll be happy."

She couldn't speak.

"Promise me, Lettie."

Her throat tightened to the point where she could barely breathe, but she whispered, "I promise."

"And you'll marry again."

She balked, but when she saw the desperation in his eyes, she willingly lied to him. "Yes." Her voice was low and rough.

The hand that lifted to her cheek trembled, ever so slightly. "Kiss me? Just once more?"

Their lips met gently, tenderly, sealing their promises of forever that had not even managed to live until morning's light. Then Jacob stepped forward, threw another scratchy blanket around her shoulders, and took her by the elbow, dragging her out of the cell.

"See that she dresses, then take her home, Rusty," he ordered tightly, shoving her in the direction of his deputy.

"Ethan, I—" Before she could finish what she had been about to say, the door slammed behind her. "Ethan!"

The last thing Lettie saw was the rigid cast of Ethan's features. And the tortured shadows of his eyes.

As soon as the sound of Lettie's departure had faded, silence shuddered within the stone walls of the jailhouse. Then Jacob took a step forward, reached for Ethan's clothing, and threw it into his lap.

"Get dressed."

"It isn't dawn yet."

"No. It isn't."

Ethan's hands tightened around the smoke-stained cloth of his shirt. "You haven't come as a marshal, have you?" When Jacob didn't answer, Ethan murmured to himself, "You've come to prove yourself to the Star."

Jacob still didn't speak; he merely stared at him with guarded eyes. And Ethan knew that, although Jacob

Grey might forgive him for many things, he would probably never forgive Ethan for touching his sister.

"Have you come to kill me, Jacob Grey?"

Jacob didn't answer for a moment, and the dim lamplight seemed to make his eyes even darker, filled with shadows, until finally he responded.

"I already told you: I'll do anything to see my sister happy."

"And you think that, by murdering me, you'll make her happy?"

"She deserves better."

"She wants me."

Silence shuddered about them. "Be that as it may, I'm sworn to uphold the law. And I intended to do just that. My way."

A quiet gloom hovered over the half dozen men who had circled their mounts around Judge Krupp. Though the long shadows of dawn cloaked their features, there was no denying the hardness of their expressions or the singleness of purpose that lay stamped within their eyes.

The clatter of hooves on the hard earth warned them of an approaching rider, and the men tensed. Only when Gerald Stone appeared around the corner did they relax.

"Jacob Grey just entered the office," Stone reported hurriedly.

"Any idea where he's been?"

Gerald shrugged. "He came from his own place behind the jailhouse."

Krupp frowned, but he could find no logical explanation that could account for the marshal's hours away from the jail. Finally he turned and squinted up at the glow of scarlet and orange bleeding into the sky. "The sun will be up soon. We'd best get this done before the whole town wakes up. Stone, take your men to the jail. As soon as Rusty Janson steps outside, I want you to begin preparations to detonate the charges. The moment you receive my signal, I want that building leveled."

"Yes, sir." Gesturing to a pair of his men, Stone

turned his mount and rode back in the direction he'd come.

"Abernathy, Butler, take the rest of the men and circle the jailhouse. You're to kill anyone coming out of the building once the signal is given."

The four men nodded and reined their mounts into the shadows. Krupp watched them as far as the corner, then glanced behind him at the ever-increasing glow of light.

"There's Janson," Tyler Butler muttered.

Ned Abernathy straightened in his saddle, squinting into the darkness. He immediately recognized Rusty Janson's spry figure. But he was not alone. Ned swore under his breath when he noted the feminine figure who accompanied him.

Evidently the other men were not so concerned with her unexpected exit from the jailhouse. They were already moving into position. They didn't see the way Ned hesitated, glanced over his shoulder, then eased his mount down a side alley, stealthily moving in the direction of the boardinghouse.

A faint streak of light seeped into the sky as Rusty Janson led his mount toward the boardinghouse and drew the animal to a halt.

"There you are, Miss Lettie."

Lettie numbly allowed herself to be lifted down from the back of Rusty's horse. Still not comprehending all that had occurred, she stood motionless, then stepped toward the house.

"Miss Lettie? Will you be all right?"

Though she heard Rusty's voice behind her, Lettie didn't acknowledge him. She couldn't. If she were to say anything, she knew she would wither and crumble into a thousand pieces. All of her energies had to be turned toward the problem at hand. She had to find a way to free Ethan. She *had* to.

Letting herself into the house, she closed the door and stood woodenly in the hall, listening to the silence of the house. Evidently, despite her pain, life went on and the boarders were still sleeping soundly in their beds.

She stepped slowly into the hall and tried to pull her thoughts together. There had to be something she could do to free Ethan. Surely there was someone she could turn to for help. Someone who would help her find a way to prevent Ethan from being taken to Petesville.

For the first time, Lettie glanced up and realized that the hall was nearly blocked by a stack of trunks, carpet-bags, and valises. When the soft sound of humming eased into the hall, Lettie stepped around the corner of the doorway to the parlor and noted the way Natalie Gruber stood primping in front of a mirror, pinning a new straw bonnet to the top of her hair.

"Oh, Lettie," she murmured when she saw the younger girl's reflection behind her. "I'd wondered if you'd return in time. I left some books in my room that I thought you'd like to have. What with my clothes and all, I simply have too much in my trunks as it is."

"You're leaving?"

Natalie fiddled with the tiny curls she'd arranged over her forehead. "Mmm? Yes. Now that Silas is dead, I'm off to Europe for an extended tour."

Lettie gazed at the woman in disbelief, astounded by Natalie's lack of grief or concern over her husband's death, but she didn't know exactly what to say. "I see," she finally murmured noncommittally.

Natalie turned and flashed Lettie a quick smile, but when she noted the way Lettie was dressed, her eyes dropped disdainfully over Lettie's rumpled cloth-ing. "Really, Lettie, you must learn to take better care of yourself."

Lettie stiffened at the other woman's insult but did not respond.

When Natalie saw her barb would have no effect, she turned and moved toward her. "According to town gos-sip, you've been spending a great deal of time at the jail." Her lips twitched. "Some say you even spent the night there."

Lettie's jaw clenched.

"I've also heard it whispered about town that you've been working above and beyond the call of simple Christian compassion—that you've offered the man more than tea and sympathy."

Taking a deep breath, Lettie tried to remain calm under the other woman's baiting.

"I've even heard a few people suggest that Ethan McGuire may have been in town longer than we have been led to believe." Natalie's eyes narrowed. "Of course, I didn't tell them that little Lettie Grey has been spending a great deal of time in the garret lately. Not to mention the mysterious creaks I've heard above my room. As if not one person had been sleeping there"— she paused for effect—"but two."

Though Ethan had tried to tell her that sooner or later people would begin drawing the correct conclusions, Lettie was not prepared for how quickly it could happen.

"You've been with Ethan McGuire at the jail all this time, I suppose?" Natalie continued.

Lettie pushed her shoulders back, refusing to appear cowed or ashamed by the fact. "Yes. As a matter of fact, we were married yesterday afternoon."

"My, my, and so quickly, too." Her eyes dipped insultingly toward Lettie's stomach. Then she made a sweeping gesture of her hand as if that fact were of no concern to her. "Perhaps it's for the best. Although I don't think you've shown the best choice in men, Lettie. Still, a woman in your position can't be too choosy."

Lettie's hands balled into fists. "Ethan is a wonderful man."

Natalie only shrugged. "Maybe so. But it's a shame he turned out to be a murderer and a thief. My lands, the things he's been doing the last few months!"

"He didn't do it. Any of it."

"Then who did, my dear? You really *do* live in a fantasy world, don't you?" Natalie shrugged. "Still, don't be too concerned about losing him. Men are as plentiful as penny candy. You'll find another soon enough."

That remark touched the fuse to Lettie's simmering

anger. Men like Ethan were not common. They were
rare. And special. But she wouldn't argue with Natalie
and give her the satisfaction of appearing superior. Not
now, not ever. Instead, she turned and marched toward
the pile of baggage.

"Let me help you with your bags, Natalie. We don't
want to keep you here any longer than necessary, do
we?"

"You're such a dear, but one of the boys from the
station is coming to take them."

Lettie ignored the other woman and reached for one
of the satchels, but her knee bumped against a pyramid
of hatboxes and the pile wavered slightly, then toppled
to the floor with a heavy thump. Lettie automatically
reached out to replace the hat and a rectangular parcel
that had been carefully wrapped in tissue.

"Don't touch that!"

Not heeding Natalie's warning, Lettie grasped the
tissue-wrapped square. Her brow furrowed when she
found it heavy and solid.

Lettie drew back as if bitten when the tissue slipped
away, revealing a corner of dull, heavy gold. *Natalie!*
The bar dropped from her hand and she stared at it in
horror, wondering if her mind was playing tricks on her,
grasping at any explanation, no matter how far-fetched.
But when she turned, Natalie's expression had become
hard. Angry.

"I wish you hadn't done that."

A cold finger slid down Lettie's spine.

Natalie took a step forward, her hand slipping into her
reticule and withdrawing a revolver. "Even so, I'm sure
I can somehow make your death look like a suicide."

"You," Lettie breathed.

Natalie smiled as if she'd just received a great compliment. "No one ever knew. No one even suspected."
She took a step forward. "Personally, I think the whole
scheme reeks of poetic justice. Five years ago, the Gentleman Bandit robbed my husband's bank and ruined his
reputation in Chicago. For the next few years, I went
without all of the things I so richly deserved—clothing,

jewels, social prominence—and I vowed that somehow I would make Silas pay for his stupidity and the Gentleman pay for his crimes.

"Then one day I realized I had the perfect weapon right here." She tapped her forehead. "Silas had become obsessed with capturing the Gentleman Bandit. He'd researched every heist the man had ever made, and each night I listened to him drone on and on. Soon I knew the Gentleman better than I knew myself. Within weeks, I'd become the Gentleman."

She took a step forward. "I was a very good thief, you know. And, being a woman, it was so easy to blend into the crowd afterward—like that night of the poetry reading. No one even knew I hadn't really attended. Once the audience began to leave, I simply slipped into the crush of people and returned home."

The revolver lifted a little higher, and Natalie's lips twitched in a smile. "I suppose, if simply stated, my escapades could be boiled down to one simple equation. I wanted money, revenge, and freedom. And how best to gain them all than to pose as the Gentleman Bandit, rob several banks in the area, then leave Silas high and dry while the authorities looked for the original thief?"

A soft chuckle melted from her lips. "Unbeknownst to me, however, my first heist started a chain reaction." She shrugged. "Who would ever have thought that so many people wanted the Gentleman dead? Not only Silas, but your brother as well. But their hate worked to my advantage. Once your brother surfaced with information that all of the circumstantial evidence pointed to Ethan McGuire, no one bothered to look elsewhere." She stepped forward, her eyes glittering. "And finally, I had the name of the man responsible for my disgrace."

She drew back the hammer with slow deliberation. "I began forming my plans with exquisite care. I was tired of waiting. It was time for Ethan McGuire to pay for his crimes. While on a shopping trip in Chicago a few months ago, I stole McGuire's watch, then left it at one of the robbery sites so that the law would have the evidence to convict him. Then, after listening to Silas brag about having found a way to bring Ethan to his knees, I formed an ally—a powerful ally in the Star.''

She took a deep breath, and when she spoke, her voice was tinged with regret. "But, like the true Gentleman Bandit, I know when to cut a good thing short and discontinue my activities—although I'm not promising I won't have . . . a lapse in Europe if I see something that catches my eye.''

She took another step forward, and Lettie began to back away from her but found her way barred by the stacks of trunks. "You won't kill me, Natalie. You don't have—''

"The nerve? Come now, Lettie. After beating my own husband with an iron bar and burning the bank down around his body, do you really think I'd hesitate to plant a bullet in your skull?''

"Like you did with Jeb Clark?''

"Actually, Clark's death wasn't my doing. I wasn't even there the night the train was robbed—trains are much too messy, you know. All that soot makes it difficult to make a clean getaway.'' She chuckled at her own joke, but when Lettie tried to shift away, her aim steadied and her smile vanished. "Silas killed him and took the gold, hoping to flush the Gentleman out of hiding so that he could be executed by the Star Council of Justice. But what Silas didn't know was that I had my own sources of information from within the Star.''

"Judge Krupp,'' Lettie breathed.

Natalie grinned. "Very good! Now, as delightful as our chat has been, I am terribly afraid that I'm going to have to kill you.''

Lettie shrank back against the trunks, her heart pounding, her breath snagging in her chest. "Don't do it, Natalie. Don't—''

"Please try to behave in a dignified manner for once in your life, Lettie.'' Natalie's eyes closed as she sighted down the barrel and her fingers tightened. "I'm sorry to be so blunt, but I simply *must* catch my train.''

When a shot exploded, Lettie's eyes closed, and her

hands rose in front of her face in a purely instinctive manner. She stood motionless, waiting for the pain.

But it never came.

Silence shuddered around her, then a muffled cry. A thump. Opening her eyes, Lettie gazed in disbelief when she found Natalie sprawled across the carpet, a crimson stain seeping from her chest. Slowly turning, Lettie looked up to find Ned Abernathy standing behind her, his fingers wrapped around the pearl handle of his revolver.

He gazed at Natalie's body for a moment, then turned to Lettie, lowering his weapon. His eyes were sad but unrepentant.

Lettie could only whisper, "How did you know?"

"I've been following the Star for months. Even entered their ranks to try and get information on who was copying my brother's methods." At the mention of his brother, he suddenly paled and blurted, "You've got to go." He grasped her wrist and pulled her toward the door. "The Star is planning to kill Ethan and Jacob at the jail. They've set charges against the foundation in back of the building."

Lettie could barely comprehend what he was saying, and Ned grasped her shoulders, shaking her as if it would help to settle some of his words into her brain.

"I've got to get help, Lettie. I was on my way to get Goldsmith when I heard Natalie." His voice became strained. "Go to the jail and warn your brother. You've got to convince him to let Ethan go and get out of the building. Fast!"

He forcibly pulled her out of the house and lifted her onto his horse.

"Ned, why?"

His features became solemn and just a little proud, and his words tumbled over themselves in a rush to be expressed. "Because I love you, dammit. But you could never be happy with me. Go save your Ethan McGuire so that I know you'll at least be happy with someone else." His eyes gleamed with a sudden pride. "And when you see him, tell him Ned Abernathy's debt has been paid in full."

His hand reached out and he slapped the mare across the rump, sending it into a startled trot. Lettie glanced over her shoulder for only a moment, before digging her heels into the mare's stomach and urging her into a race against time.

Though the horse ran in a flat-out gallop, the animal seemed to stand still to Lettie, inching as slowly as a worm along a stalk. If Ned's information were correct, then she only had a few moments to get to him before . . .

She touched the reins to the mare's neck, guiding it down the block and into the commercial center of town. Her heart began to pound in terror and her mouth filled with the taste of fear. She had to reach him in time. She had to!

Thundering toward the jail, Lettie bent low over the neck of her mount. Her heart ached in relief when she saw her brother leading Ethan out through the front door. "Jacob!" she called. "Jacob, get away from the building!"

But her brother didn't seem to hear her. Instead, he looked up, saw her approach, and shoved Ethan back into the jailhouse.

Lettie cried out in horror. "No, Jacob! Jacob!"

As she brought her mount to a shuddering stop and slipped from the saddle, Jacob emerged from the building again and stepped onto the boardwalk. "Lettie, what the hell are you doing?"

Without warning, the air shattered about them into a thundering explosion. Thrown to the ground, Lettie cried out in horror, wrapping her hands around her head as rocks and timbers showered to the earth around her. She heard the squeal of her horse, the ripping impact of crumbling stone. Shards of rock bit into her flesh and pounded against her limbs.

Then the air shuddered and grew quiet. The shower of rubble that had spattered against the ground grew still.

Slowly—ever so slowly—Lettie lifted her head and looked behind her. Jacob had been thrown to the ground a few yards away, and he pushed himself to his knees. His first glance was for Lettie.

"Are you all right?"

"Ethan!" Fighting the tangling of her skirts, Lettie pushed herself to her feet. *"Ethan!"*

Screaming, Lettie ran toward the gutted shell of the building, but before she could get more than a few yards, Jacob had dodged out and caught her, preventing her from going any farther.

"No, Jacob! Ethan!"

"He's dead, Lettie! There's no way he could have survived that blast."

"No." Her eyes grew wide and tortured, and she stared up at her brother in horror, then turned to search the rubble for some sign of life.

"He's dead," he repeated more softly.

A low, primeval cry of pain rose from Lettie's chest and seeped into the dawn. She tried to break loose, tried to lunge toward the jail, but Jacob held her fast. The last few remaining walls of the jail creaked and groaned, then collapsed in a shower of dust.

"Nooo!" she screamed, then whirled toward her brother, pounding him with her fists. "You killed him! You killed him!"

Lettie looked up to find four men on horseback circling them and edging closer, with Judge Krupp at the lead.

She wrenched free from her brother's grip. "You did this!" Lettie shouted. "Didn't you? *Didn't you!*"

Krupp drew his revolver from his holster. "My men were simply seeing that justice was served. The Star Council has been sworn to uphold the law."

"The law? What law? You're nothing but butchers! *Butchers,* do you hear me? Ethan didn't rob those banks, he didn't kill Jeb Clark. Natalie did. Natalie and Silas Gruber. And you, Judge Krupp. *You* are more responsible than anyone here."

"You're hysterical."

"I'm not hysterical. It's the truth. I swear, it's the truth! Natalie admitted it herself."

Krupp's features hardened. "Then I regret the fact that you will have to die as well."

Jacob swore and pushed Lettie behind the cover of his body, but one of Krupp's men lifted his own weapon and aimed it at the center of her head.

Without warning, the click of hammers being drawn into place shattered through the early dawn.

"Gentlemen, put your weapons down. Now."

Looking beyond the circle of Star members, Lettie noted that a much larger circle of people had arrived at their aid. Sobbing, she saw the Beasleys with rifles, Ned and Goldsmith with revolvers, Harold Beechum, Irma and Adolph Schmidt, Dorothy Rupert, and even Celeste Grey, all holding assorted Derringers, pistols, and shotguns. From a distance, she heard the first clamoring rings of the alarm bell near the church.

Judge Krupp's features grew desperate and hard. "Shoot them!" he shouted to his men, but, one by one, they dropped their weapons to the ground.

Jacob took a shuddering breath. "Take them away. Lock them in the cellar of the church until we can find a better place to keep them."

Since the sound of the explosion had brought a crowd of townspeople to the site, Krupp's men were easily overpowered and led away.

Celeste Grey moved toward her children, reaching out to draw them into her arms, but Lettie wrenched free, turning toward the rubble.

"He has to be alive!" she rasped from a throat nearly closed with tears. When she dodged toward the building, Jacob lunged after her, catching her around the waist and forcing her to back away.

"No, Jacob! I have to find him. I have to find him!"

"He's dead, Lettie."

She bucked against the restraint of his arms. "This is all you're fault, Jacob Grey. If you'd simply trusted me—trusted him—none of this would have happened. But you wanted to settle a grudge."

The words lodged in her throat and her body trembled, her knees giving way. Choking on the heavy dust and her own pain, she sank to the ground, great jagged sobs wracking from her chest and seeming to tear her heart in two.

"No," she whispered again to herself. "No."

Despite Jacob's protests, she waited, huddling with her arms wrapped around her torso, until Mr. Sorenson came from the funeral parlor to poke through the rubble. When he emerged, sadly shaking his head, Lettie felt a numbness enter her limbs and spread through her entire body. And when her mother knelt in the dust beside her and held her close, she was forced to admit that Ethan was actually gone.

Gone.

Epilogue

At the bottom of a small dip of land on the far side of the city cemetery, a simple stone marker had been placed in the earth. Though no sod had been broken, the gathering of mourners was solemn nonetheless.

From her place in the center of the group of people who stood around the marker, Lettie McGuire wrapped her arms around her waist and numbly listened to the final words being spoken by Pastor Phillips. A hot wind blew against her cheeks, reminding Lettie of the fact that she hadn't cried. Couldn't cry.

From far away, she seemed to hear Pastor Phillips's voice—". . . ashes to ashes, dust to dust . . ."—but the words seemed to patter her consciousness like the hollow promise of rain to sun-baked earth.

On the one side, Lettie's mother stood like a silent bastion of strength, her arm firmly circling Lettie's waist. On the other side, Jacob stood tall and silent. Except for the Beasleys, Ned, Mr. Goldsmith, Abby Clark, and Mrs. Rupert, the gravesite was bare of any other mourners.

Though many of the townspeople sympathized with Lettie's loss, a few still felt Ethan's death had been justified. *Once a thief, always a thief,* a woman had muttered callously. Although Lettie knew that not everyone felt that way, she'd wanted this to be a private affair.

Now that the pastor had nearly finished his remarks,

she wanted to grieve alone. The wind seemed to moan around her. The luff of the grass seemed to echo with the whispered promise of might-have-beens. And Lettie wanted nothing more than silence. Peace.

Soon the pastor's words had melted into the rustle of the grass and a few of the mourners backed away. There was no coffin, no grave, no body. Only a marker placed on a flat expanse of ground in one corner of the cemetery. Yet the sadness of the group had not lessened because of that fact. Instead, their silent sympathy and support had settled around Lettie's shoulders like the warmth of the sun.

"Lettie, it's time to go home."

Though she heard her mother's words and understood her concern, Lettie shook her head. "I'll come in a while. You go on ahead."

Reluctantly, her mother stepped away and motioned for the others to follow her toward the buggy. Soon only Jacob remained behind.

"Come home, Lettie."

"No. I need to stay. Just a little longer."

"You shouldn't be here alone."

"Go home, Jacob," she murmured softly. "I'll be fine. Please." She glanced up at her brother, and he studied her a moment before finally nodding.

Settling his hat on the top of his head, he glanced at the marker a moment before saying, "It's better this way. Although Krupp and most of the Star have been taken out of state for trial, there are still a few members who haven't been apprehended. If Ethan had been here, they would have killed him."

Lettie didn't speak. She couldn't.

"You loved him a lot, didn't you, Lettie?"

She nodded. "At first I thought I'd dreamed him. He was so . . . fascinating. So intriguing." She swallowed against the tightness of her throat.

Jacob hesitated a moment before saying, "He arranged for a wedding gift. It came this morning."

Lettie watched in confusion as her brother walked toward the buggy and withdrew a large, paper-wrapped parcel from the back. Returning to her side, Jacob placed it in her outstretched hands, waiting for her to adjust to its weight. Then his hand lifted, and he stroked the curve of her cheek.

"I never meant to hurt you, Lettie. Remember that. I only wanted to make things right." Standing awkwardly before her, he glanced down at his boots, then looked up and drew her into a quick embrace. When he drew back, he planted a soft kiss on her forehead, then strode toward the buggy. Climbing inside, he slapped the reins over the horse's rump, then guided the animal toward town, leaving his own horse for her to use when she felt like returning.

Lettie stood for long moments, staring at the ever-decreasing size of the buggy, then turned back to the simple marker. Moving forward, she brushed a faint skiff of dust from the top of the marker with one hand.

"I put you on low ground, Ethan. No heights. But, then, I guess it doesn't really matter, since you aren't really . . . here." Her voice faltered, and she took deep drags of the hot summer air. Glancing up, she could see heavy clouds piling on the horizon. Already the wind was beginning to blow more fiercely, much as it had that night she'd first hidden Ethan in the cellar.

"I received a telegram from your mother, Ethan," Lettie continued. "She seems very nice. She invited me to come and visit soon. Said she wanted to meet the woman who finally captured her son's heart and made an honorable man out of him. Hear that, Ethan? *Honorable*. Your family thinks you're honorable. Even the governor has granted your pardon, though I suppose he's a little late."

Her voice grew much softer and filled with regret. "Mama told me this morning that I should go to Chicago right away. She thinks I should get away from Madison and the talk. She even arranged my ticket. But I don't want to go." The wind tugged at her skirts and pressed the fabric against her legs. "The garret is lonely without you, Ethan. I think of you every time I step inside. But Chicago would be worse. So big . . . so empty."

Glancing down at the heavy parcel in her hands, Lettie

hesitated a moment, before tugging at the string and carefully folding the paper back. When she realized it was a thick, heavy book, she frowned in confusion, turning it sideways so that she could read the spine.

Webster's Dictionary.

"Oh, Ethan," she sobbed, and her shoulders began to shake as she fought to hold back the tears, but they cascaded over the dams of her lashes, falling with huge drops onto the cover of the book.

Taking a deep, shuddering breath, she tried to stop the sobs, tried to hold back the pain. But she couldn't. Instead, she squeezed her eyes shut and sank to her knees, clutching the book tightly against her breasts.

The wind ruffled in the grass behind her. Then a deep voice seeped through her torment.

"If I'd known you'd be so upset after finally obtaining your own dictionary, I would have sent you a box of candy."

Lettie grew still, quiet. Her eyes opened, staring out at the grass.

"Ah, Lettie. Have you spent so much of your life dreaming that you don't know when fantasy becomes reality?"

Trying to think, trying to breathe, Lettie slowly twisted to look over her shoulder. A few feet away, Ethan gazed at her from a bruised and battered face, his azure eyes filled with tenderness.

"Ethan?" she murmured, in disbelief.

"In the flesh." His lips tilted in the rare smile she'd come to cherish. One that held Christmas and the Fourth of July wrapped up in the tilt of his lips.

Clutching the dictionary against her chest, Lettie pushed herself to her feet. Still not believing the evidence of her own faculties, her eyes swept over his form from head to toe, absorbing the cuts and bruises on his face, the bandages peeking from the placket of his shirt, and the sling supporting his arm.

"You're alive?" she whispered, stepping toward him.

"Well, nearly," he muttered wryly. "With a broken arm and two cracked ribs, it's a little hard to tell."

"How? . . . Why?" She closed the distance between

them and hesitantly lifted a hand to touch a gash over his eye. He flinched, then grew still, and a shuddering warmth filled her body when she realized the flesh beneath her finger was real. Very, very real.

"Jacob had a change of heart, Lettie. When he discovered the extent of the Star's corruption, he found he couldn't stomach their ways, despite the group's original intent. He realized the Star was out for blood—my blood—whether or not they could prove my guilt, so he decided to arrange my 'death' before they could get to me." He took a careful breath of air. "Since he had evidence against Krupp and several other members of the group, he thought it would be best if I disappeared until he could arrange for the Star Council's deeds to be made public. Once he'd leveled charges against Krupp and Stone, he knew I would be a dead man. But if I were already dead . . . " He shrugged, then winced.

"Jacob was leading me out of the jailhouse so that he could hide me when you came barreling down the street." His lips tilted in a rueful smile. "He thought you were being pursued by the Star. He couldn't let them see me, so—luckily—he shoved me into the cellar before going outside again. Some of the floor collapsed, but I survived."

A short cry of joy burst from Lettie's throat and she threw her arms around Ethan's shoulders, then sprang back at Ethan's hiss of pain.

"Oh, Ethan, I'm sorry."

"So am I," he remarked, his voice husky and filled with a tender longing. His azure eyes became dark and serious. "I need to feel you, know you're with me again." He held out his good arm in a welcoming gesture. "Let's try again. More gently this time."

Slowly, tenderly, she eased into his embrace, resting her head against his chest.

"Why didn't someone tell me?"

"Jacob didn't dare tell anyone until Gerald Stone could be apprehended. He was arrested just a few hours ago in Harrisburg."

Lettie's hand ran up and down his back. "I love you, Ethan McGuire."

He leaned back to gaze down at her face. "Do you love me enough to live with the shadow of my past?"

"Yes."

"Enough to move to Chicago?"

"Yes."

"Enough to put up with my job as head security for the Wallaby Banks?"

Lettie eyed him in astonishment. "Are you teasing me?"

"No. They seem to think an ex-thief would be an excellent man for the job."

"Yes. Yes, yes, yes."

Ethan's expression grew solemn, and his eyes filled with a warm devotion.

"I love you, Lettie Grey McGuire."

"Let's go home, Ethan."

Ethan smiled and whispered, "Home."

Very slowly, he bent toward her. Careful of his injuries, Lettie slipped her hands around his nape and met his lips with her own. Softly, tenderly, they sealed their future together with a kiss. And as Lettie heard the distant rumble of thunder, she remembered her first encounter with Ethan McGuire in the barn so many months before.

At the time, she'd thought her fantasies had come to life. She'd thought she would savor a little of the adventure and excitement she'd found in Ethan's arms, then remember it long after he'd gone. Little had she known on that rainy day so long before that she would emerge from her trials to be the woman of her fantasies. One who was strong and independent. One who had managed the impossible. . . .

And stolen the Highwayman's heart.